OHARI

Praise for *Ohari*

'[T]he first financial thriller ever to be written in Malayalam … I remember this veritable page-turner well. The way it brought to readers the thrilling world of the stock markets, with such strong women characters, was really enjoyable. Such an unapologetically brilliant novel deserves to travel the world, be read by more people. And congratulations to Ministhy S. for taking a step towards making that possible with this superb English translation.'—**V.J. JAMES**

'K.L. Mohana Varma brought stock market trading into the world of Malayalam fiction with *Ohari* … a first-of-its-kind financial thriller, thick with drama and danger, fuelled by some very compelling characters who grapple with the changing tides of the share market in the backdrop of saving a company, a legacy. When it was first published, readers, including me, fell prey to its wicked charms. Now, this English translation by Ministhy S. seems to bear all the signs of enticing readers again, as it keeps alive the pulsating quality of a thoroughly entertaining and immersive tale. So, speaking of costs – miss it, but that would be your loss entirely!'—**K.R. MEERA**

'[A] captivating novel that dives into the world of the stock market, where fortune and ruin walk hand in hand. It depicts ambition, the fragile bonds of trust, and a woman's triumph over many a trial … [A] landmark work in literature, blending finance, psychology, human drama and the rhythm of the diverse cultural nuances of Kerala society in the nineties … Ministhy's simple and meticulous translation of Varmaji's inspirational work will be a real feast for readers.'—**SHEELA TOMY**

'*Ohari* is an extraordinary work of fiction based on the theme of share markets, published in the early 1990s. It also narrates the story of women who yearn to escape the clutches of patriarchy. This excellent novel is a successful attempt at interpreting financial transactions in the context of human lives.'—**S. HAREESH**

'The novel *Ohari* is a bird that flew ahead of its time. Even after three decades, it remains relevant because the inner workings of the stock market that it unravels are still the same today. In the end, what we take away from it is: not all games are lost and not all games are won.'—**BENYAMIN**

OHARI

A NOVEL

K.L. MOHANA VARMA

TRANSLATED FROM THE MALAYALAM BY

MINISTHY S.

An Imprint of HarperCollins Publishers

First published in English in India by Harper Perennial 2026
An imprint of HarperCollins *Publishers*
HarperCollins *Publishers* India, Cyber City,
Building 10-A, Gurugram, Haryana – 122002, India
www.harpercollins.co.in

2 4 6 8 10 9 7 5 3 1

First published in Malayalam by DC Books, 1998

P-ISBN: 978-93-7307-832-8
E-ISBN: 978-93-7307-816-8

Typeset in 11.5/15.2 Adobe Caslon Pro
by HarperCollins *Publishers* India

Printed and bound at
Replika Press Pvt. Ltd.

This book is produced from independently certified FSC® paper
to ensure responsible forest management.

HarperCollins Publishers, Macken House, 39/40 Mayor Street Upper,
Dublin 1, D01 C9W8, Ireland

TRANSLATOR'S DEDICATION

Late Sr. Vimala (U.M.I.), my beloved Malayalam teacher, for making me love my mother tongue.

Contents

A Word from the Author

'Ohari' in Malayalam means shares.

For centuries, Malayalis have been using this word. In fact, they have a love–hate relationship with it. Families divide their properties and possessions as per law and the members start living independently with their 'ohari', or share, of the assets. Later, the same word was used for referring to the shares in the stock market.

First serialized in the literary weekly *Mathrubhumi* in the early 1990s, the story of *Ohari* revolved around the notions of wealth and ownership prevalent at those times. The book opened up the world of the share market and stock exchanges to the public. Though in existence for centuries, terms like 'Bulls and Bears' became well known to Malayalis only around this decade.

What made me write the novel? The *Manusmrithi* says, 'Na stree swatantryam arhati'. A woman does not deserve freedom. *Ohari* was my answer to that. I had written the novel to challenge that perception.

Women have been treated as second-class citizens for a long time, incapable of taking their own decisions. This novel speaks of their emancipation and equality. It narrates the inspiring story of Kerala's first independent woman entrepreneur, the feisty Mini Balachandran. She is shown as an ordinary homemaker, hailing from a family of Ayurvedic physicians. At a very young age, Mini is married off to Balachandran, a top officer in the Central Service. Then, a tragedy transforms her from a homemaker to a businesswoman.

Ohari is also the story of Kerala's famous Ayurvedic system of healing and its fight with the super-power, allopathy. This novel captures the history of the struggle. Wealth, economics, friendship, love and even sport are the prime movers in the narrative.

After its publication, the novel garnered a roaring popularity among Kerala's reading public, and also went on to win the prestigious Kerala Sahitya Akademi Award in 1993.

I hope readers enjoy the translation by Ministhy S., published by HarperCollins. It is also my hope that my fictional daughter Mini becomes an inspiration to all.

—K.L. Mohana Varma

Translator's Note

K.L. Mohana Varma's wonderful financial thriller *Ohari* was my introduction to the world of corporate management. I would enthusiastically discuss the characters and the thrilling world of share markets with my friends during my time at engineering college.

Mini Balachandran, the smart and capable managing director of Dhanwantari Herbal Products, fighting against a hostile takeover bid; Sreedevi, the IIM Ahmedabad alumnus, who enchants us with her intelligence and percipience; the spirited and clear-headed Savitry, who plays the stocks like a gamer – were strong, unforgettable women. Needless to say, I was thrilled when *Ohari* went on to win the prestigious Kerala Sahitya Akademi Award in 1993. The book, I would like to vouch, made me pursue my higher studies in management.

Three decades down, when I was searching for a translation of *Ohari* to gift a few of my non-Malayali friends, I discovered that there was none. Thereafter, when the revered author gave me his blessings for translating his favourite creation into English, my enthusiasm soared.

The share market continues to be one of the hottest topics debated in financial newspapers today. In the world of online trading, demat accounts and a slew of IPOs, Nifty and Sensex are part of the common lingo. The public is aware of terms like RBI and SEBI. But hardly ever has one read a novel, beautifully crafted with wit and wisdom, written about the world of share markets. *Ohari*, meaning shares, stands unique in Indian literature by offering that rare treat to readers. Irrespective of one's educational background, the reader will be able to grasp and enjoy the thrill of the share market and appreciate the stories of the human beings behind the corporates.

It must be understood that thirty-three years ago, every rupee was of great value. So when Dhanwantari trades for ten rupees, we should consider it equivalent to what, today, would be a share price of a hundred rupees. When Matthews negotiates to collect two crores from the financiers, it is equivalent to a deal of twenty crores in current times. True, the world depicted by the author also shows people making STD calls. It was a time when news broadcasting and computer data analysis were just taking off. Yet the deep insights about the world of share trading, corporate governance, global markets, and the vision about upcoming technologies the story contains within it, are prophetic and awe-inspiring. For example, a character in the novel, Mohandas, has an electronic gadget which he uses to set alarms; it also throws up programmed details! (Today's 'reminder' feature in our phones!)

What happens in a span of a few days when a local Ayurvedic company based in Kerala, Dhanwantari Herbal Products, led by managing director Mini Balachandran, fights a hostile takeover bid, forms the crux of this delightful narrative. We meet through it various intriguing characters, such as Zacharia, Matthews, Vinayan, Shankaran Kutty, Savitry, Mohandas, Ramesan, with each of their stories woven seamlessly into and making for a compelling plot. Numerous aspects of the stock market are explained cogently alongside the experiences of these characters – but there is never a dull moment in that intricate web formed of numbers and greed and strategy, of concerns over profit and loss.

When I submitted the draft with great hope to HarperCollins India, an acquaintance had mocked me, saying, 'You are so gullible.' Apparently, no translator should attempt a mammoth book of five-hundred-odd pages without an offer in hand. But I have certain traits of Mini Balachandran in me. (By the way, I am called Mini by my friends and family!) Any attempt to belittle my efforts stirs my rebellious spirit. When my book was accepted, I whooped in joy and remembered Jesus Christ's powerful words about faith moving mountains.

I owe my gratitude to the author K.L. Mohana Varmaji, his loving daughter Kavita, Associate Publisher Dharini Bhaskar, and dear Rinita Banerjee, who did such a fantastic job editing the translation. What a pleasure it has been to work with such intelligent minds!

I do hope our labour of love receives a place in the reader's heart.

And now, let the game begin!

—Ministhy S.

1

The Beginning

'Guruvayurappa, please let there be no traffic jam at the high road.'

When the car neared the overbridge, Mini Balachandran closed her eyes for a moment and meditated on Guruvayurappan – the enchanting Little Krishna of the Guruvayur temple. Mini was in the habit of praying while approaching the bridge, both in the morning and in the evening.

The prayer gave meagre results, though. Two or three days of the week, she had to brake the car quite a few times in the middle of the climb up that overbridge. Mostly, it would be an autorickshaw. If there was a little space ahead, one or two scooters or motorcycles would squirm their way to the front. If the cars ahead were old and unable to negotiate the steep winding road, they would cough and sputter along, and force her to slow down. At times, her own car would shut down. The trouble was in restarting it: manoeuvring the accelerator and the brake simultaneously; more pressure on one, less on the other. The blaring horns from behind … especially when they noticed that it was a woman driver … all those mocking looks, smiles, snide remarks ... unnecessary tension! Even after crossing the overbridge, it took Mini a long while to regain her composure.

There were many drivers working for the company. But Mini's father had always gone to work driving his own car. And she never felt like changing that custom. Indeed, there was an innate stubbornness to continue all the old practices.

The Contessa was used for official purposes now. She had taken her brother's Fiat for herself, it was easy to handle. For all official trips, she could rely on the Contessa. It had a dedicated driver too. She could easily avail of it for visiting the factory located across the lagoon, beyond Aroor.

The daily drive from home to office and back held its own pleasures – especially when Mini was alone. When the eyes and limbs were intently focused, numerous intricate issues could be analysed in depth.

There was only one problem: the possibility of a major accident on the overbridge.

There were only two overbridges to cross the railway line that girdled Ernakulam city right in the middle. One in the north, the other in the south. Though there were many level crossings, most of the traffic was on the overbridges.

On the western half of the city were the offices, markets, shops, the airport, the naval base and the port. On the eastern half, a smattering of small towns crowded with people, new colonies sprouting over the swampy areas, trucks loaded with heavy material making their way from the southern hilly terrains, lorries from Tamil Nadu carrying merchandise for sale in the city markets, and so on. All the toing and froing from the port, which was the lifeline of the Kalamassery commercial zone, happened on the overbridges. A case of gross overburdening. The flow of vehicles would start by eight-thirty in the morning and continue uninterruptedly till noon. The return rush would start at three and begin abating by eight in the night. Both the overbridges would be suffocating during those hours.

Today was like any usual day, which meant being caught in the rush hour. But there wasn't much trouble. A bus trundled twenty feet ahead of Mini's car. No autos or scooters jumped in between. The bus mounted the uphill road without slowing down. Pressing the accelerator, with the clutch in the second gear, she managed to reach the summit of the overbridge.

She was happy. Today was a lucky day. When the car slowly passed the Devi temple on the right, Mini shut her eyes again in prayer. 'Devi, please save us all.'

~

By the time she had finally managed to fall asleep this morning, it was half past two. It was, in fact, a forced slumber. Mini had taken a sleeping pill. Even so, she had been haunted by a few nightmares. It was as if someone was pulling her feet backwards, dragging her through a lagoon that flowed lethargically. The cicadas chattered all the while, the sound piercing her eardrums.

Numbers, figures, charts.

The last four months had been roiling with problems. There had been a niggling fear that every phone call, every government paper were harbingers of disaster. It was a daily struggle with the bank. The finance director Adiyodi's face was glum when he quoted the figures concerning cash flow and liquidity. The plant at Thodupuzha was supposed to have started last month. But there had been no end to the glitches, right from the moment the foundation stone was laid. It might take another year before production started. The costs would escalate further. As of now, the expenses were twice the original estimates. The completion of the project was hardly seventy per cent.

The estate at Nelliyampathy was still lying in wilderness too.

Expenses, expenses.

Interminable expenses.

Every project was future-oriented. Five years, ten years, twenty-five years.

But what about now?

It was not just yesterday; an undisturbed sleep any night had long become a dream.

One could read between the lines of Suryanarayanan's report. It was evident that the company was tottering under an unbearable burden.

Every organization has an inherent limit of expansion, an optimum point of growth. Mini reflected that Acchan – her father – had known it. He would seek out new sectors when such a point was imminent. Otherwise, an inevitable decline, akin to old age, would soon take over and trounce everything.

Mini had gone through Suryanarayanan's management consultancy report, worth one and a half lakh rupees, thrice in a row. It was a solid fifty-page analysis. There were another hundred pages, including annexures, accounts, charts, and the like. The balance sheets of the last three years, cost analysis, comments on the new project reports.

Suryanarayanan had done his homework well.

When Mini was wondering whether it would be worthwhile to invest one and a half lakh rupees and get a stranger to submit a report on one's own establishment, Zacharia uncle had provided wise counsel. No player could ever assess his own full potential or limitations. That required a coach, an analyser. It was analogous to the role of the 'second' in a game of chess. Before any combat, they examined the opponent's strategies in the previous games and gathered information about the attacking style. The 'second' dug deep into the player's gaming style, threw light on their strengths and weaknesses, and helped to create a suitable game plan. Companies and business firms needed management consultants much like these coaches or seconds.

Suryanarayanan's report was replete with many technical jargons. That was pretty common. Not that it mattered much.

Mini remembered Zacharia's warning: 'Suryanarayanan will submit an excellent report. But one should pay him extra for getting him to elucidate certain sentences. You should not have to bother over the verbiage, Mini. Discard that as being merely ornamental.'

'You mean, he will be trying to impress than express?'

'Not exactly. That's the way they usually work.'

Hardly three days were left before her meeting with Aniyan Raja. The report was absolutely essential before Mini could take him on.

When Suryanarayanan was issued the final warning, he had been contrite. 'Madam, I sincerely apologize for the delay. The report is ready. I have incorporated all the conclusions and suggestions. It will be finalized today. It shall reach you by dusk.'

'If something is not timely, it's like flogging a dead horse, wouldn't you agree?'

'You're right.'

Her personal assistant, Prakashan, had arrived at eight in the night with the report from Suryanarayanan's office.

While standing under the shower, the cool needlepoints of the water had invigorated Mini.

Suryanarayanan's report had been in front of her the previous evening. It included the consolidated comments of the domain experts too.

One decision to rout Aniyan Raja … One idea. Anything to help with that…

Mini closed her eyes and meditated on the images of her father and grandfather. 'Grant me courage, strength and wisdom.'

She had a simple dinner with rice gruel, stir-fried green gram lentil, fresh grated coconut and pickled mangoes. Amma sat near as Mini enjoyed her food. These days she hardly spoke a word. The only mutterings were 'Narayana, Narayana'.

Mini instinctively felt that her mother wanted to say something. 'What is it, Amma?'

'Nothing. Everything will turn out to be okay. Lord Dhanwantari shall never let go of those who seek his refuge. Let us visit our tharavadu tomorrow or the day after. Time to seek benedictions.'

Looking into her mother's eyes suddenly made Mini feel overwhelmed. She searched for words. Nothing dawned immediately.

'There was a call from Delhi,' Amma murmured.

'When?'

'While you were taking a shower.'

'Why didn't you call me?'

'Balachandran asked me not to trouble you. He is going to Calcutta tomorrow. And then to Assam.'

'Did he say when he would return?'

'No.'

'Let me call him then.'

'He said he will be going out. Might come back late.'

Mini knew that he wouldn't have gone anywhere. The image of her miffed husband packing his suitcase appeared in her mind. Yes, he would forget something for sure! No blade in his shaving kit … Did he pack his vest, socks? And later, he would blame her for the missing item! She decided not to call Delhi.

At 9 p.m., Mini entered the office room and shut the door. She quickly browsed through the consultant's report and observations. In the second round of reading, she focused on Suryanarayanan's suggestions worth one and a half lakh rupees. Mini underlined the relevant recommendations and ruthlessly marked in blue whatever seemed superfluous. The third time, she meticulously perused every paragraph and tried to correlate them with her own experiences and know-how. Time passed quickly. Her head was a battleground of charts and figures.

The decision, the right and wrong of it, would influence so many lives! As that occurred to her, Mini felt a prickling of fear. Her strength seemed to wane, the bulwark of confidence seemed to be shaky. The desolation became unbearable.

At two in the night, Mini felt the urge to call Delhi. A silent tussle was going on in her mind. She dialled the number. When the static thrumming started, she cut the call.

No ... No...

I have to handle this ... I, by myself.

She closed the door of the office, walked to her bedroom and took a sleeping pill.

Mini had been troubled by many nightmares in the recent past. Scattered incidents, human forms ... all hazy, vague ... nothing that could be recollected at will.

Amma woke her up at eight in the morning.

She had visited a temple. Mini's mother was dressed in white and looked radiant with the sandalwood paste adorning her forehead. Even at sixty, how lovely she was!

When Mini rubbed her eyes sleepily, Amma teased her gently, 'Do you know how late it is?'

In the blink of an eye, Mini turned into a little girl. She pulled Amma towards the cot and snuggled up next to her. Then she scratched at the sandalwood paste on Amma's forehead and applied the scraping on her own forehead.

'What are you doing? Applying the holy sandalwood paste without a bath? Brat!'

Mini stretched her right hand towards her mother. Except two pointed fingers, she folded the rest. 'Amma, touch one of these.' Then she shut her eyes.

'You are crazy!'

Amma touched the forefinger. Mini laughed delightedly and jumped out of the bed.

'Amma, I'll take a bath and be out in no time. What's for breakfast?'

'Dosa.'

As she stepped inside the bathroom, Mini remarked: 'Exactly as I thought. Amma, your daughter is not one to cede defeat so quickly.'

This was a childhood habit. Her husband would often tease her: 'Mini, you have a strong gambling instinct! The same as Yudhishthir, the son of Dharma, right?'

Could it be referred to as gambling? It's not like uncertainty was associated only with the game of dice, was it?

'Mini, even if there is one chance in ten, you shall try a hand, won't you?'

She had not asked Balachandran whether their marriage fell in the same category. Maybe, to a certain extent.

Her husband would smile at her.

Only those who have known the exhilaration of gambling, of a game of dice, would appreciate it. Wasn't all human progress based on this thrill? The adventurous spirit of cladding oneself with wings and trying to fly off a mountain peak originated from the same thrill, did it not?

Mini would always test her luck, very secretively.

Yes or no?

If the leaf fell on its face … yes. If it fell on its back … no.

'Akku thikku thana varambathu…' – the childhood game of chance, played to the tunes of the ditty! You started counting the closed fists all the children in the group had placed downwards on the ground. When a particular phrase in the poem arrived, either you got hit or you evaded smartly! Ultimately, the one who survived without getting hit, would be the winner.

Shall I pass or fail in the exam?

First class?

Distinction?

If the leaf fell on its face, first class. If not, distinction.

It fell on its face … what now?

No, once more! Let's try for the best of three attempts.

Amma, I shall win.

With distinction.

~

There was no traffic-police constable at the junction. The vehicle, approaching from the opposite side, was drawing closer. Would it head right, left, or straight towards her?

If the leaf fell on its face, left! Else, right.

Mini pressed the brake and halted the car on the roadside. Seeing her car, the watchman at the gate opened the gates wide and started heckling the driver of the lorry parked nearby.

Most of the roads in Ernakulam city were very narrow. And there would always be an unceasing rush. Handcarts, heavy-carrier lorries, autorickshaws, minivans, cars, jeeps, cycles and scooters. If it was a market day, there wouldn't be space to even turn or twist! It was astounding how vehicles managed to move amidst such a melee. Give them an inch of space, and they would sidle past one another, without a scratch.

Right in the midst of all that hullabaloo was the registered office of Dhanwantari Herbal Products Limited. It was a reputed Ayurvedic medicine manufacturing company where Mini Balachandran held the post of managing director. Her mother was the chairman.

When Mini's car crossed the gate and reached the front of the office, Prakashan came running.

'Zacharia sir has been calling non-stop, madam. I have put his call on hold.'

Mini retrieved the briefcase from the back of the car and handed it over to him.

'I will attend the call from my room.'

People got up respectfully at the reception counter; she hardly noticed.

Mini felt that the call was a portent of something disastrous.

The air conditioning in the MD's room was on.

Mini picked up the phone.

'Mini here. What's up, Uncle?'

She heard P.T. Zacharia's soft-toned voice. 'I need to see you as soon as possible. It's urgent!'

'What's wrong?'

'Can't share over the phone.'

'Why not?'

'Have you been reading *The Business Times*, especially over the last three days?'

'No … I was…'

'Dhanwantari's shares are being bought at a furious pace … I don't get it. There has been a lot of interest in our shares in the past three days at the Stock Exchange.'

'In Kerala?'

'Not here. In Bombay, Calcutta, Ahmedabad, Delhi … all these places.'

'What?'

After a moment's poignant pause, Mini asked: 'Uncle, is this serious?'

'If it's an intentional strategy, then trust me, it's very serious … The company…!'

'Aniyan Raja—'

Zacharia interrupted: 'Mini, cancel all your appointments. I'm coming over. We should do something before the Exchange opens.'

'Uncle, Suryanarayanan's report…'

Zacharia raised his voice. 'Just keep it aside … One undergoes the detoxifying kayakalpa treatment only if they're alive, right?'

The call was disconnected.

It was nine-forty in the morning. The Stock Exchange would start operating at twelve-thirty in the afternoon. Two hours, fifty minutes were left to go.

Mini felt debilitated. She collapsed into the comforting embrace of the soft, flaccid executive chair. Her gaze was fixed on the dark water inside the tall, crystal glass on the table.

She did not see the glass.

2

Roots

Mini Balachandran's great grandfather, Komaru Thirumulppadu, had been a renowned Ayurvedic physician. His family home at Mavelikkara, in the middle of erstwhile Travancore, on the shores of the river Achankovilaru, had an Ayurvedic legacy. Today, members of a different matrilineal branch were residing in the place. They did the puja rituals of the Dhanwantari idol installed in their family home, a traditional nalukettu house, where an open courtyard linked four blocks.

The old-timers used to narrate many legends associated with the home – Menamvila Koyikkil – starting from Parashuram's time. Those were phantasmagorical stories, fraught with hyperboles. The vast compound was replete with serpent groves, wild creepers, screw pine bushes, medicinal plants, trees and rare herbs.

Mini had been to the family home only once so far.

A gnarled, old woman stood out in her memory, one from whose ears dangled giant, heavy, round thoda earrings. The five-year-old Mini knew a story about that granny.

The old lady used to sleep in the room in the north-west. She was totally fearless and did not care two hoots about any ghost, spectre, gnome, or ghoul! Granny would walk into the western yard and converse with these spirits at night. She would affectionately offer them honey, bananas and milk. All of these magical spirits liked her too. One day, a kuttichathan, a magical gnome, a comparative newcomer, assumed the guise of a snake to frighten the woman. Crawling into her bed, it raised its fearsome hood, aiming for her forehead. Granny did not bat an eyelid. Seizing the serpent's tail, she twirled it once before hurling it against the attic. The snake was badly wounded. The following night, the kuttichathan came to seek forgiveness for his arrogance. The old lady went to the yard, picked some random herbs and created a salve for his broken back. He was healed, and turned into her devoted helper.

During that memorable visit, Granny had asked the kuttichathan to fetch beautiful seeds from the red coral tree for little Mini.

The forestlands belonging to the family spoke of a thousand-year-old history. The heritage of Ayurveda, burnished with the wisdom of many generations, had been handed over to the healers of every generation. Komaru Thirumulppadu was one such gifted vaidyan, a healer.

The man had proficiency in not only Ayurveda but also in myriad fields. The inherent dedication that made him surrender all his efforts at the divine feet of Lord Dhanwantari, his unrelenting eagerness to master new skills, the dedication to completely immerse himself in his work, all contributed to making him an exemplary physician of his times.

In the first decade of the twentieth century, Komaru Thirumulppadu developed a friendship with the then ruler of Kochi. Both were passionate about elephants, chaturanga aka chess, and pandimelam – the classical percussion concert. The ruler – Thampuran – used to invite Komaru to his palace at Tripunithura often. The royal personage's annual kayakalpa chikitsa, that is, the holistic body and mind Ayurvedic treatment, conducted in the month of Karkidakam, was supervised by Komaru. In a few years' time, Komaru became famous in the Kochi kingdom. Soon, upon the affectionate persuasions of the ruler, he shifted his residence to Tripunithura.

Komaru Thirumulppadu was given land free of taxes and the family home, or tharavadu, with its nalukettu architecture, was built for him. In due course, Komaru established a customary marital relationship with a girl from one of the leading Nair families in the area. Mini's grandfather, Ramunni Nair, was his son.

Komaru Thirumulppadu had a thriving medical practice and grew prosperous. The number of detractors started increasing. The natives of Kochi had an inherent suspicion about the outsiders hailing from Travancore. In their opinion, these men were ruthless in disposition. The enemies poisoned the ears of the ruler through his royal consort. Nobody dared to take on Komaru directly.

The heir of the ruler died early, even before he could become the monarch. Komaru Thirumulppadu's bad times were beginning. Soon, he was struggling to make ends meet. Even so, Komaru did not think of returning to his family home at Mavelikkara. There were many penurious patients in the locality who were solely dependent on him.

'More than knowledge, a vaidyan needs gurutvam, the kindly grace and benediction of his mentors.' That was Komaru Thirumulppadu's staunch belief. He would never prescribe medicine for any disease unless he had prayed to Lord Dhanwantari. The prescriptions would be followed with suggestions for the puja offerings of his beloved deity.

In those days, a Chettiar family, well settled in Kumbalam island for generations, suffered from childlessness. The Chettiar and his wife had visited all renowned physicians, tried all the available remedies and participated in rituals at all the famous temples.

Getting to hear about Komaru Thirumulppadu, Chettiar's men approached him. He visited the hapless couple and prescribed an ottamooli, that is, a single-ingredient remedy. Further, he suggested forty-one days of puja rituals for propitiating Lord Dhanwantari. After the puja, the couple was advised to partake of the prasadam – the temple's offering.

Chettiar's wife conceived. On the twenty-eighth day after his son was born, the Chettiar invited Komaru Thirumulppadu home. He showed him the infant.

'The little one owes his birth to your blessings.'

'No, Lord Dhanwantari has blessed you. I am just a medium, Chettiar!'

Chettiar respectfully placed eleven gold sovereigns, betel leaves and areca nuts at Komaru's feet. Then he spoke: 'Now, you should accept this document too.'

'What is it?'

It was the land deed for an acre and a half of property near the lagoon, in Ernakulam. The skiffs and boats carrying merchandise moored near that deserted spot, which was run over with weeds and shrubs.

Chettiar said: 'This property is now in your name. There is a small house, a serpent grove and a pond. You should accept it for the sake of my baby.'

That was how the main office of Dhanwantari Herbal Products Limited came to be situated in the middle of a market area – a rather unbefitting place.

Komaru Thirumulppadu did not shift his residence. When they checked the auguries, it turned out that there was a ghost infestation in the premises. There was a need for exorcism.

The vaidyan died before all the ghosts could be driven out.

Ramunni Nair, his son, was eighteen years old then. Komaru Thirumulppadu had named him as the sole heir to all the properties and assets.

Ramunni was progressive by nature. He read English newspapers and magazines. The waves of the freedom struggle that began in north India, impacted him. He was aware of the Khilafat movement, and how the Indian National Congress, under Gandhiji's leadership, influenced the lives of the natives. Ramunni was averse to practices like untouchability, and opposed the barriers raised by the caste system. However, he never openly rebelled against any issue.

A few years later, Ramunni Nair shifted residence to Ernakulam. He was a father to a young child by then. His mother continued to stay at Tripunithura with her daughters. The worship of Lord Dhanwantari continued in the family home.

Ramunni did not believe in ghosts. He got the 'possessed' building renovated. On the insistence of his mother, he moved the serpent deities from the snake grove there to the grove in their family home in Tripunithura.

The city kept expanding.

Ramunni did not have the gift of healing that his father Komaru Thirumulppadu possessed. Regardless, he examined patients and prescribed medicines. His father's patients were loyal to the family. When their ailments caused them pain, they would visit allopathy practitioners or other vaidyans. Noticeably, there was an influx of new patients. They were from different religions and spoke different languages. Apart from Ramunni Nair, there was no other vaidyan in the middle of the busy Ernakulam market.

The new patients did not have time to prepare the kashayam, or herbal decoction, or create a lehyam, that is, the paste made of herbs and spices. The people of the fast-expanding city, which derailed the covenants and precedents of yore, were actively searching for new ways of healing.

Most patients were impoverished. Some were petty shopkeepers, coolies or boatmen. They could not afford the high-priced medicines. Some valuable moments of the vaidyan's time were all that they wished for.

The rush would begin by nine in the morning. On receiving the prescription, most patients would worry aloud: 'But where do we get the medicines from?'; 'Can't we find the medicines here?'

Preparing the Ayurvedic medicines was not considered a dignified task. The vaidyan was not a trader. Lord Dhanwantari's benedictions were not supposed to be bottled and marketed. But times were changing. Many were leaving their familial, traditional jobs and taking up new ventures.

'Shouldn't I adapt to the changing ethos…?' Ramunni Nair's ruminations ran thus.

The allopathy practitioners were making instant 'mixtures', selling red water in bottles. Pharmaceutical companies were selling pills and powders in attractive containers. The vaidyan just had to prescribe, the trader would do the rest. For the common diseases, it was better to have ready-made medicines which could be distributed to the patients. There was no loss of dignity in that.

Having decided the course of action, Ramunni became active. The preparations began with full gusto.

Ramunni Nair had a pretty large circle of friends in the city. Advocates, teachers, businessmen, politicians, social workers … Nevertheless, all those erudite, iconoclastic thinkers lacked money.

Everybody ardently supported Ramunni's idea. They also insisted that he should dream big even at the start. Fine-quality medicines in enticing bottles with colourful wrappers! Not just one or two, but a minimum of ten medicines to begin with.

But there were a number of complex issues to be dealt with. The land was available. But what about the workers, building, vessels, bottles, raw materials? A huge capital would be required. Ramunni and his wife spent sleepless nights working out the numbers. They needed a minimum of ten thousand rupees to start a proper enterprise.

How on earth would they collect such a huge amount?

One evening, while he was discussing the business proposal with his friends, an idea came up. Ramunni could not recollect who proposed it. Make a company, sell the shares and create the capital. There were only a handful of public limited companies in Travancore and Cochin at that time. Nobody had ventured into these turfs before, the field of shares – of ohari.

Ramunni Nair and his advocate friends started studying more about the topic. The more they analysed it, the more alluring the proposal seemed to be. No need to take loans, enough capital could be easily amassed. The patients themselves could contribute. Perhaps, ten rupees each. One ohari – share – for ten rupees.

Ten rupees was not a small amount in those days. Yet, when the need was for a noble cause, why not take the plunge? Let the patients consider it equal to loaning their vaidyan an amount of ten rupees! Instead of a document attesting to the loan, they would have a share in the company. Besides, any shareholder would be given a proper discount while purchasing medicines.

The idea expanded. Everybody was bubbling with enthusiasm.

There was no confusion about the name. Dhanwantari Herbal Products Limited.

The company was registered. Two thousand shares. Ten rupees each.

Ramunni compiled the addresses of his father's patients and his own. There were almost eight hundred of them. A share certificate, printed elegantly at a press in Kottayam, was sent to each person on the list. Along with it, Ramunni added a request of contributing ten rupees towards the company. More than five hundred people sent the needed amount over the next sixty days. Almost forty share certificates came back by post, stamped with 'recipient not available at address'. Two people sent twenty-five rupees each. One sent hundred rupees. Ten or twelve sent the share certificates back with a note that they were not interested in the scheme. Perhaps, the rest of the patients kept the certificates; but they never sent any money.

Ramunni kept a thousand shares for himself. In the accounts it was shown against the transfer of land and other facilities for the company. He distributed almost a hundred shares amongst his friends. Suffice it to say that when the Second World War broke out, there were hardly any shares of the Dhanwantari Herbal Products Limited left to sell.

The odour of herbs and sautéed oil started wafting from the small shed abutting the ghost-ridden building. Ramunni also opened a retail shop in the market.

Mini's father Raghava Menon was eight years old then. But he knew the price of every product in the shop. After school, the boy preferred to spend his time in the shop premises. He had no proclivity towards his schoolbooks or games. Raghava Menon's parents bragged that all their son wanted was to count the money and verify the numbers.

3

The Squirrels in the Mango Tree

Prakashan, Mini's personal assistant, placed the briefcase on a side table. He then turned to look enquiringly at Mini.

'Switch off the air-conditioning and open the window. Zacharia uncle will be here soon,' Mini said.

Prakashan followed the instructions silently. The grating sound of iron cables being dropped from a height could be heard.

As he stepped out, Mini said: 'Get some paan for Zacharia uncle. Also, ask Finance Director Adiyodi to come at eleven-thirty.'

Prakashan left; the door closed behind him.

The photographs of her grandfather, father and younger brother, hanging on the opposite wall, seemed to be gazing at Mini.

She ruminated:

I don't understand what Zacharia uncle meant. Who are our enemies? And why are they harbouring a resentment against the company? That, too, when the company is in such a state! Anyone who has seen the last three years' balance sheets would never purchase the company's shares at a dream price, would they? The value of the shares has remained steady in the past few years. Not just that, even when the market shares of other companies skyrocketed, Dhanwantari's shares never crossed the value of fifteen rupees.

Who is trying to cause a stir? What is the purpose?

Through the open window, Mini could see the luscious green mango tree in the front yard. She moved towards the window. Her eyes scanned the branches for a glimpse of the squirrels.

~

Mini's husband Balachandran had once suggested that they chop down the huge mango tree. They could construct a six- or seven-storeyed building in that space. The bank would readily finance the project. There could be shops on the ground floor and an underground parking area. A few floors could be leased out easily. A sort of self-financing scheme. The municipal corporation was generously encouraging such schemes lately.

Mini's acchan had responded tersely. 'Not in my lifetime. My children have been after me about such a scheme forever. But no. Not now.'

'Why?'

'I adore the sweet-as-jaggery mangoes of that tree.'

The conversation had taken place in Balachandran's Lajpat Nagar flat in Delhi.

Acchan used to drink occasionally. At first, he'd kept it a secret. Later, when the children grew up, the habit became more open. On his way back home from the office in the evenings, he would drink at a classy bar in solitude. Suresh, Mini's younger brother, would be there to drive him back. After two pegs, as they drove home, Acchan would share his dreams with his son. All the future visions he had for Dhanwantari. The man who could exhibit extreme practicality would transform into a daydreamer in the blink of an eye.

In the Delhi flat that day, Acchan had turned to address Mini.

'Mini, do you know something? When I sit down for my lunch, I open the window wide. Two squirrels scamper down the tree and perch on the windowsill. I serve them some morsels. We usually have lunch together.'

Mini recollected that once during her schooldays, she had fed those squirrels too.

'They must have died by now.'

'I don't know! Despite the passing of years, there are always two squirrels. Maybe when one dies, another takes its place. Anyway, I watch them scurry back to the tree after lunch. I am worried about their home, in case we cut down that mango tree.'

Mini's father used to visit Delhi frequently. He had many friends there. It was true that Raghava Menon had created wonders in the field of packaging and marketing Ayurvedic medicines. When a seminar or conference related to Ayurveda happened in any part of India, he would invariably attend it. He was also a member of most government committees dealing with indigenous medicines.

But Mini often felt that her father sought out reasons to visit Delhi. Wasn't meeting his daughter the main motive? Somehow, Acchan was still not confident that his daughter was comfortably settled. He needed to check for himself. Only then would he be at peace.

Mini's grandfather had been the original visionary. But it was his son, the famous Raghava Menon, who made those dreams a reality.

Fifty years. Fifty-one years to be precise. The company was growing every day.

Mini Balachandran's grandfather had registered the public limited company and blazed a new path in the manufacturing of Ayurvedic medicines by selling its shares. Mini's father, Raghava Menon, had transformed Dhanwantari Herbal Products into one of Kerala's leading enterprises. The company had issued new shares in the market thrice. At one point, it also brought out debentures, which could be converted into shares. Every four or five years, bonus shares were issued. The dividends to the shareholders were consistently maintained at twenty per cent.

Menon used to share his plans and projects with his family at breakfast. He would say, 'Just fifteen per cent of the company's shares belong to us. Another fifteen per cent belongs to the Dhanwantari Trust. That is more than sufficient. The rest belongs to the public. These shares embody the common man's implicit faith in us. In a way, the thirty per cent shares held by the government's financial agencies also belong to the community. The company should never indulge in activities that harm the stakeholders. Mere profits are not our aim. We are using the divine benediction of healing, our inheritance across generations, for serving the public. This is an action, a karma, which has to be conducted with utmost dedication.'

By then, the family had shifted into the new house that was built on the family property in Tripunithura.

Small buildings cropped up beside the main company office in Ernakulam. Cochin, Kochi or Ernakulam – the public addressed their city in many ways.

After eight years, some property was purchased near Aroor. The land was situated next to the lagoon, and the production unit was set up there. The special benefits granted to the Alappuzha district by the government, the proximity of the unit to Cochin city, and the scintillating natural beauty, were obvious advantages. Slowly, the manufacture of the full range of medicines shifted to the Aroor production unit. The Ernakulam office focused exclusively on the marketing. The availability of all the latest packaging technologies, cutting-edge gadgets and machinery, and top-notch quality control, were Dhanwantari's strengths. A new research centre was set up in Ernakulam for studying herbs.

A whole plethora of Ayurvedic products – salves, concoctions, oils and powders in tablet form – were attractively packaged in the style of allopathy medicines and sold widely. The products were available with stockists in every major Indian city, with smaller agencies in tier-two and tier-three cities, and the company's own sales depots in certain regions. The emphasis on diagnosis was comparatively less. Though five Ayurvedic doctors were appointed at Trivandrum, Kozhikode, Ernakulam, Bangalore and Madras, the sales of medicines remained the top priority. The revenues from sales started surging.

Six or seven years earlier, Menon had envisioned two new projects. A big factory in Idukki district – a specialized, autonomous department focusing on not just the production of medicines, but also the manufacture of bottles and labels. The project, originally planned at an investment of two crores, was yet to be completed. Though the shares brought to market for this special purpose were sold successfully, the venture per se had not taken off.

The second project was to purchase hundreds of acres of forestland in Nelliyampathy, in Palakkad district, and to initiate the setting up of a herbal plantation. The company purchased the land, but things did not progress as expected. No income would be ensuing from the herbal park before two years.

Meanwhile, the interest payments on the credits availed for these projects were accruing at a hot pace. The company had been reeling under a financial crisis for the past five years. The situation would hopefully change once the dual projects were completed. But what about the imminent future?

Menon had another splendid vision. He wished to establish hundreds of hospitals across India, focusing on Kerala's own special Ayurvedic treatment regimes. He also wished to introduce in them the specialties of Kerala's intricate and unique healing practices: dhara, or the process of steadily pouring a unique medicinal oil on the affected part of the body; navarakizhi, or the sweat-inducing treatment using a bolus of medicated rice; thalapothichil, or the application of a special Ayurvedic paste made of gooseberry powder, buttermilk and leaves of lotuses on the head; and thalam, where the patient's head is covered with an Ayurvedic paste while a steady flow of medicated oil is maintained. There was also the dream of bringing numerous new products made of coconut water, coconut milk and coconut oil into the market, alongside items made of coconut-leaf stems, or eerkkil, coconut husks, or chakiri, and coconut shells, or chiratta.

Menon held many discussions with famous Ayurvedic practitioners from different parts of India. He spent money in the pursuit of his dream ventures. However, the projects were yet to see the light of day. The money kept flowing from the coffers. The debts increased insidiously. Lakhs of rupees were being paid as monthly interests. But Mini's father would never disclose any of these setbacks during his breakfast discourses. His overpowering monologues were replete with great confidence and astuteness.

The target audience of Acchan's motivational speeches was his son, Mini's younger brother Suresh.

Not her, the daughter.

Mini would boil over with bitter rage then. She would swallow it, though, without ever expressing her emotions.

Mini's fury was aimed at her brother Suresh, not her father. So, when the marriage proposal came, she had protested. 'I don't want to leave my home.'

The prospective bridegroom was from the Central Services. Most of his career would be centred around Delhi.

'Don't you like the young man?'

'I told you that I won't leave this place.'

Amma insisted: 'What's the matter? If you don't like him, we will find someone else.'

Mini felt like weeping.

'That's not it.'

'Then what?'

'I want to run the company. Our company.'

The next morning, during breakfast, Mini's father said: 'Mini, business does not suit women. It has nothing to do with your ability. But the emotional issues, tension, pressures ... The world of business resembles a deep forest. Wild animals are on the prowl. They wait to pounce on those who are deemed weaker, less capable or intelligent. Physically, women are not made for this forest.'

Biting down on a retort, Mini had glared at Suresh.

As usual, he was nonchalantly mixing his idli pieces with the chutney. A disgusting sight!

'Learn to eat like decent people.'

Suresh ignored the icy remark from his elder sister. 'Chechi can design the new advertisements. Or she can be our Delhi liaison officer. We can open an office there. She can while away time.'

Suresh was in the final year of his Bachelor's degree in commerce. He did not want to study Ayurveda. Their father did not insist on it either. 'I will go for an MBA. We should engage vaidyas, real experts for our business.'

Mini had felt like strangling him that moment.

Lord, if only he hadn't been born!

After her marriage, Mini had settled in Delhi. But several months later too, it seemed her father had not forgotten that singular breakfast conversation. Whenever he dropped by, Acchan would speak in detail about the company's problems, the new products on the anvil, how the projects at Idukki and Nelliyampathy were coming along...

His son-in-law, Balachandran, was an officer of the Indian Audit and Accounts Service. A financial expert. Every time Acchan spoke on any topic, it was as if he expected a detailed analysis from Balachandran.

But Mini knew, it was all meant for her.

~

One could watch the lagoon through the window in the olden days. Many buildings sprouted, even during Acchan's time, cutting off the view. Now one could see the backyard of a godown.

Mini gazed at the branches of the mango tree. No squirrel was in sight. She shut the window and switched the air conditioner on.

The black crystal glass on the table was covered with a silken handkerchief, with delicate threadwork and pearl trimmings. A tradition from her father's time. Never had Mini taken one sip of the dark water from this particular glass. But it stayed ready in its place, as always.

Her grandfather, father and brother gazed at her from the wall.

Were they laughing at her? What had happened to the company in a year's time? The turnover had reduced by twenty per cent. The cashflow was pathetic. The debts were rising day by day – the expenses too.

What was going on? Nothing.

It was not the field for women. Biologically unfit. This was the perfect time to run away.

Mini retrieved a fifty-paisa coin from her purse and placed it on her palm.

Her eyes flitted from one picture to another.

Head? Yes. Tail? No.

She tossed the coin. It fell and, hitting the table's edge, disappeared under the carpet.

Mini knelt down and carefully pulled out the coin.

'Mini, what are you doing? Playing hide and seek?' Zacharia asked wryly, while entering the office.

Mini's face turned red with embarrassment. 'No, Uncle.'

She forgot to glance at the coin.

Was it a head or a tail?

4

Football and Politics

Mini's Zacharia uncle, P.T. Zacharia or 'Kariachan' to his friends, was a brilliant stockbroker at Cochin Stock Exchange. He always reiterated one thing: The results of our deeds are not solely dependent on our plans, capability or talent. Chance or coincidences play a vital role.

As far as he was concerned, it was a reflection of the truth churned up by life-experiences.

Zacharia was amongst the early workers of the Communist party. Even before India became independent, the party showed him the red card. Until it split, he continued to be its full-time activist.

Today, he was a highly respected member of the Stock Exchange which exemplified the capitalist system the best. China, a Communist country, had its own stock exchanges. Yet, in Kerala, Communism and the Stock Exchange were yet to see eye to eye. Consequently, his old comrades considered Kariachan to be a lost cause.

Zacharia would say, 'All the major crossroads of my life were determined by small events which were serendipitous and highly improbable!'

That was true.

Zacharia had not become a Communist by reading up the tomes written by Marx or Engels. Neither was he driven to despair by the sufferings of the unorganized labourers and farmers of his land. An improbable coincidence was behind the singular happening.

Zacharia's calculations had unexpectedly gone wrong. If they had turned out right, no one could have prophesied what might have happened. But Zacharia would never have turned into a Communist. Neither would he have developed a soulful connection with Mini's father, Raghava Menon.

The iconoclastic young men of Travancore started to get attracted to the Communist party in the period between 1940 and 1950. The party was declared illegal by the authorities sporadically. Most of the youth were passionate followers of the Indian National Congress, which was engaged in the Quit India movement under Gandhiji's leadership. Some were supporters of Netaji Subhas Chandra Bose, who was endeavouring for an armed struggle to free India by establishing his military camps in Malaya, Singapore and Burma. The Communist party was not able to lure the young blood towards itself during those tempestuous years.

Zacharia had been enjoying a glorious stint as the school football captain. He was also the defending champion in both the hundred metres race and the long jump. The school football team had gained a name for itself in Travancore province. They were the reigning champions for five years at the district-level competitions. And Zacharia was the bulwark of the team.

One year before Zacharia turned Communist, his team lost, rather, was forced to lose, in the interschool football competition held in Trivandrum. It was the story of an unbelievable treachery. Not a day passed when Zacharia would not ruefully recollect the incident.

Zacharia's position was the centre-half. In those days, there were two backs and three half positions; and the centre-half was the most prominent amongst those. But once the game started, Zacharia was found chasing the ball into every corner of the field. If someone wished to kick a ball from the right-out corner point, there was no need to worry about finding anyone at the centre-forward position to head it inside the goalpost. One could see Zacharia's head – a handkerchief wrapped around it – floating in the air. When the forward players of the other team reached the goalpost and the goalie happened to leave the post unguarded, Zacharia would be there to kick away the ball.

Zacharia was a complete sportsman. But he changed after the previous year's interschool football finals. He had never felt resentment towards anyone until then. Something happened that day.

The interschool football final round was in Trivandrum. The finalists were Zacharia's team and another from the capital. It was the first time that a team from Trivandrum had reached the finals. Naturally, the audience was rooting for their home team. They hooted at every move that Zacharia made. He didn't care two hoots either. It was all part of the game.

But when there were three offside whistles against his team, Zacharia became miffed.

In one case, it was clearly not offside. He enquired at half-time: 'Who is the referee?' Then the farce was revealed! The referee and the linesmen were all from Trivandrum. Zacharia felt a wave of obstinacy surging inside him.

There were two offsides after half-time too. Zacharia dribbled the ball past four players and reached the goalpost. Someone kicked him viciously from behind. He fell down. Though he waited for the referee's whistle, nothing was heard except the sound of applause from the audience.

That was a foul which would have granted their side a penalty kick.

Was the referee blind?

Nobody made a goal until the last minute.

In the last few moments, the opposition got a corner. Both Zacharia and the centre-forward of the other team leapt to get the ball. It hit the other player's hand and slid down Zacharia's shoulder.

Whistle.

Zacharia picked up the ball and placed it on the field for a spot kick towards the opposite side, when a roar erupted from the crowd.

He looked up.

The referee was pointing at the penalty spot. He had decreed it was Zacharia's hands that had been guilty!

Zacharia rushed to the referee in a fit of rage. Somehow, he controlled himself and did not manhandle him.

The penalty turned into a goal. Trivandrum became the state champion.

From that day, Zacharia would bristle at the mere mention of those hailing from Trivandrum.

Zacharia was the spine and soul of the school football team. It was not merely a school team; it also belonged to the whole land. The village near Mavelikkara was renowned only because of football. The school's headmaster and all the teachers were aware of this fact too. If Zacharia passed the School Leaving Certificate Examination and left the team, the whole village would face the brunt of it. So they made Zacharia repeat each grade as many times as possible. He himself was proud about it.

Zacharia was very much aware of his own importance in the scheme of things. Not just that, he also had inordinate confidence in the perpetuity of that importance. That was his mistake.

Zacharia's expertize in football and prominence at school were irrefutable. But what if something mightier than these came into the picture?

Something like that did come to pass. It was a rather silly episode.

Until then, there had been nobody nicknamed as a Communist at school. Venu was the lone student who displayed a slight leaning towards the party. He was the only son of Warrier, the Hindi teacher. A simple lad. Venu played in the football team as a forward. Zacharia liked him. He would often speak highly about Venu to the team manager-cum-school drillmaster Vakkachan.

The school was planning to celebrate the birthday of the Maharajah of Travancore, Sri Chittira Thirunal, in a grand manner. As per the headmaster's wishes, the celebrations were supposed to bring much glory to the school during a turbulent time when Netaji and Bapuji were stirring the muddy waters.

The programme was fixed:

> 10 a.m.: Flag hoisting, reciting the paean for the king: '*Vancheesa Mangalam*'. Followed by sports meet and distribution of sweets.
>
> 2.30 p.m.: Official meeting
>
> 4 p.m.: Football match between school team and Mavelikkara Young Men's Club.

The preparations began in full swing, weeks prior to the event. The football team was practising in full fervour under Zacharia's leadership.

The day before the event, they had just finished football practice. Zacharia had a favourite routine after all the team members left. He would hand over the football to the peon and smoke a beedi. That day, too, Zacharia was puffing away next to the goalpost. It was then that Venu approached him diffidently.

'Chetta, I need to speak about something.'

'Go on.'

Venu cast a wary glance around. 'Look, if you can't do it, just tell me no. But if it is a no, you should not mention that such a conversation ever happened!'

'What the heck is the matter? Spit it out!'

'Give me your word first!'

'Okay, I won't tell a soul.'

'Come closer.' Venu whispered something into Zacharia's ear. Zacharia started laughing. 'You are a smart aleck, aren't you?'

'Chetta, this is no laughing matter!'

'You expect me to weep, do you?'

'Do you agree?'

'What if I don't?'

'I shall return home disappointed, what else?'

'Nobody else to help you, eh?'

'If a person like you doesn't have the guts, am I a fool to expect someone else to help me?'

Zacharia patted Venu's shoulder. 'Don't cozy up so blatantly! Let us think of something. These fellows are all from Trivandrum, aren't they? All right then!'

Sharp at ten the next morning, Headmaster Shiva Shankara Pillai retrieved the flags kept atop his almirah, all covered up and well-preserved. There were two flags: the Travancore flag embossed with the insignia of a conch shell and an elephant, and the Union Jack of the British empire.

Vakkachan, the drillmaster, tied the folded flags to the halyard. Amidst the cheers of the crowd, the headmaster reverently shut his eyes and hoisted the flag at the mast. The students started singing the national anthem of the Travancore kingdom.

Vancheebhumipathe chiram

Hail the king of Vanchi, eternal...

Suddenly, the headmaster shouted, 'Stop! Stop!'

The singing ended abruptly. There were titters all around.

All eyes were entranced by the flags. A tricolour and a flaming red flag! There was the emblem of a charkha in the middle of the tricoloured flag. A sickle and hammer were embossed on the red flag.

The programme ground to a halt. The headmaster and village elders were wild with fury. The sports meet was cancelled. The raging headmaster and the drillmaster retreated to the office.

'The rascal removed the clay tile of the roof! That's how he slipped inside the room.' Vakkachan scowled.

'I know that! But who is the culprit?'

'Not one, but two for sure!'

'Who could it be?'

'Not the Congress fellows. Communists, definitely.'

Venu ended up being interrogated shortly. The brutal caning continued until Venu confessed.

'I was behind the swapping of the flags. It is wrong that we respect the Britishers and the king. The tricoloured flag symbolizes the Independence movement. The red flag stands for the hard-working farmers and manual labourers. We should pay our respects to them.'

The headmaster continued the walloping.

'Tell us, who was your accomplice?'

Venu did not disclose any name despite the torture.

'Who helped you to remove the tile from the roof and steal from my office?'

'Nothing was stolen.'

The headmaster sent a messenger to the police station.

'This is sedition. The minimum punishment would be banishment from the kingdom.'

Zacharia, who was loitering around with other students, stepped inside the room. 'No point in handing over Venu to the cops.'

'Hmm? Zacharia, you have no business here. Better leave.'

'No, I am the one who removed the tile and entered the room.'

'You?'

'Yes.'

'But why?'

'I felt that Venu had a point. The natives of Trivandrum don't deserve any respect. Better take it as a joke, sir.'

The headmaster might have agreed with the idea. But by then, a head constable, accompanied by two policemen, had reached the campus.

The headmaster blurted out unwittingly, 'These two fellows are Communists. They…'

The head constable patted Zacharia's shoulder with his lathi and asked: 'You, footballer! When on earth did you transform into a Communist?'

Zacharia pushed the lathi away. 'Sir, ask them to leave. We have a match coming up soon.'

The policeman standing nearby poked Zacharia's stomach savagely with his lathi. He spouted a profanity. The headmaster stood shellshocked.

'I shall see you play today! His blasted Communism!'

Venu and Zacharia spent one entire day at the lockup. They were let out the next day. There were no charges against them. But the boys thrashed around in pain for the next one month.

That day onwards, the village stamped Zacharia as a Communist. The police always looked at him with suspicion. When he went to the church, the pastor seemed to be scared while counselling him.

Zacharia tried to convince the others that he wasn't a Communist. But everyone took it as a Communist strategy to evade the issue.

Zacharia slowly grew close to the Communist movement. Over the course of time, he became a prominent member of the Communist party in Travancore.

When the party focused on arts clubs for encouraging farmers and students to join their movement, Zacharia came up with the idea of sports clubs and garnering followership amongst sports lovers. Even when the party split in the sixties, Zacharia's arena was left untouched.

Zacharia removed himself from the party membership. Yet, he continued to get unstinted support from his erstwhile comrades. He had a large friends' circle, beyond party and caste lines, inside and outside Kerala. It was while reigning as a left leaning, efficient sports lover and organizer of events that another incident occurred. It changed the course of Zacharia's life.

5

Detective Zacharia

The second major crossroads in Zacharia's life surfaced due to an incident which was fortuitous, very similar to his turning a Communist.

It was the year 1984. Whenever Zacharia arrived in Ernakulam, he would always phone his friend Hamid. Though he would call Hamid, they would mostly chat about Hamid's son Jamal, aka Jamaluddin. About Jamal's studies, friends, his games – avuncular queries. Usually Hamid would drive down to pick up Zacharia. They would head to his home.

First-class biriyani, chicken curry.

Zacharia would remark wryly, 'After eating the biriyani at Hamid's place, no other biriyani can satisfy me!'

Hamid knew that Zacharia visited his home to discuss Jamal's progress. Hamid would comment: 'You gave my son a second life. If it weren't for you, I wonder what would have happened to him.'

That story too had been unbelievable, but true.

~

There was a three-day conference in Madras to discuss the Football Federation's zonal tournaments.

Zacharia had arrived in Ernakulam to catch the evening train to Madras. He met Ibrahim Kutty, the sports reporter-cum-photographer, at the station. He was a young man who handled both English and Malayalam with ease.

There was a middle-aged man with Ibrahim Kutty. They were introduced to each other. Hamid was a slightly balding, corpulent man, who wore dark glasses. They were waiting for someone from Trivandrum.

Hamid appeared frantic. The usually punctual train was late by half an hour.

Ibrahim Kutty elucidated: 'Hamid Ikka's son has been missing for two weeks now. Jamal was last seen in school. Nobody has a clue about where he has gone or why. The cops are on his trail and the newspapers have flashed the news.'

They had scoured the house of every acquaintance. Hamid's brother had gone in search of Jamal to Trivandrum, Kanyakumari and Kovalam. He was expecting him to return by the Madras Mail. Purportedly, there was a seer who divined such missing cases, in Salem. The plan was to send his brother there, to meet the seer.

Zacharia observed Hamid's countenance. Discovering that the despondence on it was due to a missing child, he felt a stab of pity. Zacharia dug out more details.

Hamid was a businessman. Jamal was the youngest of his children. He had two daughters too. Fourteen-year-old Jamal was studying in Class Eight. One day he left school with a handbag. He had taken a shirt and pants with him. Also, around one hundred and fifty rupees.

'Had there been any squabble at home?'

'No, but his Umma and sisters said he had seemed lost in thought for the last few days. I hardly get time to talk to him. Now I feel it's all my fault.'

'Have you met his friends?'

'He does not have many close friends. Jamal is a loner who is into football and watching videos.'

Ibrahim Kutty interjected: 'Jamal's Umma hasn't eaten a morsel since he left.' He showed Zacharia the newspaper advertisement. Thick, joint eyebrows, intense eyes, and a narrow forehead. 'The newspaper also has my article. Sir, you keep it with you.'

The train arrived. They parted ways.

Zacharia forgot about everything: Hamid, Jamal, Ibrahim Kutty, and the rest. On the second day in Madras, he flipped through the newspaper and read the article. Ibrahim Kutty had written about sports councils. The journalist had captured an ordinary idea in a striking way. While folding the paper, Zacharia's eyes fell on Jamal's photograph.

Missing.

Hamid's sad face flashed in his mind.

Zacharia thought about Jamal.

What if I were a detective? Sherlock Holmes? How would I find Jamal's whereabouts? Just for fun. Nothing to do until lunch time!

Zacharia wrote down every fact he knew about Jamal on a piece of paper.

Fourteen years old.
Thinker. Father did not have time to talk to him.
Sisters. Umma.
The boy must have grown tired of being pampered.
Loner.
The eyes and brows reveal a firm character.
Hobby? Football, watching videos.
Around a hundred and fifty rupees in hand.
Started off from school by afternoon.

After reading what he wrote, Zacharia had a strong hunch that Jamal might have landed in Madras. After deducting the cost of the tickets, he must have some money left with him. There were two trains to Madras in the evening. There were no football matches recently in the area. But video, cinema? What if the film industry had attracted the lad?

Madras...? Good fun!

Zacharia began pondering. What would he have done in Jamal's place?

He would disembark at the central station in the morning. Cinema was his goal. If he hadn't fallen prey to some nefarious elements, Jamal would aim for Kodambakkam. The probability of human trafficking was low. Anyway, that was a risky assumption.

Zacharia had nothing to do for a few hours. He got dressed and tucked Jamal's photo inside his pocket. There was a gravity, very pertinent to a detective, on his mien. Zacharia grinned, looking at himself in the mirror. Then he took a bus to Kodambakkam.

When the bus made its way slowly after negotiating the bridge at Kodambakkam, Zacharia gazed outside. If Jamal had taken this bus, he might have got down here. Soon, he saw the board: Hotel Hollywood. Yes, Jamal would get down upon seeing that sign!

Zacharia got off the bus. He ordered a cup of tea from a small shop nearby. The shopkeeper was a Malayali.

'Do lots of Malayalis come here, dreaming about movies?'

The man grinned.

'Of course! What's the matter?'

Zacharia showed him the photograph.

'Maybe eight or nine every day. It can vary from day to day.'

'But they drop in here, don't they?'

'Yes, my shop is at a prime location.'

'What about this fellow?'

'No, no recollection ... I haven't met him.'

Zacharia sipped his tea. 'When kids run out of money, what do they usually do?'

'They start working. Maybe in a hotel somewhere. Nowadays every place is chockablock with aspiring actors.'

'What else?'

'Pickpocketing … stealing.'

'That requires some courage and practice!'

The shopkeeper laughed. 'That's true.'

'What if it's a boy who doesn't know anything?'

The shopkeeper brooded for a while. 'Maybe workshops, bakeries … If he is lucky, might have joined films too.'

Zacharia paid for his tea and stepped out. Hotel, workshop, bakery…? He checked his watch. There were two and a half hours until lunch. Zacharia caught an autorickshaw. He narrated his tale of woe to the driver.

'Someone I know ran away from home. The boy is working in a bakery owned by some Malayali. The place must be nearby. Let us check each shop, one by one.'

In an hour, they checked several bakeries. Most places had old-timers as workers. In one place, the owner said that the new boy had run away a few days back. But when Zacharia showed him Jamal's photo, he denied having seen him.

'No, not this boy.'

There was an hour left.

The auto driver suggested: 'Sir, let us try the Gemini round. There are a few bakeries in that area.'

'Gemini? Gemini means Gemini cinema! Why not?' Zacharia agreed enthusiastically.

Sheer luck!

By the time they reached the bakery at the end of a narrow lane near Nungambakkam, it was quarter to twelve. This was the fifth bakery. Zacharia had planned to return after visiting six in total.

The bakery's owner was not available. His brother answered Zacharia's questions.

'Boy? Yes, he came two weeks back. Ramachandran.'

Zacharia showed him the photograph.

'Yes, same boy.'

'Call him, let me talk.'

In a few moments, Jamal appeared before Zacharia. His face was drawn and dark. But he had the same intense eyes of the photograph.

'Jamal, your Vappa sent me to enquire if you were doing well over here. Are you okay?'

Jamal lifted his eyes and looked at Zacharia and the owner's brother. 'Does Vappa know that I'm here?'

Zacharia smiled. 'If he didn't know, how would your Vappa give me this address?'

Jamal did not respond.

'What should I tell your father? Do you need some money, Jamal?'

'No.'

'What then?'

'I want to talk to my Vappa.'

'Hmm?'

'Why doesn't Vappa want me to return home?'

Things became easy after that. When the shop owner arrived, he was happy too.

'I felt some doubts in the beginning. He said that his name was Ramachandran. No parents. The boy said that he was staying with his uncle and that his aunt was cruel towards him. Sounded like a movie script. See, he's wearing a watch. I also caught him reading the English newspaper. Yes, something wasn't right.'

'But you took good care of him all these days.'

'But, sir, I can't pay anything yet.'

'We owe you actually.'

Jamal went along with Zacharia. The auto driver was delighted. He cracked a coconut as offering at the nearby Ganapathy temple.

As soon as he reached the hotel, Zacharia called Ibrahim Kutty in Ernakulam.

'This is Detective Zacharia speaking.'

'Wrong number.'

'No, this is me! Hold on.'

Zacharia updated Ibrahim Kutty about the developments. He spoke to Jamal.

The next day, Hamid and Ibrahim Kutty reached Madras. Hamid's moist eyes were filled with wonder, as if he were gazing at God himself. Zacharia's eyes brimmed with tears too.

Zacharia took Hamid aside.

'Don't get angry with Jamal. What he has learned about life and dreams over the past ten days, no school could ever have taught him. Backbreaking work from four in the morning till eight at night. Just imagine!'

Hamid wept.

In the morning, when they ordered omelet and bread, Jamal whispered to Zacharia: 'Uncle, don't eat the bread.'

'Why not?'

'I know how it's made.'

Nobody ate any bread that day.

~

Even after two years, nobody consumed bread in Hamid's house.

Jamal became like Zacharia's own son. Whenever he reached Ernakulam, Zacharia would meet him or call him up. Jamal would disclose to Zacharia that which he could never share with his own father. Zacharia was both a friend and an uncle to him.

Hamid worried about how he could return Zacharia's kindness.

One day, after attending a meeting, when Zacharia reached the hotel, a message from Hamid was waiting at the reception: 'Please contact Mr Hamid urgently.'

Zacharia called Hamid.

'Sir, I shall send my car. Come home quickly.'

'What's up?'

'You please come home, sir.'

Zacharia got ready.

After dinner, Jamal went to bed.

When Zacharia and Hamid were alone, the latter asked: 'Sir, would you like to make some money?'

'What do you mean? Everybody wants money. But in the middle of the night…?'

'Have you heard about the Stock Exchange?'

'Yes.'

'Do you know that this city has a Stock Exchange?'

'Yes.'

'Sir, you should become a member.'

'Me? I have no clue about this stuff! Besides, I'm on tour mostly.'

'That's not relevant. There are a few vacancies now. Before unworthy fellows take over them, I want to get some good people in.'

'Any trouble in the future? I'm damn scared of blade companies.'

'This is no blade or razor! Sir, please fill up the form.'

'Any deposit required?' Zacharia asked.

'That's my business,' Hamid replied.

Zacharia grinned at Hamid.

'Well, if I mint money, I shall bring over a few more guys from the village.'

Hamid laughed. He spoke about stock exchanges in detail. Zacharia returned to the hotel rather late. Soon, he forgot about the incident.

Two weeks later, when Zacharia arrived in Ernakulam, a young man came to his room. Zacharia asked him to take a seat.

He sat down and offered Zacharia a cigarette. 'It is a foreign brand.'

'No, I smoke beedi usually.' Zacharia smiled.

The man did not light up his cigarette.

'Sir, you have applied for a membership in the Stock Exchange, haven't you?'

'Who are you?'

Ignoring the interjection, the young man continued with his spiel: 'You gave almost thirteen thousand rupees, right?'

'So?'

'You are not too keen to be a member, are you?'

'So?'

'If you sign this withdrawal request, I shall give you twenty thousand rupees in cash right now.'

Zacharia stared at him.

'Twenty-five.'

Zacharia grinned.

The man lowered his voice. 'Thirty.'

Zacharia spoke in the same tone: 'Come closer.'

The young man leaned closer. What he heard was a profanity that Zacharia had never used before and would never use again. The stranger's face blanched.

'Get out!'

When the man went away, Zacharia dialled Hamid.

'What's the news regarding the Stock Exchange membership?'

'It's happening. Maybe in a couple of months.'

'Well, I thought I should learn the rules of the game before setting foot in the arena. I'm coming over.'

'Very good.'

Just as he had turned Communist, by sheer chance, Zacharia became a significant partner in a massive financial ecosystem.

6

The Master of the Royal Household

'The difference between income and expenditure? Profit and loss. If you spend more than you earn – loss. If you earn more than you spend – profit. Am I right, Nanu?'

Nanu, known to the world as Narayanan Namboodiri, smiled obsequiously, showing due deference to Aniyan Raja.

It was Aniyan Raja who spoke. He was the lord and master of the royal household – the Karanavar of Vadakke Kovilakam – and one of the richest people in Pathanamthitta district. The man was nearly sixty years old. Never had he expected to become the head of the family.

Aniyan Raja's older uncle, younger uncle and elder brother had passed away within a span of just three years. Suddenly, Chathayam Thirunal Kerala Varma Thampuran, aka Aniyan Raja, had the fortune of ruling over assets worth crores: his own earnings and the entire property of the family. A high school, a few temples – all of these were under his control.

Aniyan Raja was seated in a chair near a huge pillar. Next to him was a box made of Indian rosewood, carved in the shape of an elephant. The ingredients of a paan mixture were inside. A brass spittoon lay on the floor.

Aniyan Raja was fair and handsome. A sandalwood mark graced his forehead. His lips were crimson with the paan stain. He had a tiny sixth finger, next to the little finger of the left hand.

Seeing that, Matthews remembered his father. His appan had a sixth finger too. Only, it was on his right hand.

Ignoring Matthews and Vinayan, who were seated opposite, Aniyan Raja concentrated on removing the vein of the upturned betel leaf in his hand. He continued his monologue:

'From that perspective, no gains this year. The harvest was bad at Elamala because of the drought. The rubber lies unsold for the last six months.'

Vinayan leaned forward. 'When you do the accounts, you should consider every credit that might accrue in the future as part of the gains.'

Pretending not to have heard anything, Aniyan Raja looked at the young man who stood motionless, resting against the opposite pillar.

'Unni, what about that latest income tax notice? What was the amount they were claiming?'

Unni, Aniyan Raja's nephew, wore a mundu and had casually slung a thorthu – a slim white towel – on his shoulder. Vinayan felt that the sacred white thread lying against his chest added a radiance to the young man.

Unni moved slightly forward and muttered: 'Two and a half lakh.'

Aniyan Raja spat into the spittoon. The spittle landed right inside the contraption.

'When are we supposed to pay?'

'Next Monday.'

'That's a loss.'

Then Aniyan Raja turned to Vinayan. 'What did you say, Jayan?'

Vinayan felt irritated, though it was not the suitable time for feeling miffed. He had repeated his name twice. Still, the fellow was calling him by the wrong name.

It was a technique that Aniyan Raja had mastered right from youth: call a person by the wrong name. People who approached him for their various demands would have many tricks up their sleeves. They would present their proposals with irrefutable logic and arguments. There were only two ways to disarm them: One, pretend to be an idiot. Give foolish replies, acting as if one understood nothing. Second, keep addressing the person by the wrong name, intermittently. Anyone would be discomfited when addressed wrongly. The unceasing flow of words would get interrupted midway.

As expected, Vinayan lost his composure. 'I am not Jayan ... Vinayan.'

'That's right! Vinayan. I keep forgetting names. Age is catching up, I guess. Am I right, Nanu?'

Nanu smiled and reached for the paan box.

'Nanu, I doubt if you'll like the tobacco. This is a different genre altogether, from the north. If you want some other variety…?'

'Not at all.'

Aniyan Raja smiled and looked at Vinayan. 'Ah, what was I saying?'

Nanu winked at Vinayan but he didn't see it.

Vinayan repeated: 'When you do the accounts, you should consider every credit that might accrue in the future as part of the gains. What we owe to others should also be incorporated in the calculations. That's what the rules dictate.'

Aniyan Raja assumed a naïve look. 'Did the government make those rules, Jayan?'

'Not the government, but these are basic financial principles,' said Vinayan, adding in a rasping voice, 'Not Jayan, Vinayan.'

'Yes, yes. I keep making that mistake. Vinayan. But isn't that sheer idiocy? I don't know if it is the government or a foreigner, a Sayyip, who laid out the rules! What if you can't sell the rubber? Consider that even if you sell, the cost falls steeply. Then what? How will we predict the prices? Should the accountant master astrology too?' Aniyan Raja started guffawing in mirth. 'Am I right, Nanu?'

Narayanan Namboodiri, whose mouth was full of paan, covered his lips respectfully and hummed in a noncommittal manner.

'Perhaps, I am wrong? Nanu is an expert in such matters.'

Before Namboodiri could respond, a middle-aged man, wearing a conspicuous janeyu, appeared on the scene, holding a large tray. On it were three steel glasses of coffee and a plate of fresh bananas.

Nanu quipped: 'Ah, Ettithadam, are you here nowadays? I didn't know.'

Aniyan Raja replied: 'When he arrived to attend the festival last year, I insisted that he stay back. I needed a companion for the chaturanga too.'

Ettithadam said: 'I shall get you some water, Nanu.'

'No, there is a tap in the yard.'

Ettithadam Namboodiri now worked as the junior chef in the royal household of Aniyan Raja. It was true that the man had been staying there since the last festival. Aniyan Raja was particular about the salary doled out to him. Ettithadam had demanded one hundred and fifty rupees apart from expenses. Aniyan Raja eventually persuaded him to settle for just a hundred. The chaturanga reference was true too. However, Ettithadam was the last resort. Only if nobody else was around would Aniyan Raja call on him to play.

Ettithadam went inside. Nanu headed to the tap located behind the row of rose plants and washed his face.

'Have your coffee. The banana is of good variety, njalipoovan. At least those did not throw up any surprises this year.'

Nanu lifted the glass of coffee and gulped it down without it touching his lips.

Vinayan and Matthews looked warily at Nanu.

Aniyan Raja spoke gently: 'Take small sips and enjoy.'

Matthews felt extremely offended. He had embarked on this journey only at Vinayan's insistence. These rustic fellows, who were unaware of the ABC of accounts, had crores of rupees to play with! The yokels had no clue about what to do while roosting over piles of money! But there was no point in finding fault with Vinayan. He had already hinted that Aniyan Raja was rather peculiar. But he had tonnes of money. The man appeared naïve and even foolish to boot. Nanu Namboodiri knew Aniyan Raja and had assured them that he would invest in their proposal. A pittance as commission would satisfy Nanu too.

Last week, while Matthews and Vinayan were finalizing the minutes of the company promoters' meeting, the topic had come up.

Matthews said: 'We should get the old fellow to invest a minimum of five lakhs.'

Vinayan protested: 'No, something around ten is what I am hoping for. This man, Aniyan Raja, is filthy rich as per information received from Nanu.'

In truth, there were only two promoters: Vinayan and Matthews. The rest were merely for the sake of formality. Vinayan's wife, her brother, Matthews' sister and two brothers, and Vinayan's cousin. Vinayan and Matthews usually decided the agenda and finalized the minutes. They had accounted for the expenses of the promoters' meeting as part of their preliminary expenses.

The biggest issue was the initial expenses. When Vinayan and Matthews decided to start their company, they had agreed not to spend a paisa from their own pockets. The young men were acquainted with a couple of bank managers who surreptitiously shared the project reports of a few loan applicants. The duo planned to copy and adapt their report from those documents. Awaiting them was a deluge of tasks, each of which entailed an expense: the documentation war with the Registrar of Companies, stamp duty, press charges, rent of the registered office, furniture, phones … It was then that they thought of approaching some rich folk with sparse interest in business.

There were many rich people around. They should simply finance the capital and expect payments like a regular interest. But the intelligent ones would never invest their precious money in a new company blindly, would they?

Vinayan remembered Nanu, aka Narayanan Namboodiri. There were many Brahmins flush with cash. They were loath to indulge in business activities. Typically, these men had lakhs in their fixed deposits in banks. And Nanu had good contacts with most Brahmin families.

Nanu was positive.

'Sure, I will introduce you to the right person. Not a Brahmin but a Raja. Super-rich. We will request him for an investment. But what about me?'

'You will get the remuneration, of course. This is business, isn't it?'

'You will need a car to reach his place.'

'Why not? But we should aim for a minimum of ten lakhs.'

'Rest assured about that.'

Matthews had not expected Aniyan Raja's house to be so far from the city. It was an arduous journey to first discover Nanu's house. Then they had to endure his excruciating chatter all through the trip. It was a journey of a hundred and twenty kilometres! After reaching Aniyan Raja's place, Matthews felt acutely uncomfortable. Had they come so far for nothing?

Having crossed the sparsely populated hill slopes, driving through acres of rubber groves, they parked the car under a huge banyan tree located next to a huge gateway. They crossed the gate and entered the compound. A vast front yard full of flowerpots. Removing their footwear, the trio stepped onto the verandah.

Unni was playing chess by himself. A book lay open next to him. He lifted his head and smiled at Nanu.

During the mutual introductions, Unni said: 'Please wait. Uncle will come by eleven.'

Vinayan asked: 'Where has he gone?'

'Resting inside. Some asthma trouble.'

Unni turned his gaze back to the chess board. He smiled.

'It is an old Bobby Fischer game.'

Matthews looked at his watch. It was a quarter past ten.

'If you can inform him that we have arrived … It is only a quarter past ten now.'

Unni looked up and smiled pleasantly at him. 'Do sit down. Uncle will come by eleven.'

They waited. Somehow Matthews felt a weight that prevented frivolous chatter. There wasn't even a newspaper around to while away time. He walked away. Vinayan tagged along. When they reached the car and lit cigarettes, Nanu Namboodiri also joined them.

'Thampuran is very meticulous with his schedule.'

Matthews lost his temper. 'See, we came such a long way to meet him. Asthma, my foot! The young fellow says that his uncle is resting. I felt like slapping the guy.'

Vinayan placated him. 'Matthews, we are the ones in need, right? We can't afford to lose our cool. Listen, these are men who have been lording it over others, always. Never have they done a day's earnest work. They are clueless about the modern ways.'

Matthews snapped: 'But they have sacks of money. Would God grant both intelligence and money to someone? If that happened, he'd have set out to challenge God himself.'

The hill slopes beyond the rubber trees were visible. The eastern mountains could be seen from that vantage point. In the early afternoon sunshine, the rivers gleamed darkly. They caught a glimpse of the serpentine roads winding through the hills.

Matthews griped: 'I am famished. Just had a coffee early morning.'

Vinayan checked his watch.

'The trouble involved in making money! Damn it.'

'Aren't you hungry?'

'Of course! I don't think these guys are going to offer us any food.'

'I just need some money. Nothing else.'

'Ten lakhs.'

Matthews grinned.

'We'll wait till eleven. Half an hour more.'

7

The Balancing Scale of Profit and Loss

Sharp at eleven o'clock, Aniyan Raja appeared on the porch. He had a paan box in his hand. Vinayan and Matthews had returned ten minutes earlier. Unni folded the chess board and packed the pieces. He smiled at them. They all rose from their seats and greeted Aniyan Raja respectfully.

Aniyan Raja asked: 'Have you taken a look around? There is a special way to reach Erumeli, Lord Ayyappa's abode, from here. A rarely used pathway, basically.'

Unni quipped: 'A jeep might be a better option, perhaps?'

'Yes.'

On seeing Nanu, Aniyan Raja asked: 'Ah, what about you, great one?' Then he smiled. 'Do you know the meaning of the name "Nanu"? Na Anu: The one who is not an "anu", insignificantly small. That means someone quite important! Great one. Nanu has more impact than Narayanan, wouldn't you agree?'

Aniyan Raja heaved with laughter.

Nanu Namboodiri introduced Vinayan and Matthews to him.

'They are going to start a company. They need your help.'

'My help?'

'Yes, they will explain everything. Both are highly educated, passed top exams…'

Vinayan started speaking about the company.

'We plan to establish a public limited company. It will focus on exports and other trades. The authorized capital is around fifty lakhs. We want to start small, and then expand the business. Say, some institutional finance, some public shares. See, we are thinking about five lakh shares worth ten rupees each. Fifty per cent shares should get subscribed immediately. Anyone who has a share over five thousand shall be offered directorship. That's how we are envisioning this project…'

While Vinayan spoke, Aniyan Raja sat with a rather foolish expression on his face. He slowly opened the paan box.

'I have no idea about this stuff. You want some money, is that correct?'

Matthews spoke up instantly: 'No, not that way. We need money, that's true. But not for free. Every year, you will get twenty per cent as dividends, as part of the profit … it could be more. Double the amount you get on any bank deposit.'

Vinayan added: 'Not only that. The share prices keep rising, you see. If you buy shares at twenty lakhs today, after a few years, they could have a value of thirty or forty lakhs. One can sell the shares at any time. Just give it to any stockbroker at the Exchange. Immediate money in hand!'

'Interesting. But let me ask you one thing. You need money now, don't you?'

'Yes.'

Aniyan Raja picked up a betel leaf and examined it.

'Now, the expenses are no less than the income.'

It was then that he had elaborated on his understanding of profit and loss.

After all, profit and loss stood for the difference between one's income and expenditure. If the expenses exceeded income, loss. If the income exceeded expenses, profit.

The young men, having finished their coffee, got up.

'We shall take your leave then.'

Aniyan Raja smiled at Nanu.

'All right then. Nanu, send a postcard before you come next time. It will be more convenient.'

Vinayan said, 'We tried calling you yesterday. Maybe the telephone wasn't working. Couldn't get the connection.'

Aniyan Raja laughed.

'Well, we got the STD facility five months back. Every Tom, Dick and Harry started calling ceaselessly. Nuisance. If someone has money and a phone in hand, they can trouble anybody nowadays! So, I usually disconnect the phone.'

'If anyone wants to call you urgently … then?'

'That's their problem, isn't it? I am sure they will find a way. If I need to call, I just put the receiver back to normal position.'

Nanu grinned unctuously. 'You are right, Thampuran.'

On their way out, the trio heard Aniyan Raja comment: 'Unni, let us play a game of chess. I have some relief from asthma today.'

When the car started trundling towards the main road, Matthews spewed his fury. 'Waste! The whole day has been an utter waste! Both the money and time … sheer waste.'

Nanu said consolingly: 'Don't jump to conclusions. What if the gentleman didn't like the idea of exports?'

'He knows zilch! Maybe he is aware of depositing money as fixed deposits in the bank. Nothing else. The old codger will start harping about the bank tumbling down soon!'

Vinayan was fuming too.

'Ah, Aniyan Raja is a singular specimen. I never expected someone like him to exist when we are nearing the twenty-first century.'

Matthews felt lighter after venting his resentment.

'My father had a friend. Before depositing his money, the fellow would check if the bank would lend him cash after mortgaging gold. Certain banks might not have that facility. The man refused to open an account in such banks. His argument was: How can we entrust our precious money to some banker who can't even lend us money in exchange for gold? What do you say?'

Even the car driver joined the burst of laughter.

Matthews asked: 'Aren't these people educated?'

Nanu replied, 'Aniyan Raja is an old-time BA. I think he did an MA too.'

'Really?'

'That nephew of his ... Unni, he is a CA.'

Vinayan and Matthews both gasped together.

'CA!'

'Did you notice the girl who was hovering near the door while we were talking? Unni's younger sister?'

'Seemed to be a maid to me.'

'Not a maid. She was dressed informally, though. That girl has passed top exams in the field of business, I've heard.'

'What exams?'

'Let me recollect...' Nanu tried to remember the name of the examination. 'Aren't there places in Ahmedabad, Calcutta and such ... to study business after graduation? That exam.'

'MBA?'

'Yes, that one. The girl was doing higher studies for a few years.'

Vinayan stared at Matthews. 'They were pretending to be green, while we were lecturing them about companies ... Tch! They made such fools of us...'

Matthews looked daggers at Nanu Namboodiri. 'Why didn't you tell us earlier?'

'Did you ask me?'

They stopped in front of a tea shack.

For the young men, Aniyan Raja and his royal household were a conundrum. They could not accept such people easily. Though they were outwardly respectful, an innate tendency to ridicule such men surged from within. Some festering antipathy. There was a niggling sense of jealousy, adorned with the colour of mockery.

Vinayan asked Nanu: 'After having top qualifications, why don't they work?'

Matthews sniped: 'How much money the nation must have spent on them!'

Nanu grinned.

'Let me tell you a story. A few years ago, I had approached them with a marriage proposal. The prospective bridegroom was a Namboodiri. These folks are Kshatriyas. Right from the old times, their women married only Brahmins. The precise word is "sambandham", a consensual relationship. You will find such sambandham in all ancient Nair households. Now, from the last few generations, they have started marrying from their community. In the case of sambandham, if the woman no longer liked the man, she would simply pass the message: "Do not come to sleep here at night." That was all. The man was free to seek a new relationship. So was she.'

'Pretty cool!'

'The unique factor was how two people maintained a steady relationship for long.'

'What about the children born of such relationships?'

'They belonged to the mother's family, the matrilineal system. Their mother's caste would be theirs. If we had followed the patriarchal system of the north, most of the highborn would belong to the Brahmin clan by now. There wouldn't be castes like Nair, Warrier, Ambalavasi, and so on. Everyone would have been a Brahmin.'

'I don't get it.'

'Every one of these castes can trace back a progenitor – grandfather or great grandfather – to the Brahmin lineage.'

'You mean the Nair Service Society should have been named Brahmin Service Society? That's a blast!'

'Look how strong the rules and traditions laid down by society are.'

'Now, among Nair boys, for example, the maternal uncle's daughter is their betrothed: their murappennu. In north India, she is a sister! Marry your sister? Bestial folk! That's what they speak about us.'

'In Tamil Nadu, a man marries his sister's daughter.'

'Niece? My god!'

The atmosphere lightened up as the car rumbled forward.

Vinayan reminded them: 'Today's journey was remarkable. But what about the story Nanu Namboodiri started to narrate? Do you indulge in marriage business too?'

'Everything is a brokership, brother!'

Nanu resumed his tale:

'The boy was brilliant. He was a qualified engineer with postgraduate degrees. Excellent job in Calcutta. In those days, his monthly salary crossed ten thousand rupees. Aniyan Raja's uncle was the head of the household then. A shrivelled up, old man; resembling a stick. After hearing us patiently, he remarked, "When will the boy resign from the job?" "Nobody is quitting any job," I replied. "It is a prestigious position. The girl will accompany him after marriage. He has a palatial quarter in Calcutta, with everything provided by the company." Then the old man observed: "So that means he has to toil under someone for meeting his daily needs, is that right?" I tried to argue that that was not the right perception. He didn't agree with me. The marriage didn't take place. "Let the boy quit his job and stay with us at home. They can live as they wish." As per the fellow, the girl did not need a husband who depended on someone for his livelihood.'

'How pitiful!'

'Anyway, we suffered a loss of two thousand rupees today, trip and all.'

Each of them slipped into their own thoughts.

8

Janus-Faced Commerce

Vinayan's house was near Cherthala. Amongst his earliest childhood memories were the inner room crafted from wood, the narrow black cement corridor, the shed in the back of the house, and the huge anjili tree in the yard. The house was situated in the middle of a one-and-a-half-acre plot. It was the ancestral property his father had inherited.

Vinayan's father was an impressively tall and well-built man. He was called 'Lambodaran master' by all and sundry. Though he was not a teacher, Vinayan's father showed a penchant for using a few English words in his sentences. Whenever he addressed anyone older than him, Vinayan's father would add a 'master' after the person's name. That was perhaps why everyone addressed him as 'Lambodaran master'.

Lambodaran master was a quintessential Gandhian. Even when all his acquaintances were Communists, the man did not change his stance. He never displayed any revulsion for other views, and also showed affection for the Communists. According to him, if someone was ready to forgo pleasures and endure beatings for a principle, they ought to be respected. And he believed that it was obligatory for those who had the required knowledge and wisdom to guide the misguided ones to the right path. Whether he was right or wrong was a totally different matter.

Lambodaran master's home was a safe haven for many Communists who were in hiding. It was the desire to show them the right path that propelled Vinayan's father to offer help. The comrades had no other alternative but to listen to Lambodaran master's spiel. No Communist changed their mind after listening to him. However, he wasn't frustrated by it. Rather, the man felt gratified that he could put into practice the concept of 'nishkama karma': performing actions without being attached to the results.

In Vinayan's memories, his father was half-naked at all times. When the child opened his eyes in the morning, he would be greeted by the sight of his father carrying two copper pots. There would be a khadi thorthu wrapped around his waist. His chest hair would be gleaming with sweat. Lambodaran master would be watering the coconut trees in his yard, even before the sun rose. Eight pots of water per tree. There were three ponds and eighty trees in their compound. He would water them on alternate days.

When Vinayan turned four, he was gifted two small copper pots. Five tender coconut trees were earmarked for the little boy.

It was almost ten to twelve years after India gained her independence. Travancore had become Kerala. The first freely elected Communist ministry had lost its power. Unless they joined cohorts with small parties, no big party could rule Kerala by its own strength. The fate of Lambodaran master, who was happily working on his charkha and watering his trees, transformed overnight.

Most of the prominent leaders of both the ruling and opposition parties had stepped into politics through the Gandhian path. All of them knew Lambodaran master well. He was in everyone's good books. He neither resented their progress in life nor envied their nouveau-riche lifestyles.

An intimate friend of Lambodaran master became a formidable leader of a small party. He was wont to speak for hours about

Gandhian principles. Things reached a point that whoever was in power had to take recourse to his support for political stability. The man became a minister soon enough. Occasionally, he would drop by to visit Vinayan's father. At first, these visits were for everyone to see; later, they turned secretive. During long night-journeys, the Minister would stop at his friend's home for a breather, partaking of the simple dinner he offered. The friendship between Master and Minister grew stronger.

Lambodaran master's life began changing.

He started a society. A coir manufacturing cooperative society. He purchased handlooms for weaving khadi and employed the neighbours in the initiative. Soon, Lambodaran master started providing leadership in all small-scale entrepreneurships. He took advantage of government schemes, which provided loans, subsidies and other benefits. Naturally, more and more financial enterprises came his way. Soon, Lambodaran master took on the role of a broker for the firms exporting coir. Next, he started a chit fund. Few government contracts, auctions of the excise shops ... Well, in short, Lambodaran master became the richest man in the village in a span of ten years. Both his friends and foes increased in number.

The enemies ranted that Lambodaran master's friend, the Minister, was using these businesses to divert the illegal kickbacks from politics. Whenever the political opponents raised such allegations, their own long list of corrupt adventures lost against Lambodaran master's pristine image. The Minister's party workers loudly questioned, 'Can't a Gandhian philosopher toil for his business and earn profits?'

Lambodaran master remained unruffled. There were watchmen with guns and daggers guarding his gigantic new house near the lagoon. His business spread all over Kerala. The number of close friends decreased drastically.

The Gandhian friend was continuing as Minister at that point of time. The intimacy between the friends grew to such an extent that Lambodaran master became the Minister's sole confidante in all important matters.

And then, unexpectedly, the Minister died. It was a great jolt to Lambodaran master. Amidst the period of mourning, the party leaders paid him a visit. Furtive discussions continued for two nights, extending till dawn. Vinayan, who was doing his pre-university course, heard the loud arguments echoing in his home.

Lambodaran master had a predilection for lagoon trips. When his close friends visited, he would take off with them in a boat at night. He wouldn't drink himself, but ensured a stock of fresh toddy in his boat. There would be cassettes with excellent songs and a tape recorder. No servant would be part of such trips. Very critical decisions were taken inside the boat after switching off the engine, while it bobbed over the gentle ripples of the backwaters.

Ten days after the Minister's death, Lambodaran master went to the lagoon in his boat. He was all alone. Even under torture, the watchman swore about that fact. The boat did not return to the pier even after dawn. In the morning, the boat was seen drifting northwards. Lambodaran master's corpse was found inside it; his gun lay nearby.

The experts pronounced that the man had died due to a bullet from the gun. Lambodaran master's fingerprints were discovered on the trigger.

Party leaders approached Vinayan during the funeral and ominously whispered, 'They murdered your father.'

'Who?'

'We don't know.'

That night, Vinayan had wept for long.

After three months, the dead minister's wife came home. Vinayan sat at a distance, leaving two bereaved mothers to lament. The discussion was about Vinayan's future.

There was nobody to run the multiple businesses. Vinayan was least interested in studying further. However, his mother was determined to make him an engineer.

When the Minister's wife rose to leave after tea, Vinayan heard her speak:

'We are struggling to make ends meet. I have nobody to help me. Everyone speaks only about politics.'

'That's right,' Vinayan's mother said.

The woman lowered her voice: 'My husband used to give money to Lambodaran master at regular intervals. He reassured me that even after his demise, we would be taken care of. If only that money can be returned? Not at one go … perhaps in parts?'

Vinayan eavesdropped on the conversation. His amma's voice suddenly filled with pathos. 'Aiyo! My husband never spoke a word about money or business to me. It was all men's work. And I never asked a thing.'

The woman was silent for a moment.

'I will take your leave then.'

Amma went after her.

'Chechi, please don't misunderstand me. If you need some rice or coconuts occasionally, just send word. Vinayan himself will bring them over.'

Amma searched for the driver to drop her to the bus stand. He wasn't around.

Vinayan never forgot the sight of the devastated woman walking away. He bid goodbye to his mother in his heart that moment.

A long fifteen years.

Vinayan was filled with vengeful stubbornness towards the world. More so, towards his mother. His sole hobby was to spend money. Stallions in Ooty, Pune and Bombay. Film stars in Madras. Friends and parties at five-star hotels. Cars in the latest models.

When his mother hesitated to sign away the properties, Vinayan stopped talking to her; he stopped eating. After two days, his mother would sign the required papers.

Amma was afraid that Vinayan's eyes were glaring accusingly at her. Every month, Vinayan ensured that one thousand rupees was sent to the late minister's home. Every resource was exhausted after fifteen years. Finally, they shifted to the old tharavadu that was inherited by his mother. That day, Vinayan spoke to his mother.

'Amma, you should visit that home.'

'Where?'

'The home of the late minister.'

Finally, Vinayan's mother went to the Minister's home with a marriage proposal. She was apprehensive about how they would respond. The girl's family was delighted.

One leader from the party was still a minister. He attended the wedding and blessed the young couple.

The next day, Vinayan approached his mother.

'Amma, I plan to start a business.'

'What business?'

'Haven't decided that yet.'

'By yourself?'

'Am not sure of that either.'

Amma was silent for a while. Then she remarked: 'No joint business, please.'

'Anyway, it won't be like my father's joint business.' Vinayan said that without looking into his mother's eyes.

Ernakulam city, aka Cochin, was the nerve centre of Kerala's business scenario. The small town, which was the capital of the Kochi province, had developed miraculously over twenty years. An excellent port, the facilities for merchandise to reach via water and road, industrial areas with good infrastructure, oil refinery, shipbuilding centre, many huge government enterprises ... not to mention export units of processed sea food, which changed the faces of the seaside villages ... All these contributed to making Ernakulam a modern business centre.

The city was not even an hour's journey from Vinayan's home.

Vinayan decided to start a business in Ernakulam.

9

Destiny

Problems started raising their heads one by one. Vinayan had very little money to invest. A maximum of fifty thousand rupees. If only he had a project report and an idea related to the schemes aligned with a bank's goals, he might get a loan. But the bank would demand a mortgage. The only asset that remained was the house inherited by his mother. Vinayan decided against it. No question of appealing to Amma again for a signature!

Another issue was that Vinayan was not an expert in any sector. For scions of traditional business families, there wasn't any need to search for a particular business area. Unlike them, Vinayan had no legacy in any business field. He had certain firm beliefs about right and wrong, that was all. And a few khadi clothes.

In the beginning, quite unsure of the way ahead, Vinayan had discussions with many friends. Many of them gave great advice. However, for every suggestion, there was a non-negotiable requirement: Money. Cash for expenditure, until the business turned successful.

Vinayan got a transport contract with a semi-governmental organization for three months. It involved procuring rice and pulses from Maharashtra and Andhra Pradesh. He was supposed to transport the merchandise to the warehouses of different towns in Kerala. It all seemed very simple.

Vinayan deposited twenty thousand at the firm. The concerned officer demanded an additional five thousand rupees. A 'tradition'. Vinayan promised to give him the money after the assignment was over. He was reluctantly given the contract, but with a warning: 'Don't cheat us, please!'

Three loads of rice from Nellore district. The first had to be unloaded at Muvattupuzha, the second at Shoranur, the last at Alappuzha.

There were agents in all the places, ready to help. Lorries, drivers and exact quotes. But they all needed advance payment. All the papers were intact, as per law.

Just one problem. Vinayan would be solely responsible from the moment of loading the lorries at the Nellore rice mill until the acknowledgement receipt was handed over at the godown in Kerala. It was not the sender's or the recipient's responsibility.

Vinayan tried to insure the lorry and the material. But it was disclosed that only an owner could insure the vehicle. The rates, even then, were abysmally high.

'It's just a matter of four or five days. No accident is likely to happen. Nobody ever bothers to insure. Why reduce the profit margins? Unless one takes risks, money won't come.' The Tamilian who arranged the lorries gave him this advice.

'Shouldn't I accompany the vehicle?'

'But there are three vehicles! Even if you don't go along, it will be fine. Nobody is going to cheat you. We are all businessmen. If we start defrauding one another, who shall entrust us with projects in future?'

Vinayan gave it some thought. 'That is true,' he said.

After ensuring the lorries were loaded, Vinayan returned home by train.

Vinayan planned to make a profit of fifteen thousand rupees. In the next round, he aimed to employ six lorries. Afterwards ten, then twenty … Eventually, he aimed to buy his own lorries.

Vinayan's drivers did not cheat him – God did.

One of the lorries ended up hitting a jeep. One man died and two were injured. The natives stopped the lorry. The driver and helper fled for their lives.

Vinayan got the news two days later.

When he reached the location, the villagers, cops, the owners of the lorry and the jeep, the relatives of the dead man and those of the injured, all pounced on him vengefully. They unanimously decided that Vinayan was the main culprit.

They mobbed him with demands for money. For the police. For the hospital. For helping the driver and the helper. For unloading the lorry. For loading it. For the dead man's family.

The cops seized the lorry. It took Vinayan ten days to get the vehicle and material freed.

Every resource he had, and whatever he could borrow, was soon exhausted. By the time the material reached the warehouses, they found a major discrepancy in weight. Finally, every issue was settled. But Vinayan's payments were not released. Apparently an enquiry would take place first. The officer informed Vinayan that he could take up new contracts under a false name. No issues!

Vinayan became incensed. Even if he received the full dues from the firm, he would end up with a loss of ten thousand rupees! And now, as per their new terms, to even receive the justified payment would entail months of waiting.

Until then? Who should he blame? Every rupee was gone. To get the deposit amount back, he should fulfil all the obligations of the present contract.

The officer who had granted him the contract advised him: 'Brother, don't mistake me. If you'd given the five thousand that I'd asked for, everything would have gone smoothly.'

'How?'

'Our blessings would have been there, right? Now you're all alone. Every sarkari file has certain traditions associated with it. Brother, we will give you fresh work contracts. Just bring in the five thousand for the first project and whatever is due for the second assignment. You can soon rake in profits, forgetting about the temporary loss.'

'But I don't have any money left.'

'That's an issue. What is the point of venturing into a business without enough money?'

Vinayan returned home, rather embittered.

His first business venture. A single throw of the dice, and all the money had been wiped out! What had gone wrong?

Nothing actually.

But nothing had turned out right either.

Three days later, Vinayan bumped into a friend unexpectedly near the west entrance of a temple in Ernakulam. The sun had just set. Suddenly the devotional firecracker offerings inside the temple went off.

Vinayan's friend said: 'It is the hour for worshipping the deity with lighted lamps. You won't be coming, will you?'

Vinayan did not respond. He used to visit temples as a child. Nowadays, he did not feel like it.

Suddenly, he thought, why not?

What had caused the accident in Palakkad was beyond human comprehension. What if that disaster, which had shaken his very bearings, was the wrath of God?

One cannot inveigle God with occasional prayers. He is no fool!

Vinayan stood afar from the sanctum sanctorum. Catching a glimpse of the scintillating lights near the deity, he reverently folded his hands. He stood praying for a while. An inexplicable peace filled him. Moments ticked away.

When he opened his eyes, Vinayan noticed that a tall, lean man, rather aged, was keenly observing him from near the temple's flagpole. He seemed vaguely familiar.

The old man smiled at him. Vinayan smiled back.

A broad forehead, silver hair that fell straight, gold framed glasses. He wasn't wearing a shirt. Vinayan saw the janeyu.

The elderly man came closer.

'I seem to know you. What's your name?'

'Vinayan.'

'What do you do?'

'Nothing in particular.'

'What about you, sir?'

'I am Suryanarayanan. Management consultant. Where are you from, Vinayan?'

'Cherthala.'

'Father?'

'Lambodaran master.'

'Oh my god! Lambodaran master's son! That's why you looked so familiar. It's been ages since we last met.'

Vinayan smiled. He too had a vague recollection of the man's face.

'You wait here. I will just go inside and pray for a while. You aren't in a hurry, are you? My god! Master's son…'

Suryanarayanan returned in five minutes. He gave Vinayan sandalwood paste and tulsi leaves received from the priest. Vinayan felt that meeting the gentleman was divinely dictated. He gazed at the deity and bowed again.

Suryanarayanan had been a bank manager. After retirement, he was running a management consultancy from home. The location was a prime one, where most of the city's rich lived.

He took Vinayan home and offered him excellent decoction coffee.

In the office computer, Suryanarayanan had compiled the secret data of the city's business honchos. He would give business counsel and never sell the secrets.

'Listen, Vinayan! We have to be very particular. I charge highly for my professional services. They make lakhs and crores from my expertize. I demand proportional payment. Do you know the rent of this house? Nearly four thousand.'

After sharing a few anecdotes, Suryanarayanan started reminiscing about Vinayan's father:

'I would go to your house often and enjoy the nightly boat trips. Those days! Your father, Lambodaran master, was a great man. I couldn't sleep for two days after hearing about his untimely demise.'

Suryanarayanan recounted an incident highlighting Lambodaran master's greatness.

'Those days, I was working as a bank manager in your area. One day, your father came to the office. He needed some help. A huge amount as loan. The rules did not allow such a deal. I was scared. I pleaded with him that I would lose my job. When it became clear that I would reject his proposal, he made another request. "I am planning to visit your bank's deputy general manager in Trivandrum. I usually carry ten sovereigns of gold whenever I go to see him. I am supposed to meet him tomorrow, and I hardly have the money to buy the gold. Please book me a trunk call. I should inform him that I can't make the trip to meet him tomorrow." I booked an urgent call. Lambodaran master picked up the receiver and said: "Sir, this is Lambodaran. I am handing over the phone to Swami." I took the receiver from his hand. The DGM belonged to my village. He cared for me like a sibling. The DGM said: "Surya! Lambodaran is a decent fellow. Gandhian to the core. You should help him." That was the only prompt I needed. I sanctioned his proposal. Master was happy. He invited me home that day. He would visit me sometimes too. Every time he would bring along three gold sovereigns.

Guruvayurappa! Everything is due to your divine benedictions! These are great souls. It's due to the Lord's grace that one is able to meet them.'

When it was time to depart, Vinayan said: 'Sir, I was thinking of doing some business. I tried once.'

'And then?'

Vinayan narrated the transport contract debacle. Suryanarayanan listened patiently and remarked: 'All of this is the Lord's lila – His divine games. Surrender everything unto him. Everything will be fine.'

'How?'

'If the Lord is with you, can anyone obstruct you?'

'What about the capital?'

'The Lord does not need capital, does he? Remember Kuchela's story? A friend of Lord Krishna's, also a great Krishna bhakt, who later in life, stricken with poverty, would go to meet Krishna with a fistful of flattened rice as gift? And Krishna, delighted with his devotion, would reward him with much prosperity? Devotion. Just submit everything to him.'

Vinayan remained silent.

Suddenly, Suryanarayanan said: 'I shall procure a job for you. If you are smart and have the Lord's grace, there is no limit for growth.'

'What's the job? I don't have much expertize in any field.'

'This job needs just commonsense, courage, good behaviour … Enough stoicism that you don't go overboard while victorious and topple into despondency while facing setbacks. Yes, an ability to do quick calculations will surely help.'

'I can handle that.'

Suryanarayanan smiled. Then he dialled a number.

'Kariacha! Like I told you earlier … I'm sending a young man as your Authorized Assistant. Not just anyone. My own fellow. First, you meet him. We'll discuss the rest later.'

That was how Vinayan became the assistant of P.T. Zacharia, the member of the Stock Exchange.

Matthews, who used to drop in to meet his friends at the Exchange, became acquainted with Vinayan. They liked each other.

It was at the Stock Exchange that their friendship blossomed, and grew firmer.

10

Hard Cash and Hard Work

Matthews' father was the youngest of a family with ancient roots. They had twenty-five acres of land near Poonjar as ancestral property. The terrain was both hilly and flat.

It was the most abundant land. The stream that cut across the land gleamed with pristine waters. The twenty-five acres were resplendent with a variety of trees and plants. Matthews' father, Kunjoonju, curtailed the rubber cultivation to an area of five acres. All around, his neighbours were venturing into cash crops. In his farms, Kunjoonju cultivated paddy, alongside banana plantations, vegetables and pineapples; he kept cows, and was also into honeybee production and poultry farming ... The house and farms embodied a self-sufficient rural ecosystem.

The man's spouse suited him perfectly. Rahel and Kunjoonju were always found working – right from the moment they were declared a couple at the church. They would wake up at four in the morning. As soon as they finished the prayers, kneeling in front of the Crucified One and the Holy Mother, their relentless labour would begin. The husband would walk to the compound and the wife to the cowshed. There was a maid to handle the kitchen, but someone needed to keep an eye on her. Except for the times when Rahel came to check the goings-on in the kitchen and Kunjoonju stretched himself on a wooden cot under the mango tree in the front yard for an afternoon siesta, they toiled away in the yard, hen coops, farms and the like.

Kunjoonju would say: 'What if things have become expensive? We only buy salt from the shop, that too rarely. Both my wife and I suffer from blood pressure. Can't touch salt.'

The couple did not use sugar. There was a coffee powder that was homemade, with a mix of crushed coffee beans, cumin and cardamom. It was Kunjoonju's own concoction. He cultivated sugarcane. During harvest, some of the crop would be converted to jaggery. As per Kunjoonju, if one prepared coffee with that jaggery, it was very beneficial.

Kunjoonju was a staunch vegetarian, he would not touch fish. Rahel, however, liked fish. There were two ponds in the compound. In the rainy season, when the landslides occurred, in the overflowing streams the yields would be higher.

Every Sunday, sharp at seven, the couple would attend the church. They would participate in the Qurbana. There was a shirt earmarked for Kunjoonju, and a handwoven, traditional neriyathu paired with a mundu for his wife. When the clothes became tattered, they were replaced with another set.

Kunjoonju was meticulous when dealing with church activities. He would contribute the smallest possible amount for the charity. No amount of persuasion from the pastor or the village elders could make him magnanimous. His contribution would stay the same, even when they stopped pleading.

Even amidst all that pell-mell, the couple had four children. Matthews was the eldest. There were two younger brothers and a sister. As the number of children increased, the racket and din inside the home grew proportionately.

Matthews learned to count even before going to school. Counting the number of eggs from the hen coop became the first lesson in arithmetic. He soon mastered all the tasks: milking the cows, retrieving honey from the hives, plucking mangoes from the topmost branches of the ant-infested mango tree, cutting the jackfruit and bringing it down carefully without splattering it on the ground, efficiently tapping rubber, drying the sap into sheets and the like.

While in school, Matthews used to return home promptly to help his appan with his work. But when he entered Class Eight, Matthews started exhibiting marked signs of rebellion. He became crazy about football.

He would rush to the football field every day after classes. It would be dusk by the time he returned home. His appan did not scold or counsel him. When Rahel hinted about the lad's truancy, his appan replied: 'My own father never scolded me in his life. It was my mother's territory – disciplining me. Looking after kids is a mother's job.'

Rahel tried reproaching her son. 'Play for some time after school. Then you should help your appan in his work. Listen, you have to look after your siblings and parents in the future.'

Matthews would pretend that he did not hear anything. Rahel would end up cursing herself: 'Jesus! The boy has turned into a Communist!'

Matthews would be steaming with an inexplicable rage. His resentment was mostly aimed at his father, who never exhibited any displeasure at him. Matthews could not fathom the reason behind his own angst. Every need of his was being met. There was no shortage of money. His appan would ask him to take whatever he needed from the almirah.

Matthews' appan pretended not to notice all these fluctuations in his behaviour.

There was only one way to vent that wrath. Get involved in sports. After spending his time on the football ground, Matthews would visit the nearby reading room-cum-library. There were plenty of sports magazines there. He would devour the sports page of the English newspaper. Matthews would read every word hungrily. Though he had money, he never purchased sports magazines or English newspapers. Why buy them when he could read them in the library after a few days? Matthews knew the scores of every team in the previous World Cup by heart. It would take him mere seconds to memorize everything! He believed that hoarding books and magazines was meant for those with poor memory and recollection.

Matthews relished numbers and calculations. His incomparable memory awed even his teachers. Eventually, Matthews ended up in Class Ten.

The front yard was full of harvested stacks of paddy. Two petromax lamps were hung nearby. Though the house had electricity, the frequent power cuts were irritating. Besides, there was the niggling issue of very poor voltage. So the hurricane lamps, torches and petromax lamps were always ready in the house.

One evening, a python was found near the hen coop. The farmworkers thrashed it to death. His siblings were eagerly waiting for Matthews to arrive home, to give him a spicy description of the episode.

Matthews came home very late and set off to the stream for his daily bath. Brimming with the tale of the python's murder, the rest of the lot tagged along.

Kunjoonju, Matthews' father, was taking his bath in the stream. He wiped himself with a thorthu and spoke to the boy: 'Son, come quickly after your bath. There is something to do.' Matthews did not prod any further.

As the cool waters drenched his head, Matthews surmised: 'Ah, something is about to happen today. Appan will say something nasty. I will retaliate … Even if Ammachy and my siblings plead with me, I won't let it go.'

He ignored his siblings' colourful narrative of how a chick's carcass had been retrieved from the python's jaws.

When he returned, his mother said: 'Appan is in the inner room.'

The room, almost a vault, was always locked. It was supposed to be used for storing grain. A dried sprig of paddy hung from a hook – a symbol of good fortune. There were leather boxes, some old vessels, an almirah, and a few china jars inside.

His father called out to Matthews when he saw him dithering near the door. 'Son, come inside.'

Both a big brass lamp, and a dangling lamp hitched to the attic, had been lighted. 'Close the door, son.'

Matthews shut the door.

One open leather box was filled with currency notes, old and new ones. There were innumerable stacks of ten- and hundred-rupee notes. Each set was tied up with threads.

Appan spoke:

'Son, I can hardly see properly these days. You should examine each of these currency notes. Look, we cannot trust the government or anyone these days. If they say that they won't accept the old notes, where would we go lamenting? To the Lord? These are our hard-won profits. The prosperity showered by our land. The result of your parents' sweat. It's hard to let go of it so easily.

'Listen, your appan does not believe in banks or such stuff. The scams in Kollam and Pala happened when I was a child. So many, who were hoping for high interests, turned paupers overnight. I decided then that our money should always stay with us. It is absolute foolishness to hand over one's hard-earned money to others, caught by alluring promises. All our money, without the loss of a single rupee, is here.'

Matthews was staring, almost with a glazed look in his eyes, at the bundles of cash.

'Son, separate the old notes from each stack and keep them aside. Then exchange all of them for new notes from a bank. Only you can do it meticulously.'

'Appa, there are too many bundles!'

'Do it slowly. Don't make any mistake.'

'Not at all.'

Matthews forgot that he had come to squabble with his father.

That night, very late, father and son locked the vault and stepped out.

The next one week, Matthews did not stay back to play football. He would run home after school. After taking a quick bath, he would start his work amidst the bundles of currency notes.

At first, he made mistakes in calculations. Slowly, as he separated the old and new notes and maintained accounts, Matthews felt that he was seized with an ineffable joy.

Kunjoonju did not come to the inner room again.

A week later, when Matthews finished the counting, he told his father: 'It's done, Appa.'

Kunjoonju took out another key and responded: 'There is another box. Check that too.'

Matthews entered the magical world of currency again. And from that day, Matthews wholeheartedly became a member of his family.

After his pre-university examinations, Matthews chose to pursue a degree in agriculture. When he finalized a university in north India for his Bachelor's degree, his appan was happy.

Though he studied agriculture, it was the economics behind it that attracted Matthews. He specialized in the financial aspects of agriculture for his Master's degree. His thesis was on the financial quagmire faced by Indian farmers and the possible solutions. He did his research on how capital could be collected from the rural areas.

During the vacations, Matthews enjoyed sharing his know-how with his father. He justified that he was transmitting his expertize to an ordinary farmer who was not proficient in bookish knowledge.

His father said: 'Money should never be handed over to another person or an institution ever! No matter what they promise as interest.'

'What about purchasing some land then?'

'Son, when you wish to invest in agriculture, buy land. Why waste money now on more properties? Who will look after those?'

When he returned home after finishing his postgraduate studies, Matthews realized how wise his father's commonsensical approach was. Matthews was clear that he was not made for looking after the estate and farms. There was no need for all his specialized training for doing that work. He wished to utilize his knowledge and training in a suitable venture. Matthews' younger brother, who had failed his pre-university examinations, was already helping his father manage the farms.

Matthews decided to shift to the city. Business.

Kunjoonju spoke: 'It is work that's more important than money. Hard work provides relief to both the body and the mind. Money consoles only the mind.'

'Yes, Appa.'

Matthews had a goal. It was his desire to be amongst the prominent businessmen of Kerala in ten years' time. When he became acquainted with Vinayan, that resolve grew stronger. They chose the way forward. Create a public limited company first.

The only challenge was in getting the investment. They decided to invite rich guys, not very keen on business, to invest in their idea.

Public money. Management and control in their hands.

It was against that backdrop that Matthews and Vinayan met Aniyan Raja and returned disappointed.

11

The Path to Success

Filling his pipe with tobacco and pressing it down with a matchstick, Mohandas said: 'I have decided. There is no other way.'

A new seven-storeyed commercial complex had sprung up in the west of the city, facing the backwaters. Mohandas's business administrative offices occupied the entire sixth floor. During the day, when the thick curtains were drawn around the shut windows and the air conditioners hummed away, they brought to mind the huge corporate houses in Bombay, Delhi and Bangalore.

In the block that had Mohandas's own office, his private room, his secretary's cubicle and the guest room, the colour scheme was a pale green. The carpet was plush and swanky, almost four inches thick. The sofas were so soft that they seemed formidable. Vases bloomed with fresh flowers. There was a fish tank with fishes and beautiful aquatic plants. Paintings of K.C.S. Paniker and M.F. Husain adorned the walls. The lighting in the room had an alluring quality to it; but with no light source in sight, one wondered where it was coming from. On the table were four telephones and two intercoms. Anyone who entered the room would feel slightly intimidated by the ambience. That served Mohandas's purpose.

Once, when his business empire's twenty-fifth anniversary was being celebrated, a journalist happened to pose a question to Mohandas. It was another matter that the event was a marketing gimmick and the business was actually only twenty-two years old.

'You were able to set up this vast business enterprise in such a short time. Which among your qualities helped you reach the pinnacles of success and maintain it steadily?'

Mohandas replied: 'Sincerity. Whenever I enter into a business deal with anyone, I negotiate for the most profitable terms that are beneficial for me. But having entered into an agreement, even if I have to suffer a loss, I will do my utmost to keep my word.'

The journalist grinned to himself on hearing the reply. He remembered a yarn that was pretty popular, albeit private, about Mohandas. It was true, the famed quality of sincerity, and the man's endeavours for the most profitable terms.

Everybody was aware of Mohandas's weakness for women. Since he was a perennial bachelor, presumably being too busy to get hitched, his philandering tendencies were laughed off as a joke.

It happened a few years ago, in another city. Mohandas had to spend a night there. He made certain enquiries, and they revealed that an erstwhile movie actress was in town. He invited her to his room. The rate was fixed at ten thousand rupees. Wasn't that a little too much? He started negotiating at two thousand five hundred and finalized it at five thousand. The lady agreed. There was an additional demand for Scotch–whisky.

The trouble started when the woman got ready to leave at dawn. Mohandas did not have cash in his wallet. The actress insisted on hard cash. He wanted to write her a cheque. Apparently she had been fooled by many that way before. She needed cash, pronto! Mohandas requested: 'Please relax till the bank opens. I shall continue to pay at the same rate.'

The lady was pleased and slept comfortably till ten-thirty in the morning. Mohandas paid her ten thousand rupees in cash at

10.30 a.m. Five thousand for sleeping with him in the night and five thousand for sleeping by herself in the day. The woman became an ardent fan of Mohandas after that. She would wax eloquent: 'That's called decency. A man who values his word.'

Mohandas wryly asked his accountant to earmark those ten thousand rupees as part of advertising expenses.

The journalist who knew this story tried hard to suppress a laugh. 'You're right, sir.'

Mohandas did his business negotiations inside that office. Usually, every client agreed to his conditions.

For a few days now, Mohandas found himself agitated. There was only one way to soothe that nervousness. He called his mentor Pothuval. When Pothuval came to meet him, Mohandas explained:

'Sir, I no longer find satisfaction in anything. You know that in the last three years, I have entrusted all my multiple businesses in the hands of professional experts. I did not verify their educational qualifications. Rather, I was keen about their lineage, honesty, dignified behaviour, eagerness to learn, capability of taking up responsibility and capacity to work twenty-four by seven. All are youngsters. They must be between twenty-five and thirty years of age. They present weekly progress reports to me. Sir, the turnover of my business enterprise has grown by seven times over the last three years. Profits ... I don't have the exact numbers now. There are so many business initiatives. But, then...?'

Mohandas got up and opened a window. He drew the curtains apart and switched the air conditioner off. In the western part of the lagoon, the lights of Willingdon Island shimmered amidst the ships, boats and gigantic cranes, rendering allure to the darkness around. A cool breeze wafted inside the room, its moistness evocative of sea salt. Mohandas stood staring at the backwaters for a long time.

'I have no peace of mind. I find no challenge! Sir, you know how I nurtured every institution to its present-day success.

Innumerable obstacles, oppositions, competitions. Hardly could one relax for a moment. But there has been nothing, no challenge for the past few years. I no longer feel the urge to nourish an enterprise from its start and watch it grow. Nothing innovative about it. The last one year, it has been a welter of vacations, reading books, listening to music … I'm terribly bored.'

Pothuval did not deign to reply. His fingers drummed on the table rhythmically.

Mohandas smiled.

'I forgot to ask. What about a coffee, sir?'

'Sure.'

Mohandas pressed the intercom button.

'Yes, sir?'

'Johnny, two cups of coffee please.'

'Yes, sir.'

Mohandas had always been a loner. He had arrived in Ernakulam from an interior village in north Malabar twenty-seven years ago to enrol at the Bar. Now, the law graduate ran a huge business empire straddling eight enterprises, with a turnover of fifty crores. But he was more solitary than ever.

Four or five years after starting his business, Mohandas became acquainted with Pothuval. The latter was not employed anywhere at that point of time. He was a simple middle-aged man, contented with reading and writing. A true intellectual, without the hang-ups of one. Mohandas developed an affinity for Pothuval. It was reciprocated. Pothuval never troubled Mohandas for anything. Mohandas was very sensitive and alert when it came to helping his friend. Pothuval was well aware of it.

Whenever Mohandas interviewed candidates for executive positions in his teams, Pothuval would be invited as a member of the interview board. He would be paid a thousand rupees for each day.

'Your presence is more valuable than that.' That was Mohandas's justification when Pothuval wondered whether he was being overpaid. It was said with utter sincerity. Before making any major move in his business strategies, Mohandas would always have a friendly discussion with Pothuval.

'I gain an inner strength after speaking with you. What do you say?'

Pothuval smiled.

Mohandas continued:

'See, I can't retire from this field. Business is my life. However, I'm no longer enthralled at the prospect of setting up a new firm. No satisfaction in that. Now I feel like exploring a new path. Identify a business with sufficient potential, which is currently under a weak leadership, take control of it. Then make it very successful. That's definitely a worthwhile challenge. Far more exhilarating than creating a new enterprise. Take over a decrepit institution, fix it up and make it roar! What do you say?'

An old man in a white uniform entered the room with coffee. The breeze was chilly. The aged man poured the coffee into cups and placed them on the table.

'How are you doing?' Pothuval asked him. 'What about your daughter's surgery? Is it over?'

The man covered his mouth with his right hand deferentially and muttered: 'Yes, sir.'

'Good. It's all due to the Lord's grace.'

'Yes, sir.'

The old man left the room hesitantly.

Mohandas quipped: 'This is your uniqueness. The innate understanding you develop of others! The ability to remember the minutest facts. I can't do it. Please have your coffee. It'll grow cold.'

'Let it cool a bit.'

'I can't remember anything not aligned with profits.'

Pothuval's eyes were fixed on the red light gently casting its beam far across the backwaters. 'If you remember small matters, albeit not profitable, it will be easier to appreciate the bigger issues.'

Suddenly Pothuval felt that his words were inopportune. There was no need to indicate that he knew anything about Mohandas's old stories.

Mohandas wondered about it too. Did Pothuval know? The probability was low. But he was intelligent. Must have guessed. Out of the blue, Mohandas took a decision. Whether Pothuval knew or not, he was going to narrate that story to him. One should be sincere in not just business, but also friendship. Mohandas said: 'Sir, do you know how I got into the business field?'

Pothuval sat silently.

'It's been more than twenty-five years now. I came to Ernakulam to enrol as a lawyer, perhaps aspiring to become an Honourable Justice, fresh after my law degree. Ah, the days when I was staying in a lodge near the north railway station, enduring the terrible bites of both mosquitoes and bedbugs ... There were four of us. A little politics, beautiful dreams about the future, interesting company.

'I was better off than the rest. Even in those days, I had ten thousand in my bank account. Remember how valuable that amount was, two decades ago. Since there wasn't much work to do in the evenings, we would hire a boat and cross the river to reach Ponjikkara for our evening toddy. I made lots of new friends during that time. There was a bank accountant among them. When he got high after a couple of swigs, he told me an intriguing tale. A customer in his bank had applied for a loan of ten thousand rupees. It was to acquire the statewide agency of a top Bombay company. The Kerala agency was earmarked for him. The only formality left was paying the dues. The deadline was the day after. The head office informed the branch that the loan was denied. The customer didn't know about it. He was absolutely confident of getting the money. Poor fellow! What would happen when he heard about it tomorrow?

'When I was returning from Ponjikkara, the idea struck me. I got a draft for ten thousand rupees, created experience certificates with the letterheads of two companies, and flew to Bombay on the third day. I offered the money to the company. They waited till five in the evening. The next day, they handed over the agency to me. That was the beginning. Never have I stepped inside a court's verandah afterwards.'

'What happened to him?'

'Who?'

'The one who was supposed to get the agency?'

'Him? I heard that he collected money from somewhere and forwarded it to the company after three days. But I had started operating the business by then. I have never seen him. Before or after.'

Pothuval paused poignantly for a few moments. Then he spoke:

'He died after a few years. He never did any other business. Actually, he never knew any other business.'

'Did you know him, sir?'

'His son worked for your company once.'

'I have no idea. So that means, you knew the story.'

Pothuval smiled before replying: 'In business dealings, such betrayals are akin to surreptitious affairs. Doubts, guesswork and half-truths become the basis of everything. I heard some stories. Since they were implausible, I didn't believe them. Since they weren't unlikely, I didn't discard them either. It's an eternal truth that behind every great success there are innumerable minor perfidies.'

'That's the law of nature, sir. Nature has not granted equal strength, either physical or mental, to all. What does it mean? The strong must destroy the weak.'

'Is that so? What if the strength has been given to protect the weak?'

Mohandas got up. 'It's very cold. Shall I shut the window?'

'Why not?'

In the small silence that fell over the room, they listened to the din of the vehicles whizzing past on the road.

'Where is your nephew Ramesan nowadays?' Pothuval asked.

'Madras. He claims that the artists of the Cholamandal are all part of the establishment and that there is a need to overthrow them. He is busy with such a movement, apparently. Crazy, what else?'

'Doesn't matter. If the hot-blooded youth don't attempt crazy things, how will the world progress?'

Drawing the window curtains closed, Mohandas said: 'I'll drop you home before heading to mine. I've decided to purchase reputed firms.'

'Will the owners agree?'

'Most of the huge establishments are public limited companies. I need nobody's permission to buy their shares.'

'Sounds okay. Which company will you take over first?'

Mohandas grinned. 'The oldest reputed company of Kerala. Dhanwantari Herbal Products.'

When they got inside the car, Mohandas remarked: 'Once you had asked me about the secret of my success. I hadn't responded then. Perseverance, intelligence, efficiency in execution … there are so many aspects. But I can tell you now. There is only one answer.'

'What?'

'Luck. God's grace.' He started the car. 'If luck is on my side, with God's grace, in one month's time, Dhanwantari will be mine.'

The car sped through the broad road, which was teeming with people, aiming for the heart of the city. The vast garden near the High Court was desolate and dark. There was a milling crowd near the cinema opposite. Numerous vehicles. Mohandas slowed down his car.

'Is there any special reason for the takeover of Dhanwantari?' Pothuval asked.

When the car started picking up pace, Mohandas grinned. 'Why hide anything from you? I like that company. More than the company, the managing director.'

'Mini Balachandran?'

'Yes.'

Pothuval laughed. 'I felt a doubt. Right from the start.'

'She's worth the challenge.'

After this, neither spoke a word.

12

The Scent of Money

The last few moments of sleep were the most pleasant. The final delicate bubble of slumber ought to collapse soundlessly. Leaving behind the seven colours of the morning light, Savitry jolted awake from her dream bubble.

'There's a call, madam.'

'What?'

'Call.'

'From where?'

'Some Hindi fellow.'

Savitry jumped out of bed. The clock showed fifty minutes past six. Vikas was never going to change! He had Marwari blood in him, didn't he?

He always refused to listen to Savitry's plea: 'Do not call before eight-thirty in the morning.' In fact, he would tell her that it was profitable to call before five at dawn. The STD rates were one-fourth before 5 a.m. Half until eight. Wasn't a quarter to seven better to call then?

Savitry raced to the phone without stopping to wash her face. There was just one phone extension on the third floor. In the

Working Women's Hostel in which Savitry stayed, there were a hundred inmates and a single phone. A total of five extensions. Two on the first and second floors respectively, and one for the third.

Savitry took the call.

'Vikas, Savitry here.'

'Were you sleeping?'

'You disturbed my sleep.'

'Oh, doesn't matter.'

'What? You mean my sleep is of no consequence?'

'Ssshh, it is an STD call. Am paying the money. Just listen, okay?'

'Yes … No.'

'Savitry?'

'Yes, go ahead.'

'There is a company listed in Cochin. Dhanwantari Herbal Products.'

'I know.'

'The share price is fourteen.'

'Yes.'

'Buy as many shares as you can right away.'

'Why?'

'No questions.'

'Even if the price goes up?'

'Yes. Even if it rockets. Until I ask you to stop, keep buying.'

'What is all this?'

'Later … Fifty-fifty.'

'Okay.'

'Thank you.'

'Vikas?'

Vikas cut the call. The matter was over. He did not even check if she was doing fine. Savitry smiled to herself. Maybe it was because of this no-nonsense attitude of his that she liked him so much.

When she returned to the room, Bharti, her roommate asked: 'Who was it?'

'Oh, a business call. To buy some shares.'

Both of them laughed.

Savitry wondered. Whose assistance should she seek?

~

Savitry hailed from the very famous Kunnakkal family. Their lineage equipped her with the special skill to sniff out money.

Kunnakkal tharavadu, situated at Onattukara in Travancore, was an ancient and famous family. They were all powerful patriarchs, who had once reigned supreme. The ancient historical manuscripts kept in the archives of Trivandrum would vouchsafe that when King Marthanda Varma of Venad (later Travancore) defeated the Kayamkulam ruler, he wove the strategies of conquering the rest of the region with the help of the then patriarch of the Kunnakkal family, Keshavan Unnithan. That heyday was long gone.

All their zealous celebrations, pomp and show – the kathakali performances, grand festivals at the family temple, the ritualistic Kuthiyottam dance performances offered to the Devi at Chettikulangara Temple, the hugely admired chariot and horse effigies, feasts of puberty, marriages to Brahmins – had slowly denuded the coffers of the palatial family home.

At the start of the twentieth century, the Kunnakkal tharavadu was laid out in the ettukettu style – with eight traditional blocks of buildings surrounding a vast inner courtyard – five acres of land, and two hundred bighas of land leased to tenants for farming at Veeyapuram. When they consulted the astrologers, they discovered the sins of the forebears. All sacred atonements for mollifying the gods and serpent deities were conducted duly. Slowly, the number of infant deaths reduced in the family.

By the 1930s, the family was back on track. Sekharan Unnithan was the head of the household then. He was a dark giant of a man. A few lumps stood out prominently among his dark curling chest hair. Crimson, paan-stained lips. He would do pranayama every morning. Following his daily ablutions, the man would take a dip in the family pond. After bowing reverently before the family goddess enshrined inside the house and smearing his forehead with sandalwood paste, Unnithan would sit down on his regal armchair set out at the eastern porch of the house, holding a silver tipped staff and his money box.

A veritable crowd would have thronged the compound by then. It was mostly women. They were fishmongers who would buy fish from Thrikkunnapuzha to sell in the surrounding areas. Sometimes, certain other traders would also join the horde. Unnithan would cough meaningfully, retrieve coins called chakra – the currency in vogue – from his money box, and start counting. He would make a heap of fourteen chakras, and after creating fifty such piles, beckon the women fishmongers closer.

He knew everyone's name by heart.

Fourteen chakras were equivalent to half a government rupee then. Extremely valuable. If anyone had twenty-eight chakras, he or she could buy a heavy basket of fishes. Unnithan would distribute two heaps of chakras to each client. Man or woman, whatever be their trading purpose, would get twenty-eight chakras, or one sarkar rupee.

Unnithan never disappointed anyone. Never should any villager suffer because he does not have sufficient resources for earning a livelihood. Sekharan Unnithan would finish his task of distributing money before eight in the morning.

He would have a luxurious repast of rice gruel after. Looking after the compound, the farmlands at Veeyapuram, household activities – all this was his sister's responsibility. Unnithan would enjoy a game of cards in the daytime. Occasionally, he would visit his late wife's house and chat with his daughter, a replica of her mother. By four o'clock in the evening, he would repeat the customs of the morning: take a dip in the pond, bow before the goddess, and seat himself with staff and box in the armchair in the eastern porch.

Those who borrowed money from him at dawn would be making their way back.

Instead of twenty-eight chakras, equivalent to a sarkar rupee, each of them would respectfully place twenty-eight and a half chakras – equivalent to a British rupee – before Unnithan. He would count the money and deposit it inside the money box. The half chakras, earned as interest, would be piled separately.

This moneylending business of Unnithan was a great help to the villagers around. When they received the capital for doing business, most of the men and women started doing small trading. The whole region became commercially active. When the buyers did not have the chakra to repay him, they bartered rice, vegetables or sesame seeds, and exchanged those for money in the market. It was a time when one rupee was an exorbitant amount. If anyone made four chakras in a day, it was a windfall!

During some afternoons, when the sales were over early, some women furtively visited Unnithan in the treehouse located in the south of the vast yard. He would never change the interest rate of half a chakra for any of them. But the women whispered gleefully that, when happy, he would graciously gift them even a silver rupee!

Even when the Second World War spread havoc everywhere, the village escaped the claws of penury. Unnithan converted all the interest money to silver rupees. When thirteen silver rupees were added up, he would change it for a kuthirappavan, that is, a gold sovereign.

Legend has it that when Sekharan Unnithan died in 1946, the family had a small sackful of gold sovereigns. His sister had two sons: Raman and Lakshman. Both had turned adults by the time their uncle passed away. With the momentum provided by the gold sovereigns, both catapulted to life. Raman was deep into politics; Lakshman had an affinity towards art. Raman, though defeated in the elections, switched sides and tried again. When Lakshman's theatre troupe failed, he caught a train to Madras to go make movies. Raman floundered in the elections again. Both the brothers sat on the verandah and started building castles in the air about the next election and the next film.

By the 1960s, both were householders with families to look after.

Lakshman learned typing secretly and vamoosed to Bombay. He had asked his wife to wait for him. Raman was both happy and sad that Lakshman had abandoned him. He cleared the shrubs in the compound and set up a thatched structure; bought a few benches and desks, and started a tutorial college.

In three months' time, Lakshman took his wife and daughter Savitry with him to Bombay.

Twenty years passed.

Lakshman became an important executive in the marketing division of a huge export company. It belonged to a Marwari seth. Lakshman had started his career as a steno typist. The Seth liked the young man. He observed him closely for a month. Extremely hardworking, intelligent and reticent. The young fellow did not gabble about business secrets. 'The man is sincere,' the Seth told his wife. 'Like Lakshman looked after Sri Ramchandra, he will take care of our company.'

But Lakshman died unexpectedly. Heart attack.

Savitry was twenty-two years old. She had procured two postgraduate diplomas in business management and interior decoration after her commerce degree. Lakshman had decided to purchase a flat in Bombay. He had saved ten lakhs. The Seth had promised to help him too.

The death occurred in the office. An unexpected pain. Before the co-workers could rush him to the hospital, Lakshman passed away.

Savitry was with a friend at the time. It was Vikas Kacholia who found out where she was. He was Savitry's boyfriend, and the Seth's nephew.

Vikas took Savitry to see her father's body. Only then did she come to know about the catastrophe. It took her two days to accept the devastation. Raman and his son arrived for the funeral. All the rites were conducted in Bombay.

One day before her uncle returned to Kerala, Savitry dialled Vikas's number. Vikas's father was a member of the Bombay Stock Exchange. The son waited until he turned eighteen so that he could become his Authorized Assistant. With an innate intelligence and five years of experience at the Stock Exchange, Vikas Kacholia was now a formidable stockbroker. Apart from stocks and shares, Vikas had only one other major weakness: Savitry.

Vikas picked the call at his own office located in Dalal Street.

'Vikas, I need to talk to you. I want your advice.'

'When? Isn't it better that we speak after trading hours?'

'Sure.'

In the evening, they found some solitude in the midst of the milling crowd at the Juhu beach. Twilight had rendered a serenity to the sea.

Savitry said: 'Vikas, today you won't speak. Even if you open your mouth, don't dare to utter a word about shares or convertible debentures.'

Vikas grinned. 'Okay, go ahead.'

'I am going back.'

'Back?'

'Yes, to Kerala.'

'Go on.'

Vikas always felt that Savitry's beauty increased whenever she spoke gravely. He felt like kissing her. Catching hold of her fingers, he gently drew figures on the sand.

'Tell me...'

'I've been thinking for the past one week. Amma is incapable of making any decisions. Uncle says he'll take care of everything if we go with him. The offer could be sincere, or a mere formality. My guess is that he's sure we will stay back in Bombay. Especially someone like me, who would never adjust to a life outside Bombay. But I have decided to go.'

Amidst the commotion around, they fell silent for a while.

'My best friend, dear Vikas, do you know why? I'll go to Cochin. It's mini-Bombay. I can adjust to the place. Considering all the financial benefits due to my father, we would have around twenty lakhs. Some shares too. I plan to start some business related to exports in Cochin. With your help, of course.'

Vikas sat thinking for a while. The lover inside him gave way to the practical Marwari.

'Yes, I have an idea. Go to Cochin and join the Stock Exchange there. I'll do what's necessary. There's no need to join any other business.'

He turned eloquent.

'We shall never part, Savitry. How is it possible? The nerve centre of my business is here in Bombay. But the critical part is also centred in Cochin. Kerala is fecund, has a very fertile land for growth. A huge society of investors. There's an invisible bulwark of non-resident external accounts, which allow NRIs to deposit foreign-currency earnings in an Indian bank. A set of people who are eager to embrace anything new! We can build a huge empire. You in Cochin and yours truly in Bombay. We shall be together every weekend.'

Savitry raised her eyes and gazed at Vikas. In the twilight, his eyes glimmered with dreams.

'One can fly to Cochin from Bombay in two hours. Perhaps lesser time than it takes to reach home from Juhu beach on some days!'

Savitry asked: 'Do you believe in my abilities?'

'You're asking me whether I believe in my prospective bride's abilities?'

'Are you planning to marry me?'

'Of course!'

'Who told you that?'

'My own self.'

'But I should agree, right?'

'That's the snare I laid now.'

'What?'

'Our business relation. Once you start working from Cochin, it will become a relationship which will withstand even major fights! Then you shall conclude that it is better to marry me.'

Savitry smiled. 'I never thought that far.'

'That's the famous Marwari brains!'

When they walked back in the dark with their fingers looped together, Vikas confessed: 'I'm very happy today.'

'Hmm?'

'You expressed some love for me. That's why.'

'You are my friend. Best friend.'

'Husband?'

'Anyone can become a husband. But not everyone can become a good friend.'

That night, Savitry and her mother started packing their belongings.

13

The Invisible Enemy

It was ten o'clock.

Mini Balachandran had been sitting silently for the last half an hour. The air conditioner's subdued mutterings reverberated in the room. Zacharia's voice grew more serious and imposing. Twice Zacharia opened the window to spit out the paan juice. But he continued to speak. Mini was doodling on a notepad.

One fact stood out starkly: the problem was not normal. It was extremely grave and needed to be confronted immediately.

The enemy was invisible. Nobody knew how strong he was. His main weapon was money. Courage alone would not be sufficient for fighting him.

Zacharia elaborated:

'Today is Thursday. From Monday, in the past three days, someone has been single-mindedly purchasing our shares. Not just in one place either! Bombay, Delhi, Calcutta, Ahmedabad … in every city. Nobody would notice. But it's a clear pattern.'

True. At the Cochin Stock Exchange, the sale of Dhanwantari's shares would possibly have occurred at the most four or five times in the last three months. That, too, in lot sizes of hundred or two hundred. The price stayed steady at thirteen and a half rupees. The maximum fluctuation in the past year was the escalation of the share price from ten to thirteen and veering towards fifteen. At the same time, some companies saw their shares worth ten rupees go up to eighty or ninety rupees! Dhanwantari remained at a static price.

More than the company's balance sheet, external factors played a part in deciding the share prices. The government's economic and commercial policies, the competitive pricing of the company's products in the international markets, weather predictions, and so on, affected the share prices. But these were equally applicable to other companies that made similar products. Dhanwantari's shares had never been swayed even by such factors till now.

Zacharia said: 'I checked the old newspapers. Do you know that our company's shares have been traded just six times in the last three months across all the stock exchanges? That's without counting the Cochin Exchange. And now, in the last three days? To tell the truth, I felt furious at myself. I should have seen the pattern yesterday itself. Today at nine, when I was reading the newspaper, I saw that our share prices have reached fourteen in Bombay. I was stunned. When I checked Ahmedabad, it was the same! I felt like laughing at first.'

That was a fact. Seeing Zacharia smile after reading the newspaper in his office, the young Sikh fellow who was sitting opposite had looked askance at him. Since he was familiar with those who worked in the Stock Exchange, he didn't find anything amiss in that smile. Such people smiled and cried often after ruminations.

Zacharia's house-cum-office was situated in an old building abutting the side of a small road. It connected the main artery of Kochi, the Mahatma Gandhi Road, with its sister, Chittoor Road, lying to its east. A simple tile-roofed house that seemed to ignore the intimidating presence of multistoreyed buildings in the vicinity. A spacious yard in the front, a few coconut trees, one mango tree. An ornate gate that creaked loudly while opening.

This building and property would have been sold off much earlier. A gigantic shopping complex would have risen in its place after demolishing the structure. Out of the blue, Zacharia's friend, the owner of the building, had died. The death happened when Zacharia was paying a nominal amount as rent for the house. The front room was used as an office. There was also a guest room, kitchen and a bedroom.

Zacharia's family was in his village. He would pay them a visit once a week. During vacations, Zacharia's wife and children would visit Ernakulam.

His close friend's demise threw Zacharia into a predicament. There was no question of getting another office-cum-residence at that low a rate anywhere in the city. The Stock Exchange was within walking distance of the house. Still, he decided to enquire about other accommodations. He informed his friend's wife that he was willing to shift anytime. The lady called him home and requested, 'Please don't! You should continue to stay there.'

The farce was revealed when Zacharia dug deeper. His late friend had another wife and children. The woman to whom he had spoken was his second wife. The friend's mother was hostile to both wives and lived independently. All three women had come forward staking a legal claim over the friend's assets. The case was being fought in court now. The first wife maintained that there was no second wife. The mother insisted that neither were her son's wives. The prime property – almost twelve cents of land – had a market value of one lakh rupees per cent. The brouhaha was likely to continue for a long time.

Zacharia put up a small board in front of the building: P.T. Zacharia, Stockbroker. He regularly deposited a monthly rent of two hundred rupees in the court.

Zacharia woke up at five every morning. Govinda Prabhu, the watchman of the building-cum-cook-cum-office peon, would be snoring away. Zacharia would sneak into the kitchen without disturbing him and make a cup of tea. After finishing it, he would dress up in sportswear and pick up his tennis racket. The club was a kilometre away. By the time he would walk to the club, dawn would be approaching. There were four or five players who came to the club every day without fail. They would play till seven-thirty. Zacharia would perspire heavily. In the past, even when he was crazy about football, tennis was an indispensable morning ritual. Now, there was no football. Only tennis. By the time he walked back, the city would be waking up.

At eight-thirty, he would take a shower and have breakfast. Three idlis, chutney, tea. Govinda Prabhu would buy the idlis and chutney from the hotel nearby. The tea, he would prepare himself.

When Zacharia sat down to sip his tea, Prabhu would raise his daily query:

'How does it look today?'

'Time is not yet ripe.'

'Is it going down or up?'

'Will go up.'

Prabhu would be delighted.

The scene had been playing out unfailingly every morning for the past three years. The matter was quite simple.

Middle-aged Govinda Prabhu, who was wandering around without any gainful employment, ended up at Zacharia's place. Zacharia liked him. A Brahmin, vegetarian to boot. No drinking, and remote chances of stealing chicken from the kitchen. He demanded no salary either. Just a roof over his head, food and clothes. Soon he started working as the peon in the office.

Two years later, one day, Prabhu expressed his desire before Zacharia with a bit of trepidation.

'Sir, I have a wish.'

'What?'

'I also want to buy some shares.'

'Why?'

'Er...' Prabhu had no explanations to offer.

Zacharia was kind. 'Sure. But we won't buy it from the Exchange. The price might escalate and decline rather fast. We'll apply when there is an issue of new shares. What do you say? If you're fortunate, you'll strike it rich. That will be better.'

'Whatever you decide, sir.'

Though he wasn't paying Prabhu any salary, Zacharia was keeping tabs on the amount due to Prabhu at the rate of one hundred rupees per month. It accrued to nearly two thousand five hundred rupees over two years. Zacharia took a look at the new shares in the market that week. There was a huge hotel company that was issuing ten-rupee shares. Another additional ten rupees as premium. So each share would entail twenty rupees. One had to pay half the amount. Once the shares were allotted, the rest could be deposited.

Zacharia deposited one thousand rupees in the bank to buy a hundred shares for Prabhu. Prabhu signed the document.

There were many applicants to buy the shares of the reputed hotel company. The computer did a random selection. The company decided to allot shares to every one out of the ten names thrown up by the machine. Fortunately, Prabhu too was allotted a hundred shares. Immediately, Zacharia paid the rest of the amount and got the share certificates.

Following that day, except in front of Zacharia and his friends, Prabhu acted as if he were the owner of India's largest hotel conglomerate. When this hotel company took over a prominent hotel in Kochi, Prabhu walked proudly on the road in front of the building. He did not dare to step inside. Prabhu was well aware that having a single meal would wipe away the total cost of his ownership.

Yet, every morning, Prabhu would invariably ask: 'Sir, how is it? Growing or falling?'

Zacharia knew what the question was about. Whether the price of the hotel company went up or down, it made no difference to Prabhu. He did not wish to sell his shares. Even so, hearing that the price of the shares at the Bombay Stock Exchange had gone up delighted him no end. If he heard that the shares were down, he would be chagrined. Prabhu would start caviling against the management.

Zacharia said, 'Might increase.'

'It will increase, sir. For sure.'

'Prabhu, one day we should go have lunch in your hotel.'

'You can go, sir. I won't come.'

'Why not?'

'There is whisky, meat and much hubbub.'

Suddenly the calling bell rang. Prabhu went to check.

'Some person called Singh.'

'Singh?'

'Punjabi Singh'.

'You mean a Sikh?'

'Never seen him before.'

Zacharia washed his hands. Then he folded the newspapers. Zacharia would read the *Financial Times* and *Economic Times* only in his office, after nine in the morning. Never would the newspapers enter his bedroom. In Zacharia's view, unless there was a clear demarcation, he would end up forgetting that there was another world around.

When Zacharia reached his office room, the visitor stood up and extended his hand.

'Glad to meet you.'

Zacharia shook his hand.

'Zacharia.'

'Tarlok Singh.'

'Please take a seat.'

A lamp was lit on a small table next to where Zacharia sat. The fragrance from a few incense sticks wafted around the room since the windows were shut. Zacharia got up to open the windowpanes.

'Please proceed.'

Tarlok Singh was gazing at the pictures on the table. There was a framed picture of Goddess Lakshmi. There were pictures of Hanuman and Guruvayurappan. A picture of the crucified Christ. A photograph of Mecca with the minaret and crescent moon. Images of Buddha and Mahavira placed adjacent to each other. Then the picture of Guru Granth Sahib.

'Sat Sri Akal. I realize I have come to the right place.'

Zacharia smiled.

14

Tarlok Singh's Prophecy

Without much of a preface, Tarlok Singh announced: 'I have decided to do my trading exclusively through you.'

'Why?'

Zacharia spread the newspaper to the page containing Stock Exchange updates.

The Sardarji said, 'I have met a couple of brokers. Never have I caught a glimpse of a worshipping place with all the religious insignias.'

'I got the Sri Guru Granth Sahib image from Patiala.'

'Patiala?'

'I used to go there for the Sports Federation meetings.'

'Are you a sportsman?'

'Used to be. I am one even now. The Stock Exchange work is my profession. That's all.'

'Good.'

Suddenly, Tarlok Singh asked: 'What's your opinion about Venus Tyres?'

Zacharia did not reply immediately. The company, with a share price of ten, had been trading at a loss for five rupees for years together. In the last few years, Venus Tyres had resurrected its fortunes: with a new management, modern machinery, a long-time agreement with the labour force and huge demand of its products in the market. The share price had shot up from five rupees to eighty. Occasionally, it would dip and then rise. The shareholders had received bonus shares twice. The company had doled out thirty per cent of its accumulated earnings to its shareholders for three years consistently. The ratio of the bonus shares was one for every two current shares. It had major strategies for future growth.

Without batting an eyelid, one could proffer advice: *Perfect time to invest in the shares of Venus Tyres if you wish to make a long-term investment.*

But Tarlok Singh had not made it clear whether he wished to buy or sell. Whatever it was, the broker would receive his commission. As per the Stock Exchange rules, a broker could receive more than two per cent as commission. Usually, brokers demanded commissions ranging from one to one and a half per cent. Zacharia always charged a commission fee of one and a half per cent.

Zacharia felt that Tarlok Singh was like a highly discerning patient, capable of explaining his symptoms with precision. But he was waiting for the doctor to diagnose the disease. If he could discover the sickness, the doctor's professional expertize would be verified.

Zacharia raised a query. 'Do you wish to buy or sell?'

'Sell.'

'Go ahead and sell.'

If Tarlok Singh had said 'Buy', Zacharia would have still encouraged him. It had nothing to do with his commission. Most clients who came seeking the broker's counsel would have already made up their minds after duly pursuing the information available in the newspapers. They were not coming to obtain any guidance.

Rather, they were seeking some sort of justification for their decision, that was all. Tarlok Singh had already made up his mind to sell his shares in Venus Tyres. There was no point in discouraging him. He would simply approach another share broker.

Tarlok Singh elucidated: 'Zachariaji, I was based in Delhi. It's just been three weeks since I arrived in Kochi on transfer. I was a regular player at the Exchange in Delhi. One lakh portfolio. Nothing major. Investments in five or six shares. Haven't had many setbacks till now.'

Zacharia responded: 'One needs grit and patience to stay cool when the share prices take a dive. Things turn out okay then.'

'I used to make close to twenty thousand every month.'

'If you invest carefully and sell at the appropriate juncture, yes, one won't have losses. Twenty thousand rupees is pretty cool.'

'Thank you. Now I wish to play the stock market here. It is not just money, is it? This involves one's intelligence, knowledge, all of it. Besides, that ineffable thrill of playing a game of dice. What do you say?'

'You're right.'

Tarlok Singh got up. 'My office starts at nine forty-five. Shall take your leave now.' He shook Zacharia's hand. 'Please keep this card' – he offered Zacharia his business card. 'My address and telephone number.'

Zacharia listened while browsing through the card.

'Just a moment, Zachariaji. I'll be consulting you on companies and share values … But I might not always listen to your advice. Don't feel bad about it.'

Zacharia grinned. 'It is your money! The investor always has the final call. The broker shall advise, that's all.'

Tarlok Singh returned the smile.

'I like you Zachariaji. What's your commission rate?'

'One and a half.'

'But the going rate is one to one and a quarter.'

'Even if you don't abide by my expert advice, it'll remain top notch. That cost is included in the commission rate.'

Tarlok Singh laughed. He shook Zacharia's hand once more. And then, using the usual Stock-Exchange lingo, said, 'Done!'

'What next?'

'Zachariaji, do the first business this way. Yesterday, Venus Tyres closed at fifty-three here. Sell three hundred shares in the morning. Then buy a thousand shares of the company called Dhanwantari Herbal Products.'

'Dhanwantari Herbal?'

'A rather unnoticed share. But Bombay closing was at fourteen rupees yesterday. Please buy.'

'Why Dhanwantari?'

'I have a premonition that its share prices will double in a fortnight! Then we shall sell them. By investing fourteen thousand now, we will make a profit of the same amount.'

'But how? Nobody has cared for its shares for a few years now.'

'Please do as I say. What's the margin money? We got acquainted only today, right?'

As per Stock Exchange rules, after buying shares through the share market, there was a window of two weeks for giving the share certificates and paying the amount. Fridays were earmarked for the settlement. Under certain circumstances, the sellers might not have been able to provide the share certificates. It happened typically when the prices fluctuated hugely over a fortnight.

If one had agreed to buy shares at a cost of twenty rupees and it dipped to sixteen over two weeks, a person who bought a thousand shares would end up losing four thousand rupees. He might not pay the money. But it was the stockbroker who made the deal. He was required to settle the dues on the second Friday of the month.

Even if he defaulted, after accounting for the money in his name, the Stock Exchange would ensure payment of the share prices to the broker who sold the shares. And immediately, the Stock Exchange would recover the amount from the broker who had dishonoured the terms of the agreement.

Consequently, even if the investors developed cold feet, the broker had no alternative but to pay up. To avoid such predicaments, brokers usually charged an amount, almost one-fourth of the investment, as advance. Especially from those who were new to them. Usually, the variations of share prices would not surpass one-fourth of the outlay. In that case, even if the investor did not heed the terms of the deal, the broker could pay up without suffering any personal loss. This amount was referred to as 'margin money'.

Zacharia was still ruminating over Tarlok Singh's prophecy.

'Here is a cheque for three thousand. Hope it'll cover the risk. I have not written the company name. Please fill it.'

Zacharia took the cheque. 'Thank you. I shall call at five.'

When Tarlok Singh left, Zacharia looked at his watch. It was nine-twenty. He hailed Prabhu. 'Please bring *The Business Times* of the last two weeks.'

Prabhu went to collect the newspapers and returned soon after. Monday, Tuesday, Wednesday – the trend had started only in the past three days. There was no mention of the company before that. Dhanwantari Herbals…

Bombay Stock Exchange, Monday, the share price was thirteen rupees.

Delhi, twelve and three quarters.

Calcutta, thirteen.

Ahmedabad, thirteen.

Tuesday, there was again a surge of purchases at all four locations. The price had gone up by fifty paisa.

The phenomenon repeated on Wednesday.

Now the share value was fourteen. In Calcutta, fourteen and a half rupees.

At the Cochin Stock Exchange, not a single share of Dhanwantari had been traded.

'This striking pattern! Why hadn't I noticed it before?'

Zacharia stared at the three-thousand-rupee cheque given by Tarlok Singh for a long time. What was going on?

That someone was on a buying spree of the company's shares was no prank. If in the four prominent stock exchanges in India, a small company's shares were being traded actively, it was certainly not a coincidence. Rather, it was very much deliberate.

Not a single share had been purchased in the Cochin Exchange till now. The company was based here in Cochin and most of its shares were in Kerala. Yet, no trading had occurred in the local Stock Exchange. Was it a move to keep matters low-key here?

What if that indeed was the case?

Zacharia dialled Mini Balachandran.

She had not reached the office.

Mini should know about this immediately. She was already grappling with many problems. Should he burden her with this matter now?

Yes. If there was a hidden agenda behind this singular occurrence, it would affect the whole company. The very foundation of the company, nurtured over fifty years, would be shaken. It would toll the death knell for the whole vision and dedication behind Dhanwantari Herbal Products.

Mini was courageous.

Zacharia called Suryanarayanan. Swami, as he was referred to casually, was having his breakfast after his puja rituals.

'I always carry a handphone with me. One can speak even while having breakfast. It's been a while since we met. What's up?'

Zacharia said: 'Swami, there's an urgent matter.'

'Yes, my business caters to urgencies.'

'How much data of Ayurvedic companies do you have in your computer?'

'Kariacha, I have to check first.'

Zacharia knew that Swami was terribly shrewd. He would not divulge the smallest bit of information without charging his fees.

'I need a comparative analysis of all the Ayurvedic companies that you have. The balance sheet, fluctuations in share prices, all of it. What will be the fee?'

'All companies?'

'The companies that manufacture and sell medicines.'

Swami replied: 'I won't have much data. There's someone in Bombay who sends me the necessary information. Will get in touch.'

He was going to up his fee.

Zacharia spoke: 'I need the data today.'

'Today?'

'Ask your person in Bombay to fax it. What will be the charges?'

'That I will tell you later. But this information…?'

'Need it by eleven if possible.'

'Two in the afternoon?'

Zacharia paused for a moment. 'All right. I'm sending a cheque of five thousand straight away. Send a printout of whatever data you have in the computer through Prabhu. The rest by 2 p.m.'

'Okay, Kariacha! Then make it a cheque for seven thousand five hundred. Let it be the first and final payment. How about that?'

'Swami, are you negotiating early in the morning…?'

'Kariacha, the Bombaywala will start badgering me for money right now.'

'Okay, a cheque for seven thousand five hundred.'

Zacharia handed the cheque over to Prabhu with clear instructions. Whatever packet Suryanarayanan gave him, he should keep it safely in the office. Nobody should know about it.

Once Prabhu left, Zacharia called Mini again. She had just reached the office.

'Mini here. What's up, Uncle?'

'I need to see you as soon as possible. It's urgent!'

'What's wrong?'

'Can't share over the phone.'

'Why not?'

'Have you been reading *The Business Times*, especially over the last three days?'

'No … I was…'

'Dhanwantari's shares are being bought at a furious pace … I don't get it. There has been a lot of interest in our shares in the past three days at the Stock Exchange.'

'In Kerala?'

'Not here. In Bombay, Calcutta, Ahmedabad, Delhi … all these places.'

'What?' Mini paused awhile, and then added, 'Uncle, is this serious?'

'If it's an intentional strategy, then trust me, it's very serious … The company…!'

Half an hour had passed since that phone conversation.

Zacharia threw open the windows in Mini's office. Mini's squirrels were nowhere to be seen.

They would arrive only by afternoon.

15

The Shadow of an Accusation

'There are many ways to take over a company like ours. The management of Dhanwantari Herbal Products owns only fifteen per cent of the shares. Another fifteen per cent shares are held by the Trust. Thirty in total. Many family business conglomerates run their businesses with a mere five or ten per cent shares. The Tatas hold merely one and a half per cent in the Tata Group companies. Consequently, those trying to acquire such companies are not required to purchase majority shares. Legally, it is not permissible to buy more than twenty-five per cent of the shares in any company. One needs permission from the government to do so.'

Whenever Zacharia started his speech, he would charm listeners by elaborating the context. The style of extempore, with which he came to be acquainted during the secret meetings of the Communist party, was still a part of him.

Mini Balachandran spoke: 'I know, Uncle. Only a third of the shares are with the governmental organizations. The rest are with the public.'

Zacharia said: 'Let us think logically. If I wanted to take over this company, what would I do? There are three ways open to me. Give a direct offer to purchase all the shares of the company at a particular value. And apart from the share-market price, offer a quota of black money too. If the owner of the company is not emotionally attached to the company, that's the easiest way. The company can become mine without much publicity.'

'That won't work here. This is our company, our family…' Mini responded.

'The second is more prone to public scrutiny. Send an open letter to every shareholder. Within fifteen days of your receiving the letter, the shares that you possess, costing thirteen rupees each now, shall be purchased by us at twenty rupees each. After the deadline, we will buy them only at thirteen rupees. America and other countries usually adopt this method. There are many stories of the success of this methodology in India too. Ordinary stakeholders fall for it, since they suddenly end up getting one and a half times their investment.'

'Nobody has tried that with Dhanwantari.'

'Exactly. Here, the unknown player is using the third tactic. In the first two approaches, regardless of the share prices, the buyer will also have to shell out a handsome amount. The third method does not entail that catch. Buy the shares slowly and steadily at the existing share prices at the Exchange. If one is in a hurry, the price will jack up. Buy the shares subtly, without making much of a song and dance. If they're being bought in many different names, nobody would be able to even trace who is behind it. If one buys two thousand shares in all the sixteen exchanges of India in a day, the party will end up purchasing one and a half lakh shares of the company in a week's time. They can easily match the family's fifteen per cent shareholding in a fortnight. What's the total number of shares?'

'Twenty lakh, Uncle.'

'The calculations add up. Our unknown enemy is doing exactly that!' Zacharia rasped.

'Can we do anything to stop this buying spree?' Mini asked.

'Nothing legally. After buying the shares, when the party brings the relevant documents here for registration, the board of directors can always take the view that it's against the interests of the company and will harm its operations. However, in my opinion, that won't fly. One will have to prove in a court of law, how such a takeover is damaging the company. That won't be easy.'

'Then?'

'We have to find out who is behind this takeover bid. What's their goal? Is it merely money, or something else they are after?'

'What do you mean by "something else"?'

'Can be anything. Perhaps, an idea. Some specific medicines, their ingredients. Players who are marketing similar products might want to eliminate competition. Can't rule out personal agendas. Maybe someone is miffed with you, Mini … It can be absolutely anything.'

'Miffed with me? For what?'

'Does a man need reason to feel angry at someone? Then there is another cause – far simpler.'

'What's that?'

'The trade name of Dhanwantari. We know that Dhanwantari is the God of Ayurveda. At the mere mention of the name, anyone will recognize that the brand has to do with Ayurvedic products. In almost all Indian languages, they are familiar with that name. No new company can use this name, can they? The name alone is worth many crores!'

Mini grew pensive.

'Uncle, you're right. When my grandfather tried to register the company in this name, he was denied permission. There was a small company of the same name. He acquired that company for the sake of the name.'

Zacharia smiled.

'Maybe our guess is right. It could be a battle for the brand name. There are a number of billionaires in Europe and America who were notorious for aggressive takeovers of companies. Everyone knows of Sir James Goldsmith. He had dual citizenship of Britain and France, and owned businesses in America. He was married thrice, had quite a few mistresses, and several children. Four months in each place. What fun, eh? Goldsmith was the great shark of financial markets. Once someone referred to him as the "Attila the Hun" of stock markets. He was an incorrigible greenmail corporate raider and asset-stripper. After the hostile takeover of companies, he would immediately shake up the management.

'By selling the company's assets – whatever assets he considered unprofitable – Goldsmith would recover his investment. Purportedly, Goldsmith did most of his deals from his luxury yachts moored in the Mediterranean Sea and Pacific islands, communicating via satellites to the offices in London, Paris and New York! It was rumoured that Goldsmith chose the companies to acquire by virtue of their names. The brand value of names that are easily recollected by people is never reflected in the balance sheets of companies. And since it is not visible in the balance sheets, the brand value does not reflect in the share prices too.'

'Uncle, you hit it right on the head! Dhanwantari is Dhanwantari.'

'The player is someone who knows that the share prices of our company are very low.'

The intercom sounded all of a sudden.

'Asokan here. Mini, are you free?'

Mini hesitated momentarily. She looked at Zacharia. 'Anything urgent?'

The voice that emerged from the intercom was flush with frustration.

'Yes. Do you think I'd trouble you otherwise? I have no time to catch my breath.'

Mini looked at Zacharia again. He, in turn, looked at his watch.

'All right, you may come.'

Zacharia rose from his seat.

'Mini, see if you can dig out something. I shall tap into my contacts. We have to find out who is behind this takeover bid.'

'Maybe there is nothing nefarious underfoot.'

'I don't think so. If the field of business were that simple, anyone would triumph in this arena.'

Mini struggled to smile.

Suddenly, Zacharia regretted his words. Mini might have misunderstood what he had just said. Zacharia tactfully changed the subject. 'Listen to this! Someone asked me to buy a thousand shares of Dhanwantari today.'

'What?'

'A Sardarji. New client. It was when he spoke about it that I noticed the sales pattern of our shares.'

'Sardarji?'

'Yes, he is speculating that these shares shall double in value after a fortnight.'

'Will they?'

'Why not?'

Asokan slowly opened the door and stopped abruptly upon seeing Zacharia.

'Sorry, I thought...'

'Come in,' Mini said, 'Uncle and I were chatting.'

Zacharia greeted him: 'How are you, Asokan?'

'Fine.'

Zacharia shook his hand.

'I was leaving.'

'Uncle, just a minute. Asokan chetta, anything serious?'

Mini pretended to ignore how Asokan's eyes were hovering over Zacharia.

Asokan had been working as the marketing director of Dhanwantari Herbal Products for the last five years. He had joined the company as a cost accountant at the age of twenty-one. Mini's father Raghava Menon was fond of the young man, who was enthusiastic, bright, eager to learn and ambitious. Soon, Asokan passed the company secretary examination and acquired an MBA by attending evening classes. From a cost accountant he became a company secretary, and then a director. He currently held one per cent of the company's shares.

Asokan was efficiency personified, in his suave safari suit, expensive shoes and gold-framed glasses, flaunting a supercilious look on his face. In his behaviour and work, he was a role-model for anyone in the company. But Mini loathed him. Not only that, she was also terrified of the man.

The reason behind that fear was one of Mini's innermost secrets. It was Asokan who had kissed her for the first time.

~

Mini was fifteen years old then.

Asokan was a thirty-two-year-old bachelor. He was handsome, charming in speech, and smelled of Yardley powder. The man would narrate the stories of English movies well.

Mini liked Asokan. She enjoyed listening to the conversations between her father and Asokan; found it pleasing when he would praise Asokan openly.

It was the vacation after the Secondary School Leaving Certificate Examination. Mini had been infatuated with one of her classmates at that point of time. Though she wanted to express her fondness towards the boy, she had never done so. At the mere sight of him, she would become embarrassed and feel like fleeing. The boy's smile was enchanting. Once she saw him in the temple with his mother. Since he had removed his shirt, Mini observed his fair form. Her classmate seemed self-conscious at her presence, and Mini rather liked his flushed face.

Nowadays, Mini tried hard to recollect the boy's name. His face seemed to have evaporated from her memories. But at that time, she was deeply in love with him.

One day, she accompanied her father to the office. Her brother wanted to watch a cricket match and she was planning to see a matinee.

Asokan was present in the office.

By the afternoon, Mini's father became very busy. So Asokan was entrusted with the task of taking her for the film. It was a fun outing. He bought her ice-cream during the interval. When they returned, Mini's father had stepped out for some work. He had asked the watchman to convey to Mini that she should wait for him.

That was when it happened. When Mini was waiting for her father in Asokan's office.

Mini still wondered about the incident.

Asokan said: 'I like you Mini. Don't you like me?'

By the time her surprise turned into laughter, the man had kissed her.

Mini had read a lot about one's first kiss and had many fantasies about it. She had been shocked at the unexpected, dry and emotionless kiss.

'What nonsense is this!'

'What's the issue, Mini?'

'You are more like an uncle to me.'

Mini had run off to her father's office room. Asokan had followed her after a while.

'Sorry.'

'It's all right.'

They had not spoken another word until Mini's father returned. Indeed, never after had either of them discussed that episode.

From that day onwards, Mini remained scared of Asokan.

Asokan asked agitatedly: 'Did you read today's *Times of India*, Mini?'

'No.'

'There is a report about us.'

'Us?'

'Allegedly, real ingredients aren't being used in Ayurvedic products. There is a broad mention about companies in the south, and Dhanwantari Herbals in particular.'

'Is it an open accusation?'

'Not an accusation at all; a general report. They have mentioned the name of some consumer forum. Apparently, they have taken the initiative to bring this fact to light.'

Mini looked at Zacharia questioningly.

Zacharia responded: 'I'll take my leave. It's already ten-thirty. This news will definitely affect our share prices. Let me go and check.'

16

The Innocent Smile

Asokan closed the door of the room and sat down with his eyes shut for two minutes. The doctor had told him to do that intermittently. With your eyes closed, without thinking about anything, focus your mind on an imaginary lamp that has been lit. Anything that causes emotional turmoil will increase your blood pressure.

Asokan was prone to experiencing persistent fluctuations in blood pressure. Nowadays, more so. He had given up salt and oily food. And he was scrupulous about the portions he consumed. Even so, the pressure remained a cause of concern. And so the doctor had advised him. Blood pressure is closely linked with the mind. Learn to control your mind. Avoid unwanted ruminations.

But how could that be?

The challenges that Dhanwantari Herbal Products was facing were increasing by leaps and bounds each day. Marketing was the life-nerve of the company. The existence of the firm was dependent on the sales figures and their variations. Every week, newer Ayurvedic products were entering the market. To handle that competition, a coordinated effort across multiple areas was warranted. Inventing new medicines, packaging old medicines in more attractive ways, advertisements, the timely and meticulous preparation of medicines, ensuring their delivery to the stockists and dealers, engaging the medical representatives to network with the doctors, creating an efficient way of collecting the payments of all sold medicines and consolidating them at the head office ... Asokan was willing to handle all these responsibilities as the marketing director. He did not need anybody's help. Though it could occasionally trigger a hike in his blood pressure, never would work turn fatal. But the problem did not lie with marketing. The sort of scaffolding needed to support marketing – the factory, purchase of herbs, research, modern machinery, labour management – all had to work in tandem. What was needed was a management with foresight and vision, intelligence, leadership qualities and, enough maturity. And that was exactly what Dhanwantari Herbal Products lacked. Especially over the last one year.

Those who are incapable should never take over administrative responsibility.

Was Mini behaving like a managing director? No. Asokan felt furious and bitter. Typically, anyone would be hassled if something negative about their company appeared in a Bombay-based newspaper. But Mini was utterly impassive. There was not the slightest emotion or anger on her face.

Asokan closed his eyes again. Even then, the scene refused to vanish from his eyes.

~

'Mini, I consulted with our advocate. We should file a defamation suit against both the newspaper and the consumer forum who are behind the news. A report that mentions our company specifically, without any smidgeon of evidence, in a very superficial article alleging malpractices. This is deliberate, that's beyond doubt. It will affect the good name of our company. The advocate will issue a legal notice today itself. Tomorrow, the newspapers will carry our response to the allegation.'

Mini listened silently. After some time, she asked: 'That would again imply bad publicity, wouldn't it? Whatever is printed in a newspaper, whether it is true or false, people tend to swallow it unquestioningly. Even if we establish that the news item was wrong, the uncertainty shall remain with the readers. Will they change their minds about us?'

'This is not an emotional question, Mini. It is a news-story that has put at stake a great institution's credibility and integrity! We should not let it go just like that.'

Mini smiled innocently. 'Asokan chetta, please go ahead and do as you see fit. I just stated my view.'

'If your father were alive, he would have thrown a tantrum! He would never spare those Bombaywalas.'

A moment's pause later, Asokan had wondered aloud: 'Mini, I hope you understood the full impact and seriousness of this news snippet!'

Mini smiled innocently once more.

~

Asokan opened his eyes. It was Mini's naïve smile that rankled badly. Likc a babc in thc woods.

No. There is no other way. She should go! Mini will never resign from the post willingly. She should be thrown out.

Asokan brooded: *Of course, when I remember her father, I regret that she should have to face such a fate within one year of assuming charge. But if the same state of affairs continues, the company won't exist after a year or so. What I am doing shall be a service to the memory of Menon sir. He'll be blessing me from the heavens.*

Asokan picked up the phone and dialled a number.

Mohandas's personal assistant took the call only after seven or eight rings.

'Sir is not here.'

'Didn't he come to the office?'

'Yes, but he went out.'

'When will he be back?'

'After lunch.'

'Where has he gone?'

'I am not aware.'

'Okay.'

'Any message?'

Asokan dithered for a moment. No, it was a message that should be delivered directly. Forget the personal assistant, one should trust nobody.

'Nothing. I will call again in the afternoon.'

When he put the phone down, Asokan felt uncomfortable. He yearned to inform Mohandas about Mini's reaction to the newspaper report. Only then could he relax.

He recalled Mohandas's remark from when he met him three days ago.

'Do not jump to the conclusion that someone is ingenuous only because she is a woman. They will not approach problems in the way that we men typically do. It is a fact that some of the most determined and powerful heads of governments across the world were women. Margaret Thatcher, Indira Gandhi, Golda Meir. There are many like that in the business world too.'

'Mini is a fool. She does not have the ability to be a clerk, let alone a managing director.'

Mohandas grinned at Asokan's gripe. 'But she became the managing director, didn't she? When Menon sir died, she attained that position even when most of you were not in agreement. I have heard that there were some protests. Am I right? Even then…'

'That was a tragic time. The board of directors was overwhelmed by the simultaneous deaths of both father and son. Otherwise…'

'Perhaps. I was just saying that one should never be prejudiced against someone. Especially in the arena of business, never underrate anyone as being incapable.'

Didn't Mini smile as if she were unaware of the implications of today's newspaper report?

Asokan picked up the phone and dialled home. Aswathy would be eagerly waiting for an update.

Even yesterday, Aswathy had cautioned him: 'Chetta, you have fallen for her smile! Mini is crafty. I could sense that instinctively. She makes you toil day and night endlessly. And who is benefitting from all that work? If anything goes haywire, the marketing director takes the blame. That men can be so naïve riles me!'

Menon sir's death had been an unforeseen event. Suresh too passed away. It was Asokan who was supposed to accompany Menon that day for the discussions. A discussion with an Ayurvedic company based in Lucknow was on the anvil, about launching a joint venture. Menon sir had plans for joining forces with the company, which had a strong presence in even the smallest towns of north India. The whole of north India would become their market. The partner's medicines would be sold in south India via the Dhanwantari marketing network. Start the company's outlets at multiple places. Plan for a medical centre alongside those. The project would be beneficial for both parties. If things went as planned, in a mere five years, the sales target would exceed the present numbers by five times. After the discussions in Lucknow, there was to be a trip to Himachal Pradesh. There were several areas in the Kullu valley that were highly suitable for herbal farming. An inspection of those spots would be gainful.

But on the day before the trip, the Tamil Nadu area became problematic. The state government's new policies were creating issues for the wholesale agencies. It was imperative that Asokan sorted out the chaos. There was an urgent need to visit Madras and have a meeting with the officers at the secretariat. If needed, the company would have to approach the court for a remedy.

Menon sir said: 'Asokan, you should go to Madras and set things right. Let Suresh come with me to Lucknow. There will be many rounds of discussions before we can sign the agreement. Sharmaji is very devout and honest. But if we are not wary, he will take away all the profits.'

That day, Suresh accompanied his father; Asokan had travelled to Tamil Nadu.

Asokan would shudder often, recollecting what a narrow escape he had had. The tragic news had reached him in Madras. There was a call from the Ernakulam office. Menon sir and Suresh were dead. A helicopter crash. The pilot and the host, Retired Colonel Sukhwant Singh, had died in the accident too.

Asokan had informed Mini at her Delhi home. It was almost two years since her marriage.

After the initial shock, it was the question of the company's survival, a feeling of 'what now', that had troubled Asokan. What would be the future of Dhanwantari Herbal Products? Who would lead the company?

Mrs Menon was the chairperson of the company. Menon sir was the managing director. Mini's younger brother Suresh held the post of chief executive. The plan had been that Menon sir would take over the chairperson's seat and detach himself from the daily functioning of the company, Suresh would become the managing director and the company would continue working uninterruptedly. But now, everything had been upended! Who would be the managing director now?

The funerals were conducted in Cochin. Nobody ever saw the mortal remains of either the father or the son. There was nothing to be seen. Apparently, the burnt bodies were scattered all over.

Even amidst the rites, the onlookers were worried about the company's future. Everybody treated Asokan with a special regard.

Even Mini's husband Balachandran had checked each step with him during that hour of crisis.

There were ten members, apart from the chairman, in the board of directors. Two were government nominees. Out of the eight, five were those who did not have much know-how about the company. As in most of the public limited companies, they had expertize in business or other areas. A plantation owner, a retired vice chancellor, an advocate, a rich chettiar from Tamil Nadu, a retired chief engineer. The men were Menon sir's close friends, who loved getting together occasionally and relishing tales from their days of youth. There would be board meetings in Kovalam, Kochi or Ooty. Comfortable stay in five-star hotels, food and leisure trips. Then there were the legally mandatory travel allowances. The minutes of the meeting would be duly prepared. All the real work would be the responsibility of Adiyodi and Asokan.

As soon as Asokan had returned to Cochin, Aswathy had forewarned him: 'You have to be assertive now. There will be those who support Adiyodi. The rest of the directors are all old codgers, aren't they? Adiyodi has been a loyalist for decades. At least a few would support him for the post of MD.'

Adiyodi's qualification was a tenth-standard school leaving certificate. But he had been Menon sir's Man Friday since the age of sixteen. He knew the company inside out. Adiyodi possessed the ability to foresee what Menon sir was contemplating.

Adiyodi was also the company's finance director. There were three chartered accountants working under him.

Asokan felt that his wife was right. Even if he was less qualified, there was a chance that Adiyodi might be nominated for the MD's post. The directors, who were government representatives, would not take any sides. If they did, that would stir trouble.

Asokan called each director one by one. He formally informed them about the demise of Menon sir and Suresh. Though they were aware of the tragedy, he invited them on behalf of the company to participate in the funeral rites. Asokan updated them about the arrival of the remains and the time of the rituals. Casually, he mentioned the imminent future of the company. After the necessary mourning period, there would be a meeting of the board of directors. A formal condolence for the departed souls, then a discussion on the way forward – no complicated agenda.

Everyone responded as he had anticipated. 'Asokan, you are there to handle everything.'

Only the advocate asked, 'Is Adiyodi keen on becoming the MD?'

'Perhaps, sir. I have no idea. It is but natural, isn't it?'

'But he's neither qualified nor sharp. We should give a whole new face to the company. Dhanwantari brings to mind the face of an old man! That should change.'

Before ending the call, the advocate said one more thing. 'Asokan, I'm going to propose your name for the post of MD. I'm going to recommend it to my other colleagues too.'

'As you wish, sir. I just need your blessings.'

The other four directors did not reveal anything. But they were unlikely to oppose the advocate's proposal.

The advocate was prone to a few clandestine activities whenever the board meetings were held outside Kochi. Asokan anticipated that now those scandalous affairs would have to be handled by him. Even so, it was worth it.

He was bubbling with confidence at that time. The conviction had slowly inflated like a balloon.

17

Crashing Hopes

Asokan called home again. No response.

He tried the second number. Nobody was picking that either.

Where had Aswathy gone? She was yet to learn about the news in *The Times of India*.

The news had been Aswathy's brainchild. A defamatory news-story would cause the share prices to drop dramatically. Mohandas could buy more shares in that time with a comparatively smaller investment.

Mohandas had made one thing clear: 'Once I take over the company, there won't be any major change in the board of directors. Except that Mini and her mother shall be out. Asokan will be the new managing director.'

'Sir, you should be the chairman.'

'No, not me. I have someone in my mind. He shall be the chairman. Asokan, you should take the whole board of directors along with you. That will depend on your efficiency. True, we have the great legacy and heritage of Kerala Ayurvedic traditions, but the institutional changes should be minimal.'

'Yes, sir.'

Changes.

Changes in the administrative order were akin to revolutions in a company. Nobody liked those. It was precisely what happened at the board meeting that day.

The board of directors had met three weeks after the sixteen-day mourning period. The agenda listed only a formal condolence and nomination of Mini Balachandran in the place of Menon sir in the company's board of directors.

Asokan reminisced about inviting Mini to join the board.

He had gone to Mini's house to pick up Balachandran and drop him to the airport. Mini was standing in the verandah.

'Chettan is going on a month-long tour. What will I do all alone in Delhi?'

'That's right. In my opinion, Mini, you should settle in Kochi. Let Mr Balachandran resign and join you here. The company will be in good hands.'

In all probability, Balachandran was listening to their conversation from the inner room.

Mini smiled. 'He is allergic to the word Ayurveda nowadays.'

'Your mother can't handle the Delhi cold. Somebody has to be with her, right?'

Balachandran came to the porch with his suitcase. 'I am trying for a transfer. Minimum three years on deputation.'

'In any case, I am proposing Mini's name in Menon sir's place at the next board meeting.'

'You should bring a proposal for increasing the sitting fees too.'

'But there are some conditions under the Companies Act.'

'I was kidding.'

Everybody laughed.

~

Before the board meeting, the advocate – Asokan's well-wisher – had called. It was unexpected.

'Congratulations, Asokan! Only the retired VC was mule-headed. I managed to convince him too. By the way, the chief engineer has a relative. A good for nothing. Apparently he had been requesting Menon to find a job for that wastrel. Naturally, Menon was humming and hawing. You should see to it soon.'

'As you say, sir.'

Asokan did not mention the two bottles of Scotch he had sent to the advocate's home the day before. Neither did the man say anything about receiving the gift.

The board of directors met at the company's office room. The retired vice chancellor chaired the meeting in Mrs Menon's absence. All the directors were present. Mini attended as a special invitee.

The chairperson waxed eloquent about the intimate friendship between him and Mr Menon. He pointed out the humane aspects of Menon's personality and the fact that the company was the virtual lifeblood of the late managing director. Asserting that the board of directors was mandated with the duty of guiding the company – always following Menon's vision – he proposed the condolence agenda and got it formally passed.

Usually after the passage of a condolence item, the proceedings were held in abeyance. But Menon had always been a dynamic man who hated wasting a precious moment. The chairperson appealed that they should get on with the rest of the business without any undue delay.

Asokan had agreed that Adiyodi, being seniormost amongst the working directors, should propose the nomination of Mini Balachandran as a board member.

Adiyodi got up.

'Menon sir was like my father, elder brother and guru. I belong to him as much as I do to this company. The company was his very life. And I wish that his life-spirit shines through the company forever. Nobody could ever comprehend his great vision. He would share some bits with me, or Mini or Asokan. Suresh knew the most. But they went away together.'

Menon's speeches seemed to flow ceaselessly through the finance director's tongue. It was as though Menon were speaking through him.

'The modern man who is stricken with diseases, owing to his turning away from nature, can be made healthy only with the herbs gifted by the same nature. But where are the high-quality herbs? It is the inexhaustible treasure-chest of herbs that is made bare when forests are hacked down ruthlessly. The plantation scheme at Nelliyampathy is a first step in the fight against this mindless destruction. The valleys of the Himalayas, the mountain ranges of the Vindhyas, the Pachmarhi hills – there are unknown medicinal plants in all these places. Only through expensive research activities can these be made useful for humanity. The aim of Ayurveda is not to beat death but to create a healthy lifestyle. Establish many healing centres in villages and scenic areas. There, give new life to the sick by harmonizing Ayurvedic treatments, yoga and naturopathy. Provide personalized care to every patient.'

The audience listened with alacrity.

Adiyodi continued:

'I am being garrulous. Indeed, I have only caught glimpses of the great Menon sir's dreams. I have no idea about their immensity, or how they can be turned into reality. But I am sure of one thing. Those dreams form the lifeblood of this company. If they are destroyed, Dhanwantari Herbal Products ceases to exist.'

Adiyodi poured out the dark-coloured liquid from a plastic bottle kept on the table, sipped it, and then spoke again:

'The company is like the water I just drank. This happens to be Menon sir's invention. Cool chukku vellam – nothing but water mixed with dried ginger powder and a few other ingredients. But this special mixture can heal many diseases and quench thirst, both!

Ramacham, parppadaka pullu, iruveli, muthangakizhangu, chukku, raktachandanam – all have been added appropriately. Menon sir wished to market aerated bottles of this liquid across the nation. He was exploring foreign markets for export options. If water, an inevitable part of human life, could be used to heal, wouldn't it be the best way for ensuring the health of the nation? That was his vision.'

Four or five directors opened the bottles before them and poured out the liquid.

'It is good!'

'A little pungent. But better than beer.'

Adiyodi continued:

'So I have only one appeal to make. Let us appoint Mini Balachandran, who has the ability to dream, who shares Menon sir's dreams, as managing director for ensuring this company's survival. I have never spoken to Mini about this matter. But I request that she accepts this proposal that will foster our company's progress. Or, we should insist that she accepts the post.'

That night, when Asokan reached home, Aswathy exploded with fury. 'You are all crass fools! That woman tricked you so smartly. What did you think? That she was unaware of this move?'

Later, the advocate apologized. 'Asokan, under those circumstances, I was helpless. One, it was such a sad ambience after Menon sir's departure. Second, his daughter, their company!'

'"Their company", sir? The family has merely fifteen per cent of the shares. The rest is with outsiders.'

'But Asokan, the government directors were supportive of Mini. The government institutions hold thirty per cent shares, right? The Family Trust has another fifteen per cent. That's more than the majority number of shares.'

Anyway, it was a disaster.

'Don't get upset. Wait patiently. She is a young woman. How long will she stay away from her husband? Besides, Mini has never managed a company before. Just because her father was a whiz in management, will it run in the family?'

'You can say that easily, sir. Not a single one spoke up for me. Everybody was pleading for Mini.'

Days later, when matters settled down, Asokan felt that he had made a major mistake in blindly trusting the advocate. Perchance, Mini was innocent. She might not have wanted to be the MD. But Adiyodi, the finance director, he was the main villain! How suavely he had manoeuvred his way! Adiyodi was aware that he could not become the head himself. Who else was there, but Asokan – MBA, ICWAI, young and smart? The most suitable face to lead the company to the future. But what would happen to Adiyodi then? He would have to make a dignified exit. Nobody would dismiss him. But the previous facilities and undeserved stature would definitely be denied to him. What should be done then? Sideline Asokan smartly. How tactfully he did it! Mini would continue her father's traditions. Adiyodi would continue to retain the same position.

Aswathy was right.

'That Adiyodi should be chased and beaten up! He provides Mini all the support for any foolhardiness!'

~

Asokan brooded that he would have endured everything provided the company progressed.

That was not happening.

A company should aim for profits. The shareholders have invested their hard-earned money in the company. Their money should not go waste. Not that one should undertake unfair business practices, or indulge in corporate malfeasances. But one should not continue unprofitable ventures. It was better to scrap such practices.

The first day Asokan met Mohandas, the business doyen, he had made his view crystal clear.

'I wish to cut back on many schemes which are not gainful. For instance…'

Everyone knew Mohandas. Asokan had seen him on two occasions in the past. He had tried to get acquainted with him too. But Mohandas was rather reclusive by nature. That was why when his call came out of the blue, Asokan had been astounded.

'I need to see you, Asokan. What would be a convenient time?'

Mohandas had his own motorboat. They met one evening on the Cochin backwaters.

They talked about Dhanwantari Herbal Products.

'My company wishes to launch a new scheme. Personalized patient care. Set up healing centres in picturesque places. Separate medicines and treatment lines designed specifically for every person. It is a risky venture for sure. Usually a research company invests almost twenty per cent of its earnings in research. Yet, what's the result? Most use the term "research" for negotiating tax deductions! What they do is nothing but quality control.'

'Quality control of medicines, sir?'

'Not at all. Medicines are mass produced, aren't they? The quality control of bottles, labels and stoppers is significant. There is quality control involved in the purchase of medicinal herbs too.'

When Asokan was wondering why Mohandas had invited him to the tête-à-tête, the latter smiled.

'We should meet again, Asokan. I have a penchant for Ayurvedic medicines.'

'Same here, sir.'

The second get-together was at Asokan's home. Aswathy had been delighted.

Once Mohandas left after dinner, Aswathy said: 'Mohandas sir is going to acquire our company. Then you shall be the managing director!'

'How can you be so sure?'

'Just wait and see.'

It was three months since that episode.

Asokan tried his home number. It continued to ring. Where did Aswathy go? He called Mohandas's office. The personal assistant said: 'I don't know where sir has gone.'

Asokan stepped inside his private study and opened the fridge. He did not like Mr Menon's patented water. It did not appeal to his palate.

One peg.

He opened the bottle in the morning work hours.

18

The Leader's Words

Rameesan retrieved a beedi from the pocket of a young man seated next to him. Then he looked hither and thither, searching for a matchbox.

The leader was fulminating:

'In a capitalist system, it is the principal or working capital that controls all the activities and profits. The capital belongs to the poor, the working class, the common man. But these stock exchanges and shares are ways and means of ensuring that the control never stays with the owners. A wily tactic of the bourgeoisie to make a quick buck! Even when the companies are down in the dumps, running quite a few losses, they lavishly spend the assets of the companies for their selfish interests. The ownership of shares works in such a manner that the liabilities are never theirs! Most of the bourgeoisie run their companies with merely one-tenth or one-twentieth of the total shares. Even Tata, the biggest business conglomerate of India, does not own more than two per cent of their companies' shares. The rest is the common man's money. Birla, Ambani, Thapar, all follow the same pattern. It is the Stock Exchange that helps the system to propagate exploitation. The Stock Exchange is the symbol of resilience of the capitalist system.'

There were almost ten or twenty youngsters in the room. They differed in the way they dressed, the way they spoke, but their gaze bore a common gleam; there was the gravity of self-confidence in everything they said. Everyone was keenly listening to the leader.

The leader continued: 'For us Malayalis, the problem is rather severe. To appreciate that, one should know the historical importance of stock exchanges. I shall explain.'

Personally, Ramesan did not have any aversion to stock exchanges. But when all the suppressed resentment of a week started emerging from within him, the first enemy seemed to be the Stock Exchange. So he listened intently.

Mohandas, Ramesan's valiyachan – his uncle – had also spoken about stock exchanges. The discussion had happened last Wednesday.

Ramesan had returned from Madras and gone straight to the lodge. He shut the door and spent ten minutes wondering whether to take a bath or not. Valiyachan had called him up then. The lodge manager would inform Mohandas unfailingly whenever his nephew arrived at the lodge. Ramesan had tried threatening, persuading, pleading with the manager, to desist from the practice. It had been a futile effort.

The manager said: 'You can ask me to do anything but that! From the moment you start paying the room rent, I will follow your instructions. Until then, I am bound to follow Mohandas sir's orders. Not because I care any less about you. In fact, I don't like your uncle much. But without the regular rent, how will I run this lodge? You tell me!'

Ramesan concluded that the manager was right. When he had walked out of his uncle's house five years ago, it was the manager who had provided him a roof over his head. Mohandas paid his rent and food expenses. Initially, Ramesan had been annoyed. But he contained himself, thinking that his uncle was duty-bound to provide for him until he got gainful employment.

Mohandas was in a good mood. He insisted that Ramesan join him for dinner that evening.

Ramesan had split from his uncle on the matter of principles. But there was no need to let that affect personal bonds.

They relished a terrific vegetarian meal that Wednesday evening. All his favourite dishes – kalan, olan, aviyal – and spicy mango pickle made an appearance. The famous sweet payasam of the Ambalappuzha temple was served too.

It was after the meal that Mohandas said: 'Ramesan, today is your birthday. Forgot about it, didn't you?'

Ramesan smiled. He was prone to forgetting many things nowadays. He reflected that Mohandas's finest quality was that he treated him like an equal. His uncle never denigrated his lifestyle or opinions. One could tell him anything openly. Mohandas never displayed the arrogance that wisdom was his sole prerogative. He would patiently listen to Ramesan. His responses were open-minded. Mohandas never hesitated to apologize for his mistakes.

Five years earlier, when Ramesan left home in a huff, Mohandas had spoken sombrely: 'In my personal opinion, there is nothing wrong in what you are doing. Everyone above the age of eighteen should make decisions for themselves. But your hostility towards me saddens me. I know it will go away with time. You should not persist with your bitterness forever.'

Ramesan had been inflexible then. Later, his resentment had abated. But he had chosen to live away from Mohandas. It was very difficult to logically oppose his uncle.

During the dinner too, Mohandas had spoken warmly: 'I saw these fiery graffiti on the walls when I was returning from Trivandrum. Presume your lot is behind it?'

'Yes.'

'Where do you get the funding from?'

'For what? The wall graffiti?'

'Yes, for the lime, the colours and the brushes.'

'We collect money from the common people.'

'Anyway, good publicity! The common man is now more aware of the Stock Exchange thanks to your wall graffiti.'

'You mean…?'

'I am not saying anything. The trading of shares is progressing in proportion to your protests.'

Once again, Ramesan realized that whenever Mohandas conversed with him, his confusion increased.

'Everybody knows that the Stock Exchange is the important channel through which Kerala's capital flows to other states.'

Mohandas refuted it unequivocally:

'For one, there is no capital in Kerala. What we have is savings, and that does not have the innate nature of capital. Usually the common man deposits his savings in a bank or a unit trust. The interest flows in steadily. He will never explore *where* the bank and the institutions spent his money. The reality is that, all this while, the banks have been lending his money to the same parties whom he denounces vociferously. Then and now, the money always transformed into capital only outside the borders of Kerala. The Stock Exchange can't be held at fault for that!'

Ramesan felt that his uncle was right. Yet, he did not admit it and instead, contradicted him. 'But this money could have been invested in Kerala for creating industries, right?'

'Who would do that? To start and nurture industries, money is not the crucial factor. It is the atmosphere. The social atmosphere. Some might say the political atmosphere, but I beg to differ. Once the societal ambience changes, the politicians will soon adapt. But the probability of enterprises flourishing in Kerala is zero.'

'Why?'

'In my opinion, everyone, including the common man, the bureaucracy, politicians and cultural leaders, view the entrepreneur as an enemy. Someone who has set out to exploit the society!

Most of the small-scale industries failed despite financial support, didn't they?'

Ramesan reflected on the words. True, even Valiyachan's businesses were based on trading. Mohandas had tried to start a couple of industries earlier. Ramesan used to live with his uncle then. Revenue office, collectorate, electricity board, municipality, trade union leaders, labour office, sales tax office, Employee State Insurance aka ESI … what not! Mohandas ended up pursuing everything except his new business venture! Everyone acted like emperors ruling over their sectoral fiefdoms. Valiyachan became the quintessential slave who was a mere citizen. None of his enterprises lasted for long. After selling his machines at the available market price, Mohandas started focusing on trading.

Ramesan found his uncle's words cropping up in his mind every now and then. But he was scared to share them with his comrades. He felt it was better to consolidate an opinion for himself before expressing any view.

Mohandas had reiterated his views at the dinner: 'There are three factors that multinational companies consider before investing huge amounts in any country. Before they start ventures that generate employment. First, are the people familiar with the English language? Two, would our products find a good market there? Three, would we get cheap labour? Kerala has an edge over any other Indian state when it comes to these three factors.

'You'll find people easily conversing in English here. Kerala is a vibrant market for any new product. Even the small villages are adventurous when it comes to trying out new products. Yes, the labour costs are higher than other states but if you examine labour efficiency, the output a labourer provides against an investment of one rupee, Kerala's wages might turn out to be the lowest! Yet, not a single big conglomerate prefers Kerala for starting a new industry. Tata and Birla, with factories everywhere in India, turn a blind eye to Kerala. A rare Tata Oil Mills or Mavoor Rayons crawls forward, grappling with problems on a daily basis. What's the reason?

'No point in blaming the hierarchy of power. Whether it is the Communist or the Congress government, the leadership is just a reflection of the society at large. If you check, in the states where the same parties are in power, industries are burgeoning. But it's different here. So, it boils down to what I said earlier. The social atmosphere of Kerala is unsuitable for industries. If you need interest or dividends on your extra savings, the money invariably has to flow to other states.'

Ramesan felt that Valiyachan's logic was sound. But he was infuriated at that blunt speech. His irritation increased. The foundation of Ramesan's beliefs started rocking. Over time, that fury hardened and it remained entrenched inside the recesses of his heart.

~

Ramesan forced himself to listen to the leader.

'The total trading in this Stock Exchange is more than twenty crores daily. Twenty crores! We are freely offering this humongous amount to the bourgeoisie of other states to indulge themselves with! I have no doubts that if this money is used creatively in our state, without any external aid, we can wipe out poverty and unemployment from Kerala.'

Ramesan asked: 'Is that the only reason why nobody starts their business enterprises in Kerala?'

'Maybe not. Immature political leadership, lack of civilian participation in formulating public policies are reasons too. What do we lack, tell me! Water, electricity, labour, roads, railways, ports, communication networks – we have everything. But we don't have one critical thing: a government for the poor, belonging to the common man. That is the problem. If it were such a government, would they allow the existence of an institution like a Stock Exchange through which twenty crores are passed over to other states?'

Ramesan was incensed. How ridiculous! Twenty crores? Even if the speculative trading entailed such an amount, not even one-fifth or one-tenth ended up as shares. And if one sold their own shares, they would gain the money, right? Wouldn't money be flowing into Kerala from other states then?

He lit a beedi. After puffing a couple of times, Ramesan became lethargic and sleepy.

The leader's spiel continued: 'We are limiting ourselves to marches and protests as of now. The scale shall intensify from the next month. Unexpectedly, even the bourgeois newspapers are giving great publicity to our strike. That is good in a way.'

Ramesan found himself baiting the leader unwittingly. 'Is someone sponsoring our strike?'

The leader was struck dumb for a few moments. Then he smilingly replied: 'Ramesan, what do you mean by that? Whatever you intended, such a question arises only when one has no faith in the genuineness of our movement.'

'You misunderstood what I said. While discussing such topics, any aberration should be discussed at length.'

The meeting soon descended into chaos. Some took Ramesan's side. The majority was up in arms against him. There were snarky comments on Ramesan's bourgeois perspectives and a certain business owner called Mohandas.

Ramesan was caught in a dilemma.

For the first time, he decided to call up Mohandas. The lodge manager dialled the number for him, with surprise writ large on his face.

'Valiyacha, I want to speak to you.'

After a few seconds, Mohandas replied: 'Come over.'

19

The Chess Player's Mind

Matthews was afraid of facing Aniyan Raja. He remembered how he, accompanied by Vinayan and Nanu Namboodiri, had tried to get Aniyan Raja to invest in the new export company six months ago.

Matthews had learned two business lessons that day: One, never assume anyone to be a fool. Two, do not set up a joint business; try joint ventures instead. It is necessary to retain the decision-making with oneself, though.

Vinayan was already an authorized assistant at the Stock Exchange. Recently, he had become a member. With the commission received from the sales and purchases of shares, Vinayan was leading a comfortable life. He never ventured into big stakes. Consequently, profits and losses were limited. Even so, Vinayan bought a car. A second-hand Ambassador. The urge to rake in a quick buck seemed to have dwindled in him. Matthews realized that he could not do a joint business with his much-changed friend.

Matthews had only one goal. Ten years. He wanted to become the topmost businessman in Kerala within that time frame.

Vinayan had invited him to become a stockbroker at the Exchange. 'Join as my assistant. Deal with the game of stocks cautiously. Your father's very rich, isn't he? Even if there are some setbacks, you can survive easily enough. You'll become rich.'

Matthews did not decline Vinayan's offer. He simply replied, 'Let's see.'

Matthews used this phrase as a winning technique in business. One should never blatantly refuse any offer. Just say, 'Let's see.' The Chanakya trick in political manoeuvring: 'Let's see.'

Matthews declined the offer but it was not due to any aversion towards the Stock Exchange. One could do high-stake dealings even without becoming a member of the Exchange. He could buy and sell shares while remaining unidentified.

Occasionally, Matthews did some deals via Vinayan. More than make money, Matthews wished to analyse how his logical reasoning worked out in the share market and how sharp his predictions were. He would study a company's balance sheet thoroughly. What happened to the share prices over the last one month? What were the prospects of the company's products? Would the government policy affect the share prices? What about the labour and environmental issues? Would these cause problems in the smooth functioning of the firm in question?

Afterwards, Matthews would arrive at a decision. Whether the share prices would escalate in the imminent future or decrease. To verify and satiate his own curiosity, Matthews would purchase a hundred or two hundred shares of the company. His deductions turned out right most of the time. Matthews found his self-confidence growing, as well as his courage.

Now he was aiming at a major kill. An unequivocal attack. Totally out of the blue. The foe should not awaken from the impact of the move.

For the strategy to become successful, there were two elements that were imperative. Razor-sharp intelligence and money. He was in possession of the former. Yes, he also had enough of the latter. But an intelligent man avoids using his own money as much as possible.

Matthews was dreaming of making a major kill without investing his own money. Two months ago, unexpectedly, the path had come searching for the man.

Near the Stock Exchange, there were many bar-attached hotels; some mediocre, some excellent. On the day when the Exchange functioned, there would be a jostling horde in those places. Hopes, joys, sorrows, anxieties, frustrations would all merge in the chill of the air-conditioned darkness. The bitterness of loss, the ecstasy of victory – both metamorphosed into preparations for the next round of the game. Nobody got stone drunk in the bar. Just a small dose to help one forget. An incentive for tomorrow. That was all. Money, which was more intoxicating than liquor, tightened their bridles and reined them back.

Matthews had met Unni nearly two months ago, when he had stepped into a bar.

The young man was seated all by himself at a table near the bar counter. Since Matthews had stepped inside from bright sunlight, he could not see clearly. Most of the tables were occupied. Only the table near the counter seemed to have some space. Matthews had stumbled in the darkness and made his way towards it.

'Yes, please take a seat.'

'Thanks!'

The young man smiled. By that time, Matthews' eyes had adapted to the dim light.

'Mr Matthews, right?'

'Yes.'

'Don't you remember me?'

Matthews hesitated for a brief moment. Suddenly, he remembered.

'My god, Unni! I never thought I'd find you here.'

Unni smiled. 'Why?'

Matthews wished to elucidate. Wasn't he the shirtless young man who, wearing a janeyu, was playing chess? Aniyan Raja's nephew? The chartered accountant?

Never had he expected Unni to be in such a place. Something was rotten in the state of Denmark.

By the time he got out of the bar, Matthews realized that his own calculations had been wrong. Never judge a man by his first appearance.

Unni asked: 'Did you start the export company?'

Matthews replied: 'No, I gave up that idea.'

'Good. Exports shall be profitable only if you have the back-up of a huge capital investment and factories with modern machinery for processing and packing. Especially when we're sure that eastern European countries and Russia will soon be entering the capitalistic markets, having washed away their Communist colours. Import tariffs, various controls, banning of certain product lines … the likelihood of nations trying to protect their own markets is decreasing. A huge market war is in the offing. Newest products, all out efforts to capture the global markets using technological advantages, the tendency of governments to tango with multinational companies, the transformations in erstwhile Communist countries that had never ventured into consumer markets earlier … all of this has started a tough market war, far more impactful than the world wars or the Cold War between Russia and America.'

'You're right.'

'It's like lemon-juice sellers taking over as the commission agents of cola companies. After a decade, one would hardly find lemon juice anywhere. The poor lemons would vanish, unable to handle the onslaught of various colas.'

Matthews found himself liking Unni.

It was revealed that Aniyan Raja's decision not to invest in the export company had not been due to any of the above reasons.

'Uncle's asthma had aggravated the previous night. He'd hardly slept. He doesn't believe in calling a doctor. Ostensibly, no doctor can cure asthma. According to him, reducing the debilitating power of asthma is the lone way forward. Take only the necessary medicines for that purpose. That's his methodology. But that night, no pill helped him. You arrived when Uncle was utterly fatigued.'

'Perhaps, if Aniyan Raja hadn't been troubled by asthma … then?'

'See, I'm not sure whether he would have invested in the idea. Your project report wasn't very appealing.'

Matthews was taken aback. 'Our project report?'

'Yes, I'd gone through it.'

That day, when they stepped out of the dark bar, blinking at the bright lights of the sun and the vehicles, Matthews said: 'We should meet again.'

'Sure, with pleasure.'

Matthews met Unni almost four times afterwards. Unni visited Ernakulam once or twice every week. Matthews did not find out what his area of work was. Two topics brought them together: history and art movies. Both had a penchant for those. They shared a drink in Unni's room a few times.

There were many telephone calls all the time. Matthews did not wish to interrupt Unni's work.

'Let's go somewhere else. One can't discuss anything in peace here.'

Since Matthews did not probe further, Unni shrugged casually. 'Uncle is into multiple ventures. I'm looking after most of them these days. That's why there is not a single moment's respite.'

The last time they met, Matthews had divulged to Unni something he had been ruminating over for long.

'I have a business proposal. A big plan! My wish is you join me as a partner.'

They were strolling through the less crowded road that ran parallel to the oil tanker jetty, where the ships were moored. The western sky mirrored the gorgeous beauty of the evening. There was a gigantic ship anchored at the quayside. Cycle rickshaws, a fast-disappearing specimen much like historical monuments, rested by the roadsides. A bell clanged, indicating the arrival of the motorboat for ferrying passengers.

Unni said: 'To be frank, I prefer to be your friend without having a business relationship. Never mind. We met for the first time for business too, didn't we?'

'One can have friendship even in business. Especially between us.'

They sat next to the iron fence near the backwaters. A boy came running with roasted gram in paper-cones. They bought two cones and started relishing the snack.

'Go on.'

'We should buy a company. A recognizable brand but struggling in the recent past. We can approach the company management and give a direct offer. We'll assure them that nothing will change after the takeover. They might accept a contractual agreement. See, we'll offer the market price or even slightly more for the shares. If they acquiesce, we will sell the assets marked as low-value in their balance sheet. The properties will be purchased by one of our own companies. Nothing directly – we remain incognito. Let the purchasing price be higher than the value in the balance sheet. These assets should have no direct bearing on the company's day-to-day working. Hence this action won't affect the company's normal functioning either.'

'And then?'

'We'll create a system to sell off the assets at a single go!'

Unni remained silent for a long time. Three foreigners were gesticulating at a rickshaw-puller, trying to communicate something to him. A young couple was walking on the other side, fingers interlocked, with not a care for the world.

Unni spoke: 'Idea sounds good. Let me discuss it with my uncle. Matthews, you might have shortlisted a few companies, right? If my uncle agrees, we can discuss it further.'

'It'll be better if you can take a quick decision.'

Unni smiled.

'If Uncle smells a chance to make money, he becomes quick. I shall call you in a couple of days.'

That was how Matthews ended up in the Vadakke Kovilakam, Aniyan Raja's house, for the second time.

Eleven o'clock was fixed as the time for the meeting. Hence, there was no waiting involved.

Matthews had sent Unni the balance sheets of four companies a few days before.

On seeing Matthews, Unni said: 'Listen, I received the papers only yesterday. Just had a quick glance, that's all.'

Aniyan Raja was seated in the south porch, leaning against a pillar. The paan box lay open next to him. The spittoon had been placed below his chair.

Matthews was invited to sit on a chair nearby. Unni continued to stand. Matthews caught the silhouette of a shadow, the presence of someone near the door.

Aniyan Raja said: 'Unni was telling me something. Somehow, I could not understand much. But the children say, it's all right, not much likelihood of loss ... If so, I have no objection.'

Matthews did not respond.

Aniyan Raja started removing the vein from the betel leaf. 'But, Joseph, what's your deal in this game?'

Matthews was momentarily taken aback. 'Not Joseph, Matthews.'

'Ah, I keep making such mistakes. Yes, Matthews. Matthews, what's your deal?'

'I will be frank. I need fifty per cent shares of the new company that would be formed.'

'Fifty per cent?'

Unni looked askance at Matthews too.

'Yes.'

Matthews remained firm.

'You mean, we spend the money and you reap the profits? How can that be right?'

'Who asked you to invest anything?'

'What do you mean?'

'Let me explain. Nobody needs to shell out any money. Neither you, nor me or anyone else. We can finish the deal in a fortnight's time. There are financiers who'd lend us money against interest during that period. I will organize that. Once it's known that you, sir, with your financial solidity, are backing the venture, the rest of the moves shall be easy. I just need your word. Things will change in two weeks' time. Were I alone, I'd never have got any of these advantages.'

'What if this deal fails?'

'No question of failure. If one feels that it's risky after ten lakhs, play only till that margin. It is only when you take useless risks that anything fails. For our effort, the maximum amount I visualize is around two or three crores. If you are there with me, I wouldn't mind staking even ten or twenty. That's why I approached you. Besides, I feel very confident about working with Unni.'

Aniyan Raja spat into the spittoon and said: 'Joseph, do you play chess?'

This time round, Matthews did not bother to correct him. 'A bit.'

'Unni plays decently. Both of you discuss and finalize the details.'

Matthews looked at Unni. Unni smiled.

Matthews got up. 'Allow me to take my leave now.'

'You should have stayed for lunch. But I'm not sure you'll like our simple vegetarian fare.'

Matthews folded his hands respectfully.

Aniyan Raja said: 'Once both of you decide on the plan, talk to that Ayurveda company first. The one which Ramunni Menon's granddaughter manages. That will be good. What's its name?'

'Dhanwantari Herbal Products.'

'Yes, that one. Matthews, instead of fifty-fifty, one-fourth, okay?'

Matthews waited on the steps silently.

'You think it's too less? Well, once things turn out fine … we still have time.'

After a moment's pause, Matthews spoke.

'As you wish.'

'May everything turn auspicious. I'm confident that the benedictions of Vettakorumakan, the deity of hunting, shall be with us.'

20

The Battle Begins

Matthews felt effervescent. The war strategy, where the enemy had to be routed at one go, and the machinations of the grand finale, had to be planned meticulously and with great care. The battle was unique in another way. Even those on his side should not know who the antagonist was! Neither should the foe recognize that the end was imminent until they were battered to bits. Everything had to be extremely secretive.

Matthews noted down the problems to be handled.

One, the most important: Can Aniyan Raja be trusted?

He had given no commitment in writing. Unni had made it clear that there was no question of such a thing happening. Everything would be done anonymously. All buying and selling would be in other names. Permission was granted to reveal his identity exclusively to two people. One, the financiers who would be willing to lend an advance for a month against the promise of company shares. Two, Mini Balachandran, the MD of Dhanwantari Herbal Products, when Matthews approached her in the guise of an emissary.

If more people got to know that Aniyan Raja was behind the game, many more players would enter the arena. The share prices would shoot up. That was why there was a need for secrecy.

But what if Aniyan Raja cast him aside after the victory? Would he do that?

Matthews resolved to take that risk. He decided to put his brother's name in the 'benami' firm. He would add the names of three others as recommended by Unni, but the fourth would be his man.

Second, money.

Matthews started calculating.

Dhanwantari Herbal Products had twenty lakh shares worth ten rupees each. A third of the total shares belonged to Mini Balachandran and her mother. To them, as well as to the Trust. The government held another one-third. The rest were in the names of thousands of shareholders. The strategy was to purchase one-third of the total shares from Mini and family. The moment they managed to buy one-fourth of the total shares, the government regulations for proprietary companies would no longer be applicable. Even if there was an inadvertent enquiry, one could wriggle out of it.

So, a minimum of twenty-five per cent shares, that is, five lakh shares, should be purchased. Today's market rate was thirteen or fourteen rupees. One could offer Mini a deal of sixteen or eighteen. That meant a backup capital of ninety lakhs. If Mini rejected the offer, one could plan to purchase the shares via stock exchanges. Then the price would rise. It could reach twenty or twenty-five. Maybe thirty? Not likely. However, one could plan to buy shares even at that price. A hundred and fifty lakhs, stretching to two hundred lakhs, should be readied for a contingency. Who were the financiers who could give such an amount as advance at a week's notice?

Matthews started reaching out to financiers he knew, making his moves carefully.

Those who advanced loans at humongous interest rates never appeared in person. There were agents for everything. Anyone viewing the profile of the agents – devout and kind, humble and servile – would easily believe them to be the financiers! In reality, these men were commission agents working at ten per cent of the interest charged. There were many professors and chartered accountants amongst them; even some of Matthews' closest friends. Their business activities were surreptitious. The real lenders were connected to smuggling rackets, politics and liquor contracts. Many engineers and doctors would reroute their black money through such agents to the lending market.

When Matthews got in touch with the agents, all of them pretended helplessness. 'There's no money! Who informed you that I was into lending? I stopped the business a long time back.'

Something was amiss! The lending market was active. The lethargy after the decline of the 'blade companies', that is, the loan sharks, had settled down. The number of small-time financiers had not decreased. There were huge projects taking shape in the city every day with the support of wholesome funds. What was the reason behind the setback?

Suddenly, Matthews remembered Suryanarayanan. The retired banker who worked as a management consultant, referred to as 'Swami' by his friends. Friend of Vinayan's late father. Vinayan's mentor, who had guided him to a steady career, after meeting him at a temple. Matthews had met the man twice before.

Matthews called Suryanarayanan. Suryanarayanan was praying. He agreed to meet him at seven in the evening.

Matthews took along a bottle of Scotch for the rendezvous.

Suryanarayanan listened intently to Matthews' demands.

'Two crores? Well, if I ask what's it for, you won't tell the truth. My principles include avoiding lies, speaking or hearing them, especially at dusk. See, two crores happens to be a huge amount. I have a friend. Let me check with him. Lambodaran master's son's friend is like a son to me. And you are seeking my help for the first time. I will make this my priority.'

Suryanarayanan went inside. A glass almirah stood against one end of the drawing room wall. In it were many fat books with hard covers. Did Suryanarayanan read all of them? Matthews enjoyed the beauty of the marble sculpture depicting Sri Krishna's discourse with Arjuna in the Gita. Suryanarayanan returned soon.

'You came at the right time. Got someone to arrange the money. Not a tiny sum, is it? Big risk too. But he will get it done.'

Matthews spoke: 'I will ensure that the conditions are followed.'

'That is important. They are rigid about those. You should keep your word. If not, they will haunt you and me both.'

'Sure, go ahead.'

'One, they need a three-day notice to get the money.'

'Okay.'

'They need more than shares as surety. Some immoveable property. Or, it should be someone they trust. When you demand money, they want to know about your assets.'

Matthews did not respond.

'Also, a draft for ten lakhs in the name of the company they suggest. In return, they will give a receipt. It will show that they are going to sell a fishing vessel called *Jal-Kiran* to you in a month's time. That the ten lakhs were received as advance payment against the price of the shipping vessel, which costs two crores. Whether you use the two crores or not, the ten lakhs shall be theirs.'

'Ten lakhs?'

'Yes, they are real Shylocks! Cut-throats. If possible, try to avoid dealing with these sorts.'

'There is no option!' Matthews exclaimed.

'No separate interest for the borrowed money. It is for a month.'

Matthews took out the Scotch from his bag. 'My friend got this from Singapore. Not the smuggled stuff that you get here.'

Suryanarayanan gazed at the bottle's label. 'Guruvayurappa, may everything turn out to be okay.'

Matthews queried: 'Just asking. Is there actually a trawler called *Jal-Kiran*?'

'Yes. It sails occasionally. Once or twice a month.' Suryanarayanan grinned. 'It is the easiest way to turn black money into white! Buy shipping vessels. They catch fish every day. Show the money as profits made by selling the harvest. No need to sail, or sell fish! The sea does not demand receipts for the fishes caught, does it? Your paperwork escapes scrutiny.'

Matthews got up to leave.

Suryanarayanan said: 'Inform me a week before you need the money. My fee is just a nominal amount of fifty thousand rupees. You can pay me while submitting the advance for ten lakhs.'

Matthews lost his sleep that night. *Ten lakhs and an added fifty thousand for Suryanarayanan! White money too.*

What should he do?

Matthews sent a telegram to Unni. 'Call me immediately.'

Unni called. They discussed the matter.

Unni consoled him. 'Let me talk to Uncle. Will call you back tomorrow.'

The next day, Unni called Matthews.

'Uncle will handle it. But he says, the expenses shall be booked in your account.'

'What does that mean?'

'The ten lakhs were not in the initial plans. Whether the business works or not, it'll be booked under expenses. If there's a loss, we'll be hit, right? So Uncle says, if we gain profits, the ten lakhs shall be deducted from Matthews' account.'

'Er...'

'Think about it. Old-timer's rules. What can I do?'

Matthews replied: 'Yes, in any case I have ventured into deep waters.'

'Okay.'

Matthews scribbled 'Solved' against the second problem on his sheet.

Third, modus operandi.

Where and how shall the battle begin?

Better to finalize the strategy after fixing the modes of attack and defence.

Mini Balachandran had two choices. First, get ready to sell the shares. Second, refuse to do so altogether.

Going by emotions, she would not accept the first alternative. To sell off a family legacy one fine morning for the sake of money? Nobody would do it. But what option did Mini have? She should be persuaded by being told that if she does not sell, the shares will be purchased from the public. If she sold three quarters of her shares, one was willing to cede certain conditions. Things would proceed without much commotion.

One, let the purchases be made in the name of a Trust. Nobody needs to know that it is Aniyan Raja's.

Two, give word that there will be no change in the company's board of directors.

Three, the money involved in purchasing the shares at a higher rate shall be handled in such a way as to avoid paying extra taxes to the government.

Four, the proxy of shares bought can be given to Mini herself. She will thus be legally authorized to vote on behalf of that shareholder and retain the same authority in her annual board meetings.

Five, the two hundred and fifty acres of land belonging to Dhanwantari Herbal Products at Nelliyampathy and the lands purchased outside Kerala for new retail outlets should be sold at one and a half times the amount shown in the balance sheet to a company we prescribe at the time of purchasing the shares. The reason shown can be the expansion of the new factory at Idukki or the modernization of the Aroor factory.

Will Mini fall in line?

She should. Maybe, another bait can be dangled. After exchanging the real estate properties, if Mini wants, these shares can be sold back to her at the current market prices.

Mini will agree. Does she have any another choice?

If Mini desists their attempt at acquiring Dhanwantari, one should start a hostile takeover bid. Start purchasing the company shares via different exchanges. The share prices will shoot up. Mini will start buying shares too, to defeat the attack. There will be another surge of prices. One should have lots of money at hand or enough financiers to fall back upon. Mini's business sense, courage and financial security will be tested at this stage.

After assessing many permutations and combinations, Matthews could not assume that Mini would reject his offer.

Unni had suggested that Matthews himself undertake all the necessary negotiations with Mini. Aniyan Raja's name should not be exposed at the beginning.

Matthews made an appointment with Mini.

The visit happened a week later.

It was at Dhanwantari Herbal Products' office.

At the very first glance, Matthews told himself that behind the façade of the innocence was someone with a strength of mind and sharp intellect. If one took the simple attire and soft-spoken nature at face value, it would be dangerous.

Matthews had pictured a top corporate honcho in his mind. But Mini surprised him with her simple salwar kameez, sandalwood mark on the forehead, and open smile.

Matthews was determined that the mistake he had made of stereotyping while meeting Aniyan Raja and Unni for the first time should not repeat itself. He should not fall into the trap of imagining Mini Balachandran as naïve.

Matthews spoke: 'Madam, your time is precious. So I will go straight to the topic.'

'Yes, please.'

Mini looked at Matthews' visiting card. Financial Consultant and Investment Analyst.

'Are you a share broker?'

'One can say both yes and no. I am not registered formally with the Exchange. Nor do I have a membership. But occasionally I play in the share market. Big cases mostly.'

'The trading of our shares is rather dull. You must surely be aware of that.'

Seeing Matthews gaze at the reddish dark liquid in the glass container, Mini explained: 'That is some sort of medicated water. My father's invention. Good for quenching thirst and easing digestion.'

Matthews smiled. 'Yes, I have heard much about Menon sir. He put forth many innovative ideas in the field of Ayurvedic treatments, did he not?'

Mini nodded.

After a few moments of silence, Matthews said: 'I will tell you the purpose of my visit. I have come with a big offer. Good for both of us. Take a look at this sheet. It has every detail.'

As Mini read the document, Matthews keenly observed her face for any reaction.

Transfer the lion's share of four lakh ninety thousand shares which Mini and her mother possessed – both theirs and the Trust's – to a new Trust. The current prices of shares, at thirteen rupees – nearly sixty-four lakhs in white money – as well as an additional five rupees per share – around twenty-five lakhs in black money – shall be given to Mini.

There will also be an agreement. Mini shall have the voting rights for all these shares. There shall be no change in management. Within the next six months, she should sell all the immoveable properties purchased by the company for setting up retail outlets outside Kerala, as well as the Nelliyampathy estate, at one and a half times the value of the assets shown in the balance sheet. The buyer would be someone recommended by the new Trust. Six months later, the new Trust would be willing to sell back all these shares to Mini at the market price of the day.

Mini read the sheet fully. Her face remained impassive.

'Are you serious?'

'Yes.'

A moment passed. Mini returned the paper.

'Who is behind this?'

'Aniyan Raja. You must have heard about him.'

Mini remained silent for a long time. At the first reading, she had not quite gauged the gravity of the matter. Only someone with two crores to spare could even think about such a move. But on hearing the name 'Aniyan Raja', she felt a tremor of fear.

Mini spoke: 'My father knew him. Why is he so interested in this company?'

'I don't know.'

'Aniyan Raja suffers from asthma attacks now and then. My father would often send him special medicines. How is his health nowadays?'

Matthews lied. 'He is doing well.'

'I shall meet him one day in the coming week. Meanwhile, let me discuss the matter with my mother.'

When Matthews stepped out of the room, a sense of incompleteness stung him. Wasn't everything out in the open? There was no hint of what Mini was thinking. Did she intentionally divert his attention by mentioning asthma?

It was time to watch his step.

21

The Trading Inside a Lover's Heart

Seated on the train, Shankaran Kutty repeated the sentences he had learned by heart the previous night. Where to raise his pitch, where to restrain himself with meaningful silences, where to pause and smile – he had prepared everything. He scrolled through the scribblings inside the diary again and again. The other passengers gladly grabbed the Malayalam newspaper that he usually read during the train journey. Shankaran Kutty had totally forgotten about it. When the train neared Ernakulam, he enacted the final rehearsal mentally.

Shankaran Kutty planned to catch an autorickshaw to Jos Junction. It was a walkable distance. But if he walked, he would end up perspiring. The stench of talc mixed with the sweat might be unsettling. While appealing for love, the ambience should be fragrant. Though he was not carrying a bouquet of roses, at least travelling in an autorickshaw would help him avoid the repellent smell of sweat.

Savitry would be near the STD booth situated at Jos Junction. Whether it rained or snowed, she was to be found near the booth every day at nine, calling many people. Was she calling Calcutta, Bombay or Madras? He had not asked her. Even if he did, Savitry's reply would be that enchanting smile of hers.

Then she would say: 'Mister Kutty, would you like to hear a secret? Titan's shares are going to leap today. Buy as many as possible.'

Shankaran Kutty knew that Savitry was connected to Bombay and a huge brokerage firm at Dalal Street. She preferred to call from a public booth for whatever reasons.

Today, he decided to wait at a distance while Savitry was busy in the public booth. When she emerged, Shankaran Kutty planned to approach her. He imagined their conversation:

Good morning, Savitry.

Good morning, Mister Kutty. How's life?

He planned to latch on to that bait.

I want to talk about it.

About what?

About life. Come, let's have a cup of coffee.

He would take Savitry to a restaurant. While sipping coffee, he would say:

Savitry, I want to confess something.

What?

I love you. I want to marry you. It was love at first sight for me. You needn't give me an immediate answer. Don't tell me whether you love me or not. Just think about it. I shall wait for your reply.

No, he would not add anything more. Let Savitry take her time.

Shankaran Kutty ruminated that Savitry's family and background was more prosperous than his. But in this Stock Exchange, a broker could turn into a lakhpati overnight. His inauspicious days were behind him. Good fortune was in the air.

Shankaran Kutty believed in the turns of fortune.

~

There was no work that Shankaran Kutty had not tried at least once after finishing his degree in political science. For fifteen days he worked as a rubber merchant's accountant. Then, as a bill keeper in a bar-attached hotel. He had run a newspaper agency, taught at a parallel college meant for students who had failed to secure an admission in universities, and contributed as a partner in a grocery shop. Finally, he became the proprietor of a hardware shop. Whether it was business or a job, Shankaran Kutty could not persevere beyond the first six months. The stars would turn inauspicious.

The hardware store was in Ernakulam. Shankaran Kutty managed to last there for one and a half years. Then the sales tax and income tax officers started harassing him. Even at a loss, he had to continue running the store. Helplessly, Shankaran Kutty sought refuge with a chartered accountant.

For the next one year, the CA convinced both the income tax and the sales tax fellows that Shankaran Kutty was a pauper. In the melee, he took as fees the last two thousand rupees in Shankaran Kutty's bank account.

Shankaran Kutty announced solemnly to the CA that day: 'I'm shutting down my shop from today.'

'What then?'

'Will rot at home.'

The CA thought for a while. Then he spoke:

'Shankaran Kutty, become a member of the Stock Exchange.'

'What's that?'

'The place where the shares of companies are bought and sold. One can buy and sell only through share brokers. These brokers get commission. If you work honestly, you can make a handsome amount every month.'

'How much does "handsome" mean?'

'Ten thousand rupees minimum.'

Shankaran Kutty became excited.

'Ten thousand monthly? I'm ready. What should I do?'

'Become a member of the Stock Exchange. There are some vacancies. I'll help you.'

'If you expect some money for giving bribes, better stop right now.'

'Listen, just a hundred rupees for application fees. And seventeen thousand for deposit. No bribes needed.'

'Forget seventeen thousand, I hardly have seventeen rupees in my hand.'

The CA took out one hundred rupees from the fees that Shankaran Kutty had paid him.

'I'll get you an application form. But Shankaran Kutty, you better manage that seventeen thousand from somewhere. Such a golden chance will not come again in life.'

'But how?'

'That I don't know. Sell your house, steal, do whatever!'

The application form arrived by evening. Since he was sure of never being able to collect seventeen thousand rupees, Shankaran Kutty did not bother much about it. Shutting his shop and dumping the receipts and bill book in his bag, he left town.

That was when good fortune showed up.

One day, as Shankaran Kutty sat nonplussed, unsure of what to do next, a scooter stopped in front of his house. Two well-dressed young men got down. As Shankaran Kutty wondered if there was more income tax trouble, they stepped inside the compound.

'Is this Shankaran Kutty's house?'

'Yes.'

'Mr Shankaran Kutty?'

'I don't know. He's not around,' he wanted to say. Instead, he said, 'Yes, please.'

The young men introduced themselves. They were from the bank. Development officers, in charge of new schemes.

The older one among them asked: 'Mr Shankaran Kutty, are you still interested in breeding rabbits?'

The other young man said: 'There is such a lot of open space here. It is perfect for breeding rabbits, sir.'

Shankaran Kutty sputtered: 'I don't understand.'

'Two years ago, you had applied for a bank loan for breeding rabbits. Our branch has been allotted such self-employment schemes only now. We shortlisted ten applicants from the old papers. You are one among them. Are you still interested in breeding rabbits?'

Without blinking an eye, Shankaran Kutty asked: 'A loan for twenty-five thousand, right?'

'The bank loan is twenty-five thousand and the government subsidy is five thousand. They shall also provide you with a litter of baby rabbits for free.'

Shankaran Kutty said: 'I'm interested in breeding rabbits.'

'Right. Come to the bank at ten o'clock tomorrow.'

It was after the officers left that Shankaran Kutty was hit by the gravity of the situation. Once upon a time, he had the habit of blindly applying for everything, including projects for rabbits! He had absolutely no idea about that creature. What would he say tomorrow if they asked him about the subject?

Having sworn to surrender ten per cent of whatever he got in the Ettumanoor temple coffers, Shankaran Kutty went to the bank. He had no trouble there. The bank officials' knowledge on rabbit breeding was limited to the circular they had received. A rabbit hutch was required, and eighty per cent of the loan would be allotted to building one. If Shankaran Kutty brought a proforma invoice proving that he had purchased material for building a rabbit hutch, the bank would issue a cheque in the name of the shop. The bank officers would be carrying out a periodic inspection. Then the government would be giving him a litter of baby rabbits.

Shankaran Kutty had the bill books of his hardware store. He submitted a proforma invoice in the bank the very next day. The bank issued him a cheque in the shop's name.

Twenty thousand rupees.

Shankaran Kutty devoutly submitted two thousand rupees in the receptacle of the Ettumanoor temple. He paid seventeen thousand rupees at the Stock Exchange and kept the remaining thousand in his hand. That was how Shankaran Kutty became a member of the Stock Exchange.

He did not indulge in speculation. Shankaran Kutty would methodically serve his clients and manage money with precision. Never did Shankaran Kutty end up with any liability on the Fridays when accounts were settled. His dealings were systematic. A member could have up to four authorized assistants. Shankaran Kutty collected seventy-five thousand as deposit from each of his assistants. Fifty thousand was shown in the accounts since that was refundable. The rest he kept for himself.

With some money from that collection, Shankaran Kutty started his rabbit business too.

Sometimes he would brood that it was time to stop the Stock Exchange work and settle down with Savitry. If he negotiated well, the membership card would easily fetch him a sum of no less than fifteen lakhs. That was a comfortable amount. Honeybee farming, poultry, dairy farming ... he could do anything.

However, for doing that...

~

Shankaran Kutty did not realize when the train had slowed down at the station. When his co-passengers got up, he woke up from his reverie.

Catching an autorickshaw, Shankaran Kutty reached Jos Junction.

Good luck. Savitry was in the STD booth.

He waited.

Shankaran Kutty repeated the sentences once again in his mind.

When Savitry stepped out of the booth and paid for her calls, Shankaran Kutty approached her.

'Good morning, Miss Savitry.'

Savitry took the receipt.

'Good morning. How's life today?'

'Life! I wish to talk about—' Suddenly Savitry interrupted him: 'How many shares of Dhanwantari Herbals do you have, Mister Shankaran Kutty?'

'What?'

'Dhanwantari company. How many shares would your clients be having right now?'

Savitry got into an autorickshaw.

'Aren't you coming to the Exchange?'

Shankaran Kutty climbed in too.

'Why are you so pale?'

'Am I?'

'Yes, very pale.'

'Not at all.'

'How many shares?'

'Of what? For whom?'

'Didn't you hear what I said? How many shares of Dhanwantari would your clients have at this moment, Mister Shankaran Kutty?'

The edge of Savitry's dupatta rose in the breeze and gently caressed Shankaran Kutty. He looked up.

All the love-soaked words that he had rehearsed for proposing to Savitry surged upwards. But when he gazed at Savitry's face, the words scattered.

'A decent number.'

'Five thousand? Ten thousand, maybe?'

'No, no. Five thousand possibly.'

'Okay. I shall buy those shares. For fourteen rupees each.'

'But the clients should agree to that.'

'That's where you show your efficiency. Increase it by fifty paisa or another rupee if you wish.'

'Why this sudden fondness for Dhanwantari?'

'Why look a gift horse in the mouth? You'd get the commission, wouldn't you?'

The autorickshaw turned the corner aiming for the Stock Exchange. The traffic constable gestured for them to stop.

'You can't go there.'

'Why?'

'Strike.'

'Strike?'

'Satyagraha. Dharna before the Exchange.'

As they disembarked and walked towards the Exchange, they heard the slogans booming in the air.

'Stop transferring Kerala's money to other lands!'

'Stop the Stock Exchange!'

'Drown the serpents of capitalism in the Arabian Sea!'

Shankaran Kutty said: 'These fellows are Naxalites. There was a rumour that they would be protesting today.'

'That's all right. So five thousand shares of Dhanwantari purchased at fourteen rupees, okay?'

Shankaran Kutty smiled. 'Fifteen?'

'Fourteen and a half.'

'Fifteen.'

'Okay, done!'

Through a verbal contract, they agreed to buy a thousand shares of Dhanwantari at fifteen rupees right on the roadside. By the regulations, the Stock Exchange would start trading only at 12.30 p.m. But verbal contracts flouting that rule were part and parcel of the Stock Exchange. Nobody violated such contracts. In the next few days, Shankaran Kutty was supposed to hand over five thousand shares of Dhanwantari to Savitry at the rate of fifteen rupees under the rules of the Stock Exchange. Even if the price escalated or decreased, both parties would continue to abide by their agreement.

Suddenly Shankaran Kutty looked at Savitry.

'Miss Savitry? Shall we have a cup of coffee?'

'No, no! I don't want to miss the thrill of a satyagraha and a strike. Come on!'

Shankaran Kutty followed Savitry.

22

The Dice of Speculation

Zacharia stepped out of Mini Balachandran's office. He made his way through the crowded Market Road and reached the autorickshaw stand. When he clambered inside an autorickshaw, his glance fell unwittingly on the board at a distance.

Dhanwantari Herbal Products Limited.

The familiar words, omnipresent across Kerala.

There was an attractive signboard, in orange and green, next to the company name. Zacharia had not seen it before.

Perhaps it was Mini's idea. Or was it the brainchild of some new advertising company that had been entrusted with the job?

The words were good.

> *Health in the Nineties.*
> *Dhanwantari is the insurer.*
> *Policy-holders need not pay any premium; just reap the profits.*

Zacharia grinned to himself. There was a gentle reminder of death. The fear of death was the mirror image of insurance, was it not? Death strongly reminded one of health.

But now the imminent need was to insure the company itself, not the common man's health.

One thing was crystal clear. Somebody was planning a takeover of the company. Would Mini be able to resist such an attack under the present circumstances? If Menon sir were alive, he would have handled the crisis courageously. He would have won the game. But, what about Mini?

Mini was intelligent. Maybe the enemy presumed that, being a woman, she was not to be taken seriously. That would be helpful. The presumption 'Oh, she's a helpless woman' would aid Mini in getting decisions made in her favour and rout the opponent effortlessly and unexpectedly. Mini knew it rather well. Besides, she had the full force of the family legacy behind her.

Suddenly Zacharia was struck by a thought. What if he also played a move? Maybe he could rake in a few lakhs smoothly. Should he? Why not?

A majority of the stockbrokers indulged in speculation or what is known as 'trying out one's luck'. Though not part of the official task, if one yearned to make a quick buck, turn into a crorepati overnight, the share broker could play the game of dice called speculation. Such fortune-seekers were called Bulls and Bears in stock-exchange lingo.

The Bulls raised their horns towards the sky. Those who bought shares, expecting their prices to rise, were referred to as Bulls. The phenomenon of the share prices increasing steadily was known as a 'Bullish market'. The Bear was the opposite. The Bears always stared at the ground. They expected stock prices to fall. They sold shares, expecting the prices to start decreasing soon. That was a 'Bearish market'. There was something unique about these Bulls and Bears. When they prepared the agreements for selling and buying, they would not actually have the shares in their hands. Zacharia had never belonged to this breed who got ready for losses and profits by virtue of mere paper contracts.

Only once in his life had Zacharia indulged in such a speculation. It was an unforgettable experience. A great lesson too.

~

The event unfolded a few years ago. There was a football tournament in his village. A sort of tradition, running for years. The tournament was in the name of Venu, who had paved the way for the football player Zacharia to be hailed as a 'Communist' by all and sundry. Over the years, the antipathy that many had exhibited towards the Communist party had transformed into a heartful embracing of its philosophy. However, many comrades had been martyred, without having witnessed their dreams coming true. Venu had not died from police brutality.

The poor villagers fished in the local pond. There was a sacred grove nearby, and a small idol on a stone pedestal, rather decrepit. A few villagers decided to grant a new lease of life to both the grove and the idol. They wished to carry out a reinstallation rite. The auguries revealed that the idol was of Lord Shiva. Purportedly the deity was furious with the treatment that had been meted out to it. If remedial actions were not undertaken, misfortune would rain on the village.

It was the time when there was a veritable race of discovering ancient temples and reconstructing them. A small temple came up in the grove. A pujari was appointed and the coffers started filling up. The temple committee decided to install the idols of Ayyappa, Sri Krishna and Ganapathy too. They planned for festivals. When they started collecting funds from the public, Zacharia also contributed five hundred and one rupees to the kitty.

The whole episode would have subsided quietly. But out of the blue, someone had the grand idea of cleaning the nearby pond and declaring it as the temple pond! Venu was an active member of the Communist party. His family were devout temple-goers. They were also assigned the traditional cleansing activities inside the temple. But when it came to the pond, Venu would not budge.

'If anyone wants to take a bath in the pond, that's all right. Let the pujari and devotees use it as a temple pond. But nobody shall stop the routine fishing in the pond.'

The temple committee was taken aback. Catch fish from a temple pond? That could not be allowed. Both parties went to the court. The cops started visiting the place frequently. Soon, the villagers were more familiar with the temple pond than the temple itself. There was simmering discontent all around. For the first time, there was a clear rift among the natives.

When the fishing was stopped for a fortnight, Venu and his clique became assertive. The police and the temple management safeguarded the sanctity of the temple pond with a night vigil. How long could the situation go on? One night, when the cops were not around, someone shattered the petromax lamp. Unknown people cast fishing nets.

Mobs attacked one another with cudgels and daggers. The hands of those who cast the fishing nets were hacked. There were counter-attacks. The village stood on the edge of panic that night. Young men went on a rampage. Like the dance of the mysterious Kapalika sect, shadows intertwined horrendously near the grove.

Two were murdered. One was Venu.

The annual football tournament was in Venu's memory. Zacharia sponsored the main trophy. He regularly attended all the games, which were meant to reignite the glory of football in his land. It was before he joined the Stock Exchange. Later, he would visit the village only on weekends.

There was no getting away from the Stock Exchange. Every moment was valuable. Some smart aleck remarked: 'Even if one's pater conks off, please ensure that the pyre is lighted only after four in the afternoon!' No broker could afford to leave the premises of the

Exchange during the working hours. In mere seconds, stock prices could change devastatingly. Some might have raked in lakhs in that interval. If one wasn't around then, it would mean a heavy loss.

Zacharia, however, chose to go home on a working day. It was the final of the football tournament. He could not keep himself away.

Following the game, the trophy distribution and the general chitchat, when Zacharia reached home, his son, Jayan, an eighth-standard student, updated him.

'Appa, there were three calls from Ernakulam.'

'Who was it? Didn't you ask?'

'Vinayan chettan.'

'What's the matter?'

Zacharia had trained Jayan in telephone etiquette. The new generation had to be conversant with it. Ever since Jayan turned seven, he would pick up the receiver.

First, he would spell out the home number. If the other side responded with their identity, well and good. Else Jayan would ask: 'Good morning. Who is speaking, please?' ... 'Appan is not here. Any message? Is it urgent? What's your number?' ... Jayan would note down every detail diligently.

Now, he read out from a sheet of paper: 'Kirti Ambani arrested in Bombay. No chance of securing bail. The charge is of allegedly conspiring to murder Nusli Wadia. The police have sufficient evidence.'

Zacharia had just begun to ponder over the news when the call arrived.

'No further news. Maharashtra government is adamant. He is in jail.'

Zacharia replied: 'I'll reach early morning.'

He could not sleep that night.

Two of India's major business conglomerates were at war. The Ambani group, which was registered in 1966, had purchased the latest technology from the America based DuPont company for manufacturing terephthalic acid (TPA), a raw material that was used in the production of polyester yarn. Soon, it became a major player, capable of deciding the rates of the textile industry.

With the famous Vimal brand in textiles and the petrochemical factory, and converting whatever they touched to gold, the Ambanis soon rose to become the third among India's top business families. Their share prices skyrocketed all of a sudden. Until then, the raw material used for polyester yarn had been DMT. It was manufactured by Bombay Dyeing, a company boasting a hundred-year-long legacy and grandeur. The owner was Nusli Wadia, whose maternal grandfather was Mohammad Ali Jinnah, the founder of Pakistan.

Both parties were equally influential in government and business sectors.

The war was over the power to fix tariffs in the Indian textile industry.

Two hundred and sixty-five rupees was the market price of a Reliance share with the face value of ten rupees! Eighty-seven rupees was the market price of a Bombay Dyeing share whose face value was twenty-five rupees.

It was in 1988 that the intriguing event transpired. The conspirator was a distant relative of the Ambanis. It was Wadia's moment of triumph. The share prices of Reliance would crash tomorrow; the prices of the Bombay Dyeing shares would shoot up.

Zacharia tossed and turned all night. When his wife asked if he was all right, he pretended to be asleep. He reached Ernakulam early morning.

Zacharia listened to the All-India Radio news at dawn. Kirti Ambani was in jail. He scoured through the newspapers. Delhi was rocked by the news. What was the prime minister's stance? Who would he help? The newspapers were replete with conjectures.

That day, Zacharia played his first and last speculative game.

He used a 'Bear trade', when everyone was focusing exclusively on Reliance and Bombay Dyeing shares. Kirti Ambani, though a distant relative of the Ambanis, was not in a prominent position in the company hierarchy. But Zacharia was in the know of a top secret. The Ambani family was purchasing bulk shares of Larson and Toubro in a bid to take over L&T, and the arrested relative was supervising the deal.

The market price of the L&T shares, with a face value of ten rupees, was a hundred and twenty-five rupees.

Zacharia threw his dice.

'I'm willing to sell L&T shares worth a hundred and twenty-five rupees at one hundred and twenty rupees.'

In moments, he was mobbed by buyers.

Zacharia sold almost fifty thousand shares in a span of ten minutes. Mere contracts. He did not have a single L&T share with him. Only a prayer in his heart.

Zacharia expected the share price of L&T to dip to at least one hundred and fifteen in the next half an hour. The Maharashtra chief minister would keep Kirti Ambani in jail for a long time. That was for sure.

But the price did not fall. After one hour, the news came. Kirti Ambani had got bail. Delhi might take over the case. The CBI will be the investigating agency.

The computer screen flashed with the share prices in the Bombay share market. The L&T shares were at one hundred and twenty-seven rupees.

In one hour, the loss was three and a half lakhs. Seven rupees lost per share for fifty thousand shares.

The next morning, Zacharia was supposed to deposit the 'margin': one-fifth of the total traded amount. It was meant to discourage those trading without the share certificates.

Twelve and a half lakhs!

Either share certificates or cash had to be surrendered. Or he would be disallowed from working in the Stock Exchange.

Somehow, good luck pulled Zacharia through.

He pledged numerous share certificates and borrowed money at exorbitant interest rates. And yet, he was short by two lakhs.

Just to get that amount, he persuaded two friends to sell their shares at high prices. Zacharia had to vouchsafe that he would bear the burden if they suffered losses.

Zacharia did not know a moment of rest for the next ten days. Never had he lost his bearings in the way he did during those black days. He desperately beseeched God every moment. Zacharia swore that if he got out of that mess, he would stop playing the dice of speculation forever!

The newspapers stopped carrying Kirti Ambani's news.

The price of the L&T stocks fell slowly.

Before the deadline of the fortnight when the shares had to be exchanged, the prices fell to one hundred and seventeen.

God saved Zacharia.

He repurchased all the fifty thousand shares at that price. Though it fluctuated between one hundred and eighteen and one hundred and nineteen at the start, he conducted the deal without suffering any loss. Neither was there any gain. After paying the interest for the borrowed sum, it was back to square one. Only the ghastly nightmares of a fortnight lurked in his memory.

Never had Zacharia indulged in speculation afterwards.

~

When the autorickshaw trundled to a stop before his office, Zacharia proffered a five-rupee note to the driver and laughed heartily.

'What's the matter, sir?'

'Nothing.'

While walking to his office, Zacharia wondered: What if I play a game of dice? Not for me. For Mini. For Menon sir. To help Dhanwantari survive…?

Govinda Prabhu was waiting with the printouts that Zacharia had asked for.

23

Curb Trading

Savitry was part of the crowd thronging the gate of the Stock Exchange building. There were four or five men shouting the slogans. Most were onlookers. There was a police jeep and a posse of cops. From the screaming headlines, she had been expecting a riotous mob of ten thousand revolutionaries tearing down the Stock Exchange.

There was a hubbub from the compound. Most of the audience moved away. The youth, pumping their fists in the air, as if doing a formal duty, gazed around listlessly.

'End the bourgeois capitalism!'

'Let the land's money stay in the land!'

'Long live the revolution!'

'Down with the north Indian invasion!'

Savitry walked towards the source of the sound. The Stock Exchange functioned from the second and third floors of the huge building. There was a massive coconut tree next to it. It had a few dried leaves, having been diseased for long. Some people were bringing down the tree. They were singing in tandem: '*Elessa, Elessa*...'

There was a small pit dug in the vicinity. Next to it was a coconut sapling.

Savitry felt an inexplicable sense of peace. She remembered what Vikas had once told her in Bombay: 'Trees and stock exchanges are inseparable from one another.'

~

Nowhere did the government or the public respect the brokers who bought and sold shares while charging commission for their services. They were considered to be dalals, middlemen, fortune-hunters who gained by gambling on the sweat and hard work of others!

In the beginning, before the passing of the Companies Act, there were five or six brokers in all. The market was trading in bonds of the East India Company, Commercial Bank, Chartered Bank, and also in the shares of bonded warehouses and steam-tug companies.

The share brokers hardly got any space for conducting their business. In Bombay, almost a hundred and fifty years ago, they worked under the cool shades of the banyan trees situated in front of the Horniman Circle. Apparently, the prop roots of the banyan tree were as smooth and shiny as chairs.

The brokers were always shouting at the top of their voices. Sound and enthusiasm go hand in hand in the Stock Exchange. Even today, there stand a couple of majestic banyan trees that silently witness the uproar, when brokers dealing with shares worth almost one lakh crores shout themselves hoarse in the impressive building situated on Dalal Street. The birds, unafraid of Bombay city's incessant sounds, do not perch on the banyan branches during the trading hours.

In Bombay, it was a banyan tree. In Kerala, a coconut tree. It was apposite.

That day, Vikas had joked:

'These banyan trees are the symbols of fortune's vagaries. Once a year, the leaves ripen and fall. One might fear that an end is imminent. But come monsoon, there's the cool breeze again, green leaves sprout anew. The banyan trees regain their youthful vigour and vitality quickly. Exactly like the Stock Exchange. One crash, and it seems like doomsday! Rare heart attacks, blood pressure cases, a suicide. Everything looks bleak. Then, a monsoon wind wafts by at twilight. Water rushes in. The dams fill up. The harvest is good. The common man's income grows. There are new products to consume. Businesses boom. Companies make profits. Share prices rise.

'The banyan trees are enlivened yet again. The fortune seekers smile inside the Stock Exchange.'

~

The coconut tree fell precisely as planned.

Even the slogan-shouting youth forgot their protest and rushed ahead.

The crowd was growing. It was a narrow road. On one side were the police, the hordes, parked cars and motorbikes. Youngsters crowding to watch the morning show in the theatre. A merry pandemonium.

Savitry tried to bypass the rush. Suddenly, she observed a young man hurling a stone, without any provocation. Nobody else seemed to have noticed. The man's face was impassive, and now he was gazing at the fallen coconut tree.

The stone hit the policeman standing in the back. He flinched.

One moment passed.

Three cops rushed into the crowd.

'Who threw the stone?'

Savitry gazed at the wrongdoer. He continued to stand nonchalantly, as if he had never heard the question.

The policemen repeated the question. Nobody responded.

They caught hold of a young man nearby. 'Was it you?'

He shook his head.

'Cat got your tongue?' A cop started heckling and pulling him.

The crowd turned aggressively at the policemen.

A few moments ticked by.

The sloganeering began again:

'Stop police atrocities!'

'Sack the police who lick the boots of the bourgeoisie.'

Savitry felt terrified, but could not help staring at what was going on. The cops and the public ended up in a tussle.

Someone remarked: 'What these fellows need is a good walloping!'

Another opined: 'It's all a facade. The Exchange, cops, protestors, journalists – all of them! Tomorrow the headlines will scream: Strike. Police lathi charge. Unrest. Injustice.'

A callous indifference to both the government and the frequent strikes was in the public's blood, habituated as they were to all such fracas. They did not bother about the boundaries of right and wrong. It was similar to the small pamphlets brought out by brokers when new shares were in the market. Everybody knew – nothing was hundred per cent true.

Some of the protestors climbed into the police jeep. It was as if they were waiting for that step.

One of the fellows who had ranted earlier raised his voice again: 'Tomorrow the Stock Exchange news will appear on the front page. Usually it's relegated to the middle pages.'

When Savitry crossed the road and started climbing the steps of the Exchange, she cast a look at the crowd. The young man who had hurled the stone stood there calmly.

Suddenly Savitry wondered: Was the speaker right? Was this show of protest and the ensuing ruckus a part of some publicity campaign?

Maybe the story was different.

When the Stock Exchange started in Kochi ten years ago, only a handful of people had come forward to become members. Hardly any shares were traded those days. The general public was totally unaware of the mechanics of the Stock Exchange. Nobody considered investing in shares as a profit-making measure. They were aware only about fixed deposits in banks or routing money through blade companies.

The newspapers highlighted only negative news about the share market. 'Share Prices Crash, Companies Wiped Out...' In those days, big companies run by Malayalis were few and far between. People knew only about the British tea plantations and some shipping companies. Trading in those shares were very rare too.

In those times, advertisements were needed to make the public cognizant of stock exchanges. People typically paid more attention to the news about police brutalities and strikes.

Savitry reached the verandah where the stairs ended. She browsed through the magazines and newspapers lying around. A huge universe of shares, businesses and companies. Most were English magazines that showcased the glamour of that world.

She hesitated, wondering if she should pick up a business paper. No, there was no time for anything today. Buy as many shares of Dhanwantari as possible – that was her aim.

Vikas would be able to know the rates at Bombay as of yesterday evening. The newspaper would highlight only the official share price. That was the price when the trading closed yesterday afternoon. But even after the official trading hours, the brokers and their agents bought and sold shares. It was known as curb trading.

If there were buyers, the share prices would go up. If there were more sellers, the prices would go down. The curb trading in Bombay could upend the share prices before trading started officially the next day.

Bombay was India's biggest stock exchange. Half the total value of shares traded across India was concentrated there. The stock exchanges in Calcutta, Delhi, Madras, Ahmedabad and others, implicitly followed the trend set by the Bombay Stock Exchange.

Curb trading existed in all the stock exchanges. As per law, it was not acceptable. But everyone ignored that stricture. Anyone could indulge in curb trading. But members and assistants were needed to settle the shares legally after the Exchange opened. One could say that the major part of the work in a Stock Exchange consisted of legalizing the shares bought and sold during curb trading.

Savitry mused: Maybe some others, besides Vikas, were tipped off too. It was likely to reflect in the curb trading of Dhanwantari shares at the Kochi Stock Exchange today.

Savitry hurried to the space between the cubicles meant for members. That was the hot spot of curb trading.

The members' cubicles were on the second floor. Open rooms, twenty-five or thirty feet wide. A few small tables, stools, telephones, a television screen mounted on the wall. In ten minutes' time, the details of the share prices of prominent companies in all the important stock exchanges would appear on the screen.

Savitry looked. The television screen was yet to flash the news. It was only a quarter past ten. A few young men and women were at work in the cubicles. But the curb trading had begun.

From among the crowd of twenty, one young man gazed at Savitry. When Savitry's eyes met his, he came forward.

'Orkay, Orkay.'

Savitry did not respond. But she did not withdraw her eyes.

'Orkay, Seller, forty-two.'

Savitry stood motionless.

The man repeated: 'Orkay, Seller, forty-two.'

Savitry was impassive.

The man's voice changed a bit. 'Orkay, Orkay.'

Many names echoed throughout the place.

'Apollo Tyres.'

'Neeraj Petro.'

'Reliance Capital.'

'Reliance Petro.'

'Videocon.'

'Seller, Seller…'

'Buyer, Buyer…'

People were wrestling for a space for themselves in the crowd. None of the young men or women were looking at one another.

Savitry focused on the glitter in the man's covetous eyes. She observed the imperceptible movement of the lips.

The man said: 'Orkay, Seller, forty-one fifty.' He had reduced fifty paisa.

Savitry responded: 'Forty.'

The youth became excited. Savitry wished to buy Orkay shares at forty rupees. His original negotiating price was forty-two. He had reduced it to forty-one and a half. How low would he go? How much was Savitry willing to shell out?

The man repeated: 'Orkay, Orkay, Seller, forty-one fifty.'

Savitry replied firmly: 'Forty.'

The man's eyes scanned Savitry's.

'Forty-one, Orkay. Forty-one, forty-one.'

Suddenly, a middle-aged man approached him from the throng and asked: 'Seller?'

The young man left Savitry instantly. 'Orkay, Seller, forty-one.'

The middle-aged man asked: 'Forty fifty?'

The youth shook his head.

'Forty-one.'

'How many shares?'

'Five hundred.'

The young man was happy. The customer was willing to buy the shares.

'Forty-one.'

'Okay, done,' said the middle-aged man.

They moved aside and jotted down the details. Now, when the Stock Exchange opened at twelve o'clock, five hundred shares of Orkay would be exchanged at the rate of forty-one rupees. Two brokers authorized to carry out the contract would inform the centralized computer via their official accounts. There was a fortnight's time to exchange the share certificates and settle the money. The brokers would receive the commission of the shares sold and bought.

Nobody paid attention to Savitry.

In the Stock Exchange, nobody cared at these moments about beauty, femininity or allure.

Only one sound.

Seller. Buyer. Rupees.

Savitry listened with eagerness.

A voice emerged in the melee. 'Dhanwantari, Buyer, fifteen … Dhanwantari, Buyer, fifteen…'

Savitry looked around. Shankaran Kutty was nowhere in sight. Who was the buyer, then? That meant, in the curb trading at Bombay Stock Exchange yesterday, Dhanwantari shares were traded.

There were buyers. More would troop in. She should buy as many as she could before that happened. Savitry raised her voice. 'Dhanwantari, Buyer, fifteen fifty.'

Vinayan came closer.

'Dhanwantari, Buyer, fifteen fifty.'

Both were buyers.

The calls of Dhanwantari buyers were soon lost in the pandemonium around.

24

The Game Is On

Govinda Prabhu was waiting for Zacharia in the office, with the report of the management consultant Suryanarayanan.

The balance sheets of the last three years, of five of Kerala's most prominent Ayurvedic companies, a data analysis of their assets, an evaluation of their ability to accrue money for a potential takeover bid, the inherent strength of their management, the money value of the companies' brand names and their products – all the information lay impassively in the computer printout. Zacharia browsed through the notes quickly.

Then he started analysing each company profile, one by one.

Among the five, there was only one public limited company. Two were trusts, and the rest were private limited companies. The public limited company had a plethora of agencies and sales outlets in every corner of the state. The agencies outnumbered its own retail units. The company had invested heavily in advertisements and other indirect expenses. There was no reason to be afraid of such a company. They did not have the wherewithal to swallow Dhanwantari Herbal Products.

Both the trust companies were competing brethren from the same family. Two different branches of one Ayurvedic legacy.

The balance sheets revealed that both were strong and resourceful. Their real assets would turn out to be ten times more valuable than what was shown in the balance sheets. One company was focused on Ayurvedic research whereas the other was aiming at treatments and clinics. Both had very experienced management professionals in their teams. Either could easily acquire Dhanwantari Herbal Products. The finances wouldn't be much of an issue for these companies. But, why should they do it?

Both the companies had made good names for themselves. They had their rich family legacy too. The duo were modernizing their medicine manufacturing units. The packing and handling of medicines were all mechanized by now. But they were twenty years too late in catching up with the trends. The managements acted as if the organizations were adapting to the requirement of the times unwillingly. How would an acquisition of Dhanwantari help either of the companies? They were at each other's throats constantly. It was evident that each party aimed at trouncing the other in business. They were on a hyper-alert mode twenty-four seven. The story of their internecine warfare was a joke in the Ayurvedic business industry. They did not wish to defeat anyone else. Most of their staff owed loyalty to both companies equally.

A grin spread over Zacharia's face as he read the printout.

Prabhu, who was waiting with a cup of tea, asked: 'Why are you smiling, sir?'

Zacharia drank the tea. 'No, I was just thinking. Prabhu, you have read all the puranas, haven't you? What are the reasons behind the most bitter fights?'

Prabhu paused for a moment. 'The poet sings: "Due to gold and women, fights are rampant in this world." That truth has remained unchanged for ages.'

Zacharia said: 'There's one more reason.'

Prabhu took a ripe areca nut and spliced it neatly. Zacharia focused on separating the vein of the betel leaf.

'The most acrimonious fights break out among those who are the most intimate. It could be over gold, women, a bad word, a doubt, anything at all. The ones closest to us do not forgive what outsiders might forgive easily. Isn't the fight between husband and wife after a split, or between siblings, the most venomous of all?'

'Yes.'

Slicing the areca nut into small bits, Prabhu deposited the slivers on the table.

'Which company is this, sir?'

There was a glossy advertisement of some company's new issue of shares. Extremely eye-catching design.

Zacharia took the sliced pieces of areca nut, blew away the dust and tossed them inside his mouth.

'This is a new company, headquartered in Calcutta. They want us to believe that they invented cement! Some smart advertisement company has done a good job, I'd say.'

Prabhu took away the teacup.

'I'm not interested in cement.'

'You want another hotel, I guess?'

'No, something good ... like this computer.'

Zacharia looked at the printout and remarked: 'The golden age of companies is going to arrive soon. The cold war and hot war are going to be between companies in the future. Haven't you seen what happened in Europe? It's all about corporate governance. The identity of nations has vanished. The European economic community rules the roost. They'll aim for a single company now. Limited company, fixed liability. In East Europe, Communist nations are all being Balkanized and weakened internally. India and China might face it too. So companies arise to take care of countries. A big Russian company, a huge Indian company ... Individuals will become less important. We can call it economic survival. Political societies focusing on survival. Isn't America a forerunner of such a concept? So, Prabhu, for our sheer survival, we need companies more than any philosophy.'

Prabhu could not make head or tail out of what Zacharia had just explained. But he was used to listening to Zacharia's abstruse monologues. He would nod along like an intellectual.

'Originally the fight was between nations. Between kings, leaders ... "The ruler of the world" was the title which Alexander, Genghis Khan, Napoleon and Hitler aspired for. It will no longer belong to individuals any more. Companies will grab that instead. Oil companies, grain companies, milk companies ... Water, electricity, textiles, education, health – all the sectors are being taken over by corporate companies. Companies ruling computer systems shall take over human intelligence, people's thoughts and opinions! Prabhu, the companies shall rule the world soon enough!'

Prabhu nodded. 'Yes, of course.'

'A war shall break out soon. The war between companies. One will swallow another, annihilate, devastate. Eventually, all the weak ones will vanish.'

Zacharia walked out to spit the paan juice. On his return, he gazed at the computer printouts again.

'Nothing to worry about here. The two trust companies are trying to destroy each other. Dhanwantari has no cause of concern from this duo.'

Now what remained were the two private limited companies. They belonged to two different individuals. Both were doing rather well. The first had been registered just seven years ago. An Ayurvedic medicine manufacturing company, run by an engineering graduate. Zacharia had met the young man once. He had approached Zacharia to help him convert it into a public limited company. Zacharia's friend had introduced them. They had joked that day about an engineer handling medicine.

The engineer's family, which had been practising Ayurveda for generations, was in possession of two single-shot remedies, or ottamooli. His uncle was the physician. The mechanical engineer had designed a machine for his uncle. He had made the first prototype himself. Everyone praised him effusively. After obtaining a patent, the youth had begun a small production unit in the family compound. Very few came to buy the machine. He ended up selling one per month. Occasionally, three or four. There were no profits to continue the business. But he did not have the fortitude to shut the business either.

The young man started making medicines using the machine. First, he focused on his family remedies. He invested in excellent advertising. The response was astounding. Soon, he registered a private limited company with his uncle as chairman. Every year, their turnover doubled. Now the company was stepping into automatic packing and labelling. They were also trying to sell Ayurvedic medicines in allopathy mode, that is, in the form of pills. The company was seeking loans via government agencies for further expansion. This company was firmly grounded and planned every step after strategic discussions. Perhaps, after five or ten years, the engineer's company might become the numero uno among Ayurvedic companies in Kerala. Even so, right now, he would never attempt to take over Dhanwantari. The very character of the young man's company was different.

Zacharia eliminated the engineer's company from his final list.

Now, what remained was a renowned pharmaceutical company. This private limited company made all sorts of medicines. The founder, a vaidyan, still believed that the medicines in the bottles mattered more than the packing or labelling. Forty years ago, when certain districts banned liquor, the arishtam, or liquid medicine, the company produced had become very popular.

The vaidyan had good connections in the political circle. He was a good friend. Fine behaviour. Humble. A charming smile. Even his foes liked his arishtam. Though the liquor ban was withdrawn from Kerala, the vaidyan's medicine continued to have many fans. Later, Tamil Nadu banned liquor totally. The arishtam continued to sell in bottles with Tamil labels, doing exceptionally well. This company had a few subsidiary companies too. Suryanarayanan's report showed their details in footnotes.

One export company was running at a loss. The vaidyan was using it as an excuse for touring Singapore and Hong Kong – nothing mala fide there.

A cinema company produced two movies. The first scraped through, the second flopped miserably.

One plantation. Rubber. The tapping should have started last year. But there was a labour strike going on.

Zacharia brooded over the details of the company for a long time. Though the figures in the balance sheet were not favourable, the vaidyan could easily procure money from the market. Maybe he wished to take over a firm dealing in the same area, like Dhanwantari. The vaidyan had the proclivity for such a move. Possible. If at all any Kerala company was behind the aggressive purchase of Dhanwantari's shares, it had to be the vaidyan's company known for its arishtam!

After discovering the enemy, one could plan a suitable battle strategy.

One question, however, remained: If it was the vaidyan who was behind the takeover bid, would he keep it such a secret? Judging by his pompous nature, the man would have boasted about it to quite a few! Instantaneously, through the business grapevine, the news would have spread.

By afternoon, Suryanarayanan would provide more details of the other prominent Ayurvedic companies of India. Zacharia decided to make up his mind after receiving that information.

It was eleven-thirty in the morning. When Zacharia was about to start for the Stock Exchange, Vinayan's call arrived.

'Sir! Curb trading happening at full strength for Dhanwantari shares. Thought I should inform you.'

'Who's the party, Vinayan?'

'Desai and Kacholia from Bombay. I think both are involved. Our Thomachan is also actively trading. That's why I called you. He usually does only line trading. That means the north Indians are up to something.'

Thomachan was Zacharia's friend. It was Zacharia who had introduced him to the Stock Exchange. Thomachan used to work in Kuwait. A friend of his was now a partner in Desai and Co., the famous stockbrokers of Bombay. When Thomachan became a member of the Cochin Stock Exchange, the friend made him an unofficial representative of Desai and Co. He did 'line business', following only the instructions passed on by brokers from other exchanges over the telephone. Their commission was a meagre percentage of the traded amount: 0.5 per cent or 0.75 per cent.

'Enough. I'm not greedy. The money I made in the Gulf under the scorching sun is not meant to be spent lavishly in share market speculations. I'm happy with whatever I get. Desai ensures that I get a commission of nearly twenty thousand rupees in a month. Kariacha, I'm content with rum. I never insist on whisky or champagne. Having taken a couple of pegs, I wish to sleep well. No avarice in my heart. I'm happy with the line business.'

That was Thomachan's take on the issue.

Zacharia instructed Vinayan: 'I'm coming over. What's the rate now?'

'Sixteen.'

'Do one thing, Vinayan. Sell twenty thousand shares of Dhanwantari in curb.'

'Sell?'

'Yes, the share price is increasing, right? Let's see if we can hold back the rates! What if it's all a joke?'

'I don't think this is a joke.'

'Anyway, try a seller offer. Watch the reaction.'

Vinayan wanted to say something, but he muttered, 'Yes, sir,' and hung up. Though he was an independent broker now, Vinayan took Zacharia's counsel in everything. He followed his instructions unquestioningly.

Zacharia smiled to himself. This was a game! How long since he had played one? The thrill of the game…

Zacharia the centre half, who once controlled every move in the football field. The red-card holding member of the Communist party who tricked the cops and vanished among serpent groves and screw-pine bushes!

Thrill!

Zacharia felt he was shedding his years. Old age moved away from him.

Now, he wished to play a game, but cautiously, slowly … It could be a Desai, a Kacholia, or any invisible monster … they will meet their match in Cochin.

Zacharia walked to the Stock Exchange.

25

Skyrocketing Shares

Leaving Savitry to watch the dharna, Shankaran Kutty walked to his cubicle on the first floor of the Stock Exchange.

He could not confess his love to Savitry. But one good thing had happened. They could travel in an autorickshaw together. Savitry's mind was on Dhanwantari's shares. It was not the appropriate time to offer his love. There was more closeness now, though, wasn't there? Didn't she ask for five thousand shares of Dhanwantari? He had agreed too. Didn't he gasp, 'Okay, done!' in the excitement of the moment?

Now, Shankaran Kutty had to manage those shares.

An acquaintance quipped on seeing him: 'Why are you smiling, Shankaran Kutty?'

'Nothing.'

Actually, it was a self-congratulatory smirk. It had emerged as a wide grin. Savitry was his sweetheart, future wife and, of course, love was blind. But even she could not manipulate him to selling for fourteen rupees, could she? It was the Lord of the Ettumanoor temple who had granted him the strength to overcome the allure of her smile. He had negotiated a higher rate of fifteen, without agreeing to fourteen fifty.

Shankaran Kutty warmly congratulated himself. The satisfaction had emerged as a grin.

There were two small tables, one chair and a few stools in Shankaran Kutty's cubicle. Also, many colourful pamphlets and application forms. These belonged to companies bringing out new shares in the market. Shankaran Kutty picked up two pamphlets and dusted the table. Then he flicked at the grimy plastic board.

S.K. Associates.

The name was rather impressive. Shankaran Kutty Associates did not carry the same aura. Many clients, even those who had dealings with other brokers, were attracted merely by the name on the board: S.K. Associates.

~

A curious incident had happened a year and a half ago.

There was not much rush that day. Shankaran Kutty had seen an old man gazing at the cubicle from afar. He was dressed in a long white shirt, an upper cloth, wearing an ear stud, holding an old umbrella, and his silvery hair was bristled up.

Shankaran Kutty had mastered a lesson early in his career as a stockbroker. Address people as 'Sir'. Most would be charmed.

Shankaran Kutty smiled at the old man.

'Sir, are you waiting for someone?'

The aged man looked intently at Shankaran Kutty.

'Who is the broker of S.K. Associates?'

'Yours truly.'

The old man stepped inside the cubicle and sat down on a stool.

Srinivasa Kurup of Omalloor was leading a serene, retired life. He had five acres of rubber plantations. His wife was old and sickly. Their only son was settled in the Gulf. He would visit once every two years. Kurup had one weakness: he loved watching films. His son had gifted Kurup a VCR and the old man watched two films every day. Kurup adored the world of cinema. He had also spoken directly to a movie star. That was how he came to be associated with the Stock Exchange.

Ten years ago, a movie star had arrived in Pathanamthitta in connection with the inauguration of a business enterprise based in Kochi. The proprietors had brought the glamorous film star for attracting investors. The strategy worked out. Many people who had never invested in any company bought shares of this particular company. The movie star spoke to Kurup for ten minutes. That was the most memorable moment in the old man's life. Kurup had withdrawn forty thousand rupees lying in his Post Office savings bank account and handed it over to the film star. He was given four thousand shares worth ten rupees each.

The new company started with much fanfare. But progress was at a crawling pace. By the time the shares reached the market, the share price fell. Kurup feared he would lose his investment. When the price reached three rupees and fifty paisa, Kurup wrote to the movie star. Since he was busy with shooting, Kurup received an autographed photograph as reply. Disappointed, Kurup visited the Cochin Stock Exchange.

The prices of a number of shares were climbing steadily and their investors were minting money. Soon, the world of shares enchanted Kurup more than the world of movies. He started investing what his son sent him from the Gulf, along with profits made from his rubber plantations in the share market. Kurup would never keep any shares for more than three months. Whenever the share prices of the companies he had invested in dipped a bit, he would sell the shares at hand and purchase other shares of a lower price.

Kurup had entrusted all his deals to a local fellow – someone who was his son's classmate. A few months later, Kurup grew worried about the lad's integrity. The money from the sale of shares never reached him on time. The amount that was to be received in a fortnight's time, took longer. Something was not right. Was the young man double-dealing him? Kurup took a decision. One should never put all their eggs in one basket. He needed more brokers.

It was at that time that he saw the plastic board. S.K. Associates.

Srinivasa Kurup evaluated Shankaran Kutty. He asked: 'What's your name?'

'Shankaran Kutty. What's yours, sir?'

Kurup liked Shankaran Kutty. Usually the brokers he dealt with called him 'Uncle'. In front of others, they addressed him as 'Mr Kurup'.

Kurup told his wife later that Shankaran Kutty displayed his inherent culture by hailing him as 'Sir'.

Slowly, all of Kurup's stockbroking ended up with Shankaran Kutty.

~

S.K. Associates.

Shankaran Kutty wiped the plastic board nicely. Then he opened the briefcase and took out the diary. Savitry needed five thousand shares of Dhanwantari Herbal Products. How many of these shares did his loyal clients have? He flicked through the pages.

One usually sold or bought shares in multiples of fifty. Fifty, hundred, one hundred and fifty. But sometimes, companies distributed bonus shares to their stockholders. It would be at a ratio of one bonus share for two shares or three shares held by the person. Thus, some would have shares which were not exactly in multiples of fifty. Certain companies borrowed funds from the public in particular years and returned it as shares and money on specific dates. Again, shares which did not fit into multiples of fifty would be distributed. These were rare and few in number, but provoked much headache among the brokers.

Shankaran Kutty examined the figures.

Four or five of his customers had almost five hundred of Dhanwantari's shares; a seventy here, a hundred and ten there, two hundred and twenty with another … Muthassi, aka Granny, had twelve hundred shares with her.

Muthassi was a neighbour, back in Shankaran Kutty's village. A distant acquaintance. Shankaran Kutty had met her in front of the Ettumanoor temple some years ago. She had invited him home. Muthassi was living in a traditional nalukettu house. Her children and grandchildren were well-settled in various towns. She lived with her widowed daughter and a differently abled grandchild. Muthassi did not own much gold or money. But coconuts and pepper were plenty. Her kith and kin gave her money whenever they visited.

When Shankaran Kutty went to meet her at home, Muthassi said: 'You're familiar with the banks, aren't you? I need a favour.'

Shankaran Kutty was gobbling down boiled tapioca with a mixture of crushed chillies, salt and coconut oil. The tasty food was accompanied by piping hot coffee. When the pleasure of the chillies had scalded the tongue, he had agreed.

'What do you want?'

'Here, take five thousand rupees. The lone savings of my daughter's late husband. Put it in some bank as a deposit and ensure that the interest reaches us on time every month. I don't have much trust in chit funds, that's why I'm requesting you.'

Shankaran Kutty smiled.

'Muthassi, don't worry at all. Shall I buy shares with this money?'

'What are shares?'

'Well, they are shares of companies. When the price of various items increases, their shares swing up. So, if it's a good company, just like interest payments, we'll get dividends. Our investment or capital will increase too.'

'I shouldn't lose my money, that's all.'

Shankaran Kutty invested the five thousand in the shares of two companies whose prices were likely to shoot up soon. In two weeks, the prices increased by ten per cent. Shankaran Kutty sold the shares and bought some low-priced shares. In three months' time, very carefully, he exchanged shares five or six times. Only once did the speculation go wrong. Three months later, after deducting his commission of one per cent, Shankaran Kutty took the earnings back to Muthassi.

This time around, Shankaran Kutty was treated to a sumptuous meal. Eight thousand and five hundred rupees.

'So much interest in merely three months?'

'Not interest, Muthassi. The net gains after selling and buying shares carefully.'

Muthassi said: 'Isn't there a machine which crushes rice nowadays?'

'Mixer?'

'Yes, get me one. The rest you can deposit into that contraption. What's it called?'

'Shares.'

'Yes.'

Shankaran Kutty bought her a mixer. The remaining amount, he cautiously invested in shares again.

This was the fourth year since he had met her. Muthassi's home currently boasted a new refrigerator, cooking gas, pressure cooker, grinder, television and a VCR. Muthassi had shares worth almost forty thousand rupees. And the old woman had changed too. She knew about companies and would enquire about share prices and debentures. The newspaper she read had one page dedicated to the share market. Muthassi was aware of Tata and Reliance.

She would tell Shankaran Kutty proudly: 'My children think they are the only smart ones around. Now they realize that they have inherited my intelligence. What do you say?' She would advise Shankaran Kutty judiciously: 'Invest prudently in good companies.'

Shankaran Kutty would listen sincerely. Due to the mixer and grinder, he was fed with new delicacies every time he paid her a visit. He liked to hear the aged woman talk. Based on the newspaper reports, she would astutely analyse companies and shares. He had succeeded in introducing her to a new world!

But recently, there had been some trouble. Muthassi had started commanding him.

Last year, she said: 'Buy the shares of an Ayurvedic company.'

'Why?'

'If I fall sick, at least I can stay in a hospital that belongs to me!' She grinned after saying that. 'Try that Dhanwantari company. I want that company's shares.'

'Muthassi, I don't think it's a good idea.'

'Doesn't matter. You buy a thousand shares for me.'

Shankaran Kutty purchased twelve hundred shares. He got them at a steal, when the share price was twelve and a half rupees.

Once, when he asked whether he could sell at fourteen, Muthassi had forbidden him. 'No, don't sell the medicine company's shares.'

Shankaran Kutty was now determined to sell her shares. Especially after Savitry's demand. *I should coax Muthassi to sell at fifteen. If she feels like purchasing more, we can always do it later.*

Now, he had to find another three thousand-odd shares. He had given his word to Savitry. It had to be kept. Shankaran Kutty scribbled in his diary: Three thousand three hundred Dhanwantari.

He shut the diary. There was time for a coffee.

The canteen was at the other end of the cubicles. As Shankaran Kutty wove his way through the crowd involved in curb trading, he could hear the shouts:

—Orkay.

—Titan.

—Videocon.

—Apollo.

—Reliance.

—Dhanwantari.

Shankaran Kutty had only contempt for those indulging in curb trading. Speculators! Was stockbroking similar to lottery or gambling?

In Shankaran Kutty's view, the dignity of the share market, the Stock Exchange and accountability towards the stakeholders mattered most. The share market should ensure that white money flowed into healthy businesses. Shares had the power to change a nation's future, ensure progress and uplift the living standards of the public. They should never be played like pawns in a speculative game.

Shankaran Kutty disregarded the yelling and walked towards the canteen.

Someone called out: 'Dhanwantari, Buyer, seventeen.'

Shankaran Kutty did not hear it.

26

From Kashi to Kerala

Aniyan Raja was afraid of only two things in his life: one, his wife; second, asthma.

Both entered his life at the same time. When he was twenty-four or twenty-five years old. Mysteriously, without any forewarning.

It all began in Kashi.

Aniyan Raja had gone to Banaras Hindu University for his MA degree. Before the first year ended, Malati stepped into his life. Mahesh Chand Bhartiya was the first friend he made in Banaras. It was he who introduced Aniyan Raja, who did not know much Hindi, to Kashi's narrow gulleys and the soothing flow of the Ganga.

When the close friends went to Bhartiya's palatial home in Satna, Madhya Pradesh, during Holi, Aniyan Raja had caught a lightning-like glimpse of Mahesh Chand's sister Malati. The day after, when Aniyan Raja was sitting in his room, five or six girls entered like a tempest. Before he could get up, colourful liquid, spurting from the pichkaris, splashed all over him. Moist laughter filled the room. One girl – her clothes wet and face smeared with a myriad colours – took out sindoor and rubbed it all over Aniyan Raja's face and hair. Then, casually pulling at his shirt, she daubed his chest and back too with the sindoor. For a moment, Aniyan Raja stood nonplussed. Then, he had his revenge. Taking a pot of coloured liquid from one of the girls, he poured it over the villainess. She giggled and frolicked about. The gaggle of girlfriends started laughing helplessly. Aniyan Raja and the vivacious girl started attacking each other with colours. The girl's name was Malati.

Three months. Aniyan Raja became Malati Bhartiya's husband.

Their marriage lasted for only four years. Unexpected medical complications arose during the delivery of the first child. Aniyan Raja was in Calcutta then. Had Malati been taken to Allahabad, she might have survived. Malati died in the same room where she had laughed with Aniyan Raja – in her palatial home in Satna.

Aniyan Raja bid goodbye to north India in a month's time. But the four years he had spent there gave him a new lease of life.

Every moment of the four years had gone by in utter terror of his wife. Not the trepidation experienced by any husband or wife in relation to the spouse. Malati belonged to a renowned business family that had forged new paths in the arena of enterprise. It was her great grandfather who started the first coal company in the Vindhya valley. The Central India Coal Company. The Vaishya community of north India had started taking interest in the sectors once dominated by the whites. Bhartiya belonged to the same echelon as that of the Birlas, the Goenkas, the Mahindras, the Bajajs, and so on. Coal, textile, jute, chemicals, cement, sugar: these families were leading another revolution, even as Mahatma Gandhi and others readied the common man for the freedom struggle.

Whenever the Bhartiya family started a business, a clear pattern was discernible. The fundamental principles were non-negotiable. Similar to the rules of chess. But even within the purview of those rules, there could be a million combinations of moves. Otherwise referred to as 'the efficiency of doing business'.

Aniyan Raja became a member of the Bhartiya business clan. It was then that the fear of his wife set in. Every time Aniyan Raja applied a business tactic and shared it with her, she seemed to be in the know of it. It was a skill she had inherited through her bloodline. Aniyan Raja was terrified that she would discover his naivety when it came to business.

Calcutta was the nerve centre of the Bhartiya family's business enterprises. The family business was just taking off in Bombay. Aniyan Raja made many friends in both places. He became an inseparable part of the Marwari family.

Four years. Aniyan Raja mastered business lessons worth four hundred years.

One: Never spend your own money for business or commerce. Use the money of the public, government, banks, whosoever's you wish. But not yours.

Two: Your liabilities should be defined and limited. Even if the business fails, you should not be devastated. So, conduct business via public limited companies and trusts.

Three: Do not make enemies of any political party or government.

Four: Everybody – be it an idealist or a foe – has a price associated with them. For some, it's money. For others, power. For a third, fame. Foresee the price early. That is the recipe for success.

Five: Always follow the law. One can always find legal loopholes with the help of expert lawyers. Use those well.

With every additional bit of knowledge, Aniyan Raja felt the thrill of defeating his wife. It took him merely two years to master the family inheritance of 'business prowess'. It was Aniyan Raja who pulled the reins when the Bhartiya family decided to venture into two new sectors: cigarettes and vanaspati.

A huge factory for manufacturing vanaspati was set up in Maharashtra. The most important ingredient of vanaspati was cottonseed oil; then, a portion of mustard oil; and another portion of groundnut oil. The cotton seeds were profitable; and so, ninety per cent of the mixture comprised that alone.

Three companies were organized for the purpose. One for setting up the factory, the second for running it and, the third, for selling the products. Advertisements were launched, praising vanaspati and highlighting the impeccable business background of the Bhartiya family. The shares of the three companies were traded at both the Bombay and Calcutta stock exchanges. One-tenth of the total shares were reserved for the Bhartiya family.

Aniyan Raja highlighted the legal loopholes in his project report. For the next two decades, despite minting crores of profits, taxes would not need to be paid. In the next five years, three more factories could be set up. The public and the banks would provide the funds towards that.

Offer debentures to the public. These were long-term debt instruments promising higher returns than banks. Of course, one should repay the interest without fail. After five years, convert half of the total number of debentures into shares. If, for example, the shares with a face value of ten rupees were worth thirty in the market, instead of debentures, offer the public shares at the market value of twenty rupees. Those with debentures would happily accept the offer. After ten years, convert the rest of the debentures into shares too. No need to return the borrowed amount as cash. The difference between the face value and the market value of the shares would enhance the financial stability of the company too. A win-win situation for all stakeholders. Even if the company ran at a loss, there would be no obligation of repaying the borrowed amount.

The Bhartiya family liked Aniyan Raja's proposal. Aniyan Raja was scared that when he presented the idea to his wife, she might poke a hole in it. But time was very short. Malati passed away.

Many relatives tried to persuade Aniyan Raja to marry Malati's younger sister, as was the custom, and continue in the business. But Aniyan Raja left north India.

He confessed to Mahesh Chand that he couldn't imagine anyone else in Malati's place. Sometimes, Aniyan Raja felt that if asthma hadn't been his nemesis, he might have continued in Satna, Calcutta or Bombay.

The first incursion of asthma had been in Kashi, a few months before meeting Malati. Aniyan Raja was facing the bitter north Indian cold for the first time in his life. He did not have sufficient woollens. By the time he bought them, the infection had taken hold of him. It started with a niggling cough, which turned into acute suffocation. Aniyan Raja took medicines. His suffocation increased.

The asthma, along with Malati, was his constant companion for those four years.

Even after his wife left his side, the asthma did not. It would aggravate during new moons. Sleep eluded Aniyan Raja then, and he would spend the whole night wheezing.

Forty-odd years. Countless medicines, treatments – all futile.

The greatest of allopathy experts tried their hand. More than two hundred needles must have impaled Aniyan Raja's body. Finally, they concluded: 'Listen, you have an allergy. The pollen of new plants irritates your system. Please try to live somewhere where these aren't in the surroundings.' There was even a piece of humorous advice: 'Why not try sailing? No pollen in the sea, is there?'

The Ayurveda practitioners left no stone unturned. They made him ingest both the liquid kashayam and the semi-solid lehyam concoction.

Homeopathy. Unani. Ottamooli. Acupuncture.

No matter the treatment regime, every twilight, the breathlessness would begin unfailingly. The disease would rasp, 'Hello, I am still here.'

Aniyan Raja would swear: 'I shall beat you yet!'

Then he would wheeze all night.

Most who approached Aniyan Raja for any work were familiar with his asthma. He had a natural proclivity towards those who narrated the latest cures for asthma. Aniyan Raja was percipient enough to recognize his own weakness.

Today, Aniyan Raja was being presented with a new ottamooli cure. The school's biology teacher was going gaga over the topic.

The fellow had been teaching in Aniyan Raja's family-owned school for the last three years. Since he had only a second class in MSc Botany, he had applied for a teacher's post. The deposit amount was sixty thousand in those days. When Aniyan Raja took over the school management, he tweaked the requirements a bit. No need for any deposit or receipt. Based on a calculation fashioned by Aniyan Raja – depending on the power and stature of various deities – the applicant should deposit the proportionate amounts in the holy receptacles of the five temples owned by the family. There were many advantages to this method. The applicants could resort to black money. Nobody would probe further. The earnings of the temples would increase. There would be no uncomfortable details in the school accounts either.

The biology teacher recently found a new job in Madras. He wanted to quit the present job and get his deposit back. The resignation was no issue but asking for the deposit of sixty thousand to be returned was tricky. The teacher brooded long over the problem. There was no legal way of getting the money back. It all depended on Aniyan Raja taking a lenient view.

The biology teacher, hence, was going on full steam on the subject. He had purportedly spent the last two weeks in a hilly forest. He was appraised about the herb. One just needed to crush the leaves and drink the juice. The crushed leaves should be chewed at leisure. Apparently, if this ritual was followed for fifteen days in a row, asthma attacks would cease.

The man had brought a few withered green leaves wrapped up in banana leaves.

Aniyan Raja asked: 'What's its name?'

'The tribals call it kothuvatty. No scientific name. It appears that if any mosquito – or kothuku – lands on this plant, the leaf on which the mosquito lands curls around it and crushes the pest to death. Hence the name.'

Aniyan Raja examined one of the leaves closely. Slightly bigger than that of a thumba plant. Brownish green. He chewed a bit. Sour. Aniyan Raja spat it out.

'What's this? It doesn't taste like a leaf.'

The biology teacher elaborated: 'Few people have started exporting these leaves, much like tea leaves, to Europe. A hush-hush affair. I don't know whether the herb is sold in the form of leaves, a juice or as a powder. But it is true that people are collecting it assiduously. No clue about the reason.'

'Might have medicinal value. Or it has intoxicating effects like marijuana.'

'Yes.'

The leaves worked. The biology teacher got his deposit back.

Aniyan Raja sent some of the leaves to Pune for testing. His friend was a director of an Ayurvedic ashram there.

What are the specialties of this leaf? Is it a drug or an intoxicant? After jotting down his query in a letter, Aniyan Raja smiled to himself.

The Maharashtrian friend too suffered from asthma.

27

The Investor's Helplessness

When Zacharia reached the Stock Exchange, the second floor was thrumming like a bustling wasp's nest. Men and women thronged the brokers' cubicles. The crowd had taken over the corridors and the corners. Neither was anyone paying any attention to others. The day was just beginning. The fragrance of talc and eau-de-cologne was yet to be overpowered by the stench of perspiration. After some time, the ruckus would spread to the third floor. Exactly at twelve-thirty, when the official trading hours started in the Stock Exchange.

When it came to the clamour around, there was no discriminating between a male and a female. It did not matter if someone was a believer or an atheist. There was no difference between a handsome man and an unattractive one, a woman who was gorgeous and another who was ordinary-looking. Everybody screamed at the top of their voices. Friend, foe, husband, wife, siblings – everyone was part of the deluge of sounds in this place. The ears caught only the nuances of the disparity when the names and prices of the company share were yelled. The same goal, same focus, same salvation: money. The overarching deity called money. The invocations and paeans were all to attract money to oneself.

Zacharia remembered a witty anecdote about the mayhem prevalent in a Stock Exchange.

Bang opposite the Stock Exchange was a five-star hotel. And abutting that, a gents' salon. In fact, the salon primarily offered haircuts. The only difference between a barber shop and the salon was that the latter charged five times the cost. However, pretty young girls did the haircuts there. So, money did not matter.

Ulahannan Mappila, a traditional Christian gentleman, treated himself to the special haircut once every four months. That was the day meant for his family's outing in Ernakulam. After sending off his daughter and wife for shopping, Ulahannan would drop in for a haircut. He was nearing seventy. After ingesting a large peg, he would settle into the extremely soft seat of the salon. When the slender fingers of pretty young girls, who chatted nineteen to a dozen in English, caressed his head and neck, Ulahannan Mappila considered the extra money charged as a worthy investment. There was an added thrill in enjoying all that attention without his wife's knowledge.

He had noticed the commotion in the neighbouring building the very first time. When he arrived after four months, the uproar had not lessened. During his third visit, Ulahannan observed that the chaos had only aggravated. After his haircut and a second peg, the gentleman decided that matters should be taken in hand.

Ulahannan Mappila marched to the Stock Exchange gate and called the watchman, who was strutting about in his smart uniform.

'What's their demand, tell me!'

The watchman stood confused for a moment. 'What do you mean, sir?'

Ulahannan Mappila kept a friendly hand on the watchman's shoulder.

'See, I've been noticing this hubbub for some time. Nobody to listen to the poor fellows, even after protesting for months at a stretch? What happened to the newspapers and political leaders of this place? What's their demand, tell me!'

The watchman surveyed Ulahannan Mappila from head to toe carefully. Okay, the old geezer was drunk out of his mind. No worries. The man was used to handling such cases daily.

The watchman grinned. 'Uncle, this is not a strike or protest.'

'I have been watching for almost eight months now. All this sloganeering … People are on a strike! Usually they arrive at some sort of a compromise by this time.'

The shouting at the Stock Exchange sounded like sloganeering to strangers.

Zacharia grinned to himself recollecting that Ulahannan Mappila's 'strike' was growing from strength to strength every day.

Nobody asked Zacharia why he was smiling. Here, laughter, sorrow, hubris, disappointment – all appeared on different faces, alternately. The one who smiled today, cried the next day. The one who wept today, would burst into laughter tomorrow. It was like the law of nature. Unchangeable.

'Fifteen and a half. Everyone is astounded.'

'Buyer for the twenty thousand shares?'

'Yes.'

When news spread that someone was out to buy the shares of Dhanwantari Herbal Products, the share prices bounced upwards quickly. Fourteen rupees was the market value for the share with a ten-rupee face value. In the morning's informal curb trading, buyers had appeared out of the blue. Naturally, the price rose. The trading had started even before the Stock Exchange started. Zacharia had given a 'buyer offer' to find out who was buying the shares and their motive behind doing so.

'Ready to sell twenty thousand shares of Dhanwantari!'

The steep climb of share prices stopped. When more shares came into the market, the share price stabilized. In fact, it reduced by fifty paisa.

Vinayan said: 'Bombay figures are yet to arrive. The price might go up again.'

Zacharia did not respond.

The bald man seated in front of Vinayan spoke: 'By the way, you didn't give me a definite answer. I refuse to budge from here without getting one. What sort of baloney is this?'

'I told you that I can't do anything about it, didn't I?' Vinayan replied.

'Good God! We are speaking about my lifelong earnings. I suffered a hell of a lot of bed bugs to make every paisa! I trusted you with the amount. It's the cost of my lifeblood, do you realize? You can't just give up so easily.'

Vinayan bit down his retort.

Zacharia asked: 'What's the matter?'

The bald man elucidated: 'Sir, I shall explain. You don't know me. Please settle the matter.'

The bald man was a government clerk who retired eight or nine months ago. He had started his career as a junior clerk and eventually turned into a senior one. After adjusting the loans taken for his daughter's wedding and building a house, there was not much left in the Provident Fund. Only four thousand rupees. He received a gratuity amount of forty thousand rupees. The man's lifetime earnings were close to only fifty thousand rupees in total.

His children were grown up and settled in towns. If the man had deposited the money in a bank, he could manage well with the regular interest. He also had two cows, a few coconut trees in his compound, and had cultivated some vegetables. At this point, confusion over which financial firm to invest his money in arose. The co-operative bank offered one and a half per cent more interest than government banks. The Unit Trust run by the government offered an additional two per cent returns. The bonds of certain government companies, which came out with full-page newspaper advertisements, offered more interest to the investor. The poor man became thoroughly confused.

There was a finance company near his house. Once upon a time, it was in the category of a 'blade company': a fly-by-night firm that promised exorbitant interest rates and cheated clients. When the nation's laws took such companies to task, the company's board changed. Their rate of returns lessened. Even so, if someone deposited money as a fixed deposit for three years, they would give him twenty-four per cent interest on the principal amount.

The old man remembered Vinayan at that juncture. He had known Vinayan's father Lambodaran master. He had been a beneficiary of the great man's generosity. The man was aware that Vinayan worked at the Stock Exchange. He approached Vinayan for expert advice.

It was the time when Vinayan had started portfolio management. The investor had a specific amount in hand. The broker would use his intelligence, prudence and experience to invest the money in shares, debentures or bonds. He would sell and buy at the appropriate time. The investor was not required to keep track of anything at all. He would get his returns in a timely manner. The success of the portfolio management was dependent on the broker's skill and luck.

The old man liked Vinayan's counsel.

He entrusted Vinayan with the fifty thousand rupees.

Vinayan invested five thousand rupees each in the shares of four companies. The rest of the thirty thousand he used to purchase the new shares introduced by five well-known companies in the market.

Eight months had gone by.

The bald man spoke: 'Sir, I gave fifty thousand rupees trusting his word. Eight months have gone by. What have I got in the meantime? See, a cheque of five hundred rupees!'

Zacharia said: 'Please don't get upset. Let me look into the matter.'

He analysed the problem.

Out of the four companies in each of which five thousand rupees had been invested, only three had declared temporary dividends. Two among those were yet to give the share certificates in the client's name. That was why the man had not received the dividends. The company that had issued his share certificate, had paid a dividend at ten per cent and sent him a cheque of five hundred rupees. The fourth company had converted the money to shares too. But they had not declared any dividends yet. There was no fluctuation in the share prices of these four companies. Consequently, there was no point in selling these shares at the moment.

Zacharia mollified the client. 'The four companies are doing well. The cost of the shares is likely to double in a year's time. There would be no loss.'

'Does that mean I survive on air till then?'

The Zacharia of old would have snapped in response. But now, he had mellowed down. Besides, why should one blame the old man? It was his lifetime savings. His didn't put his faith in the companies but in the share broker. The investor's strength lay in the broker's integrity and reliability.

Zacharia asked Vinayan: 'What about the thirty thousand?'

Vinayan said: 'Sir, I have paid the application fees for the new issues of five excellent companies. If the shares are allotted, the market value shall be thrice the investment. But I can't do anything, can I?'

Whenever companies started new ventures, or spent much money in expansion of operations, they issued new shares in the market. Owing to the government's generous trade policy, almost every month in the last few years, twenty or thirty new issues were appearing in the share market. A majority of these were highly successful companies. The investor had a plethora of choices before him.

The middle class had started accepting shares as an investment option only in the recent past. The share issues were in small lots allowing investments in thousand rupees, two thousand rupees and upwards. Along with the application, the applicant had to pay for a hundred shares with a face value of five rupees. If the shares were allotted, he was supposed to pay the remaining five rupees per share. A total of one hundred shares at one thousand rupees. The market value of these shares was about twenty-five rupees. Clearly, it was a good investment.

Companies preferred small investors. Owners of two hundred and three hundred shares. Capital owners who were faceless and numerous were scattered across India. They would never assemble to question the company. It was virtually impossible to get these shareholders together, to buy their voting shares. Usually, companies were started by an individual or a family. To oppose the owner, the stock owners should co-operate. That possibility was averted by creating innumerable small stakeholders. They were satisfied by regular dividends. Owing to that fact, companies resorted to countless tricks to attract small investors.

The old man said: 'I put thirty thousand rupees in five companies following Vinayan's advice. Eight months have gone by. I got a letter that hundred shares have been allotted in one company. The others are absolutely silent.'

The companies happily advertised that their initial offers were stupendous successes. They could only offer shares to one in fifteen that applied.

The customer griped:

'Sir, I don't understand one thing. I crosschecked everything before filling up the application forms. This boy from a reputed family is my broker. All the companies are big names in their fields. The directors of the companies are famous. There are also government representatives. It is the government's own bank that is accepting the money. I gave the money knowingly and trustingly. Maybe there are many applicants. But if they can't allot me shares, shouldn't they return my money? The form clearly mentions that in case the shares are not allotted to me, they shall return my money within forty-five days. Forget forty-five days, four months have gone by now! Where is my money? You may please tell me, sir.'

Most companies behaved deplorably: they retained the money received along with the application even after forty-five days. Can small-time investors drag a gigantic corporate to court for this egregious error? Could a small investor afford the legal fees? Of course, the company would promptly return the investor's money when the court notice reached them. Nobody dared to take on the corporates after incurring heavy legal costs.

Zacharia replied: 'You're mostly right, sir.'

'"Mostly right"? I visited State Bank yesterday. That is where I paid for the three companies' shares. SBI is our own bank, isn't it? They had put out a big advertisement that they would be managing the sale of these shares. I'm sure they received the commission for their work. I'm a fool to have trusted all of them! This is simply cheating. They are making idiots out of small investors. The manager told me that they have nothing to do with my predicament. He asked me to go to the court. How does that sound? Can a feeble investor like me drag the bank and the company to court to get justice…?'

Zacharia interrupted: 'Sir, there are rules for everything. But the common man might not be in a position to make it work. The Stock Exchange has the power to blacklist such companies. But who will bell the cat? If someone takes such a step…'

A relentless tolling of bells was heard then.

Vinayan checked his watch.

Twelve-thirty.

The uproar in the hall shifted to the top floor.

Zacharia got up.

The bald man asked: 'What did you say, sir?'

Zacharia smiled.

'If the Stock Exchange starts blacklisting companies that do not follow the rules, can you imagine the ramifications? Hardly any organization would be left out of that list.'

The old man stared at Zacharia. His eyes were brimming with abject helplessness.

Zacharia was familiar with the feeling of such powerlessness. In the olden days, when he was an active member of the Communist party, he had seen the same helplessness in the eyes of the poor farmers and villagers of the Travancore region. The manifestation of the heart's desolation.

28

The War Trumpets Blare

Mohandas sipped from the glass and laughed. 'I'm truly happy today. Whatever I wished happened.'

Ramesan gazed at the sand-filled boat floating on the Aluva river. The heat of the afternoon sun did not affect them due to the trees. The cool breeze blowing from the east was pleasant.

Water boiled with basil leaves, sugar and salt, with a few drops of lemon juice in it. Mohandas took another sip.

Ramesan sat silently.

Lonappan had bought murrels especially for him. He still acted as if Ramesan were a young boy.

Ramesan had not expected to visit this place.

Picketing and protests were planned in front of the Stock Exchange. His friends were all participating. Ramesan had differences of opinion with them. But he hesitated to cut all contact with them. Who was at fault?

Ramesan had never dreamt of such a sea change in his uncle when he asked whether he could return home. He was still struggling to handle his oscillating beliefs, his notions regarding the capitalist-bourgeois-proletariat, ideas cherished across decades, philosophies that were a hundred years old…

The arguments began at the dinner table every night without fail. But his awe and respect for Mohandas was growing day by day. His uncle had deep knowledge to speak confidently about Marxism. Ramesan often wondered whether the fire-spitting, revolutionary leader of his party cohorts had an iota of that proficiency.

Ramesan asked Mohandas directly about the matter. 'Ramesan, I have to understand Marxism because my livelihood depends on it. For your small-time leaders, a lot of noise and less know-how would suffice.

'Worker, owner, capital – even the preceptors could not admit that the differences between the three were merely a matter of interpretation, not mutually exclusive. That was the crux of the problem.

'When the theory of Marxism was being formulated, not many cars were around. Of course, no point in blaming them for not envisioning the petrol economy that transformed the world capital markets. The revolution of the computer chip followed. The world shrunk into a single entity. The information revolution garnered details of consumer goods and brought them to the customer, even in the deepest of forests.

'It's difficult to turn the greedy human mind away from its thirst for the latest comforts. So, worker–owner conundrums don't hold much water any more. The worker is the owner. Crores of common people own capital via the share markets. Conflict doesn't serve any purpose in such a world. There's no need for any confrontation.'

Today, while having breakfast, Ramesan asked: 'Are you off to the office or do you have some other plan?'

Mohandas extended the newspaper he was reading to his nephew. 'Here, take a look. *Times of India*. There's a two-column news article about how Ayurvedic companies are not using authentic herbs. There's a subtle reference to Dhanwantari Herbal Products and other south Indian firms.'

Ramesan asked: 'Isn't that the Ernakulam-based company? Who knows, might be true.'

Mohandas laughed. 'Come, we have to settle certain matters today. I'm not going to the office. Let's go to Aluva and think it out. This is the right time.'

Ramesan had visited the Aluva house six or seven years ago.

A vast, verdant compound, which almost looked like a wilderness. An old building inside the yard. The external façade was misleading but the interior boasted of every modern comfort. Two air-conditioned bedrooms, television, VCR, fridge, cooking range, state-of-the-art bathrooms, a balcony opening on to the riverfront, and a mini-bar that was always replenished.

The only connection the old house had with the external world was through Lonappan and the telephone. Lonappan slept near the phone. He never knew when his master would call or who would be his guests. Ramesan was aware that a number of his uncle's business acquaintances dropped in frequently. He also knew that Mohandas brought his favourite girls to that house.

Ramesan wandered around the lush compound. Everything seemed to be the same, including Lonappan, the evergreen Man Friday.

Lonappan was overjoyed about Ramesan's visit. He was hard at work in the kitchen from the morning.

During the journey from Ernakulam, nobody had spoken a word. Mohandas had driven the car himself.

'Just a moment's carelessness and that would be the end. When on earth will the traffic management get better?'

Buses, lorries, autorickshaws, scooters, cycles ... He had stopped the vehicle in front of the Edapally church. Mohandas had given Ramesan a silver coin.

'Go ahead, offer it in the holy receptacle.'

When he started the car again, Mohandas had been grave.

'I've learnt from experience. There's a deciding force, which is overarching and supreme. A force that decides the flow of fortune. Every action entails a faith, a prayer. The realization that, ultimately, we do not get to decide what happens to us.'

A log came floating through the river. Apparently, it had escaped being stolen by avaricious hands.

Mohandas asked: 'What are you contemplating so deeply?'

Ramesan smiled. 'Nothing. There's picketing going on in front of the Stock Exchange right now.'

'Are you missing it?'

'No.'

'Then, let's forget it.'

Mohandas gazed at the river for a few moments. Then he spoke. 'I want you to achieve something I could not. That's why we are here.'

Ramesan lifted his face eagerly.

Mohandas said: 'You can start working at the Stock Exchange if you wish.'

Ramesan grinned and shook his head to express his disinterest.

His uncle continued: 'I have one wish. See, I founded many establishments. Property, relationships, power, fame ... I have it all. I have achieved all that was once considered unthinkable for someone from our background. Kerala praises me as a very good businessman. But...'

'But?'

'These are mere trading firms. Commerce and trade. They are not manufacturing centres. I wanted to start a successful manufacturing unit here. I tried it twice or thrice.'

'I know.'

'Never got off the ground. Ramesan, you should run a full-fledged production unit and make it successful. My experience, capital, expertize ... all of that is at your command. I don't mean an enterprise focusing on services like hotels, schools, hospitals or a fleet of private buses. A manufacturing unit. What do you say?'

Ramesan did not react.

'I know it's difficult. Very difficult. Every government tries to bring in attractive industrial policies. How many incentives are in the offing! Anyone would be tempted to jump right in. However, without a fundamental attitudinal change, no industry will take root here. It's not in the policies or interest subventions or subsidies that a change is required, it's the human mindset that needs changing. The political parties and the common man should change their approach.'

Ramesan looked askance at his uncle.

Mohandas took another sip of the tulsi water.

'You don't get it, do you? Everybody implicitly believes that the owner of a factory or enterprise is someone who ruthlessly exploits others. Both the right and left are in total agreement over this fact! Naturally, the bureaucracy and the populace at large view the owner of the capital as a slave driver. They forget that an entrepreneur is not always a crorepati; he can also be a small-time owner, who purchases a small machine and starts a mill to grind wheat and rice. Even if he employs one worker, suddenly he turns into an exploiter in the eyes of all! Obviously, emotions run high against the evil man! It's not easy to break down the barricade of negativity. Even the public who contribute in creating the capital by buying shares, look at the industrialist as an exploitative figure.'

'You may be right.'

'Not "may be" right, definitely right. But I have a wish. A sort of challenge. Start an enterprise in Kerala and take it to the pinnacles of success. Why not? Let us demolish this attitudinal barricade. If you are with me, I'd like to give it a try.'

'Me?'

'Yes.'

'There are intriguing characters in your friends' circle, willing to get beaten up for their philosophy, right? You, too, belong to that category. But they have started eyeing money for elections and other purposes, have they not? You'll always be troubled by that truth. Why don't you try to create a successful venture instead?'

Both were unaware of Lonappan standing behind. He coughed discreetly. Mohandas turned to look.

'Is lunch ready?'

Lonappan nodded.

'We are coming. Serve the food.'

When Lonappan left, Mohandas got up.

'There's no need to start from scratch. I have planned it out. As a pilot, take over a sick company. Let us try running it. It will be both an experience and a challenge.'

Suddenly, Ramesan asked: 'Valiyacha, are you behind the news in *The Times of India*?'

Mohandas placed a hand on Ramesan's shoulder.

'Just wait for a month. You shall be running Dhanwantari Herbal Products. The foundation of our future establishments.'

Lonappan had prepared the murrell fish with plenty of spices. To accompany the rice, there was a delicious menu of aviyal, fried pearl spot, lemon pickle, curd and papad.

Even as they had their lunch, Mohandas was garrulous.

'The news has come out in the papers. The company prices will dip in two days' time. Another piece of news will be published then. A rebuttal from the company. Nobody will believe them, of course. The prices will fall further. I've arranged to buy as many shares as possible in the Madras Stock Exchange. After we purchase almost ten per cent of the shares, we shall try negotiating with the present management. Let's see if we can take control without any confrontation.'

'Will they agree?'

'Yes.'

Mohandas smiled.

'One needs a Vibheeshan to win any war. Even Sri Rama sought the help of Vibheeshan to defeat Ravan, didn't he? Our Vibheeshan is no less!'

'Who's that…?'

The telephone rang before Mohandas could reply. This telephone connection was under Lonappan's name. Very few people were privy to the number. Lonappan took the receiver and turned to Mohandas. 'From your office.'

Mohandas said: 'Tell them I'll call back.' He smiled. 'My assistant won't call unless there's a crisis. But I don't want to mess with the taste of Lonappan's curries.'

Mohandas, however, hurried with his lunch and called the office. Ramesan was watching him keenly.

After listening to his personal assistant, Mohandas turned to look at his nephew.

'I don't understand.'

'What?'

'Dhanwantari's share price has increased steeply in Madras.'

'Shouldn't it have fallen?'

'It's risen instead.'

A moment later, Mohandas said: 'Come on. Let's go to Ernakulam.'

29

The Investigations Begin

Finance Director Adiyodi had dropped by Mini Balachandran's office room to discuss the imminent meeting at the labour commissioner's office. He knew Mini since she was a child. Whenever he would go to their house to see Menon sir, little Mini would grin at him toothily.

'Uncle has come!'

Adiyodi would always have some surprise for the toddler. A few grapes, a guava, sweets … Mini would stretch out her tiny hand. When Adiyodi gestured that he had no gifts, her bright face would turn sad. Adiyodi would then spring a surprise and the little girl's face would light up again. The sweet milk-toothed grin would flash once more.

Little Mini had transformed into Mini Balachandran now. The managing director of Dhanwantari Herbal Products. Even so, the first memory that would rush into Adiyodi's mind was the baby grin. The delight at getting a few grapes.

Adiyodi spoke: 'The department has called three trade unions for the meeting. I was studying the charter of demands. We have objected to inviting the trade union that we haven't recognized formally. Most of the points in the agenda are about their demands.'

Mini was doodling on a pad.

Adiyodi's behaviour was typical. He would make it obvious that he did not want to disturb Mini with important issues. An overprotective style, as if she were a toddler, who would fall down if left to play alone in the yard. Strategic moves had been made against the company by some unknown people, threatening its very existence. But the finance director was absolutely clueless about it.

Mini often reflected that, in an institution, every individual could rise only to the level of their own potential. If they rose beyond that level, it proved harmful for the institution itself. She recollected reading something pertinent to this topic.

A few top Marwari companies never let any underperformer go. They would create some superfluous posts for them, with no responsibilities, higher salaries and perks. Their participation in the company's management would be a façade – just for the sake of it.

Mini considered that it was time she found some such post for Adiyodi.

Mini Balachandran did not discuss Matthews' offer or the alarming selling pattern of Dhanwantari's shares in the stock exchanges today.

'Uncle, it's better that you attend the labour commissioner meeting. I know you'll handle it well.'

Adiyodi became happy.

'I didn't want to disturb you. But you should be aware of it. Isn't it the most important matter regarding the company? Yes, I shall handle the trade unions by myself. Mini, you just don't worry about it.'

'Thank you, Uncle. A big relief indeed.'

Mini wondered for a few moments.

Should she discuss the issue with Adiyodi? He was sincere and honest, no doubt. The old man would always stand by her. But secrets were to be guarded as secrets. Sincerity alone would be of no help in combatting the crisis. One's moves should be cryptic and strategic. It was better that a select few people were taken into confidence.

Mini said: 'Uncle, two more things. This is the management consulting report prepared by Suryanarayanan. The report cost us one and a half lakh rupees. I read it last night. I'm not sure I understood it properly. Maybe you can give me your comments in a couple of days.'

Adiyodi took the report and replied: 'Let me see. Couple of days? Mini, there's the issue of audit and labour problems … I'm very busy. But this report's important and I have to study it myself. I'll get back to you after a week.'

'All right.'

Mini was relieved. Adiyodi would be busy gnawing at the report for a week or so. Good.

'What was the second thing?'

Mini asked: 'Is our share register updated?'

Usually, the practice was that the details of all the buyers and sellers of the company's shares were sent to the headquarters. There, they would crosscheck the signatures of the buyers with the records available with the company. If there was nothing legally amiss, the purchasers' names would be added to the register. Most of the trading in the Stock Exchange avoided this part. The reason was that most deals were speculative in nature. But a majority of the investors insisted on getting the shares registered in their names. The legal mandate was that the company should immediately heed their request. Usually, before the company's annual general body meeting, the share register would be frozen. The voting rights belonged to those who had bought shares until that day.

Adiyodi responded: 'There are possibly a few shares pending to be updated. I'll check.'

'No, you please concentrate on Suryanarayanan's report. Send me the share register. Let me take a quick look.'

'Sure.'

After Adiyodi left, Mini looked at her father's photograph, gazing at her from the wall opposite.

What would Acchan do during such a contingency? Wouldn't he fight back if it were a case of an aggressive takeover? Of course! There was only one way to defend oneself. Money. Fight money with money. One can make lakhs by selling the shares in hand. Use that money to buy more shares. But how long will the strategy continue? If the enemies don't retreat, the prices shall keep escalating. Till what level? Zacharia uncle had mentioned his Sardarji client's prophecy – that Dhanwantari's share prices would double in a fortnight's time. If there are buyers even then, the price will hit the skies. Would Acchan have adopted such a strategy? No, it's futile to second guess Acchan's move. My father's no longer alive. This is my time.

Mini closed her eyes.

I need only my father's blessings.

Mini called her personal assistant through the intercom.

'Prakashan, don't let anybody inside for some time. Don't connect any calls either. I have a headache. I'll take some rest.'

'Should I get some medicines?'

'No need. Is anyone waiting to meet me?'

'The doctor who visited our Nelliyampathy estate for research purposes is waiting to meet you. I shall ask him to come after half an hour.'

'Okay.'

Mini picked up the receiver of the direct line.

Matthews' number.

He had apparently gone out.

'Kindly ask him to call me immediately when he returns.'

She dialled the next number.

The city reporter of a prominent newspaper.

She muffled the sound of her voice by placing a handkerchief over the speaker of the phone and spoke gruffly:

'You'll get an interesting story at the Stock Exchange today. A takeover bid by a north Indian company, trying to swallow a local firm. A coordinated attack from all the stock exchanges across the country. Some rich men from Kerala are also involved in the deal. Try to sniff out the details. It will be hot news. It's the first time such a bold move is being made.'

The reporter asked about her identity.

'Why look a gift horse in the mouth?'

Mini tried another number.

In a few minutes, reporters from three top newspapers rushed to the Stock Exchange.

Next move.

Mini Balachandran opened her diary and traced the number.

When the person she was expecting took the call, she asked: 'This is Mrs Balachandran. Hope you remember me. I'd met you once in Delhi.'

The friend remembered. He had come to Kochi on a transfer just a year ago. He had been a close friend of Mini's husband. They had undertaken the foundation course at Mussoorie Academy together.

After leaving Mini in Cochin to manage the company's affairs and before boarding the flight, her husband Balachandran had given her a piece of advice.

'Just ring him up during any emergency. Don't worry that he's a cop! He'll be a friend in need.'

Mini had had no reason to call the top police officer until now.

Now the friend said: 'Balan keeps in touch. At first, I expected a call from you too. But I found out that you were handling everything by yourself. Both of us felt good about it.'

'But I need some help now.'

'Please tell me.'

'I need to be updated about the moves of four people over the next four days. Who are they talking to? Which numbers are they calling? Sounds like a detective novel. Is it possible?'

The friend did not ask for any justification.

'Let me call you back in fifteen minutes.'

Mini wrote down the names on a pad:

> Asokan, marketing director
> Adiyodi, finance director
> Zacharia, broker
> Matthews, investor

Right, that was all as of now.

She checked her watch.

Mini called Prakashan.

'Send the doctor in.'

The doctor was young. A lanky young man with a beard. With a loose bag on his shoulder, he could have passed for a revolutionary.

The doctor gave Mini a four-page report in Malayalam about his research into the herbs at the Nelliyampathy estate. He kept on gabbling. Mini's mind was elsewhere.

'I'll go through the report,' she assured the doctor.

Matthews' call arrived as she was browsing through the report.

Mini said: 'Matthews, we decided to discuss your offer after three days, right? Why can't we make it earlier?'

'What?'

'I have a few more offers. Let's meet tomorrow at five in the evening.'

'I'm not sure if Aniyan Raja can make it so quickly.'

'I'm not insisting. I shall wait for you only till 5 p.m. tomorrow. Okay?'

Mini put the receiver down without waiting for Matthews' response. The telephone rang immediately. It was the friend.

'Tell me the names and details.'

Mini read out the names and all the details she had with her.

'Yes, I want them tracked for the next four days. Kindly let me know about the expenses involved. I will ensure the payment's by cash.'

The friend paused and asked after a moment.

'Can I tell Balan when he calls?'

'Of course.'

The friend laughed.

'Don't worry. The first update shall be given at eleven at night. I will call you personally with the information. Is that fine?'

'Thank you.'

Mini gazed at her father's photograph after disconnecting the call. The smile on his face was serene and steady.

Suddenly she remembered that Adiyodi had not sent her the share register yet. It had been more than an hour now.

Mini called him over the intercom.

'Uncle, where is the share register?'

Adiyodi sounded perturbed.

'I've been searching for it for the last one hour. It's gone missing. There is one more almirah which is locked. The store clerk has the key. He's on leave today.'

'How would a store clerk have custody of the company's share register, Uncle? Check once more. Didn't the secretary entrust you with all the keys when he went on leave?'

'Sorry, Mini. I'm on it.'

A smile blossomed on Mini's lips inadvertently.

30

Half an Hour's Windfall

Suryanarayanan tapped on the computer keyboard.

Dhanwantari Herbal Products ... Equity ... Letters and numbers filled the screen.

He stared at the names and the figures. An expletive emerged from him unknowingly. Nobody heard the abuse. The room was soundproof.

Tche! He started cursing himself. There was sufficient reason for that.

Suryanarayanan was the leading management consultant in Kochi. Among his major tasks were making project reports for new joint stock companies and enterprises, arranging for finances from banks and government financial corporations, analysing reasons for overspending in firms and getting to the roots of inefficiency.

Suryanarayanan lived in the city's richest housing colony. The office was located in his house. There were several computers and a fax machine to get in touch with a Bombay-based consultancy company. Suryanarayanan had once been a top banker and had fallen in love with computers while working. The first thing he did while starting the management consultancy services following retirement was procure the latest computer models.

Suryanarayanan delighted in keeping himself updated about computer systems. Any information that he felt was invaluable for the future would be immediately keyed in.

He would often say: 'Knowledge is the most vital factor in my line of business. Information about companies, products, management. Knowledge is money.'

Consequently, Suryanarayanan kept every bit of information a secret. One should also have the ability to use the knowledge appropriately. Only then will it transform into money.

Today was a good day.

Zacharia's manservant Prabhu had come with a cheque of seven thousand five hundred rupees. Zacharia needed some information about Ayurvedic companies. Suryanarayanan sent a fax to Bombay since the computer-call did not connect. He was asked to wait till afternoon. Suryanarayanan gave Prabhu the details of Kerala's top five Ayurvedic companies.

Computers were like humans. They were prone to virus attacks. If the virus was not routed, the data would get corrupted. Zacharia's servant had arrived while Suryanarayanan was readying some defence strategies against a possible virus attack.

After some time, Matthews came to meet Suryanarayanan.

He had brought along a bank draft of fifty thousand in Suryanarayanan's name. There was also another draft of ten lakhs, made in the name of a benami company, meant for the lender willing to loan two crores.

Suryanarayanan made photocopies of the drafts.

'I hardly put such stuff in my computer. Got to destroy them after the purpose is served.'

Matthews seemed rather nervous.

Suryanarayanan made a receipt for the agreement with *Jal-Kiran*, showing the ten lakhs as an advance for the two-crore loan. The power of attorney of the benami company was in Suryanarayanan's name.

'The money is ready for you, starting today. Whatever shares you buy, send us the documentary record as security. For the final settlement, we need money. Is it understood?'

'Yes.'

Matthews left.

In half an hour, Suryanarayanan connected to Bombay via a computer-call. *The virus had not attacked the system, thank god!*

Suddenly it struck him: Were Zacharia and Matthews after the same goal? They were in opposite teams, that was for sure.

Suryanarayanan asked sharply: 'Tell me, did trading happen for an Ayurvedic company in Dalal Street today? Something that hasn't happened before?'

It was twelve in the afternoon. The Bombay Stock Exchange had just started working. He received the reply in five minutes.

'There are buyers for Dhanwantari Herbals.'

'Thanks.'

Suryanarayanan tapped the keyboard. The figures pirouetted in front of his eyes.

Dhanwantari Herbal Products. Managing Director – Mini Balachandran. Fifteen per cent of shares in the Family Trust, fifteen with the MD. He scanned the numbers on the balance sheet.

Cash reserve – less than average. The working capital ratio did not look so good either. The assets were few. The figures were solid. Estates, buildings, plots in different cities.

Broker advisor – P.T. Zacharia.

Suryanarayan grinned. *Ah, is that the way the wind blows?*

Someone was hurriedly purchasing the shares of Dhanwantari Herbal Products. The market value of the share price was rather low. The value of the company's assets was shown to be very low in the balance sheet.

There was something intriguing about the whole escapade. Who was behind the buying spree? Matthews and his invisible team?

Suryanarayanan dithered for a moment. Should he inform Zacharia that Matthews's coterie was about to bring two crores into the stock market?

No.

Zacharia had given him exactly seven thousand five hundred rupees. He should be provided with services in accordance with that amount. Sincerity should always be within limits. Else, it entails losses.

Suryanarayanan dialled a number. When the call got connected, he spoke:

'Ambi, buy ten thousand shares of Dhanwantari Herbal Products immediately. Don't worry about the price. Buy them quickly, okay?'

Of course, there was nothing wrong in making some good money with his inside knowledge, was there? Anyway, there were a few players buying Dhanwantari's shares intentionally. The share prices would go up for sure. One could sell the ten thousand shares comfortably tomorrow or the day after. A neat profit of three or four rupees per share. In a few days, a profit of thirty or forty thousand rupees. One should not be greedy. Ten thousand shares would do for now.

The Bombay line became markedly active.

The computer screen displayed the details of India's top ten Ayurvedic companies. Suryanarayanan carefully took printouts of each. Quickly glanced through them.

All were huge companies. Any of them could easily swallow a small player like Dhanwantari. Poor Zacharia was going to struggle today, trying to decipher the predator among them. The real enemy was very close. By the time Zacharia realized the truth, the company would be under the control of Matthews and his allies.

It was all God's will.

Suryanarayanan put the reports inside an envelope and called Zacharia's office. He asked Prabhu to collect it.

Ambi's call arrived.

'I bought the shares, Uncle.'

'What's the price?'

'Five thousand for sixteen rupees. Two thousand for sixteen and a half. Three thousand for seventeen.'

'Okay.'

After a moment's pause, Suryanarayanan said: 'The price will shoot above twenty tomorrow. Sell them all.'

'As you say, Uncle.'

Suddenly, Suryanarayanan had a doubt. 'Did you buy some Dhanwantari shares for yourself?'

'Three thousand.'

'Good, but not more.'

'All right, Uncle.'

Suryanarayanan replaced the receiver in the cradle.

A real fine day. Everything had turned to gold upon a mere touch.

Seven thousand five hundred as commission from Zacharia in the morning. Fifty thousand from Matthews. Another forty thousand from Dhanwantari, soon! One lakh rupees in a day. Not bad. Now, he could have some food, indulge in a siesta. But as he sat down for lunch, Suryanarayanan got a call from Matthews.

'Sir!'

'Yes, what's the matter?'

'Can we get the money today itself?'

'Today?'

'Yes.'

'Sure.'

'Thank you.'

Suryanarayanan reflected for a moment and pressed his handphone. Ambi's assistant in the Stock Exchange answered the call.

'Ambi sir is on the floor. The trading's begun.'

'Ask him to get in touch, very quickly.'

As he was relishing rasam, Ambi's call arrived.

'Uncle, what's up?'

'Ambi, Dhanwantari's price is going to rise in half an hour. Sell all the shares when it crosses twenty. Don't wait!'

'Okay, Uncle.'

'You should sell yours too.'

'As you say, Uncle.'

Suryanarayanan poured rasam into his cupped right hand and slurped it.

No greed at all. Tomorrow, the share price might reach twenty-five. Thirty, perhaps. But there was the Almighty above, watching everything. Nobody should forget that.

The present profits were good enough. Forty thousand in half an hour. One should feel contented.

'Guruvayurappa, protect us all!'

Suryanarayanan's doctor had forbidden him from enjoying curd.

Now he wished to rest.

Suryanarayanan settled into his armchair comfortably with *The Times of India*.

31

The Trading Ring

The trading ring of the Stock Exchange was on the third floor. Shares could be sold and bought only in that space.

The Kochi Stock Exchange traded from half past twelve till a half past two in the afternoon.

There was the drawn out trill of the bell at twelve-thirty sharp. It caused a ferment among the thronging hordes, standing in the corridors and cubicles, stretching their necks towards the television screens affixed on the walls. The major stock exchanges in Bombay, Delhi, Calcutta, Madras and Ahmedabad worked between twelve and two. During the trading hours, the latest share prices of the stocks would be displayed on the TV screens. The figures helped to gauge the direction of the stock prices by the time official trading began here.

Zacharia would say:

'The Marwaris and Gujaratis have a deep bond with the share market! Most of their great-grandfathers were stockbrokers. They have been engaging in the share business over many generations. In Bombay, Ahmedabad and Calcutta, the important brokers are either Gujaratis or Marwaris. The situation is different in Kerala.

Here, engineers, doctors, professors, navy officers are all attracted to this new gold mine. They yell themselves hoarse to grab their bit of the profits! These people have no formal training in share markets. The best help provided to newbie traders was fixing the trading time at Kochi Stock Exchange to twelve-thirty. It was safer to trade after observing the trends of shares at the stock exchanges in Bombay and other places.'

The narrow staircase leading up to the third floor was overflowing. The watchman was diligently checking the identity card of each person.

Only two thousand-odd people were allowed inside the trading ring. Nearly four hundred and seventy members and the authorized assistants – four – allotted to each. In case a broker failed to submit the trading figures and associated money on time, they would be banned from trading further, until the dues were settled. The temporary embargo also applied to the authorized assistants. The watchman would verify the identity of such members and colleagues against a special list in his hand.

The watchman grinned upon seeing Zacharia.

By the time he reached the top floor, the faces and sounds had assumed the guise of strangers. Nobody greeted anyone. Nearly two thousand people, mostly young men and women, their eyes glittering with intensity, like those of a rapacious gambler. Their gaze flitted alternately between the large television screen fixed high at a corner in the vast hall and the computer screens and blackboards behind the counters on either side. Sometimes the eyes searched for other eyes in the crowd. In a matter of moments, one could amass thousands or even lakhs. Or lose the same. Everyone smelled equally of hope and despair.

Pictures of various deities, associated with different religions, hanging on the pillars in the middle of the hall, were silent witnesses to the intriguing ambience of joy and sorrow.

Behind the long tables on either side of the hall were counters. Every counter had a few letters from the English alphabet marked on it. A, B, C for the first counter, D, E, F for the second, and so on. After selling or buying shares of any company whose name started with the letters A, B and C, the brokers or their assistants would submit the papers at the relevant counter. The company name, number of shares sold, and the agreed price would be written on the blackboard. The details of the brokers and other nitty-gritty were fed into the computer immediately. That was how information about the shares could be passed around easily.

Usually, crowds would throng the counters where speculative trade of certain companies would be carrying on at full throttle. There was a huge rush before Reliance, TISCO and Apollo Tyres. Zacharia did not pay much attention to the crowds there. He stood near the pillar on which pictures of the goddess of the Chottanikkara Devi temple, the Blessed Mother of Velankanni Church and the deity of Sivakasi were displayed. He gazed at the counter dealing with D, E, F.

The official figures of curb trading and line trading would emerge soon.

Sounds danced around Zacharia.

'Reliance, Buyer.'

'Forty-five.'

'BPL Sanyo.'

'Chougule Tea.'

'Seller, Seller.'

'Grapco Granites.'

'Forty. Buyer.'

'Forty-two, forty-two!'

Suddenly a name rose, unheard before in the trading ring.

'Dhanwantari Herbal.'

'Buyer, Buyer.'

Zacharia watched alertly. The face seemed familiar.

The man faced him and said: 'Dhanwantari, Buyer. Fifteen, fifteen.'

Zacharia turned towards counter D, E, F.

The blackboard displayed the name.

Dhanwantari. Thousand shares. Fifteen rupees.

Who had bought them?

Zacharia made his way through the crowd towards the counter.

It was Savitry. Zacharia was acquainted with the smart young lady, her hair in two loose braids, who ran about the trading ring, speaking pidgin Malayalam, with a mixture of English and Hindi. He knew that she was a prominent broker who did line business with the Bombay Stock Exchange.

Yes, Savitry was actively buying Dhanwantari's shares for some Bombay firm. Or was she indulging in speculation, after being informed about a potential buying spree in Bombay? If she purchased at fifteen today and sold after four or five days at twenty, how much profit would she make? If one bought ten thousand shares, maybe it would be a deal worth fifty thousand rupees. Was that the plan?

Those who had done curb trading were submitting the documents according to their verbal agreements.

The Dhanwantari share prices were going up.

Zacharia looked at the blackboard.

> Thousand shares. Fifteen.
> Five hundred. Fifteen and a half rupees.
> Thousand. Fifteen and a half rupees.

Zacharia approached the television screen displaying the share prices at the Bombay Stock Exchange.

There had been a rumour that the government might de-control steel products, and hence the shares of TISCO were fluctuating wildly, doing some interesting dance steps, right from the morning.

In the turn of events when crores of rupees were at stake, expecting news about a small company like Dhanwantari seemed ridiculous. Even then, Zacharia waited.

Small letters appeared on the screen. Hard to read.

Zacharia checked if Vinayan was around.

He had to buy a thousand shares of Dhanwantari for Tarlok Singh. The man had paid him the margin money of three thousand rupees. He had not specified any particular price at which Zacharia should buy. Just hinted that the price was fourteen rupees at the Bombay Stock Exchange yesterday. Venus Tyres was at fifty-three rupees now. He had wanted to sell three hundred of his shares.

Zacharia went to the counter with the letters U, V, W.

The blackboard showed that someone had bought Venus shares at fifty-four and a half rupees just a little while ago.

Zacharia shouted: 'Venus. Fifty-four fifty. Fifty-four fifty. Seller.'

Three or four people surrounded him immediately.

One minute.

An agreement was made to sell three hundred shares of Venus Tyres at fifty-four and a half rupees. By the time Zacharia returned after submitting the paper at the counter, the price of Dhanwantari's shares had escalated to sixteen rupees.

Zacharia paused for a moment.

A broker's sincerity and integrity formed the foundation of a healthy stock market. The share prices went up and down during the official trading hours at the Stock Exchange – from twelve-thirty to two-thirty. The price at which one person bought a share would be different from the price at which another bought that share. Newspapers published the final rate of the shares during the previous day's trading. Even if many people dealt in a particular share or the rates changed multiple times, the common man got to know only the final rate of a day.

Imagine that Zacharia purchased the shares of Dhanwantari at sixteen, and the closing rate at two-thirty became twenty. Now, if Zacharia told Tarlok Singh that he had purchased the Dhanwantari shares at twenty rupees, he had no option but to believe what his broker said. If he wished to ferret out the truth, Tarlok Singh would have to write to the Stock Exchange. If the broker wasn't honest, the investor would end up in deep trouble. The broker had to merely submit documents to the Exchange tantamount to him purchasing shares at sixteen in some other client's name, and the rest in the Sardarji's name, at a price of twenty. Nobody could raise a finger in such a case.

Generally, everybody trusted their broker. An odd black sheep among the brokers might trick the investor, taking advantage of his naivety, and make a quick buck. The broker could always charge a lower commission and befool the client. Typically, no broker would do such a thing. Zacharia had never even dreamt of such a situation.

He bought a thousand shares of Dhanwantari for his client. The price rose to sixteen and a half rupees.

The ruckus inside the trading ring increased every moment. The shares of four companies were being traded actively. In the case of TISCO and Reliance, there was a lot of speculation going on. A news report about a potential foreign investment in a local company caused its shares to shoot up. The fourth was Dhanwantari Herbal Products.

Zacharia slipped outside the hall to the balcony for a quick smoke. Vinayan approached him.

'I was searching for you everywhere.'

'Why?'

'Dhanwantari is trading in Bombay and Ahmedabad. It's reached eighteen in Madras.'

'Here?'

Vinayan spoke softly: 'I have a niggling doubt. You know my friend Matthews, don't you?'

'Yes.'

'Matthews's broker is chasing Dhanwantari in a big way.'

'What do you mean, "in a big way"?'

'Very big way.'

Zacharia stared at Vinayan.

'But that's not possible.'

'I have no idea. He has already purchased twenty thousand shares.'

Zacharia was silent for a while. He could see the newly planted coconut sapling from his vantage point on the balcony. The water that nourished it some time ago, had dried up. The watchman took a break and sat on the stub of the hacked coconut tree as the sun's glare moved away from it.

Zacharia spoke: 'Let's sell Dhanwantari shares in lots of thousand or two thousand. Twenty thousand, thirty ... fifty thousand. We'll do it after the share prices cross twenty rupees. The moment the prices start dropping, we should stop selling. We should try to raise the price till twenty-five. Let's see.'

Vinayan said: 'Going by the present trend, it'll reach twenty-five.'

'But be cautious. Sell only in small lots.'

'What about Madras?'

'Same offer in Madras too. Try an STD call and ensure the plan works.'

There were brokers who worked in different stock exchanges, kept in touch with one another. A broker in Cochin could conduct business in Delhi, Bombay or Madras. They amassed thousands due to small fluctuations in prices. This was commonly referred to as 'line business', where the broker charged a comparatively small commission.

Vinayan laid out his offer at the Madras Stock Exchange too, in a matter of minutes.

Willing to sell Dhanwantari shares in small lots.

The number of buyers was astoundingly large. The price of Dhanwantari shares escalated fast.

By the time trading stopped at the Cochin Stock Exchange, Dhanwantari shares with a face value of ten rupees had a market price of twenty-four rupees.

Twenty-three and a half in Madras.

Twenty-three in Bombay.

Twenty-three and a half in Calcutta.

Twenty-three in Delhi.

Twenty-three and a half in Ahmedabad.

Zacharia smiled to himself as he climbed down the steps.

Suryanarayanan's report about the north Indian companies must have reached his office. Did he need it now?

~

Zacharia went to his cubicle. Avarachan came to sit beside him, as if he had sniffed out his presence.

Avarachan took out a betel leaf to prepare a paan mixture. Lowering his voice, he spoke: 'Just tell me the amount you need.'

Zacharia laughed.

Avarachan was a broker, long associated with the Stock Exchange. Currently, he had stopped trading shares. Just one job. Financier. He would lend money to speculative traders.

'How much do you need?'

Zacharia replied: 'I'll answer tomorrow.'

'Sure, sure.' Avarachan raised his left hand and showed four fingers.

Zacharia understood perfectly. Amount of four crores ready.

Zacharia grinned.

'Okay.'

32

Breadcrumbs in the Street

It was three in the afternoon.

The trading ring, where shares were bought and sold, became desolate like a festival ground after the display of fireworks. The television screen and the computers closed their eyes. A few people stuck around, as if looking for a lost dream. The officials behind the counters were busy settling the accounts of the day's trade: preparing files, entering data into the computers, taking printouts, updating their financial records. The uproar started on the lower floor again.

There was only one subject that was being discussed in the brokers' cubicles, corridors, canteen and every other sundry place.

The shares of Dhanwantari Herbal Products.

The brokers, their assistants, the thousands who tried their luck in curb trading without entering the trading ring: all of them were chatting about the same matter. There had never been a day like today in the history of the Cochin Stock Exchange. A low-profile local company, which had been unnoticed before, had its share prices climbing to twice the original value in a couple of hours! Not only that, the shares had become a favourite in almost all of India's prominent stock exchanges too. Those two hours had been every speculative trader's dream come true. Now, what?

Only thirty-odd people had bought or sold Dhanwantari's shares in the last few hours. They were not alone in worrying about tomorrow. Most of the speculators were regretful of having missed out on purchasing Dhanwantari's shares in the morning. Also, many were cursing themselves on not taking the risk of selling the shares as the prices went ballistic.

Will the prices rise or fall tomorrow?

What is the situation in Bombay? Madras?

Every day, a broker created an imaginary balance sheet of his own activities. The bold amongst them shrugged off the losses of the previous day and never carried them over to the day's accounts. Most visited the bar next door. They would swig a couple of pegs and return. One could indulge in some curb trading after verifying the share prices in Bombay and Madras. Some believed that fortune hunting should never be postponed for the next day.

The young journalist seated in Zacharia's cubicle raised a question:

'Do you know the reason behind the never-seen-before trading that we witnessed today? You're known to be closely associated with Dhanwantari Herbal Products. Am I right?'

'You're right.'

Zacharia elucidated:

'Most of those who bought and sold the shares today were clueless about what sort of a company Dhanwantari is, what it manufactures, or even about its management. They are least interested in any of these aspects. None of them has any share certificates at hand even. But the pattern will repeat itself tomorrow. More people shall trade in Dhanwantari's shares.

'Somebody has set out to acquire this company. I have no idea if the protagonist is based out of Bombay, Delhi or Cochin. Anyway, that move has triggered a new life in the share market. Many, lost in deep slumber, have been jolted awake. This fresh lease of life might last for a fortnight or even a month. Nobody cares about the takeover of the company. Money is the only stake here.'

The young man started noting down Zacharia's observations. They ignored the shouts emerging from nearby cubicles. Zacharia's phone became active in between. Prabhu informed him about receiving Suryanarayanan's second report.

Zacharia replaced the receiver.

'Just take a look around. The thirst for money! Every eye, ear and mind happens to be focused only on money. The greed for money is very natural to a human being. No point in denying it. Many journalists try their hands at the Stock Exchange, don't they?'

'Yes.'

Zacharia grinned.

'One journalist wrote about the share market some time back. It was more or less a factual report. Somehow, the writer appeared to have an axe to grind against share brokers. He alleged that most were cheating their clients. Maybe he's right. Which sector is free from cheating? Several people threw a fit after reading the missive. But I felt amused. Do you know why? The cost of the membership card went up suddenly after the article was published!'

'What do you mean?'

'We have around four hundred and seventy members in this Stock Exchange. They have the sole right to conduct the trading of shares. Most have acquired the membership after paying seventeen thousand rupees as deposit. There are various reasons behind limiting the number of stockbrokers. Suffice it to say that someone should give up his or her membership for a new member to join. Forget the seventeen thousand rupees of yore. Today, apart from the Stock Exchange deposit, unless ten lakhs are paid, no broker will sell his membership card. But within days of the article getting published, the price climbed to sixteen lakhs! A difference of six lakhs in a single stroke.'

'Why?'

'Like I mentioned, the report had alleged that most stockbrokers were cheating customers in various ways. Maybe the public realized that there was much scope for double-dealing in this area. The prices went up overnight.'

Both of them laughed.

Zacharia said: 'What happened today, the trading of Dhanwantari shares, is a rare phenomenon in the Cochin Stock Exchange. The situation poses a challenge for the brokers and traders regardless of who the real player behind the game is. A bright opportunity for those who want to rake in lakhs overnight. Or lose terribly too.'

Zacharia retrieved a betel leaf from a drawer, carefully removed the veins and started applying lime paste on it.

'Every fortune-seeker who ventures into the arena is fully aware of the share market. They are conversant with financial reports, documents, theories. But nobody can make lakhs from abstract concepts. All sorts of people are found here: students, engineers, lawyers, artistes, politicians, government servants, soldiers, teachers, housewives. Many MBAs and CAs. However, education, knowledge, circumstances and notions do not hold much significance here. One needs a system, a discipline. Patience.

'One target that can be felled in a single bout. One victim. One hit. One game. Not more. So, patience is the most relevant factor. Supposing you fail in that single attempt, do not give up. Face it courageously, openly. Do not sob over your losses. Wait for the next chance. You shall not fail in all the rounds; neither will you ace it every time. This is a brawl over crumbs of bread in the street.

'There is no friend in this game. Everyone is a rival. Even your closest friend is your enemy. Today was such a day. An opportunity for the seeker. Your luck might turn any moment. It is war, over Dhanwantari's shares.'

The journalist smiled.

'May I report what I have heard?'

'Of course! Even the one who won today is preparing for tomorrow's battle. Nobody has the luxury of celebrating today's winnings. The anxiety about tomorrow has already got him in its clutches.'

'Will the share prices of Dhanwantari rise or fall tomorrow?'

Zacharia got up.

'If I had such divine prophetic powers, I would have been a crorepati by now.'

Near the staircase, the young man probed yet again: 'Do you know who's behind the takeover move?'

Zacharia stopped momentarily. Suddenly, he asked: 'Do you come here every day?'

'No.'

'How come you're at the Stock Exchange today? Is it a coincidence?'

'No, someone gave us a call. Gave a tipoff that one would get a juicy story during the trading hours at the Stock Exchange today.'

'Who was the caller?'

'Did not reveal their identity. Not just us, two other newspapers were informed. They are here too.'

Zacharia spoke: 'It's a secret, but I'll speak my mind. In my opinion, a very famous Ayurvedic medicine manufacturing company based in Lucknow is behind this takeover bid. If they succeed, it will be a setback for us Keralites. Dhanwantari Herbal produces medicines following the Kerala Ayurvedic legacy. If that changes, it'll be an irreparable loss to all of us.'

'I can report this, right?'

'Sure. I want you to be specific for the sake of our state and Ayurveda.'

~

Back in Zacharia's office, a sheaf of computer printouts was awaiting him. Suryanarayanan's report. The business details of prominent north Indian Ayurvedic companies.

They did not seem so relevant at this juncture. Though the enemy was unidentified, one had had a glimpse of their power. What then was Matthews' role in the melee? Was he the agent of the north Indian company? Most likely not. Did that mean that the enemy was closer home? Somebody in Kerala trying to take over Dhanwantari Herbals?

Zacharia called Mini.

The call was made straight to her personal number. As soon as she picked up, Zacharia spoke:

'Did you hear about it, Mini? It was utter pandemonium at the share market today. Everyone was chanting Dhanwantari, Dhanwantari...'

'Uncle...?'

'Do you know where the share prices reached today? Closing was twenty-four. The north Indians are playing with sackfuls of cash, I presume.'

'What shall we do, Uncle?'

Zacharia was silent for a while. Then he shook himself out of the reverie. This was no little girl, flitting about like a butterfly, perching on one's lap. Mini was the owner of the company. A strong and powerful personality. She was intelligent, and fully aware of her capability.

Zacharia said: 'Mini, I'm your uncle. But that's a personal matter. I'm also the official stockbroker of your company, isn't it?'

'Yes, of course! What happened?'

'No, I'm very serious. I'm obliged to merely offer you advice. The final decision is yours to make.'

Mini paused for a moment before acknowledging what Zacharia said.

'Yes, I understand.'

'Okay, then I'll proceed. It's not exactly a do or die situation. The share prices will climb up tomorrow too. How far will the Bombay guys go? There has to be a limit. By the way, those journalists that you sent to the Stock Exchange, they'll come out with some interesting reports tomorrow. The speculators shall further raise the price of our shares.'

'How did you make out that I was behind that?'

'Well, I would have been disappointed if you hadn't done it.'

Zacharia laughed.

'Let me assess the situation once again. I shall give you my counsel by six o'clock.'

'Call me home by seven. I have a meeting at the Chamber of Commerce at six o'clock. It will be seven by the time I return.'

Before he put the phone down, Zacharia asked: 'Mini, do you know someone called Matthews?'

Mini laughed.

'That's Aniyan Raja's agent.'

Zacharia replaced the telephone receiver.

Good. It should be worthwhile to inform the journalists that Aniyan Raja was also present in the arena. Once the news was published, it would be a universe of avarice all around.

How far would the share prices rise?

Thirty, forty, fifty?

Until everyone ran off, scared out of their wits.

33

The Weight of Dreams

Shankaran Kutty was perturbed.

The devotion to his sweetheart was on one side of his warring heart. In a mere two hours' time, the share prices of Dhanwantari had risen by nine rupees! The other side of his heart was heckling him about the huge loss incurred. And who had caused it? His sweetheart.

Naturally, it was a situation where every lover would lose their footing.

Savitry had asked him whether he had Dhanwantari's shares to sell, precisely at the moment when he was about to profess his love. Shankaran Kutty knew that Savitry was in touch with the Bombay Stock Exchange. She had been tipped off well in time. That was why she had agreed to buy shares of Dhanwantari early in the morning, offering an additional one rupee to the last trading price yesterday.

Love was indeed blind!

Shankaran Kutty was overcome with self-recrimination. One should have wondered, using the broker's intelligence, why Savitry was hell bent on buying Dhanwantari shares. Well, he had not and was suffering the consequence.

They had made a verbal agreement to sell five thousand shares at fifteen rupees. He had also submitted the documents for transferring two thousand shares at the counter immediately. Now the closing rate was twenty-four rupees!

'Dear Ettumanoorappa!' Shankaran Kutty hailed the Lord of the Ettumanoor temple fervently.

Surely, Savitry had anticipated the escalation in the price. Yet she had made the contract early morning, without batting an eyelid. Lightning shot through Shankaran Kutty's ruminations. Was it intelligent to plan a lifetime with a girl who was so secretive?

Forty thousand rupees! His innards burned upon recollecting the loss.

There was a fortnight's period for exchanging the share certificates. The second Friday. The price should decline before that. Surely it would slump? The Lord of Ettumanoor would not let go of him. He would not cast his devotee into an abyss of frustration. Share prices were as likely to tumble as they were wont to zoom.

Shankaran Kutty ignored the ruckus of the cubicles and prayed to the deity of the Ettumanoor temple.

'Mister Shankaran Kutty, are you sleeping?'

Shankaran Kutty almost jumped out of his skin. He rubbed his eyes.

Savitry. She stood smiling in front of him. Whenever she smiled, dimples flashed on her cheeks. And her eyes flickered luminously.

A tremor seized hold of Shankaran Kutty. It was as if he had stepped on a live wire. Shankaran Kutty shut his eyes with great will power. Then he said: 'Miss Savitry! Do you know the closing price of Dhanwantari Herbals today?'

'Yes.'

Savitry murmured: 'That's why I have to come to see you, Mister Shankaran Kutty.'

'Hmm?'

Shankaran Kutty opened his eyes. The dimples were not visible any more. No smile played on Savitry's lips. Her eyes were still. Shankaran Kutty sighed. 'Miss Savitry! You shouldn't have done that to me. You got the news from Bombay. Of course, you shall earn the line-business commission too. No loss for you. But what about me? The share price increased by nine rupees today. You knowingly pushed me into the trap, Savitry. You know that I don't do speculative trading. Forty thousand rupees! Just imagine. Never did I expect that you'd behave like that.'

Shankaran Kutty was close to tears. There was a catch in his voice. He stared at Savitry.

One moment. The smile, dimples, dancing eyes … those were on full display.

Shankaran Kutty closed his eyes again.

Savitry spoke:

'Can you please hear me out for a second?'

The cubicles and corridors were overflowing with people. There were almost three thousand men and women prattling away in the not-so-big hall on the second floor. The postmortem exercise of the gains and losses of the past few hours. The perfect solitude to exchange secrets was bang in the middle of all this pandemonium. Nobody was paying any attention to anybody else. Everyone was engrossed in his or her own voice.

Savitry divulged: 'I never expected the price to soar so high. But Mister Shankaran Kutty, I'll share a piece of inside information.'

Shankaran Kutty did not open his eyes. 'Go on.'

'There will be heavy purchases in Bombay, Madras and here tomorrow. The price will rise steeply yet again. It may even touch fifty.'

'Is that true?'

'Yes.'

'Really?'

'Yes. There are two parties trying to take over the company, in both Bombay and Madras. There is apprehension that someone's out to play here in Cochin too. When there are doubts in the air, speculation increases. So, if you buy shares now, you can sell them at a good profit tomorrow or the day after. What you're lamenting as a loss shall turn out to be a profit.'

'Are you sure?'

'Yes. But you must ensure that the shares you buy today and tomorrow morning are sold by tomorrow evening. Do not keep those with you.'

Savitry smiled again. Her dimples made Shankaran Kutty crazy in a matter of seconds. The Stock Exchange, the crowd and the chaos turned into a turbulent sea. The flow of air stirred by the ceiling fan seemed to be the cool western breeze. Shankaran Kutty felt as if he were lazing by the seashore.

He gazed downwards.

'Savitry, you're very nice. No other broker would have shared such a secret. This is a tip worth lakhs. I know that you like me. It's only because you care about me that you revealed this inside information. Let us leave this world of money. I have a small house and sufficient land. A big pond. Some rubber trees and decent agriculture. Nobody is there at home. My only sister is married and settled in Trivandrum. My aged mother will never trouble anyone. I'm not extremely rich. But I can sell my Stock Exchange membership card. Why do we need this tension? There's no end to greed here. Everyone is minting money for money's sake. We shall turn old before thirty-five, under these circumstances. Today, I can get sixteen and a half lakhs for my membership card. The demand will keep rising. I plan to wait till it touches twenty lakhs.'

'What price did you say?'

Shankaran Kutty jolted awake. Vinayan was standing in front.

'For twenty?'

Shankaran Kutty gazed around.

Savitry was not to be seen anywhere.

'Who are you looking for?'

'Nobody.'

'Are you planning to sell your card?'

'What card?'

'You just said that you wanted to sell your membership card. Do it fast.'

'No … I…'

Shankaran Kutty suddenly recollected Savitry's words. Dhanwantari's share prices would soar tomorrow.

'I'm a buyer for Dhanwantari shares. Do you have any?'

'Closing was twenty-four, right?'

'I'll buy for twenty-four.'

'How many?'

'Ten thousand. Wouldn't mind even more.'

Most people knew that Shankaran Kutty was among the rare stockbrokers who did not indulge in speculation. It was the same man who was buying more than ten thousand shares of Dhanwantari Herbals at such a high price!

Vinayan grinned.

'I saw Savitry leave. Are you buying on her behalf? I'm not playing with Dhanwantari. Too risky. If tomorrow is riotous too, the Stock Exchange will have to take some tough steps.'

The stock exchanges could regulate the speculation only to a certain extent. Some brokers would recklessly push the share prices too high or too low. It was a step fraught with a potential loss of crores of rupees when brokers did speculative trading. They did it without checking the financial status of the company, or any other external factor affecting the share prices. Undertaking regulations to control such irresponsible speculative trading was one of the important duties of the top honchos of the Stock Exchange. But it was not always possible. Most of the top management consisted of stalwarts in speculative trading themselves! Even so, on rare occasions, stock exchanges stepped in with some checks and balances. The authorities could order stoppage of trade in the shares of certain companies for a few days. Vinayan was hinting at such a situation.

'I don't have any Dhanwantari shares with me. I'm not going to touch those now. Likely to get burned. Are you serious, by the way? Any idea of disposing off your membership card, Shankaran Kutty?'

'No.'

'They are planning to start a Stock Exchange in Coimbatore. More are planned in Trivandrum, Thrissur and Calicut. Maybe even in Kottayam. The rules will continue to undergo changes. The number of members at Cochin Exchange shall increase. We might even have an additional Stock Exchange here. So long as the Indian government encourages privatization, the number shall keep increasing. The probability of the membership card becoming more valuable in future is low. If you really mean it, I have five or six customers looking for a card.'

'No.'

'Okay.'

When Vinayan went to Zacharia to inform him that Shankaran Kutty was looking to purchase ten thousand shares of Dhanwantari, he found Zacharia talking to a young man. He listened to their conversation for a little while. Vinayan guessed that the young man was a journalist. Zacharia liked the exuberant company of youth. He was loath to let go of the behavioural patterns of aging politicians. Such men were prone to bore their youthful audience in the urge to convince them that their intelligence and knowledge were still untouched by age. The listeners would tolerate the lecture, out of consideration for the speaker's advanced age. Zacharia was still in the grips of that habit.

Vinayan decided that enough was enough. When there was the temptation to rake in tonnes of money and also lose equally, it was better to take the car keys and drive home. He wished to lie supine on the white sand of the temple yard. One could see the skies growing dark and the stars sprouting slowly. The songs of the wind caressing the coconut leaves. When the darkness covered the world with its thin cloak, one could immerse himself neck deep in the temple pond's cool waters. Then the world of shares, commissions and speculative trading would appear like a fantasy land.

Matthews was waiting for Vinayan in his cubicle.

'Where were you? I've been waiting for such a long time!'

'Was just taking a breather.'

Matthews got up. 'Lock up everything and come with me.'

'What's up?'

'Come on.'

'I was thinking of going home.'

Matthews laughed. 'No, you can't go home today.'

'Why?'

'I'll tell you. Come along.'

Once the car started moving on the Mahatma Gandhi Road, heading southwards, Matthews said: 'Vinayan, remember, I used to brag that one day I'll become one of the top ten businessmen of Kerala?'

'Yes. You used to see many such dreams. What about it?'

'I'm going to acquire a big company. I've taken the first step towards it.'

Vinayan did not reveal that he was aware of Matthews' agent buying Dhanwantari Herbals' shares.

There was a huge rush before the movie theatre. Which movie was playing tonight? Vinayan strained his neck to read the poster. He failed to decipher the name.

The car stopped. The traffic policeman was helping two schoolchildren cross the road. Horns blared from both sides.

'Almost three crores are ready to buy the shares. Once I reach twenty per cent, I shall take over the company.'

'Why are you telling me all this?'

'I must tell someone. The burden is unbearable.'

They reached Matthews' house. After parking the car, Matthews said: 'You should buy the shares for me. Might want to engage other brokers.'

'Which company?'

'Dhanwantari Herbal Products.'

Before Vinayan could say a word, a boy stepped out of Matthews' home and approached them.

'Sir, someone called and asked that you urgently get in touch.'

Matthews gazed at the paper the boy extended and responded: 'The managing director of Dhanwantari! I'm coming.'

When he stepped out of the car and hurried inside, Vinayan could not hide his surprise.

Matthews definitely had a role in the astounding share trading that had happened at the Stock Exchange today.

34

Suspicions

'What can we do now?' Ramesan wondered aloud.

The aroma of expensive tobacco clung to the chill of the air-conditioned room. If one tugged at the thick window curtains, they could catch a glimpse of the bay, where the lagoon met the sea. The sunlight shimmering silver-like on the greenish lagoon waters created a lovely ambience. However, neither Mohandas nor Ramesan tried to pull back the curtains.

Mohandas had been brooding ever since he reached his Ernakulam office. His personal assistant had placed all the important letters on the table. There were three unopened letters among those. Mohandas simply ignored everything. His eyes were fixed on the picture of the racing horses on the opposite wall. It was an M.F. Husain sketch. Mohandas had purchased it for twenty thousand before the paintings had become costly. Today, it would fetch him five lakhs easily. But though his gaze remained steady, Mohandas was not looking at the picture. His fingers moved intermittently, playing with a matchstick. He was trying to light up his pipe.

Ramesan had never seen his uncle so pensive ever before. Mohandas would always solve any problem with logical answers, with a half-smile flitting about his lips.

Mohandas spoke:

'I wanted to buy Dhanwantari's shares at the Madras Stock Exchange without much hue and cry. I expected that the negative publicity caused by *The Times of India* report would adversely affect the share prices. The plan was to buy nearly two lakh shares over a fortnight, rather unobtrusively. No confrontation or conflict. Cooperate with Mini Balachandran, the company's MD. When we came to possess ten per cent shares, she would have no other option but to listen to us. Ensure that two of our men were in the board of directors. Slowly, get under the company's skin and understand all its secrets. What is its Achilles heel? Who are likely to be hostile? The marketing director Asokan is part of our team. Use him as a pawn in our game. Keep buying more shares very silently, under various names. Confront Mini with the proxies of all the accumulated shares in the next annual general body meeting. She will have no other choice but to sell her own shares to us at whatever rate we dictate. But now...'

Mohandas laughed suddenly.

'The starting itself became faulty. I had not mentioned any specific price in Madras. Just instructed them to buy as many shares as possible. Apparently, they bought almost fifty thousand at an average price of twenty-one rupees. I'd never imagined the price going beyond fifteen. Neither did I anticipate the rising prices in Bombay. We lost nearly three and a half lakhs today. Nobody knows what's going to happen tomorrow. Could the speculators have guessed our move and started this aggressive strategy? Or someone else is trying to take over the company like me. What should we do now?'

'We can't retreat now, can we? We'll end up losing three and a half lakhs.'

Mohandas did not respond immediately. He was smoking his pipe. It was a top-variety tobacco, a single puff of which was highly invigorating. His friend had prepared the tobacco mixture in his own factory. Export quality. An exclusive grape flavour, gifted to politicians, government servants and close friends.

The loss was not the problem. He could ask his brokers to sell the shares tomorrow. The price might rise to twenty-four, and he could make a neat profit too. The issue was whether to go ahead or withdraw from the battlefield.

Ramesan was silent.

Mohandas rose from his seat. He tugged at the thick green curtains of the window facing west. The lagoon shimmered in the light cast by the sun. A huge bird was circling above the monstrous ships anchored at Willingdon Island. He stared at it. No, it was a helicopter.

Mini appeared in front of Mohandas's eyes. He had seen Mini Balachandran only three times in his life. The first time was during her wedding. All brides looked similar during wedding ceremonies. The poor girl would be embarrassed, half-smiling, covered with layers of makeup. Mohandas had observed the bride's father more. Menon sir was standing at the entrance of the hall, welcoming every guest. Mohandas had wished him warmly and left as soon as the ceremony was over. He did not even remember Mini's face then.

The second time was after the funeral of Menon sir and his son. Mohandas had gone to Mini's home to convey his condolences. He met Mini's husband Balachandran and exchanged sympathies. Mini was seated on a sofa nearby. No makeup or jewellery. She was wearing a white sari and blouse. Inadvertently, Mohandas found his eyes running over Mini's cheeks, neck, bosom and arms. Her form never vanished from his heart afterwards. Mohandas found himself getting agitated when he was alone.

He had seen Mini for the third time during a seminar conducted under the auspices of the Chamber of Commerce and Industries. Mini Balachandran had become the MD of Dhanwantari Herbal Products. She was the cynosure of all eyes. A naïve housewife, who turned into the top honcho of a big company by a twist of fate.

Everyone was hovering around her. Mini was dressed in a salwar-kameez. A carelessly draped dupatta. There was a watch on her left wrist and a string of black beads around her neck. She seemed lovelier than before. Mohandas noticed the black mole on the neck. It still glowed in his memory.

Mohandas did not withdraw his gaze from the backwaters. He spoke:

'No question of retreating from the arena. We should run a successful business venture. It will take a long time to start something new and make it work. There would be many issues to handle. That's why we decided to take over a firm running into losses and turn it around, right? A challenge.'

The telephone rang. It was his personal assistant.

'Sir, Mr Asokan is on the line. It's the fourth time he has called today. Should I connect him?'

'Okay.'

Asokan's jubilant voice echoed through the telephone line.

'Sir, I've been trying to get in touch with you desperately since morning. Couldn't get through.'

'I was out.'

'Sir, things are moving as we planned. The news appeared prominently in *Times of India*. There will be another news item tomorrow about the legal department issuing a notice against the consumer society for defamation. Everything is proceeding according to your strategy.'

Mohandas did not respond.

'Sir, are you there?'

'Yes.'

'What am I supposed to do next, sir? The MD is a fool. I don't think that she's even aware of the implications of the news report.'

Mohandas felt a twinge of fury. Without expressing it, he asked: 'Mr Asokan, you have been in the office throughout the day, I presume?'

'When? What's the matter, sir?'

'Were you there during the last two hours?'

Asokan could not reply instantaneously.

What could he say? Mohandas was waiting to anoint him as the future MD of Dhanwantari. Of course, he could not lie to him. If Asokan fibbed, his whole credibility would be at stake. But it was difficult to confess the truth. Asokan had visited his home surreptitiously during office hours. It would stir up many problems if he revealed the true reason.

Asokan's suspicions had been triggered ever since Mohandas visited his house. He could understand Aswathy's excitement in catering to the distinguished visitor. Her husband's future was important. The whole family's prosperity was dependent on him. It was an enthusiasm which any housewife would display during such a delicate occasion. That's what Asokan had surmised. So long as Mini Balachandran remained MD, Asokan could never hope for a promotion. No wonder that Aswathy became overwhelmed when Mohandas mentioned his future plans. But nowadays, Aswathy waxed eloquent at the mere mention of the name 'Mohandas'. Her face would brighten up, eyes sparkle, cheeks flush with a rosy hue … Perhaps, it was all his conjecture. But…?

'Mohandas sir will save us all, no doubt. He will remove Mini from the seat of power.' That's how Aswathy would gabble. With a wave of awe, devotion.

There were a number of salacious stories regarding Mohandas, which spread through the grapevine of social circles and clubs. All the tales were linked to his penchant for voluptuous, gorgeous women. Bachelor, crorepati, a lone tusker. A lot of middle-aged women showed a marked proclivity towards Mohandas. But Aswathy? Not that Asokan suspected his wife. But her incessant paeans of Mohandas irritated him much. He would try to swallow his vexation.

Trivial matters had started provoking Asokan lately. He would call Aswathy intermittently from office. Asokan noticed that the phone was engaged for ten seconds usually. He wondered whether Aswathy's voice was fraught with guilt, when she replied. He had called her around eleven in the morning a few days ago. Nobody answered. Asokan tried again after five minutes. Aswathy had taken that call after almost a minute. She told him that she had been in the shower. But didn't she usually bathe at four in the evening? He did not probe further.

That day, Asokan suggested that they get a new servant. Someone to stay home full-time. Now, for every small need, Aswathy had to visit the market herself, didn't she? The maidservant they engaged left home after completing her chores by ten-thirty in the morning.

Aswathy reacted immediately. 'No need! Once you become the MD, we'll keep a couple of servants under company expenses. Mohandas promised that you shall become the MD within two months of the takeover, didn't he?'

Mohandas! Asokan felt more sorrow than anger. Did Mohandas visit Aswathy when he was away at work, he wondered. Was Aswathy visiting the town frequently to meet Mohandas secretively?

Asokan had been caught in the grips of a silent despair. Today, he had called home to inform Aswathy about the news report in *The Times of India*. Nobody answered his call. Asokan immediately tried Mohandas's number. The personal assistant told him that he was not aware where his boss was. Asokan kept trying both Aswathy's and Mohandas's numbers. Filled with helplessness and frustration, he had downed a couple of pegs in the office itself.

Are they both rolling around on the soft Dunlop mattress in my own bedroom? Asokan had set off for his home immediately. When he reached the verandah, he stopped. Mohandas's car was not to be sighted anywhere. He pressed the doorbell. An autorickshaw slowed down near the gate. Aswathy stepped down with a few bags of groceries. The maidservant opened the front door.

Was Aswathy's gaze wary? When she enquired about his unexpected presence, Asokan had struggled for an answer. He felt remorseful that he had doubted her.

'I tried to call you many times. I got scared.'

Aswathy laughed.

'The maid's afraid of the telephone. She thinks it will give her an electric shock.'

Asokan stayed home for a couple of hours, almost as an atonement. He helped Aswathy cook and they enjoyed their lunch together.

How could he tell all these stories to Mohandas?

So Asokan said: 'Sir, I wasn't in the office. Had a client. I took him to lunch.'

'No issues.'

'What's the matter, sir? Any problem?'

'Nothing.'

'Sir, everything is moving as per plan. Mini is already nervous. She was frazzled by the news report. Following your guidance, I have prepared the list of every stakeholder with more than a thousand shares. An updated list. The share register has been under my custody for the past few days.'

Mohandas looked at Ramesan. He started grinning.

'The shareholder list must be long, right?'

'Yes, sir. Thirty pages, closely typed.'

Mohandas laughed.

'Do you have a shredding machine in your room, Mr Asokan?'

'What?'

'A shredder?'

'No.'

'Matchbox, perhaps?'

'Why, sir?'

'Set fire to that list.'

Before Asokan could respond, Mohandas cut the call.

35

Poison Pill

Zacharia was reading the computer printout with the details of India's top ten Ayurvedic companies – the report that Suryanarayanan had procured from Bombay.

All the companies were far bigger than Dhanwantari. Not a single Ayurvedic company in Kerala would be able to match them. Two companies were based in Lucknow, three in Calcutta, two in Delhi, another in Bombay, and one each in Bihar and Madhya Pradesh respectively. They had enough reserve funds for handling any liquidity challenge. Though the shareholders were in the thousands, there was a single decision-maker in most of the companies. Almost all of them desired to enter the south Indian market. Kerala had a great legacy in Ayurveda. The Malayalis were keen on trying new products. If one acquired a Kerala-based company, the business would surely expand. All ten companies were capable of a hostile takeover.

How would you discover the real adversary? There were some traditional strategies for defeating the enemy. Increase the quality of one's own products, lower the prices, unleash an advertising blitzkrieg and capture new markets, reach out to the challenger and negotiate a compromise. The Indian business scenario was familiar with such competitive tactics. But after Independence, a new lot of youngsters entered the battlefield. They had lost their families, their inheritance and homes in the Partition. There were many refugees from western Punjab and Sindh. They made their aggressive presence felt, with nary a thought of family legacies and traditions.

Not satisfied with India, these young entrepreneurs spread to Canada, England, the Gulf and other countries. They were willing to work unceasingly and set down roots everywhere. In a way, they were similar to the young men who had fled Europe centuries ago and settled in America. The new America did not have the traditions of old European business houses. Similarly, according to Zacharia, the new Indian business families were drastically different from the traditional Marwaris, Gujaratis or the southern Chettiars. They never felt any prick of conscience while ruthlessly destroying their competitors. Even India's gigantic companies were terrified of these Young Turks biding to win at all costs. They were willing to do anything to influence the government and the regulatory bodies.

If there were any companies headed by someone like that, one definitely had to be wary of that institution. This would be no dharma yuddha – a war fought fair and square.

Zacharia started examining the names of the directors of each company. It was then that Vinayan made his entry.

As soon as he put his foot inside the room, he gasped: 'Do you know who's behind the Dhanwantari takeover? Matthews! He approached me. Ready to invest three crores liquid cash.'

'And who's behind Matthews?'

'I don't know.'

'There is someone.'

After scanning the papers before him, Zacharia mused: 'The prices will shoot up again. Matthews will feel the heat.'

'Why?'

'I am sure. There's more than one party trying to take over Dhanwantari. The prices will zoom frighteningly. Only one among them can win, right? Or all of them might end up losing, a scenario that's more likely in fact. A huge crash is imminent. Many are bound to be devastated. Heart attack, suicide, insanity. Nothing unusual in places like Bombay. Pretty common in Tokyo and Wall Street in America. We're growing big too, aren't we? One shouldn't be surprised if something similar happens here too.'

Zacharia became deeply immersed in thought.

Vinayan was silent. He was thinking about the man sitting in front of him.

Zacharia was a man of many personalities – each strikingly different from the other. Excellent football player, Communist worker of yore, efficient organizer, warm householder who charmed children and friends equally, impassive share broker who worked equably in the avaricious atmosphere of the Stock Exchange. How could Zacharia remain so endearing even in the midst of such a variety of dispositions?

Prabhu appeared at the door. He conveyed the silent query: Do you need tea?

Vinayan half-closed his eyes and threw him a sidelong glance. Then he winked his right eye twice.

Prabhu understood the gesture. Tea and banana fritters. He grinned and went away. Vinayan and Prabhu communicated nonverbally mostly. In exchange for Vinayan's insights on stock markets, Prabhu was supposed to teach him Konkani. Vinayan would learn a few words of Konkani whenever he came to visit Zacharia.

Once, Zacharia had joked: 'Prabhu, won't strangers master your business secrets if you teach them Konkani? Malayalis are notorious for pulling the rug from under your feet.'

Prabhu retaliated: 'Oh, the businessmen in my community use another language. No worries.'

'What's that? Code language?'

'Yes, even some of our own community members can't understand it. I don't intend to teach Vinayan sir that code language.'

Zacharia said: 'The share prices of Dhanwantari shall soar. There will be cut-throat speculation since there are likely to be more than three competitors vying for the takeover. There are players at the Bombay Stock Exchange. They will buy blindly during such a crisis. These men aren't interested in the company or the takeover. Their sole wish is to make a handsome profit overnight.

'Consider the scenario: those trying to take over a company and the owners fighting off the acquisition bid. Both are desperate to buy a majority of the shares. The players shall sell their shares at high prices to either party when the fight reaches a peak. They will make crores in a matter of weeks. There is one calamity in such a situation. If the takeover does not happen, say, due to a surreptitious understanding between parties, and the buying spree stops, everything goes for a toss. The fortune-hunters shall run helter-skelter with their high-priced shares. Who would buy those? When there are no buyers, the prices shall plummet. A catastrophic loss of crores.'

Vinayan asked: 'Guide me, sir. What am I supposed to do? Matthews has entrusted me the job of buying Dhanwantari shares.'

A smile appeared on Zacharia's face.

'The answer is simple. Vinayan, you are a share broker. Somebody who buys and sells shares for the customer. A worker, essentially. The client gives you a commission for your task. Is that all there is to your profession? In a country like India, a share broker has an added responsibility. He can use his intelligence and knowledge to create roadmaps for the nation's progress. He should, I'd say.

'In my opinion, more than any politician or leader, stock exchanges can play a far more vital role in ensuring India's future.

Democratize the Stock Exchange. To achieve the true aim of the Communist party – that of empowering the last man, the one left behind – stock exchanges can show the most straightforward path to prosperity. The small savings of the worker, the common man, the farmer, turn into capital here. The public invest in banks, insurance policies, post office savings and gold. This saving ultimately reaches the stock market, transforming as bonds and shares. The investor doesn't know that it is his hundred rupees, deposited in a bank, that is loaned to a company! The bank, like a middleman, lends the common man's savings to a company of its choice as working capital. The insurance companies invest the money – which they receive as premium payments – in the stock market.

'Many companies, with no moral compass or societal obligations, indulging in activities against the national interest, use the common man's earnings in whatever way they wish! Herein lies the share broker's relevance. He can control the unchecked flow of capital by guiding the investor to buy shares using his hard-earned savings. He should crosscheck the company and its mission to protect the interest of the common citizen. Thus he democratizes the rampant capitalist system. Empower the farmer and worker to profit from his earnings. Only a stockbroker can ensure that.'

Prabhu brought in banana fritters and tea.

'In India, a share broker can ensure that the principles of socialism are implemented. Much better than any Communist.'

'Sir, your ideas are thought-provoking. But they are not practical. Human greed, the unlimited hunger for money – nobody can stop that rapacity.'

'You're correct.'

Both sipped their tea in silence.

Zacharia spoke again:

'No point in shrugging away Matthews' offer. If not you, someone else shall buy the Dhanwantari shares on his behalf.

They will learn only when their hands get burned. Let the game play itself out. Vinayan, just ensure enough margin money so that you don't end up hurt.'

Vinayan was deep in contemplation.

'Yes.'

A few moments later, he asked Zacharia: 'Sir, what's your prediction? Will this takeover bid succeed? Will someone seize the ownership of Dhanwantari Herbals?'

'It depends. The adversary's strength and intensity of purpose are critical. There's a cost to everything. An optimum point. They should have the forbearance to hold on until that point. The takeover experts in the Indian business scene: the Ambani, Chhabria, Swraj Paul families, they too wait for an optimum point. After reaching it, they either seek a settlement or withdraw from the attack. I can't prophesy whether such a situation might evolve in Dhanwantari's case.'

'Dhanwantari's managing director is young. Will she have the wherewithal to handle such a battering?' Vinayan wondered aloud.

'Don't come to a conclusion so easily. Mini is smart and intelligent. She also has the backing of her family legacy. The attackers are aiming at control and power. Mini is fighting for survival. The difference is striking. My brain tells me that Mini will fail. It is such a strong offensive. But my gut feeling is that she'll win. I'm in any case trying to make her the victor.'

Vinayan smiled and got up.

'And I'm trying to ensure her failure. I can't let go of Matthews. Wish you luck.' Upon reaching the door, Vinayan turned to look at Zacharia. 'But I'll pray that she wins. Somehow, I don't like money being used to destroy something vital.'

Vinayan went away.

~

Zacharia started making notes on his writing pad. What are the ways to tackle the takeover bid?

One, a knight in white armour, protecting the damsel in distress. The takeover lingo referred to such a party as a 'white knight'. A third party steps in to save the beleaguered company. He buys a lion's share of the company's ownership. Once the enemy is routed, the white knight returns the ownership. A third man, willing to help and with money to boot. If Menon sir were alive, a few of his friends would have come together to play that role. Mini did not have such personal associations, did she? No. Then what? Zacharia scribbled:

Try Aniyan Raja.

Wasn't Mini speaking about some proposal he brought forward? Explore the offer. No harm.

Second, greenmail.

The antonym of blackmail. Get in touch with the enemy and buy back his shares at a premium. The foe gains handsomely and the shares are returned in a block. If the enemy's aim was only money, this was an effective strategy. But liquid funds were a prerequisite. That tactic might not be effective here. There was a limit to the money that Mini could arrange. He scratched out 'greenmail'.

Third, special voting rights.

Give special voting rights to certain categories of shareholders. Maybe the workers who held shares. Individuals who retained Dhanwantari's shares. But the conundrum was that the enemy could always approach the courts. The snares of law would catch everyone unawares. The battle would become prolonged. The ultimate result could go against the company. No, that would not work.

Four, poison pill.

The enemy would realize that it was poisonous only after swallowing the pill. Make an agreement to sell most of the company assets, currently shown as low value in the balance sheets, to a third party. The moment it seems like the enemy is winning, execute the agreement. The value of the shares bought by the enemy will crash drastically. What's the use of a company that has sold off its assets? The rival will run around frantically, trying to spit out the poison. The shares will return to the market at a low price. The owner can buy back his shares.

He circled the fourth point. Poison pill – yes, that would work here. He should guide Mini to make an agreement to sell off Dhanwantari's assets. It would be a cakewalk from that point onwards.

'Sat Sri Akal.'

Zacharia was startled.

Tarlok Singh. The investor who had tipped him off about Dhanwantari in the morning.

'Zachariaji, did you buy the stocks?' he asked.

'Yes.'

'For how much?'

'Sixteen and a half.'

'Right, I was passing by. The prices will touch thirty by tomorrow afternoon. Sell all the shares immediately.'

Zacharia stared at the man. 'What about waiting for a few more days? The prices will rise further.'

Tarlok Singh grinned. 'There's a Punjabi proverb about avoiding greed, whether it is for money or for women. I know how much I need. I'll tell you which company's shares I wish to be bought with the gains. I shall call you tomorrow morning. Okay?'

'Sure.'

Tarlok Singh shook his hand.

'Zachariaji, you are a good man.'

'Thank you.'

36

The Beginning of Fear

Matthews tried to make an STD call to Aniyan Raja's number once more. Engaged.

The infuriating man had obviously disconnected the receiver from the phone. When would he ever learn! One was playing a game of dice with a borrowed capital of three crores. Anything could happen. The D-day when things could either nosedive or soar beyond expectations had arrived. Yet, the old geezer's phone was still disconnected. And he was asthmatic to boot. If he continued with his outdated antics, which ended up scorching people, surely he would catch more deadly diseases!

Matthews became frantic. How would he inform Aniyan Raja about the happenings in the Stock Exchange? ... There was one way.

He booked a trunk call to Aniyan Raja's number. Now, let the telephone exchange fellows sweat a bit. If they apologized that the number was engaged, one could implore them to connect some neighbour's number.

Matthews wished to tell Aniyan Raja the following:

Almost twenty thousand shares of Dhanwantari have been purchased. The price escalated unbelievably over a few minutes. The first lot cost sixteen rupees. When the trading hours closed, each share was selling at twenty-four rupees. There was a different price during curb trading. I arranged to buy another twenty thousand shares today itself.

The share broker had warned him already: 'There is a huge probability of speculation.'

Matthews wanted to convince Aniyan Raja.

This is the first time in the history of the Cochin Stock Exchange that so many speculators are trading in a small company's shares. There is talk that not just us but many strong players are trying to take over the company. As the proverb goes, you do not give the hyena meat to watch over. Most of the brokers will be out hunting tomorrow. The share prices will rise further. Only the Lord knows what the price will be by the time the matter is settled! If things go through the roof, I'll be finished. So…'

The broker needed forty per cent of the total traded amount. They took margin money from the investors. The Stock Exchange would take legal action against the broker if the amount was insufficient during the exchange of share certificates. It was but natural that the brokers took care of themselves.

Matthews had paid the broker forty per cent margin money. A cheque for four lakhs which was inclusive of the shares he intended to buy. He had already paid off ten lakhs to Suryanarayanan for arranging the finances. His commission was extra. Matthews felt a surge of fury.

And, amidst it all, the dignity and composure that reverberated in Mini Balachandran's voice. Her calm and steady words troubled Matthews even now.

'I'm not insisting. I shall wait for you only till 5 p.m. tomorrow…'

What did she mean?

Matthews' confidence in his own abilities seemed to totter slightly. It had stood by him ever since he had decided to be the richest businessman in Kerala.

By the time he smoked his fourth cigarette, the phone rang.

'We can't connect the trunk call. It's engaged.'

'Any other number? Please connect to a neighbour's number. Someone has passed away. It's an emergency.'

The man in the rural telephone exchange felt a wave of sympathy. He said: 'Even the nearest number is two kilometres away from Aniyan Raja's house. My duty will get over soon. I shall inform him myself, since I have a bicycle.'

'That's so nice of you.'

'Who died?'

Matthews paused for a moment.

'Not died. He's on the verge of dying. The man's name is Matthews. He wishes to see Aniyan Raja or Unni urgently. That's all.'

'What's the disease?'

'That's an English name. Even I couldn't catch it myself. Brother, can you just tell them what I said? You should mention that he's breathing his last.'

'Sure.'

'Thanks.'

Matthews hung up.

Half an hour. His cigarette packet became half empty. Matthews leapt as the phone rang.

Unni's voice came through. 'Hello, Matthews! What happened?'

Matthews could not contain his frustration and anger. 'What are you doing? I'm getting burned over here … Lakhs of rupees are at stake. And one can never reach you! Where were you?'

Unni consoled him. 'Today is holy for us. We have an old Shiva temple in the family. We visit the place every month on a special day. I was about to drive to the temple when Ibrahim Kutty came.'

'Ibrahim Kutty?'

'The telephone operator. He was my classmate. When he told me that you were sick, I panicked for a moment. Then I thought, how could it be?'

Matthews lost his temper. 'You and your bloody … One is getting scalded here!'

'If you're upset, Mr Matthews, we shall speak later. We'll return by eight in the night. It'll be better to call after that.' Unni cut the call.

Matthews was trembling. What the hell could be done now? He was getting angry quickly. Now, that was not allowed in business. That, too, with one's friends.

Matthews cursed himself. 'I should apologize.' He dialled Aniyan Raja's number.

Aniyan Raja's number was engaged. The receiver had been disconnected again. Now he would be forced to wait till eight at night.

One could not go ahead without discussing matters with Aniyan Raja. He could be in the dark about what was happening. There was no chance that the news of the unexpected surge in Dhanwantari's share price had reached that remote place. What was the point in blaming them?

What a day for a temple visit!

Matthews opened a fresh packet of cigarettes. By the time he smoked the second cigarette, Matthews came to a decision. There was no other way. He had to meet Aniyan Raja in person. After detailed discussions, they could decide on a strategy. He called a friend who owned a taxi company.

There was the evening rush, when people departed from the city, clad in clothes soiled with sweat and exhaustion. When packed buses crawled on the roads, Matthews, seated in a taxi, cursed himself. Had it been anyone else, he would have ingested two pegs. No, it wouldn't do in this case.

The taxi took almost twenty minutes to cross the overbridge and traverse the three kilometres to the east, over the pothole-ridden road. Slowly, through many bylanes, it trundled to the villages. Matthews lowered the car window. A cool breeze. There was a lush green, passive ambience outside. Nobody was in a hurry. Matthews closed his eyes.

By seven-thirty in the evening, Matthews reached the densely dark entrance of Aniyan Raja's house, which was dimly lit by a single bulb. The desolate-looking palatial home reminded him of the ghostly bungalows in folklore. There was a surfeit of sounds emerging from all sides, as if in a forest. Matthews waited.

At exactly 8 p.m., he heard the rumble of a car approaching the gate. Unni was driving. Aniyan Raja was in the front. Two women were seated in the back. One elderly, the other young. Matthews could not see their faces. He guessed they were probably Unni's mother and sister. Both were in traditional dresses. Matthews presumed that the young woman was the MBA-degree holder.

Unni looked mildly surprised by Matthews' presence. He said to Aniyan Raja, who was disembarking: 'That's Matthews. My friend, who's managing the takeover of Dhanwantari Herbals.'

Aniyan Raja smiled. 'Yes, I remember.' He called Matthews closer.

'My asthma grew bad since evening. Now with this journey, I don't think it will let me sleep tonight. But I can't miss the special prayer, can I? The priest at the Shiva temple got a job in the bank. Had to conduct an interview for his replacement. I decided to get it done at the temple premises. Luckily, that was successful. That's why we got slightly late. Go on, apply a little bhasma.'

On a sliver of banana leaf was that sacred ash, some bright red ixora flowers and leaves of the holy bael tree. Matthews extended his hand.

'Don't worry. The mind needs an occasional medicine. The greatest strength is to appreciate that a divine power is controlling every action of ours. This is a symbol of that indomitable power. Go on.'

Matthews applied the bhasma on his forehead.

Aniyan Raja said: 'Both of you discuss the matter and decide what to do. It must be chaotic at the Stock Exchange, right?'

'Yes. Not just that. You might have to take the trouble to come to Ernakulam tomorrow.'

'Tomorrow? No way. There is a Chakyar Koothu performance in the temple in the morning. A disciple of our Madhava Chakyar. Supposedly very good in his act. Unni, you have seen him, haven't you?'

'Yes, once in Ernakulam.'

'Let me rest now. Though I shall hardly get any sleep.'

Aniyan Raja was breathing heavily when he walked. After a few steps, he turned back to gaze at Matthews.

'Best of luck. Good night.'

Matthews heard himself respond: 'Thank you, sir! Good night.'

When Aniyan Raja went away, Unni spoke: 'Come, the guest room is ready for you. Let me park the car. Get fresh in the meantime.'

When Matthews went to the guest room, he saw it was vast and spacious. An old caretaker accompanied him. A silk bedsheet was draped over the Dunlop mattress. There was a blanket kept neatly folded on a side.

The old man said: 'The heater's on. You can take a warm shower.'

Matthews hesitated for a moment. 'Did they know I was coming?'

'Yes. Before leaving for the temple, I was told that you would be coming from Ernakulam.'

Matthews did not reply.

The room had the facilities of a top-class hotel suite. Matthews took a shower. There was a lungi and shirt kept for him in the dressing room. As he changed, Matthews found his resilience returning. The shares of Dhanwantari were going berserk in some other world. But the situation did not seem beyond control.

Fifteen minutes. Unni arrived with his sister. They carried food trays. After depositing the tray he was holding on a side table, Unni introduced the young woman. 'My sister, Sreedevi. This is Matthews.'

Matthews smiled. 'Hello.'

Sreedevi served chapatis, potato curry, stir-fried lady's fingers and green chilli pickle. One small katori of curd too. Unni grinned.

'Sreedevi did her MBA at IIM Ahmedabad. She pretends to have mastered many Gujarati recipes over there. One of those culinary delights happens to be this chilli pickle. Try one! Not spicy.'

Matthews bit into one. He smiled. 'Good!'

Sreedevi pulled a stool and sat nearby. Unni asked: 'How many shares did we buy in all?'

Matthews was flustered. For the last thirty-odd minutes, he had become oblivious of the world of shares. Ever since that warm shower. Then, there was Sreedevi – without a touch of makeup. Matthews had never expected that simple white clothes and an ash mark on a woman's forehead could have such a mesmerizing effect on his senses. Rather dazed, he lifted his head to focus on Unni's question.

Unni probed: 'Twenty thousand?'

Matthews replied: 'No, almost twenty-five thousand. An additional twenty in curb trading. But the price? It was utter madness! It opened at fourteen and closed at twenty-four.'

'In Bombay?'

'Almost the same pattern. I guess two more players are in the arena.'

'Mini? Has the company itself set out to fight?'

'I don't know.'

Sreedevi offered two glasses containing water boiled with cumin seeds.

Matthews remarked: 'Mini Balachandran called me today. She has some ace up her sleeve. Now she insists on having the discussion about our offer tomorrow, instead of three days later as originally planned. When I told her that would be inconvenient, she said she would talk to me tomorrow and no later. So we can forget about any discussion if I don't meet her at the hour she has fixed.

Unni was silent for some time. Matthews continued: 'What should we do now? See, we have spent almost twenty lakhs already. The broker might increase his margin money. What if tomorrow's market is the same as today? What if the trend remains the same afterwards?'

'We have to put an end to the escalating price. If we have to give more than twenty rupees per share, it'll burn us badly.'

'You mean we should also consider selling?'

'I don't know. I was just thinking aloud. There's only one way to reduce the price. The public should be convinced that there's something seriously amiss in the company. The government goes against the company, some labour trouble, the reputation of the company's products goes down the drain, something or the other.'

'But these can't happen overnight.'

A few moments passed in silence. Amidst the chirping of the cicadas, the trio heard the rumble of an approaching vehicle which then stopped at the gate. They looked at each other with curiosity.

By then, they had finished dinner. Sreedevi removed the plates. Unni and Matthews went off to wash their hands. There was a knock on the door.

A lean, middle-aged man smiled at them. He was dressed in a long white shirt and shawl, and his lips were stained red with paan juice. His hair had started greying. He introduced himself.

He was the district correspondent of a prominent newspaper based in Ernakulam. The journalist had been asked to verify a particular fact and report to the headquarters. The man and his family had been readying to attend the feast at Omalloor church when the critical call came. But it was a matter of his livelihood.

Was a journalist ever lucky to enjoy a festival? Fate! He had caught a jeep and immediately set off to meet Aniyan Raja.

'Come inside, please.'

'No, I'm in a hurry. I just wanted to crosscheck a fact with Aniyan Raja.'

'My uncle is sleeping. He is not keeping well. You can tell me.'

'Nothing special. The Cochin office wants to know if it's true that your uncle is buying or is planning to buy a company called Dhanwantari, that's all.'

Unni remained silent. Matthews intervened: 'Is it for the newspaper?'

'How do I know? They asked me to confirm and I came over. Is it true?'

Unni replied: 'No.'

'Okay. Then I'm leaving. My newspaper's sources must have got it wrong. A useless trip in the evening.'

The man had reached the last step when he turned around.

'So, it wasn't your uncle who gave the news in today's *Times of India* about Dhanwantari's medicines being substandard, right? The bilge people whisper!'

'*Times of India*?'

'Of course!'

The man grinned at the shocked faces in front of him.

'I'll go now. Maybe I can still make it to the festival with the kids. I tried to call but your phone was out of order. Tell your uncle that there is some real issue with the phone. It never works. I tried the telephone exchange too. The exchange told me that many calls amounting to ten thousand rupees or more must have been booked in your number yesterday and today. Please check. I'm going.'

The man vanished in the dark.

Unni and Matthews gazed at each other. Fear coloured both their faces with the same hue.

37

Vibheeshan's Effort

Mohandas did not need the list of Dhanwantari's shareholders any longer. Someone who had been after Asokan's life every day for the same information was insolently asking him to burn it.

Asokan lost his bearings. He bitterly cursed himself after ending the call.

As the marketing director of Dhanwantari Herbal Products, he should have kept such a list ready much earlier. The company secretary was on leave. The section clerk would have needed just a clear instruction. Please type a list from the share register. Everybody obeyed the marketing director. Typically, nobody had his networking ability and contacts. But Asokan had not taken the risk of getting a third party involved. What if the clerk blurted it out unwittingly? What if it reached Adiyodi's ears? Even Mini's? Why give them a chance for suspicion? That was why he had taken the time to type out the list himself.

All the effort had been in vain. Mohandas had rejected the list.

Asokan contemplated lighting a matchstick. But he did not have to wait for long to discover the reason. His wife called.

It was very rare that Aswathy called him up at work. It must be something extremely urgent.

'What's the matter, Aswathy?'

'Chetta, someone called and checked if I'm willing to sell my shares in Dhanwantari. He promised to give a good price.'

'And then?'

'I asked him his name and details.'

'Okay.'

'Some man called Shankaran Kutty. A share broker.'

'What did you say?'

'Told him that you were in office. He took your office number.'

The call that rattled Aswathy was the twelfth call that Shankaran Kutty had made after the trading hours. Savitry had line business with the Bombay Stock Exchange. Had it not been for the temporary blindness caused by his love for her, Shankaran Kutty would never have sold five thousand Dhanwantari shares to her in the morning for a mere fifteen rupees. The price had touched twenty-four rupees by the closing hours. A loss of nine rupees per share. Savitry had advised him to buy as many shares of Dhanwantari as possible and sell them by the next evening at a higher price. He would cover his losses and rake in lakhs in profits.

Shankaran Kutty remembered the quip of the old woman who was actively into share trading. 'What you lose in sesamum, you make up in barley.'

The farmer and the stockbroker were similar in many ways. The wisdom of generations and one's own calculations only aided till a point. Both needed a good downpour for progress. Water for agriculture and prosperous villages for a strong share market. New consumer products would sell only in affluent villages. Manufacturing picked up only when there was sufficient demand. The profits would grow and the share prices would rise.

Shankaran Kutty was working hard to implement Savitry's timely tipoff.

Usually, the brokers who indulged in speculation operated without actual share certificates. In two weeks' time, when they had to settle the money with the Stock Exchange, they made documents to show the purchase or sale of shares depending on the price. They would suffer if the prices went down. And they would buy if the prices were favourable.

Shankaran Kutty was inherently averse to such speculative trading. The fear of playing without actual shares in hand triggered a feeling of panic. Shankaran Kutty actively searched for contacts in his old diary. Were there any names and addresses of Dhanwantari shareholders?

Eight hundred shares of Dhanwantari were in Aswathy's name. Shankaran Kutty had interceded for another broker one and a half years ago. Her name and address were jotted down in his diary.

Shankaran Kutty called Aswathy. He did not know that her husband Asokan was the marketing director of Dhanwantari Herbal Products.

That was how Asokan came to know about the news. Many were competing to acquire the shares of the company. Not just Mohandas, lots of other people.

What should be done now? Had Mohandas been keen on taking over the company, he would not have asked him to burn the shareholder list, would he? Maybe others had stepped into the battlefield after seeing Mohandas's interest. They could always sell their shares to Mohandas at a higher price.

What if Mohandas withdrew?

Should he invest money beyond a point?

What after?

Asokan decided that he had to be very careful. The first heads on the guillotine, after a company takeover took place, were those of the managing director and the marketing director.

Asokan took the directory and called Shankaran Kutty.

Shankaran Kutty could not believe his ears. While he was pleading to the Lord at the Ettumanoor temple for Dhanwantari's shares, here was an offer for five thousand shares! Some fellow called Asokan. An extra eight hundred shares that belonged to his wife were also on sale. Twenty-four rupees each. What incredible luck!

Who was Shankaran Kutty buying the shares for? He told the truth. Asokan was going to sell him five thousand and eight hundred Dhanwantari shares tomorrow, wasn't he? The broker was not obliged to disclose the name of the person they were buying for. Even then, Shankaran Kutty disclosed the facts: It was for a broker called Savitry, who engaged in line business with a Marwari broker at the Bombay Stock Exchange. Asokan prodded further, asking whether someone local wasn't involved. Shankaran Kutty affirmed that that was not the case. He also promised due offerings to his Lord at the Ettumanoor temple.

Asokan became thoughtful. Twenty-four rupees. If the share prices went up so crazily, Mohandas would retreat for sure. There was nothing to motivate him to buy Dhanwantari at any cost, was there? He must have bought some shares today. Seeing the trend, he must have stopped soon. What then? One should know the truth.

If the north Indian lobby was behind the takeover attempt, it should be fought off.

Suddenly, Asokan recollected seeing Zacharia in Mini Balachandran's room in the morning. His face had been grave. Maybe Mini was in the know right from the start. Asokan shuddered, remembering that he had spoken about *The Times of India* news dramatically. What had been Mini's facial expression then? Absolute innocence. A wide-eyed look of wonder, like a child who did not know anything.

Maybe Aswathy was right. 'Mini is not as you men assume! She's one whip-smart woman. How coolly she stole the MD position which should have come to you!'

Not a day went by when Aswathy did not remind him of the excruciating day when Mini Balachandran was chosen as the managing director of Dhanwantari Herbal Products.

Now what?

Asokan was not involved in the Stock Exchange. The only shares he had were of Dhanwantari Herbals. He did not think that investing in stocks was a good idea. Typically, he converted his savings into gold. For thousands of years, saving in gold has been the practice across the world. The eternal yellow metal, which never loses its value. It is easy to mortgage too. Asokan had a good deposit of gold as investment.

Naturally, he did not have many contacts among share brokers. There was one friend named Govindan. Asokan had no idea whether he was still into stockbroking. He would know the nitty-gritty of the share market war.

Asokan tried Govindan's number. He was informed that the broker was busy. Someone noted down his name and number.

Govindan was always on the go. Asokan had met him four months ago. That day, Govindan had confessed that he was on the verge of committing suicide. Asokan had scoured the obituary columns of the newspapers for the next few days. Govindan's name did not feature anywhere. Afterwards, he had forgotten about him.

Govindan radiated youthful vitality both mentally and physically. Brilliant in studies and good in sports. He participated in college politics and sang well too. A rather good-looking young man. He was keen on exploring new horizons. Someone gifted to be a natural leader. Govindan had joined the Cochin Stock Exchange two years after it started to function. He became a member soon. The first month, his way of work was awe-inspiring. He would analyse the last four years' balance sheets and the share-price trends of top companies, indulge in comparative studies of different companies producing similar products, and work extremely hard. He would toil till three in the morning. And then, the young man would arrive sharp and ready at the Stock Exchange early the next morning. In speculative trade, he easily aced the game in a matter of weeks. Experienced share brokers looked askance at the upstart's progress. Astute, bright, incomparable! Every day, Govindan was garlanded with many encomiums.

The first month, Govindan had reaped a profit of seven lakhs. People hung around him, overtly and covertly, waiting for his counsel. In the second month, the profits reduced to one and a half lakhs. No worries. Certain shares did not play out as expected. In the third month, a veritable windfall! Ten lakhs in gains. Those waiting for Govindan's fall from grace were left disappointed.

In the course of time, the game changed. In a game of cards, the Ace, King, Queen and Jack never end up in the same hand all the time, do they? The losses began. After six months, the accumulated setback reached thirty lakhs. Govindan's colleagues gazed gleefully at the fall of Icarus. An old broker advised him heartfully, 'Son, sell your membership card and make good your escape! This job is not meant for you.'

The phone rang. Asokan awoke from the reverie.

'How are you, Govindan?'

He heard Govindan's laughter echo through the phone.

'You won't believe it! I was going to speak to you today. Look at the miracle! I get a note saying that you'd called me.'

'Go ahead. Why did you wish to speak with me?'

'Your company share prices increased by more than ten rupees today. From fourteen to twenty-four! Why's that? Have any idea? Any inside information?'

'I was about to ask you the same question!'

'My guess is some Bombay player is trying to increase the share prices. Maybe more than two entities are involved. Anyway, these are not small-time players for sure. What's your company's approach? In case the real goal is a takeover, will you be defending or attacking?'

Asokan did not react for a moment.

'We haven't decided on any clear course of action. You know, we're still discussing the matter.'

'Do inform me in case of any plan. Day or night doesn't matter. You know my home number, don't you? Let me see if I too can make some hay while the sun shines.'

'Someone's drowning, and you...?'

'Hey, it's one man's fall which delights another, am I not right?'

'Don't philosophize, please. If you get some tipoff, let me know.'

Govindan agreed. When the call ended, Asokan took some decisions.

All the company managers would join forces at this critical stage. If any north Indian company were to take over Dhanwantari, surely the purchase and sales heads would be their own trusted men. They might entrust the fields of research, engineering and medicine production to the local personnel. However, when it came to accounts, and departments which impacted company finances directly, like sales and purchase, these would be with their tried and trusted hands. Manipulating the prices, under-invoicing, over-invoicing, creating favourable contracts for family companies, and many such furtive deals would be part of the deal. The local chartered accountant, smart and efficient, would be entrusted with creating the documents, receipts and audit certificates as per Companies Act – perfect and flawless. Good pay and status would be offered to them. But the real numbers would be saved in the Marwari bahi khata: the long red-calico-bound register. Only the company loyalists would be monitoring at that level. It was beyond doubt that if a north Indian company took over Dhanwantari, Asokan would either have to resign or be relegated to some powerless assignment.

No, that could not happen.

Asokan went to Mini's room.

On seeing him, Mini asked: 'What happened? You look unwell!'

Asokan sat down.

'Mini, you know about our company's share prices.'

'Yes.'

'I'm really upset. What should we do?'

Mini's face looked more childlike than ever, Asokan thought.

'What can be done? You suggest a way. I shall follow whatever all of you say.'

'If only Menon sir were here.'

'But my father is not here, is he?'

Mini smiled.

For a moment, Asokan was stumped.

'You're right. Now, we have to decide. Shall we call a board meeting?'

'That will require a formal notice. Zacharia uncle informed me that someone, may be two or three firms, are fighting desperately to acquire our company.'

'Shall we call Adiyodi? Let us pool our ideas.'

Mini gazed at the wall clock.

'I have a chamber meeting at five o'clock. Just half an hour left. It is at the Malabar hotel. If there's a traffic jam, I won't be able to make it. Do one thing. Why don't you discuss the matter with Adiyodi uncle and Zacharia uncle? After that, you all should decide what to do next.'

The phone rang before Asokan could react. Mini took the call.

'It's for you.'

Mohandas's voice came through. 'Asokan, I'm sorry. I was rude to you earlier.'

Asokan stared at Mini. She was occupied in arranging some papers.

'Sir?'

'I have to speak directly to Mini, Asokan. Please fix an appointment for me immediately.'

Asokan's gaze returned to Mini once again. 'Madam is going to the Malabar hotel for a meeting now.'

'Meeting? The one conducted by the Chamber?'

'Yes.'

'Okay, I'll meet her there.'

'Sir...'

The call was disconnected.

Mini raised her head. 'Who was it?'

'Mohandas. He was requesting an appointment with you. Something urgent.'

Mini did not respond.

She kept her briefcase on the table and pressed the call bell.

Mini Balachandran did not ask Asokan the obvious question: 'Why did Mohandas call you to get an appointment with me?'

Asokan felt a tremor of fear.

38

The Game in the Tennis Court

Zacharia stood under the shower to let the water cool his body. In vain. The overhead tank was heated by the afternoon sun. The water from the city pipeline would be cooler. He turned the shower off. After opening the tap, Zacharia waited for the cool trickle to fill the bucket.

Water, unending flow of water! How many rivers Kerala was blessed with! There was no reason for a drought-like situation even if the monsoons played truant occasionally. There was great scope for a properly run water resources management company.

A water company.

The public would buy the shares. A public limited company with a management comprising qualified professionals, the government merely playing an advisory role; a check and balance for preventing exploitative profits.

Zacharia poured cold water over himself.

Weren't communism and capitalism fundamentally the same? When the capital belonged to the common man, was there any disparity? When classes disappeared, did a class war make sense?

A water company. An electricity company. A public health company. A transportation company.

No need for any subsidies. Why burden an unsuspecting public with debts accrued due to poorly performing government companies, running into crores of losses annually? But what would that mean for the rulers and administrators? A government in which the public representatives were limited to creating legislations that regulate companies? No political party would ever agree to such a concept.

Zacharia smiled to himself.

When he emerged, Govinda Prabhu, standing by the bathroom door, smiled back.

Zacharia said: 'I'll be at the club. If anyone calls, give them the club's number.'

Prabhu coughed discreetly.

'What's the matter, Prabhu?'

'Sir…'

'Go on.'

Prabhu had a small smile hovering on his face. Greed gleamed transparently in his eyes. The same glint that was visible in the eyes of the stockbrokers and investors.

'I heard that many people made huge profits from the Dhanwantari shares today. Is that correct, sir?'

Zacharia grinned at his Man Friday.

'Why, do you want to buy some shares?'

'Perhaps a hundred? The price rose by ten rupees. Is that correct, sir?

'Yes.'

'Thousand rupees in a day. What if I bought two hundred shares, sir?'

Zacharia continued to smile.

'Now, a share costs twenty-four rupees. It will cost you four thousand eight hundred rupees. Do you have the money?'

'If I mortgage my ear stud and ring, that will be a handsome amount. Almost two sovereigns of gold. I will reclaim them tomorrow. A profit of two thousand rupees.'

Zacharia responded: 'Anyway, let me come back from the club. You think about it one more time. What if the price crashes tomorrow by ten rupees?'

Prabhu's face turned bleak.

How many would lose sleep over Dhanwantari's shares tonight?

When Zacharia started for the club, he quipped: 'No point in calling to the Lord at Thirumala, Prabhu. I don't think the deities dabble in stocks and shares.'

The city had donned its evening gown. During the day, Mahatma Gandhi Road reeked of petrol and diesel. There was a surfeit of advertisements on the telephone posts, dividers, lamp posts and walls. All of them were of the newest consumer products that promised to make life finer.

The tennis court at the club was in action mode. Zacharia sat in a rattan chair on the verandah parallel to the court. His usual bottle of beer and a glass arrived.

A game was in full flow. The marker boys were the best players in any club. But they would get a chance only when not enough players were around. Even so, by practising when the courts were free, they became quite skilled. Here, too, the marker boy was serving swiftly and sharply. Nambiar, on the opposite side, was failing miserably. The boy slowed his serve.

Zacharia sipped from his glass. Dusk silently draped the city. The lights blinked to life inside the tennis court.

One set ended. Two new players stepped in. Nambiar and the marker boy withdrew.

Nambiar wiped his neck with a towel. Looking at Zacharia, he spoke:

'Were you trading today?'

Zacharia nodded.

Nambiar settled beside him. He clapped his hands to attract the attention of the club's attendant and gestured for a drink.

'One here.' Then he turned to face Zacharia. 'Some fellows are going to crash-land soon.'

'Hmm?'

'The trading of Dhanwantari broke all records. Take it from me, many are going to the pits soon.'

Nambiar was a member of a legendary family in the area. In the field of culture or arts, business or trade, nothing happened without his family playing a significant role. Naturally, Nambiar became a member of the Stock Exchange when it began.

A member could appoint four authorized assistants. They could officially trade in the Exchange. But there was one catch. Whatever buying or selling the assistants did, the ultimate responsibility rested with the member. In case anyone ended up losing in speculative trading, the member would be expected to pay the concerned amount to the Stock Exchange.

Nambiar had appointed four assistants charging fifty thousand rupees each. All four were brilliant. Nambiar was praised as a business-savvy broker.

A year passed. One Friday it was discovered that an assistant had defaulted on a payment of seventeen lakh rupees to the Exchange. It had accrued over a few weeks. Nambiar had not given it much thought. The Stock Exchange demanded that Nambiar pay up the missing amount. He did not have any money. The assistant promised to get the money from home and left town. When the young man went missing for a fortnight, Nambiar set out to trace him. There was no one by that name in the address the youth had provided.

That day onwards, Nambiar was suspended from the Exchange although he continued to be a member. He would get notices intermittently from the Exchange. Occasionally, the man would respond to them. Nambiar was planning to sell his membership card and settle the debt. However, he went to the Stock Exchange without fail. With great fervour, he would proclaim to all and sundry that speculative traders were going to be devastated any moment.

Zacharia asked: 'Nambiar sir, didn't you try a hand?'

'Me?' Nambiar lowered his voice. 'It seems you're unaware of the game. Let me explain. The Bombaywala is behind it. The price shall increase until it hits, say, seventy rupees. Then the prices will be reined in. On the day the brokers have to submit the share certificates for settlement, wait to watch the bloodletting. They won't be having any share certificates, will they? They will have to pay up the price that day, almost seventy. All who sold today and are planning to sell tomorrow, will be shattered. The ones who sold in Cochin will lose, and the Bombaywala will benefit.'

The brokers who always had a back-up of considerable money played a significant role in the Stock Exchange operations. Without any external provocations they could raise and lower the stock prices. Many companies found it imperative to show high share prices. When the prices were high during the issuing of bonds, non-convertible debentures or IPOs (initial public offerings), the public invested more. Brokers played a vital role in ensuring high share prices during such critical times.

The stock exchanges were supposed to regulate such tactics. They could even come up with a rule that one has to pay twenty or forty per cent of the total share value purchased as cash before registering the sales of the shares. Spot trading, buying and selling assets at the current market price, aka spot price, could be enforced. But all laws had loopholes. Mostly, the regulators themselves were the fences that ate the crop.

Zacharia asked: 'Any inside information? What if somebody in Kerala is trying to take over Dhanwantari?'

'No, no! I know this is a totally Bombay-based action. They loathe the fact that our small stock exchanges are growing in scope and impact. Even though we started out late, aren't we the third largest when it comes to trading?'

'But that's more in speculation, right?'

'Yes, but even that needs some guts, doesn't it?'

The progenitors of the Indian Stock Exchange were those who handled the bonds of the East India Company in Calcutta towards the end of the eighteenth century. During the period of 1861–65, a huge amount of share trading took place in Bombay and Calcutta. The victory and defeat of speculators began in those times. Many turned into lakhpatis and many, paupers. Trading was mostly conducted in an unorganized manner.

In 1875, the first Stock Exchange came up in Bombay; Ahmedabad had its Exchange in 1894, and Calcutta in 1908. Madras got its Stock Exchange in 1937. Usually, one had the leeway of paying up the amount of share trading over a period of time. But the Madras Exchange had very strict norms, a maximum of two days for settling accounts. That effectively discouraged speculative trading. The interval for raking in profits from high share prices was severely limited to two or three days in Madras. The other exchanges gave a relaxation of over ten days. Hence, the trend in Madras was always starkly different as compared to other exchanges.

The second set started. Nambiar did not participate. A niggling knee pain.

'Dhanwantari has a good range of salves. You can buy some shares and make enough money to establish a vaidyasala.'

Nambiar smiled.

'No way, you know what happened in Madras today.'

'One of my fellows told me in strict confidence. Till closing time, the price was twenty. At the last minute, some party started a buying spree. At twenty-three and a half rupees! Fifty paisa more than the Bombay rate. Tomorrow, the newspapers will publish only the closing rate. The public will presume that the Madras share prices are very high. But in reality, they sold twenty thousand shares under twenty. Only the last hundred shares were sold at twenty-three rupees. But what will be the published information tomorrow? Twenty-three and a half.'

Zacharia grinned.

'That means it is war.'

'What about entering the arena tomorrow?'

The waiter came running. 'Sir, phone.'

Zacharia said: 'I'll be back soon.'

It was Mini's call.

'Uncle?'

'Yes.'

'You seem to be in a good mood.'

'Some beer, that's all.'

'I need some help. You know Mr Mohandas, right?'

'Yes.'

'He's adamant on saving our company somehow. I haven't a clue why. Can you find out what's behind his extraordinary interest?'

'By when do you need the information?'

'In half an hour's time. I'm speaking from Malabar hotel. Mohandas is coming over to the club to meet you. Please wait.'

'Okay.'

Zacharia was steeped in thought when he replaced the receiver in the cradle.

39

A Bachelor's Mind

'The transformation in the Indian government's outlook towards trade and commerce has been remarkable. The socialist idea was to throttle the life breath of the private sector. The new approach is a harbinger of hope. Also, the changes in policy for exports and imports, even the foreign exchange policy, augur well for the business community. Now foreign companies are being welcomed with open hands to start investments in our country. In Kerala, for those with sound infrastructural backgrounds, this is a good time. Make a working agreement with multinational companies or specialized foreign investors who are keen on a new product. Our sectors…'

Mini Balachandran did not listen to the rest of the speech. It was a seminar under the auspices of the Chamber of Commerce and Industries. It had started at 5 p.m. sharp.

The top businessmen and traders of Kerala chitchatted in the pleasant coolness of the Malabar hotel. Most were companies focusing on exports: Coir, marine products, coconut oil, spices, processed goods. A few like Dhanwantari Herbal Products.

There were many cheerful faces, delighted by the positive outlook of government policies. The falling rupee in the international market gave hope to the exporters. The nitty-gritty of export-related rules and regulations was less formidable nowadays.

Mini's mind did not follow the speaker. She had wondered whether she should attend the seminar. The real challenge was to get to the bottom of the share price game in multiple stock exchanges. It was the question of Dhanwantari's survival.

In the office, befuddled about the next step to be taken, Mini had gazed at her father's picture.

Suddenly, she remembered visiting Trivandrum with her father.

Mini had just completed her pre-degree examinations. Acchan had to visit Trivandrum urgently. A loan case, which had taken up a year's efforts. One of the common dining-room topics was the challenge of arranging for a loan. He wanted to initiate a scheme near Adimali, before the Nelliyampathy project started. Acchan was exhibiting signs of nervous tension. The desperate attempt at securing a loan finally worked out. He had to visit the bank's head office in Trivandrum the next day.

'You're having holidays now. Why don't you join me on the trip?'

During the car journey, Mini's father had waxed eloquent about the minor details of the new project at Adimali, which he hoped to implement after securing the bank loan. It was a huge sum, and he had all his hopes pinned on this dream project. He was in top spirits. When they reached the bank at eleven, the divisional manager extended a paper.

'Sir, I tried calling you in Ernakulam. This is a telex message from Bombay denying the loan. Some unexpected government regulation regarding environment clearance.'

Mini's father did not utter a word. He thanked the manager politely. He never displayed the devastation of his plans being shattered.

When they returned to the car, Mini remarked: 'How sad! What will we do now?'

Acchan replied: 'We have time until the evening. Let's visit the zoo. You wanted to see the baby giraffes, didn't you? Let's go now. We can visit our local office later. I want to shift our sales office and showroom to a better building.'

Her father forgot about the loan. They saw the giraffes. Then they scouted for buildings for shifting their office. Never did her father waste time lamenting over a year's hard work that had gone down the drain.

Recollecting the incident, Mini had decided to attend the seminar at Malabar hotel.

~

Mini did not remember Mohandas. Perhaps she had met him earlier, or even seen an occasional photograph of his in a news item. Why did he want to meet her, that too using Asokan as an intermediary?

The car did not stop at the overbridge. From the backseat, Mini watched the new ships in the yard. They appeared as small specks in the sea.

Suddenly, she became alert. Asokan had been bubbling in the morning but had looked slightly depressed by evening. Was he involved in the takeover bid?

What about Mohandas? He was Mini's father's acquaintance. A lone tusker. He had built a business empire single-handedly. Was Mohandas married? Mini hadn't heard anyone mention his family. Married to business, perhaps!

Her father had once commented: 'Unmarried people are incomplete. They are always yearning to fill the void in themselves with someone. And it is an unending thirst.'

If Mohandas was a bachelor, it was likely that he would be ruthless during a takeover. Was the endeavour to destroy or help?

Why would Mohandas step into a relatively new field like the production of Ayurvedic medicine?

She was listening, albeit indifferently, to the active discussions on how the central government should run its department of finance when Mini heard someone address her.

'Excuse me, madam. I am Mohandas.'

Mini turned to look. She smiled. 'Oh, yes. We have not met officially before.'

'I did not have the good fortune or opportunity until now.'

A glimmer of innocence was visible on Mini Balachandran's face. As Mini was about to set down the teacup she had been holding all this while, Mohandas quickly took it from her hand.

'Thanks.'

Placing the teacup on the table, Mohandas spoke:

'I have seen you. But unfortunately, those were all in adverse situations. So we could never be formally introduced to each other. I attended your wedding too. How is Mr Balachandran?'

'Fine, thank you.'

'Still in Delhi?'

'Yes.'

'No chances of a transfer?'

'Perhaps. But it all depends on the government.'

'You are right.'

They walked to the foyer.

'I have always wondered. A woman like you, extremely beautiful and brilliant, stepping into business, instead of enjoying herself in creative pursuits. In the jungle infested with wild animals ... I don't know. Are you happy?'

It was the moment when dusk touched the sea. Watching the guiding ship's lights flicker as it paved its way through the bay, Mini smiled. Her eyes lit up with wonder.

'Uncle, did you call me to ask this particular question? My father used to speak a lot about you. That one should learn from you, rising from challenging circumstances to scale such heights of success in business. To be frank, I am not happy. But what can I do? Both my father and brother … This is our family business. Legacy. Can one run off from such a heavy responsibility?'

Mohandas stood shell-shocked. 'Uncle' was a form of address he had never expected in his wildest dreams! Mini was speaking like a naïve kid. To hide his emotions, Mohandas tried to light his pipe. It did not catch the flame.

Mini continued:

'Take today for example. Our share prices are climbing steadily in all the stock exchanges. I cannot understand why! The company's financial status is not good. It is also a highly competitive field. Who is behind this phenomenon? And for what reason? Do you know, the share prices doubled by the evening? I'm scared.'

Mohandas was gazing at Mini Balachandran as if she were some strange creature. Was she acting? This obvious naivety, her childlike confession? If so, she was a smart cookie. He recalled Asokan's comment. 'A chit of a girl, rather foolish. She acted innocent even when the board decided to make her the MD of Dhanwantari Herbal Products. Anyone would like her. A damsel in distress.'

Mohandas tried to catch her eye. Mini's gaze was fixed on the horizon where the darkness met eternity. She turned her head.

'Sorry, Uncle. I bothered you with my unnecessary griping. Why did you wish to see me? When Asokan chettan asked me to meet you, I was truly astounded.'

'Mrs Mini Balachandran, do you call everyone chettan or uncle?' Mohandas laughed.

Mini's face displayed a five-year-old girl's innocent smile.

'Our company is like a family. I have grown up seeing all of the staff. Acchan would say that the business aspect came later. It is a way of life. A relationship based on a strong, fundamental idea. Nobody has ever been dismissed for non-performance.

Maybe that is a liability. But Acchan insisted that if there are four siblings in a family, all of them would not be gifted equally. Does that mean one feeds less food to the dull one? He wanted everything to be idealistic. So, everyone is a relative to me. Uncle, chettan or chechi.'

The pipe finally lit up. Mohandas took two puffs. There was a rhythm to the waves lapping against the wall near the grass meadow. The reflection of the yellow lights from the boat moving to Cochin threw alluring shadows in the lagoon waters.

Suddenly, Mini said: 'Look, that's a dolphin for sure! The water is churning.'

Mohandas stood stupefied. 'What?'

'Over there ... No, I was mistaken. Not a dolphin ... What did you want to discuss, Uncle? Was it about the problems the company is facing?'

'Yes.'

'What should I do? Tell me.'

'I will be frank with you. I knew Menon sir very well. Let us say that I respect only a few people, and your father stands out tall among them. A dreamer and a business visionary. Though I could never catch up with him, I have the same attitude. I feel that it is my responsibility to help when his company is undergoing trouble. Mr Asokan had spoken about the issues. I told him that I would discuss them with you and arrive at a solution. That is why we are here now.'

Mohandas could not see Mini's face clearly. In the shadows cast by the lawn lights, he caught the rhythmic tapping of her slender fingers on her vanity bag.

Mini said: 'Money is the name of the game. Unless one wins in the share market, things won't be sorted out. Dhanwantari is reeling under liquidity issues. All the money is locked up in fixed assets. Even the bankers are unsure. Sometimes I feel they don't have enough faith in me.'

Mohandas said: 'I will help.'

'How?'

'The expenses don't matter … Whatever it takes.'

Mini turned effusive. 'Uncle, thank you so much … With no strings attached?'

'Yes.'

'Thank you. I knew God would not let go of me. You should take on one additional trouble for my sake.'

'Yes.'

'There is Zacharia uncle, who is my advisor.'

'Another uncle, eh?'

Mini smiled.

'He is a stockbroker. An old friend of my father. Old-time Communist, footballer. You should get in touch with him and decide the future course of action. I will go with whatever you both decide.'

'P.T. Zacharia?'

'Yes, do you know him?'

'I have heard quite a lot about him. We will talk … Do you have his number?'

'Zacharia uncle must be at the club. Let me check.'

Mini called Zacharia and returned.

'Zacharia uncle will be waiting for you at the tennis club.'

'Good.'

When Mini made her way towards the seminar hall, Mohandas commented: 'One moment, Mini. I am not old enough to be your uncle.'

Mini smiled sweetly.

'Sorry. You seemed like my father in both wisdom and knowledge. Apologies. I shall call you chettan from now on.'

40

Speculation in Love

For the first time in his life, Shankaran Kutty broke his routine. His friends, travelling in the Kottayam passenger train they took daily, played cards without their core member that evening. Initially they had been hesitant to start without him. Maybe their friend had run late and managed to get into some other bogey at the last minute? When the train halted at Tripunithura station, all of them stretched their necks to check for Shankaran Kutty. He was nowhere to be seen.

What happened? Did he fall sick?

Shankaran Kutty disliked the city after six o'clock. But what could he do? He had to stay back. Today, he had indulged in speculative trade for the first time in his life.

Trusting Savitry, he had bought ten thousand Dhanwantari shares in curb trading. The Stock Exchange working time was over an hour ago. Curb trading was carrying on in full swing on the second floor.

'TISCO.'

'Apollo Tyres.'

'Dhanwantari Herbal Products.'

Shankaran Kutty diffidently searched for sellers of Dhanwantari shares.

Three thousand shares for twenty-four rupees. Four thousand for twenty-five. Three thousand for twenty-five and a half rupees.

The doubts started to creep in when he returned to his cubicle after exchanging the informal paper slips. They crawled inside Shankaran Kutty's mind like lugubrious earthworms. What if luck turned and the price crashed tomorrow? This morning it was fourteen. What if it became thirteen tomorrow? What then?

Shankaran Kutty hopped about, as if he had stepped on hot embers.

He hadn't smoked in a while. He stepped out and bought a pack of cigarettes. How costly cigarettes were nowadays! Almost double their old price. Like Dhanwantari's share prices.

Shankaran Kutty forgot to check his watch. He also became oblivious of the fact that usually he would be gobbling down ghee-roasted dosa at the Udupi restaurant near the railway station. Hunger had long abandoned him.

He scoured the *Economic Times* again and again. Yesterday, Dhanwantari shares had been trading in Bombay, Ahmedabad and Delhi. Savitry was most probably right. Two parties were trying to acquire the company.

Good, let the price shoot up. Tonight, just for tonight, let them continue with their takeover bid. Until tomorrow afternoon. Shankaran Kutty planned to sell the ten thousand shares by that time. After that, even if the takeover bid went to hell, it would not matter.

Shankaran Kutty closed his eyes and meditated on the Lord of the Ettumanoor temple. He needed His benediction at this critical hour. There were feral animals around in this wild jungle. Just being alert with one's eyes and ears open would not suffice. One needed the bulwark of that invisible power. Even if we insisted on walking the straight path, unexpected obstacles could crop up on the way. The Lord should constantly be by one's side. That was very important.

Shankaran Kutty remembered an incident that had shaken him badly a year before.

~

There was an investor called K.S.P. Nair. He lived in Calcutta. There were two thousand shares of a Bombay company in his name. When the shares costing ten rupees rose to sixty in the share market, his brother K.S.V. Nair sold them following the instructions of his older sibling. Shankaran Kutty was the broker who sold them. He had also charged his commission. After two weeks, on a Friday, he submitted the accounts to the Stock Exchange with all the duly signed documents for transferring the share certificates to the buyer. The buyer's broker handed over the cheque. K.S.V. Nair, the younger brother, got the money.

A month and a half later, the broker who bought the shares approached Shankaran Kutty. The company headquarters had apparently returned the share certificates. Allegedly, the signature of the person who signed the certificates was different from what was in the original record. Such a sale was illegal. Now the shares cost ninety rupees – thirty rupees more than the sale price. Sixty thousand rupees in total for two thousand shares.

They searched high and low for K.S.V. Nair. The man was not to be found. He had gone abroad. When they called up the elder brother K.S.P. Nair, he revealed that he had no idea what was going on. His younger brother had been a crook since childhood. Why don't they file a criminal case against him? He offered to help. Shankaran Kutty became frantic with worry.

The buyer was adamant about receiving his due shares. K.S.P. Nair wrote to Shankaran Kutty from Calcutta: *I shall help you out. I will sign the share certificates. Pay me today's price.* He wanted an additional sixty thousand rupees! Frustration, fury and helplessness roiled inside Shankaran Kutty. He wanted to file a case. But he didn't even know the fugitive's address. The incidental expenses and the difficulties were another story. The constant pressure of the broker and the buyer. Maybe both the brothers were involved in the conspiracy. Who could tell!

A month later, the elder brother came to Kerala. Sitting in the bar, he thoroughly abused his younger sibling. By that time, the price had gone down to eighty rupees. Shankaran Kutty sought help from some mediators. Finally they reached a compromise. Shankaran Kutty was also at fault partially, wasn't he? Why did he sell the shares without checking with the owner K.S.P. Nair? The signature which the younger brother produced was also forged. The older brother acknowledged that he too was to be blamed. Didn't his brother steal the share certificates easily? He offered to endure a loss of ten rupees. Shankaran Kutty should step forward and suffer the same. Finally, they settled for seventy rupees. The share certificates were exchanged.

Shankaran Kutty suffered a loss of twenty thousand rupees. He filed a criminal case against K.S.V. Nair. But he had no great hopes about it. The advocate sent his bills on the dot. Whenever he received those, Shankaran Kutty would contemplate withdrawing the case.

What if the share prices had gone up from ninety to a hundred and twenty instead of decreasing to eighty? The Lord's grace was essential during such circumstances.

Shankaran Kutty smoked another cigarette.

He went to Savitry's cubicle. It was empty.

What should he do now?

Shankaran Kutty decided to book a room in a lodge. Buy a shirt and a mundu. Take a shower, wear the new clothes and visit

Savitry at her hostel. Go to a nearby hotel for dinner. Dhanwantari Herbals should not figure anywhere during their conversation. Wasn't it better to take her to the temple instead? Or should they go to Subhash Park, gaze at the backwaters and ... There should be serenity around. His heart had to open up before her. One needed a divine ambience. The Lord's benediction was essential for this matter too.

Shankaran Kutty arranged the papers on his table. Folding the newspaper, he tucked it inside his briefcase. A few young men were at the curb trading corner. Most of the cubicles were deserted. On the third floor, where the president and the office bearers of the Stock Exchange sat, the lights were still blazing bright. All of them were in the office.

The staircases that used to be choked with the rabble of eager buyers and sellers were desolate now. Even the watchman was missing. Shankaran Kutty took a look around. A few red flags – remnants of the morning strike – could be glimpsed lying here and there. A couple of vehicles – two motorcycles and a car – were parked on the opposite side of the street.

First, take a room in a lodge. Then buy some clothes. Shower.

Savitry.

He stood at the junction near Mahatma Gandhi Road. While he waited for an autorickshaw, someone tapped his shoulder.

An acquaintance. An authorized assistant at the Stock Exchange. Shankaran Kutty could not recollect his name. He smiled at the young man.

The man's face made it evident that he had visited the bar recently. But he was not too tipsy. He asked: 'Are you interested in Dhanwantari shares?'

'Hmm?'

'I have five thousand shares to sell.'

'Price?'

'The closing was at twenty-four. But I'll give you at fifty paisa less.'

'Twenty-three and a half rupees.'

'Yes.'

Shankaran Kutty was shocked. The man did not notice his expression.

Exactly half an hour earlier, he had bought three thousand shares at twenty-five and a half rupees. Now they were selling at twenty-three and a half! What on earth was happening? Were the prices crashing? Good lord!

Shankaran Kutty responded: 'I don't need any. Already bought some.'

'I'll give you for twenty-three.'

'Are the shares falling?'

The man said: 'Sir, you're sure you don't want any, right?'

'I don't want any.'

'Let me tell you. The prices are going to fall soon. Better to sell to avoid much loss.'

'How do you know?'

'Oh, the share price in Madras was not more than twenty. At the closing time, some fellow bought some fifty-odd shares at twenty-three and a half and escalated the costs. The price has gone down in the curb trading in Bombay too. I bought five thousand at twenty-two. I just want to save my neck now.'

An autorickshaw ambled closer. Shankaran Kutty seated himself inside.

'Where do you want to go, sir?'

'Go straight.' He mentioned the name of the ladies' hostel.

It was when they had gone quite a distance that reality hit Shankaran Kutty. He had not booked a room. He had not bought new clothes. Taking a shower too would not be possible.

Never mind.

Here, moments were worth money. Who knew what losses would accumulate with further delay. He still had time to take Savitry to the temple, park and restaurant. Far away from the world of TISCO, Dhanwantari, Genelec and Titan ... Now, Dhanwantari was the burning topic.

He waited for almost ten minutes in the waiting room at the hostel. When Savitry stood at the door, rather bemused, evidently having taken a fresh shower, Shankaran Kutty's heart started beating faster.

One moment.

It was time for intelligence and prudence to exert iron control over one's passions.

Savitry saw him. A smile. His heart throbbed quicker.

'What? What happened?'

'Savitry, the price is twenty-three now.'

Savitry looked askance at him. She sat down in a chair nearby.

'What?'

'Just now I bought ten thousand shares of Dhanwantari in curb for twenty-five and a half. But ten minutes later, it's become twenty-three! Maybe it'll slip down further. Your information wasn't correct.'

'No, it can't be. Vikas would've definitely called if there had been a change in trend.'

'Who's Vikas?'

'My ... my friend in Bombay.'

'Let's call him.'

Savitry became engrossed in thought for a few moments.

'No. If there's any change, Vikas is sure to call. It's better to wait here than go to a booth to ring him up.'

'What about me?'

'If I get any tip, I shall immediately inform you. Where are you staying?'

Shankaran Kutty did not hear that question.

'What if this Vikas fellow tricks you?'

'He won't.'

'Is he a Malayali?'

'Marwari.'

'Oh, Marwari? Then don't fall for it. Am not too sure if they can be trusted.'

Savitry smiled. Her dimples flashed, eyes sparkled. The water clinging to the locks of her hair resting on her forehead, slowly trickled into Shankaran Kutty's heart. He became flustered.

Savitry said: 'Mister Shankaran Kutty, I'll share a secret. If you promise not to talk about it.'

He nodded dumbly.

'We're going to get married. Vikas is my boyfriend. I have known him for almost five years now. In a year's time, we'll get married in Bombay.'

Shankaran Kutty sat shell-shocked. He did not even notice the circling fan overhead. Savitry got up and patted him on the shoulder.

'If there's any inside trading in Bombay, Vikas will inform me by seven o'clock. Or after ten at night. Give me your hotel number. I shall keep you updated. No worries.'

Darkness encroached on Shankaran Kutty's eyes. Everything was shaking. He did not understand a word of what Savitry was saying.

He lifted his face. Savitry smiled again. This time, he did not notice her dimples.

'I'm leaving.'

Savitry reacted: 'Mister Shankaran Kutty, you should sell today's shares only after Vikas calls me.'

Vikas! Vikas! Shankaran Kutty walked out fuming in silence.

One should never trust women. All these years she was secretly in love with someone. They were apparently getting married soon! That, too, a Marwari. How did Savitry garner the courage to do all this? He must have lured her with inside information from the Stock Exchange. Otherwise, would such a lovely, intelligent young woman fall into a Marwari's trap? Anyway, he was not going to let it go so easily. This was just a passing fancy.

Shankaran Kutty decided to show Savitry that he was better than her Vikas when it came to using one's intelligence to make money. Then she will come to her senses. The sheen of infatuation will be removed from her eyes. *Vikas! Useless fellow! He and his blasted phone. Tonight or tomorrow morning, Dhanwantari prices will crash. Savitry's shares will remain unsold. But I will have sold every share I bought. I shall sell them at a good profit tonight itself. Now tell me, who's smarter? Vikas or Shankaran Kutty?*

'Are you about to kill yourself, bloody fool!' An autorickshaw almost grazed against him.

'There's a footpath on the side. If you want to kill yourself, why choose my auto? Go west. There's a lagoon.'

Shankaran Kutty leapt to the footpath. He had been walking on the main road until now.

Whatever it was, he was determined to sell all the shares immediately. No thanks, he did not need any of Vikas's tipoffs.

The sales should not cause any loss. He should not become a loser before Savitry.

Shankaran Kutty walked to a nearby telephone booth. He ruffled through the telephone directory.

Dhanwantari Herbal Products. Managing Director. Personal number.

Shankaran Kutty dialled the number.

41

Herbalism

At the office of Dhanwantari Herbal Products, the last light to be switched off was typically that of Finance Director Adiyodi's room. When Mr Menon was alive, he would stay back till eight at night. After office hours, he would call Adiyodi. They would chat leisurely for forty-five minutes. Usually it was Menon who talked. Adiyodi would hum and haw in accompaniment.

Those days were long gone. Ever since Mini Balachandran had taken over as managing director, she would leave the office sharp at six. It was Adiyodi who insisted that she should go home on time. A helpless young woman. Due to a cruel twist of fate, she had been burdened with such a heavy responsibility. Wasn't there a limit to what a woman should endure? Even her husband was not around for support.

On the first day, Adiyodi had generously advised Mini: 'Mini, don't be afraid. Just come to office at your convenience. We shall handle everything.' Mini had respectfully listened to him.

However, Adiyodi did feel aggrieved from time to time. Mini often took decisions without consulting him. But Adiyodi consoled himself thinking that those were around insignificant matters.

For the important issues that affected the company, his own opinion remained the final word.

Adiyodi's vexation lay in whiling away time after six in the evening. When Menon sir was there, he would listen to that flowing Ganga of words. An occasional smoke. A hot mug of tea flavoured with cardamom. Now it was utterly desolate after six o'clock. The office files left him cold. He wished to talk with someone. He needed a big mug of tea. Only then that feeling of completion would emerge.

On rare occasions, it would come true. Like today, for example.

The company estate at Nelliyampathy was lying forsaken for all these years. There was a need to create a working plan and establish a herbal garden there. The main cell of the research wing was supposed to work from there. Menon sir had been toying with that idea for almost twenty years. He had purchased the property fifteen years ago. But things had not panned out as he wished. Money issues had cropped up.

A small office at the Nelliyampathy estate, guest house, research laboratory, residential quarters for research officers and staff, road, electricity, telephone: all entailed heavy investment. It was a long-term project, which would take almost ten years to come to fruition. There was a delay in funding the project. Cash flow problems had always pestered the company.

After Mini became the MD, she had appointed a young doctor as a researcher.

One morning, the young man had approached Adiyodi without any recommendation letter. A lean, bearded young man, with a serene expression. He had earlier worked as a researcher in the herbal plantation of a Lucknow company at Pachmarhi. He had a degree in Ayurvedic medicine. But the young doctor preferred to do research than take care of patients.

During the interview, Mini asked him: 'Why did you leave the previous job?'

'Purely personal, madam. Nothing to do with my professional work.'

When he left the room, Mini had appreciated his honesty. The man had been appointed immediately.

Every three months, he would come to discuss his progress.

The young doctor had met Mini this afternoon. Adiyodi had asked him to wait till five for their meeting. It was six o'clock when Adiyodi called him inside his room.

'Now we can talk without any disturbance.'

The young man started talking. Adiyodi ordered tea, after keeping aside the report the doctor had submitted.

'Herbalism is a concept much acclaimed internationally. A nation's health lies in her herbs and plants. Ayurveda, based on scientific processes, will show the way ahead. Ayurveda never accepts any medicine that triggers sickness while seemingly healing the body. Cleansing and detoxification procedures in Ayurveda make use of herbal medicines exclusively. The fundamental texts like *Charaka-samhita* and *Susruta-samhita* have elucidated upon such aspects. I found many rare herbs in our Nelliyampathy estate..'

Adiyodi smiled.

'I know that. When Menon sir was vacillating between the property in Adimaly and Nelliyampathy, it was I who insisted on buying the Nelliyampathy estate. My judgement has proved correct.'

The young man beamed. Usually it was rare to get a patient audience. Typically, people laughed at him. They referred to him as a 'bore' behind his back. But someone who was slightly crazy often turned out to be a maverick, proposing brilliant ideas and providing leadership to the world.

The young doctor went ahead at full steam:

'There are references to sixty-seven herbs in the Rigveda and seventy-two in the Yajurveda. Two hundred and thirty-nine is what the Atharvaveda expounds. Six-hundred-odd herbs are mentioned in the *Charaka-samhita*. An equivalent number is cited in Susruta's treatise as well. In Vagbhatacharya's works, we read about a hundred plants.

'Most Ayurveda professionals are in the dark about the herbs in our own backyard. There's a fair estimate that seven lakh flowering plants exist in our world. Ayurveda believes that every plant has medicinal value. It's just a question of matching a plant with what it can be best used for, that's all.

'Only a minuscule part of the plant family has been researched till now. In Kerala, almost fifteen hundred plants have been found. Just seven hundred have been thoroughly researched and used. That means, another eight hundred herbs are waiting to be studied for their healing properties. We have nearly two hundred plants in our Nelliyampathy estate. We can bring up innumerable herbs easily. I have created a list of plants for the purpose. There's an annexure to the main report.'

'What about medicines for invigorating the system and dealing with geriatric problems? Maybe step into non-herbal terrain?' Adiyodi asked.

The young man replied: 'Yes, sir. Mud, sulphur, rock water, metals, why, even human wastes are sometimes included in the vast repertoire of Ayurvedic preparations. But the rule is not to use anything except milk for longevity and maintaining the balance of the body. Only for treating sexual disorders has there been a legacy of using meat and liquor.'

A smile appeared on Adiyodi's face. 'That's intriguing.'

'In my opinion, if we improve our packaging and make it look classier, there's great scope in the European market. We can't fight with allopathy companies abroad. But China, Japan and South-East Asian countries follow our culture, more or less. Their bodily ailments are similar to ours too. For example, there are very few Asians free from asthma or such respiratory troubles. If we can develop a single patent for multiple allergies, we can market it all over Asia.'

Adiyodi sat upright. The young man was intelligent and sharp. To what extent would his ideas work in practical life?

'Look, we have our own legacies, like the sacred ten flowers, the dasa-pushpa, which we use for our rituals. I did some research recently and produced a medicine. In fact, I tried it on some of the estate employees and they got much relief. Immediate relief for asthma in a week's time! I repeated the trial in a week's time. Basically it is the crushed juice of a rare herb's root. The Adivasis often use this plant. Upon chewing the leaves, one doesn't even feel the pain of wounds. I tried the roots as a cure. Very effective for asthma.'

'Did you divulge your extracurricular activity to the MD?'

'No, she didn't seem to be in a good mood. Well, Madam assured me that she'd read my report.'

'She's a woman, what can we do? But she's intelligent. After all, there's something called family legacy.'

'I've made some samples.'

'Do you have them with you?'

'I will bring them tomorrow.'

When the doctor was about to leave, the phone rang. The telephone operator usually left at six. Four lines were linked to the security after that. One was connected to Adiyodi's office.

Adiyodi gesticulated to the doctor to stay put and took the call.

'Adiyodi speaking.'

'I am Shankaran Kutty. Sir, are you the finance director of Dhanwantari Herbals?'

'Yes, who are you?'

'I am a broker.'

'Broker?' Adiyodi raised an eyebrow and looked at the doctor. He grinned.

'Yes.'

'I don't need the help of any brokers.'

'I am a share broker.'

'Go on.'

'Do you need shares of your company?'

'What are you blabbing about?'

'I called the managing director. Nobody answered the call. Someone from the security answered the other numbers. Somehow, I got through to you. Do you need Dhanwantari's shares?'

'Why would we need our own shares?'

'Ten thousand shares at twenty-six rupees.'

Adiyodi contemplated the offer for a while.

'No.'

Disconnecting the call, he complained to the young doctor: 'Some drunkard. He wants to know if we need ten thousand shares of our own company! For twenty-six rupees. Selling us our own shares!'

Some time passed. Then Adiyodi said: 'Liquor's the curse of this city. Drinking in the evenings has become a fashion these days. Disgraceful!' He sounded preachy.

The doctor smiled.

Meanwhile, Shankaran Kutty was staring at the telephone receiver in utter bewilderment. The company's own management wasn't bothered to save it!

42

An Attempt at Dacoity

'Having listened to all of you, I think it's best we sell all the shares that have been bought until now,' said Aniyan Raja. 'The share price will definitely escalate tomorrow. The Bombay brokers are fighting on behalf of one or two north Indian companies. Both shall try to keep the prices high. If we jump into the fray, we'll only end up hurt. Yes, it sounds like defeat, withdrawing at this stage of one's initial business venture ... Pardon me, I forgot your name.'

'Matthews.'

'Yes, Matthews. You should wait and watch. When the price becomes unbelievably high, sell off all the shares. That makes business sense. Are we mule-headed about taking over Dhanwantari? No. We made an attempt, that's all. The timing went awry since the north Indians entered the arena at the same time. Bad luck. Now let's get out without any injury.'

~

Matthews, Unni and Sreedevi had chatted only for five minutes after dinner. They had been astounded by the latest news. What the journalist shared was like a bolt from the blue.

First, a planted news item in *The Times of India*. Second, the news that would be flashed in every newspaper tomorrow: about the takeover bid of Dhanwantari Herbals and the role of Aniyan Raja in the game.

The first news item was aimed at lowering the share prices of Dhanwantari Herbals. The second, on the other hand, would provoke a sharp increase in share prices. The Bulls would rush in on hearing that a takeover was being played out. The share prices would grow by leaps and bounds. Both those who wished to take over the company and those who wished to fight off that attempt needed the shares. The Bulls would increase the prices so long as there was a buyer in the market.

Unni said: 'Let us discuss this with Uncle.'

Aniyan Raja was glancing through some documents when they entered his room. Aniyan Raja's bedroom also functioned as a drawing room. A wide hall, large enough to house four rooms. A huge bathroom was attached to it. Black cement flooring, smoother than marble. Gigantic glass almirahs full of books. There was a TV and a VCR in one corner. The television was arranged so that Aniyan Raja could watch it from his bed. A centre table carved from rosewood and two sofa sets. An easy chair next to the cot. A small side table with a computer and cordless phone on it. A few bottles of medicine and a small paan box.

Aniyan Raja breathed laboriously. It made his asthma evident. He smiled at Matthews.

'Come and take a seat. You must have been miffed by the dinner.'

'Not at all. It was pretty good. My family prefers vegetarian fare. My father does not touch meat. But my mother can't cook such excellent dishes.'

Aniyan Raja folded the documents in front of him.

'I'm thinking of getting a dish antenna. This was paperwork in that regard. Involves an investment of around a lakh. One shall be able to watch CNN without any ado. Now the government decides when we watch the news, doesn't it? With a dish antenna, I can watch the news whenever I wish. That's good.'

Matthews looked wide-eyed at the aged man.

Aniyan Raja asked: 'Did you discuss the matter? What have you decided? Seems like I will have to endure the asthma till the new moon now. But I tried a new medicine. Very effective, I must say. Go ahead, tell me your plans.'

Matthews explained: 'From this morning, the share prices have been skyrocketing. A bullish market has been the trend recently. But Dhanwantari was not in the picture at all. Yet, the company's share prices became almost double by evening. This is not just the brokers manipulating the scene. There are solid players behind what's happening. Not just in Bombay, the shares are actively being traded here too.'

Unni informed Aniyan Raja about *The Times of India* news article and the journalist who had dropped in just a while ago.

'The news will be out tomorrow. The share prices will go berserk afterwards.'

'What's the attitude of the girl who runs Dhanwantari? She will be in real trouble soon.'

Matthews replied: 'The managing director Mini Balachandran appears very confident. At least that's what I judged through the telephonic conversation. She told me that we should discuss our business proposal by five tomorrow, or she's not interested.'

Aniyan Raja smiled. 'Maybe that's a tactic to intimidate us.'

'Perhaps. But I suspect that, in the meantime, she's making some secret moves.'

'When someone is pushed into a corner, they will fight ferociously. Even the antelope will attack a tiger.'

'What should we do? We have spent over twenty lakhs till now. Also, I have committed to buying more shares in curb trading. Tomorrow morning…'

The electricity connection snapped unexpectedly. A moment later, the lights blinked on. Matthews was pleasantly surprised.

'I thought the electricity was gone for good. Even in Ernakulam city, it takes quite some time before the connection is re-established.'

Unni responded with a smile. 'Oh, it is brutal here. This is the electricity produced by our own gobar gas plant. When the original line is reconnected, the system switches off by itself. Won't suffice for the whole house, but we can manage comfortably in the meanwhile.'

Aniyan Raja said: 'Sreedevi, what's your view? You heard everything, didn't you?'

'Yes,' responded Sreedevi.

'If you were the managing director of Dhanwantari, what would you have done?'

Sreedevi paused for a moment. Then she said: 'I would not let go of my company.'

'Okay, but you don't have money to fight off the takeover bid, do you?'

'I have two alternatives. One, fight with money. Either borrow, or mortgage my shares in the company, ensuring liquid cash…'

Matthews shook his head. 'That's difficult.'

'Maybe. But I'll try. I prefer the second alternative though.'

'What's that?'

'I shall find out why someone is trying to take over Dhanwantari. Not who, but why. If I know who's behind it, I have to tackle them with money. If I discover the reason, I might be able to fight with my intelligence.'

Aniyan Raja looked at Sreedevi. 'Go on, please.'

'What could be the motive of those trying to take over this company? Typically there are four reasons why someone tries to take over a company. The first is the goodwill. If one uses the name and fame of an established company, it becomes easy to dominate the market. Dhanwantari has a good name. But its name and fame are limited within the state of Kerala. The company is not that popular even in other southern states. My guess is that the takeover is not for the goodwill associated with the company...'

Sreedevi waited, as if expecting a response from her uncle. Aniyan Raja stretched himself on the easy chair and shut his eyes.

'That's right.'

Sreedevi looked at her brother. Unni smiled.

She continued:

'The second reason: something purely personal. To defeat the company's owner by hook or by crook. The fundamental cause would be a grudge. Destroy the company and the owner along with that. But it does not ring true in this case. Dhanwantari Herbals is a family-owned enterprise. Only a mother and daughter remain in that family now. Having a personal vendetta against the daughter, well...'

'You're right,' remarked Unni. 'Why should anyone nurse a grudge against Mini Balachandran?'

Matthews was staring dumbly at Sreedevi. She was not a stunning beauty. Neither was she unattractive. Not dusky, nor very fair. Modest and shy. With each passing moment, her allure was increasing greatly.

Sreedevi clarified: 'The third reason: simple business. Dhanwantari is a company with deep roots. Competition can be done away with by merging with such an enterprise. The unnecessary expenses in marketing and research can be avoided. Just a single showroom for both the companies in the future. Pool in all the know-how and resources. A pure business takeover. However, such attempts can be predicted early. Usually they establish contact with the management before setting foot in the share market. Similar to Lord Krishna acting as an emissary. Didn't we offer a scheme to Dhanwantari too? Our ultimate motive was slightly different, that was all.'

Aniyan Raja did not open his eyes. 'Your deductions appear logical,' he remarked. 'What about the last reason?'

Sreedevi's voice turned grave.

'Fourth reason: make a kill in the process. Take over the company and sell off the valuable immoveable properties. These would be shown in the company balance sheet at abysmally low values. Grab these precious assets which never reflect in the share prices. Just plain dacoity. Our motive too was similar, wasn't it? Perhaps the Bombay businessmen planned like us.'

Matthews felt affronted on hearing Sreedevi refer to their efforts as dacoity. He reacted sharply: 'No, our goal was different. We planned to sell only those assets which were not significant for the company's growth. How can that be termed as dacoity? We were strategizing a proper financial management of the company, that's all.'

Sreedevi's answer bubbled with half suppressed laughter. 'Mr Matthews, all dacoits offer that simple argument—'

Aniyan Raja cut in: 'Don't pick up a fight now, children. So, you're saying that it's an attempt at dacoity. I agree with her, Matthews. We too are dacoits. There are more in the field. Sreedevi, what would you do in such a case?'

Sreedevi replied: 'I shall provoke the dacoits to fight one another. In fact, I shall do everything possible to create such a scenario. Meanwhile, I shall ensure that their goal is rendered utterly worthless. Both the winner and loser shall gain nothing.'

Matthews gazed intently at Sreedevi. Then he looked at Unni.

Unni gasped. 'You mean, they will sell off all the assets during this interval?'

'Yes.'

'How? Where's the time for that?'

Matthews jumped in: 'There are many legal steps to be followed before selling any company's assets. The approval of the board of directors is mandatory. A notice to that effect should be submitted to the registrar. How many such formalities are involved! The time for all that…?'

Sreedevi responded firmly: 'This is war for one's survival. I think she will do it. Mini Balachandran is pushing all of us into the battlefield. Meanwhile, she has kept a Brahmastra, something which shall never fail, ready in her armour.'

For a while, nobody said anything.

Aniyan Raja started breathing normally. He opened his eyes.

'Having listened to all of you, I think it's best that we sell all the shares that have been bought until now. The share price will definitely escalate tomorrow. The Bombay brokers are fighting on behalf of one or two north Indian companies. Both shall try to keep the prices high. If we jump into the fray, we'll only end up hurt. Yes, it sounds like defeat, withdrawing at this stage of one's initial business venture ... Pardon me, I forgot your name.'

'Matthews.'

'Yes, Matthews. You should wait and watch. When the price becomes unbelievably high, sell off all the shares. That makes business sense. Are we mule-headed about taking over Dhanwantari? No. We made an attempt, that's all. The timing went awry since the north Indians entered the arena at the samc time. Bad luck. Now let's get out without any injury.'

Matthews felt both joy and sorrow at his words. The pungent taste of defeat at the first venture, the bitterness of a wrong decision.

'Are you going back tonight, Matthews?'

'Yes, I have a taxi waiting. Then, tomorrow morning...?'

'Yes, let us not delay.'

Matthews got up and folded his hands.

'Your asthma problem seems to have eased a bit.'

'Yes, a new powder. An ottamooli. I just took it once. Big difference!'

Unni smiled.

'Let us take over Dhanwantari and market this powder.'

Everybody laughed.

43

An Offer of a Bribe

'Let's have some beer, if you don't mind.'

When he sat on the soft sofa in the spacious guest room next to Mohandas's office room, Zacharia felt like he was tumbling down to the ends of the earth. This was the first time he had come to Mohandas's office. Of course, he had heard about Mohandas. In fact, Zacharia had once spoken to him over the phone, about sponsoring a children's football tournament. Zacharia felt respect for Mohandas. The guest room and office were not ostentatious but elegant. The office reflected the character of the man.

Mohandas retrieved two cans of beer from the fridge.

'Mr Zacharia, you look far younger than I expected. Are you still playing tennis?'

'One needs some exercise in the morning. Else I will get a potbelly.'

'I am a loner. I can't say that I don't play due to lack of time. Somehow, I never got round to doing it.'

'Those at the top rungs are bound to be loners.'

Mohandas poured the beer into a mug.

'I always want to do something creative. Doesn't happen. At once the gains and losses associated with the venture come to my mind. I don't know if you still remember. You had once called me for sponsoring a children's football tournament. I agreed immediately because of the income tax exemption under Section 80. Also my new T-shirt brand was going to be promoted in a big way when thousands of children came to watch the matches. I can't think of any investment without calculating the profit and loss involved.'

Someone knocked at the door gently.

'Yes, come in.'

It was Ramesan. He smiled at Zacharia.

'My nephew, Ramesan. This is Mr Zacharia. Sportsman, Communist, share broker, all in one.'

Zacharia grinned and said: 'Not just that. Also a father and son. And a husband.'

Mohandas laughed.

Sipping his beer, Mohandas spoke:

'I shall speak without much preface, okay? I'm interested in Dhanwantari Herbal Products. It's not just a casual interest. I'm dead serious. I want that company. I have both the money and brawn for acquiring it. This has been a secret ambition for a while.'

'Why Dhanwantari? Your businesses don't enter into the realm of Ayurveda at all.'

Mohandas got up.

'Let me open the window. Why use the AC when there is such a pleasant sea breeze? We are all prisoners of our environments, aren't we?'

Zacharia sat silently. Ramesan switched off the air conditioner. He pulled the curtains aside and opened the window panes. Willingdon Island gleamed in multicoloured lights. The wind was crisp.

'At first, I did not feel any special attachment to Dhanwantari. I always yearned to run a successful manufacturing business in Ernakulam. You know that I have many business enterprises in

Kerala, don't you? Either they are into trade or service. Nothing dealing with manufacturing. I have always wanted to make a success of such an enterprise.'

'Didn't you try?'

'Did I not, indeed! My god, I will tell you a story. Happened two decades ago. Rubber products was the hot topic then. I sought the advice of the Rubber Board officials too. Collected information about potential schemes and government support. I wanted to start small and then expand it later. I leased land near Mulanthuruthy for setting up a crumb rubber factory. Water, electricity, the building plan, raw materials. Well, let's say that what the panchayat and government offices should have done in two months, they did in two years. The expenses I had originally estimated doubled. But I was bloody determined. Then I applied for the Central Excise licence.

'When weeks passed by, I visited the office. The officer was young and well-behaved. "You are a law graduate," he said, followed by, "Why choose to do this business? Idealists will drown in such a sector. Listen, I am not discouraging you." He sanctioned the licence that very day. When I stepped out, a peon came running after me. "Sir, I know you. That's why I'm advising you. You shall make profits only if you know how to evade excise duties. I shall tell you the ways. When should I meet you?" To be honest, at that moment, I lost my self-confidence. Nothing to do with the right and wrong of tax evasion or the tricks of the trade. A society's perception of someone who sets out to start a manufacturing business! I knew then that it won't work. There were more reasons to close the factory. I felt defeated. That was the important factor.'

Zacharia smiled.

'Our savings are like the money-order of the olden days. It used to arrive from Malaya, and north India, later from the Gulf and America. The flow of money to Kerala from those who toiled in foreign lands. The rubber estates started yielding profits. The money circulated in the system. It never transformed into any products or manufacturing ventures. That's also a reason for the common man's aversion to manufacturing.'

Mohandas spoke:

'True, but to continue what I was saying ... I don't like to be defeated. I wanted to retire in the recent past. You know, settle down with books and gardening in some remote area. But I know I would be restless. I want to run a successful manufacturing company. Only then my life will find purpose. Then I contemplated taking over a business based in Kerala, which was not being managed properly. Dhanwantari fit my needs.'

'Oh, okay.'

'My first idea was to offer money and buy the shares belonging to the family. A decent offer, without loss to anybody. Now, seeing the stock market trends, that would not be practical. Now it's clear that there are other players interested in Dhanwantari.'

'Yes, but so what?'

'I have another offer.'

'Go ahead.'

'Tomorrow, I shall be buying almost ten per cent of all the Dhanwantari shares through all the exchanges of the country. Two lakh shares.'

'Irrespective of the price?'

'Yes, immediate delivery wherever possible. I can arrange for spot cash too. It's okay even if the share price goes up to forty rupees. Mini Balachandran's thirty per cent shares added to my ten per cent would make the total forty per cent. Government institutions have thirty per cent of the shares. Even if the new party buys all of the outside shares, he would be limited to just thirty per cent, right? The government will always stand with the majority stakeholders. After some time, the new party will bring their shares back to the market for sale. The price of the shares will plunge.'

'Then?'

'Ramesan will become the company's executive director in charge of production. That's my only condition. No other change. Any policy decision related to production will be finalized by Ramesan. Of course, he will work under the guidance of the board of directors and the managing director.'

Zacharia sipped his beer. He could glimpse the darkness in the sky outside.

Mohandas attempted to light his pipe. The flame of his lighter was extinguished by the west wind.

His voice gathered force.

'You're probably wondering why I am being stupid enough to invest almost eighty lakhs for a directorship in the board of Dhanwantari. We shall re-examine the arrangement six months later. I will be bringing my shares into the market when the prices are favourable. You'll be in charge of selling them. Ramesan would have picked up the necessary skills by then. I will create a new production company. It might or might not involve Ayurvedic medicines. It's up to him.'

Zacharia was busy calculating the bribe Mohandas had offered him slyly. Shares worth eighty lakhs to be sold. One and a half lakhs as commission.

Mohandas asked: 'Mini Balachandran said she would agree to whatever decision you make. What do you say?'

Zacharia pulled a packet out of his shirt pocket.

'Would you care for some paan?'

'Sure, it's been a long time.'

Zacharia prepared the betel leaf and offered it to Mohandas. He smeared lime on it.

'What if the share price goes above forty?'

Mohandas folded the betel leaf carefully.

Mini's profile as she gazed at the backwaters, standing on the Malabar hotel lawns. Alluring eyes. A dimple, which appeared when she smiled. The promise of enticing curves, hidden in some secret treasure trove.

Mohandas spoke:

'I will risk it. It does not matter.'

Her eyes, half-closed now. Trembling lips. Blushing cheeks. Power in my encircling arms. I become complete. How can I be a man without you?

Mohandas was caught in the thrall of some other world.

Zacharia asked Ramesan: 'What is your line of work?'

Ramesan looked at his uncle. Mohandas answered: 'An intellectual with a muddled brain. Rather, the more knowledge he acquires, the more confused he gets! But now I've convinced him that it's better to bring about a revolution through manufacturing than to create a revolution in the manufacturing sector.'

Zacharia tossed the tobacco inside his mouth and grinned.

Ramesan asked: 'What's your response to my uncle's proposal?'

'As far as I'm concerned, it's okay. Mini will agree too. This is the strongest support she can get from anyone under these circumstances. Though the old Communist within me warns me that I am helping a bourgeois thrive, I agree fully with your idea. I shall not allow someone outside Kerala to take over Dhanwantari with the brute force of money.'

Mohandas said: 'Thank you. I shall do the needful then. Hearing you mention a bourgeois, I'm reminded of an anecdote.'

'What is it?'

'Once upon a time, before philosophies or traditional employment came into vogue, some tribals were living in a valley. Our ancestors. There was a lake on the summit of the mountain. When it overflowed, the water would trickle down to the valley through streams. Everyone used it for drinking and bathing. The men and women would set out to hunt in the morning and return with their prey by evening. They would roast the wild meat and settle for the night. No thoughts of tomorrow, neither any worries.

'In their midst was a fellow who was lame. He was lucky if someone offered him a portion of the meat. One day, he brooded for a long time. I should make myself useful to these people, he thought. There should be something that I provide, which they want. What could that be? Usually, when the people returned after hunting and foraging, there would not be sufficient water in the streams. They would be forced to climb the mountain to collect water from the lake. They would often get exhausted.

'The man came up with an idea. He gathered bamboo stalks and made pipes with those. Then he dug up a vast pool in the village. He brought water from the lake to the pool. Everyone was delighted by the endless supply of water. Then the man said, "I don't need anything except one-tenth of whatever you hunt. Take as much water as you wish." Everybody started offering him one-tenth of the meat like he had asked. But he couldn't eat so much, could he? He dried the meat and preserved it. Meanwhile, he cleaned the animal skin and crafted vessels from them for collecting water. Slowly, he became rich. The bourgeois in charge of water.

'The rainy season came. Nobody could get out of their homes to hunt. Lots of water, but no meat. The lame fellow said, "I shall give you dried meat. But on one condition. When you start hunting again, you should give me one-fifth of the prey instead of one-tenth."

'Problems began when the lame man started taking advantage of his compatriots' hardship. He should have stopped at that point. But we aren't like him. We are not annihilating competition at all. Competition is imperative for a healthy business environment. The quality of products will improve. The prices will come down. We are coming together to defeat some unseen bourgeois fellow! To help the consumer.

'So, let us proceed. A merger; a coming together of identical minds. Zacharia sir, if you don't mind, let us celebrate this agreement. Let us have dinner together. We can discuss other details too. Future plans…'

Zacharia called Mini. She was neither at home nor in the office.

She had left the Malabar hotel more than half an hour ago.

'No issues ... I'll invite Asokan, the marketing director.'

Zacharia said: 'I have to go home. Mini might have called on my home number. I shall return soon.'

'Use my car then. We will go for dinner together once you come back.'

When Zacharia left the room, Mohandas called Asokan.

'Sir, Asokan here!'

'Did you finish dinner?'

'No, sir.'

'Then come over for dinner. By eight-fifty, perhaps? Do bring Aswathy along.'

Asokan was flustered. But he replied politely: 'Yes, sir.'

Zacharia reached the road. He told Mohandas's driver not to bother driving him home. Instead, he caught an autorickshaw and stopped at the first telephone booth.

He called Mini's personal number. She took the call.

Zacharia laughed.

'I called from Mohandas's office some time back. You might have guessed it.'

'Of course. How did the evening go?'

'The rascal wants to swallow us whole. Not in a single go. Like a python, inch by inch, while the victim is still alive. Our dear friend is aiding him.'

'Who?'

'Asokan.'

'I had my suspicions.'

'I am going for the celebration dinner.'

'Who all are attending?'

'You tell me...'

'Asokan, hmm ... Aswathy too.'

Zacharia laughed.

44

A Simple Solution

It was nine in the night.

Mini Balachandran reached home by eight-thirty. She did not drive that night. Her mind was troubled. The lorries and buses were not prone to dimming their headlights. The glare affected one's sight. A moment's misjudgement meant disaster.

The driver dropped Mini at home in Tripunithura. Amma was waiting for her. As usual, she was leaning against the pillar on the foyer. 'Narayana, Narayana…' The Lord's name was on her lips.

'I'm famished!'

'Go ahead and freshen up. Relax a little.'

Amma fetched Mini a cool glass of buttermilk. Mini opened the plastic container on the dining table and picked up a sautéed papad.

She enjoyed the shower, it helped soothe her frayed nerves. While drying herself, she heard the incessant ringing of the telephone.

Amma called out: 'Mini, it's Balan. From Shillong.'

Mini hastily draped herself in a fresh mundu and raced outside.

'Hello.'

'Yes, Mini here.'

'What's the trouble, dear?'

'What trouble? Nothing. How are you?'

'Bored. Bored to death.'

'Had your dinner?'

'Nope.'

'I just came home from work. Was taking a shower. Came running.'

'One moment. Let me take a look at my wife.'

'Hush!'

'Now, tell me. Should I fly down? What's happening?'

'Ah, your friend seems to have called you.'

'Yes.'

'I'm handling it.'

'Mini.'

'Hmm?'

Mini wanted to scream out loud: 'Please come to me. Be my strength and support…' Instead, she said: 'There's nothing to worry. Several stock exchanges saw heavy trading of our company's shares today. The share prices shot up. I'm managing well. Zacharia uncle is around to help me. But since it's a matter of money, one can't trust anyone blindly. I asked your friend to keep an eye on those very close to the company. There are problems, but…'

When Balachandran spoke, his words were everything Mini was waiting for. The life-giving sanjeevani.

'I know, Mini! You have the strength and ability to tackle the situation. I was curious about the detective work going on. I know you can do it.'

'Thank you, dear.'

'Best of luck.'

There was a sweet kiss that travelled across two distant lands, and then the telephone went dead.

Tears welled up in Mini's eyes.

Her mother had prepared a special yam curry with kanji-rice porridge that night. Mini's grandfather used to adore the dish.

Mini gazed at her mother. She was reciting the Lord's name with her eyes shut.

Amma had intentionally prepared the dish to remind Mini of her grandfather. What better day to empower her daughter with their ancestors' memories?

While having her dinner, Mini looked at her mother again. Had she ever been able to understand her mother?

'Amma.'

Her mother stopped murmuring the prayers and looked questioningly at Mini.

'Amma, many people are trying to buy Dhanwantari's shares across different stock exchanges. They are after us, in Bombay, Delhi and here in Cochin.'

'Who bears such a grudge towards us?'

'It's not a grudge. It's competition. Maybe the greed to make money. It could be a bit of everything.'

'You mean others want to make money by taking over our company?'

'Yes.'

'Then why don't we do it ourselves?'

Mini sat stunned, forgetting to chew.

What did Amma say just now? Yes, that's it! The simplest solution to the problem! Did she say that mindfully? If others have a strategy to make money out of the takeover, why not replicate the same method? That would stop them, would it not? Yes, definitely.

'Who all are involved?'

Amma's question awoke Mini from the reverie.

'There are some north Indians.'

'Sharmaji in Lucknow was closest to your father. Perhaps he's behind it.'

'If he was close to Acchan, would he do this?'

'Mini, competition and jealousy always happen between those who are intimate. Haven't you read the Mahabharata? The smallest reasons provoke the ones who are close.'

'Amma, you know Aniyan Raja, don't you? He's also in the arena.'

Amma was silent for a few moments.

'Aniyan Raja?'

'Yes.'

'You mean, he's trying to take over our company on the sly?'

'Not secretly. He's made a direct offer.'

Amma did not speak till Mini finished her dinner.

'Did Aniyan Raja speak to you?'

Mini was preoccupied with Zacharia, who was having dinner with Mohandas.

'What?'

'Did Aniyan Raja speak to you?'

'Someone called Matthews approached me on Aniyan Raja's behalf. Anyway, like you said, let's explore what we can do with our own company. I'm going to make some phone calls.'

Amma said: 'Don't work too late into the night. Let's go to our family home tomorrow morning. We should light a lamp before the deity. Lord Dhanwantari will make everything right.'

It was nine o'clock. The news in English was being telecast on TV. Mini listened to the headlines. She started dialling a few numbers.

Dhanwantari's board comprised nine members apart from the chairperson and managing director. Finance Director Adiyodi and Marketing Director Asokan were part of the company. Two were government nominees. They always supported the majority view. Usually, they would never support a move against the status quo. There was no point in calling them up and stirring confusion.

There were five other directors. They were all Menon sir's close friends. The Chettiar from Tamil Nadu, the retired vice chancellor, the lawyer, the retired chief engineer, and the plantation owner.

The first three were directors in several companies. As per the Companies Act, one could not be a part of more than twenty boards of directors. But for that preventive clause, they might have joined more.

Among them, only Chettiar was wise enough to provide counsel.

Mini called Chettiar's Coimbatore number. Chettiar had a second wife and children in Salem. Today was the birthday of one of his children from the second wife. He had gone there with his first wife and family.

Someone in the house told Mini that Chettiar was in Salem. Mini called him right away. Chettiar sounded pleased and happy when he answered the call.

Mini narrated to him the sequence of events. The trade of Dhanwantari's shares that started a few days ago, the news article in *The Times of India*, the suddenly active share market, how the share prices of Dhanwantari reached twenty-four rupees from fourteen…

'I'm going to fight this takeover bid to the best of my ability. Any advice for me, Uncle?'

'Don't worry, my dear. Just go ahead. Your father was not just a friend, he was also the saviour of my son's life. He's alive only because of Dhanwantari's Ayurvedic medicines, did you know?'

'No.'

'Well, I'm behind you one hundred per cent. Do not hesitate to ask for money, in case you need it.'

'No, Uncle. I need only your blessings.'

'Lord Ayyappa will protect you. But be careful of those around you. They are all Malayalis! Remember that favourite story of mine?'

'Which one, Uncle?'

'The export of crabs?'

Mini laughed.

'Oh, yes. Shall be alert about that one!'

Mini smiled to herself after putting the phone down. Chettiar would always be loyal to the family. There was no doubt about that.

The crab story had been retold in a million ways. A Kochi exporter got a new export order. Live crabs for a foreign country. First shipment, a thousand crabs. The cartons were stacked with crabs in open polythene bags. The buyer's agent arrived from Bombay to crosscheck the shipment. He got infuriated at the sight of the cartons with big holes in them.

'What's this nonsense? Repack everything at once! The crabs shall escape through the holes.'

The exporter consoled the man.

'These are stacked with native crabs from Kerala. If one starts climbing a bit high, the rest will definitely pull it down. Forget escaping, no crab would even be able to make it halfway to the top.'

Chettiar loved to share that yarn. Mini thought it was a befitting story. She should be wary.

Next, she tried the retired vice chancellor's number.

The gentleman had gone to bed. Yet he picked up the extension and conversed with Mini for half an hour. He morphed into the professor of yore. The VC gave a lecture on the history of companies.

The first companies were formed in Europe. In England, Spain and Holland. The concept of shares started at that point of time. All were maritime companies. The merchants used to lend money to the brave sailors venturing to distant, exotic lands in search of spices, silk and black gold. Natural disasters, pirates, strange lands … there were many challenges. Most of the seafarers did not return to their homelands. And those who made it safely back, brought in humongous profits. The moneylenders decided: let us bear the costs of all the ships at one go. No need to make one merchant responsible for the risk of one ship. All ships for all merchants. Even if a few sunk or never returned, dividing the profits brought in by the vessels that did come back successfully, ensured good gains for everyone. Depending on the shares taken, the profits and losses were distributed among the stakeholders.

That was the beginning of the saga of companies, which took over the world with the tagline of limited liability.

The vice chancellor was still living in the era of his teaching days. He started yammering about the phenomenon called 'takeover'. Fifteen minutes were already gone.

Mini tactfully interjected: 'I shall proceed as per the guidance, Uncle.'

'Yes.'

Mini bid him good night hastily, not allowing the old man to start yammering again.

Next, the lawyer. Should she call him or not? Either way, it augured trouble.

The lawyer was closely connected to the Stock Exchange. The courts heard a number of cases related to the Exchange every day. When money rushed in, the greed for power increased proportionately. That stoked petty competitions and conflicts which ended up in the courts. The High Court in Ernakulam was a stone's throw away from the Exchange. The advocates were the beneficiaries of the disagreements between the plaintiffs and the defendants. Some local advocates became experts in company law, counting among the best in the nation.

The lawyer, who was also a director at Dhanwantari, belonged to that category.

Mini called him. He reassured her.

'Don't worry a bit, Mini! Even if someone tries for a takeover, we won't let it happen. Tomorrow I shall get an order in our favour from the High Court, instructing the Stock Exchange to stop the trading of Dhanwantari's shares for a week. Leave it to me.'

'How's that going to work out, Vakil uncle?'

'I'm a shareholder of Dhanwantari Herbal Products. I will convince the court that this speculation is harming the company in which I have a stake. We can get an order issued.'

'Thank you, Vakil uncle.'

The plantation owner was next in line. He had two numbers – in Kottayam and Thodupuzha.

The first number went unanswered. Someone answered the second. The servant informed Mini that the gentleman was not at home. No, he did not know his whereabouts.

No issues.

The last was the retired chief engineer. He was astounded at the update.

'Our company? Takeover? Why?'

'I don't know, Uncle. But I'm going to fight it out.'

'Adharma should be vanquished, Mini. That's what even the Lord exhorts in the Gita.'

The engineer's main work nowadays was to interpret the Bhagavad Gita. And, of course, lend money. Most of it was black money. He would offer tonnes of free advice about both his ventures.

'Mini, handle it bravely. The Lord always supports the one who takes action.'

Mini called Zacharia at home. He hadn't returned from the dinner.

She opened her briefcase and took out the Nelliyampathy report. The phone rang. It was Zacharia.

'Mini?'

'How was the evening, Uncle?'

'Bastard! Sorry.'

'No problem.'

'Mohandas is a smart cookie. A truly cool customer. He had the audacity to offer me a bribe.'

'It is business, after all. What happened then?'

'I pretended to go along with his plans.'

'If he is cool, we are cooler.'

'Mini, it's already late. Get some sleep.'

'You take some rest, too, Uncle.'

'I will sleep after a while. If at all I can.'

'Why?'

'I have a friend. A financier. I need to meet him.'

Mini bade Zacharia good night. It was later that she realized that they had not talked about Asokan.

Mini opened the Nelliyampathy report. First page. The phone rang.

It was her husband's friend.

'Mini?'

'Yes.'

'Here's the update. Zacharia is close to Mohandas. So is Asokan. They all had dinner together. Matthews left the city at five-thirty in a taxi. The destination is supposedly near Kottayam. He made a trunk call.'

'To Aniyan Raja, of course.'

The friend chuckled.

Mini asked: 'What's up?'

'When I enquired about Mr Adiyodi, we found out something funny. How old is he, by the way?'

'Nearly sixty, I guess.'

'This old fellow is having an affair.'

'Affair? Adiyodi? Impossible!'

'The woman is a widow. Was married to an employee of your company. Do you want her address?'

Mini laughed.

'No, please.'

'I have updated Balan.'

'Yes, thanks. Chettan called me.'

'Good night.'

Adiyodi's secret love affair!

Even when she switched off the bedroom light, Mini couldn't help giggling.

45

A Sleepless Night

Many people, who were affected by the shares of Dhanwantari Herbal Products, did not sleep that night. Even those who managed to catch a wink did not find it peaceful. They woke intermittently, haunted by nightmares.

After finishing dinner at the five-star hotel abutting the backwaters, Mohandas spoke:

'Asokan, please drop Zacharia sir home. We'll wait for you.'

'Yes, sir.'

Zacharia wished him good night and set off with Asokan.

Mohandas said: 'Ramesan, let's arrange for three or four brokers immediately. Buy almost ten per cent of the shares. In lots of five thousand, ten thousand. Let's limit the negotiable price. Only once I permit them should they buy a share costing more than thirty rupees.'

He checked his watch.

'Why don't you try now? Don't waste time until Asokan is back. Here are the numbers of some brokers I know.'

Ramesan took the paper and walked out of the hall. Mohandas smiled at Aswathy.

'Did you enjoy dinner?'

Aswathy nodded.

Mohandas lit his pipe. The aroma of expensive tobacco wafted in the air. In the background, a popular western music band of the city was playing. The ambience was languorous.

'Aswathy, if I asked you something would you give me an honest answer?'

Aswathy became nervous. Asokan and Ramesan were not around. Though the restaurant was a public place, she had been expecting an overture from Mohandas. Yes, undoubtedly the man had a soft corner for her. He hadn't dropped a hint yet. A lack of opportunity, presumably.

Aswathy blushed like a teenager.

'No answer?'

Aswathy shook her head.

'What's your opinion about Zacharia? A woman's intuition? You've observed him for more than an hour. Can we trust him?'

Aswathy could not fathom what Mohandas meant. Mohandas pulled his chair closer to her.

'Women have a heightened sense when it comes to judging people. Can we trust Zacharia?'

Aswathy leaned against the table and spoke. 'He's very close to Mini Balachandran.'

'Yes, Zacharia was her father's friend. But does that mean he has the same loyalty to the daughter?'

'Oh, Mini is pretty good at charming anyone! You don't know her. After Menon sir's death, Asokan chettan should have become the managing director in his place. But the board of directors completely ignored him. All of them fell for Mini's smiles and tricks. Everyone knows about her mediocre qualifications and lack of experience. Why did the directors stand behind her when Asokan chettan was toiling for the company day and night?'

Mohandas put his hand on Aswathy's thigh.

'Aswathy, we're trying to rectify that error now, aren't we? By the way, when you speak so passionately, Aswathy, you look stunning! So, please stop. Or I might forget that there are people around.'

When Mohandas's fingers pressed harder, Aswathy flinched. She fixed her gaze on the remnants of the black coffee in the cup before her. Mohandas casually pulled back his hand.

'We need more opportunities to get closer. I don't know ... For the last one hour, your presence has given me a sense of completeness, a new strength.'

Aswathy lifted her flushed face. Mohandas continued:

'In this battle with Mini, you would have been a better opponent, Aswathy.'

Aswathy's heart beat faster. What was she hearing? In five minutes, the whole world was changing. Everything appeared colourful and vibrant. The background music acquired a new tempo.

Aswathy spoke:

'I am more educated than Mini.'

Ramesan entered the hall.

Mohandas said: 'I shall call you tomorrow at eleven.'

Ramesan had called up the brokers. They would wait for clear instructions early the next day.

~

Aswathy was bubbling over with joy and excitement that night. She did not let Asokan sleep. Seeing her vivacity, he asked: 'How come you're in such a great mood?'

'Chetta, you shall become the managing director. I felt reassured for the first time today.'

'Did he tell you something?'

'Who?'

'Mohandas.'

'Tell me what?'

'Did he mention anything when I went to drop Zacharia?'

'What are you saying?'

Embracing Asokan warmly, she rendered his questions futile.

Asokan did not sleep. *What was behind the ploy of bringing in Ramesan as a director? Was the goal to make him the MD? Could it be that Mohandas was training his nephew for the post?*

Aswathy could not sleep either. She imagined various scenarios of ousting Mini Balachandran from the office. Of course, one should bid her farewell with dignity and propriety. She visualized herself seated in the MD's chair. By the way, what would she do with Asokan? Poor man! Maybe she would form another company and appoint him as the MD.

~

Before going to bed, Mohandas asked Ramesan: 'Can we trust Zacharia?'

Ramesan had been pondering the topic since dinner. So he was quick to respond. 'He will never betray Mini Balachandran. I am sure of that.'

'Why? There's a price for everything.'

Ramesan was silent for a few moments. Then he explained: 'The idealists who know about the power of money tend to be cynical towards it. Zacharia happens to be such an idealist.'

'What does that imply?'

'So long as Zacharia believes that we are going to do good to Dhanwantari and to the MD who embodies the company's ideals, I guess we can trust him.'

Mohandas wrestled with sleep. Mini's face and figure haunted him. He tried to think of Aswathy but failed miserably. Finally, he popped two sleeping pills.

Ramesan was having trouble sleeping too. His mind was caught in a whirlpool of emotions. Ever since he had stepped into the business world, his mind was grappling with problems. Today's dinner discussions were over medicines that would affect the health of lakhs of the common people. Amidst the chaos caused by the shifting share prices, change in management, profits and losses, the poor man was using Dhanwantari's medicines. The commoner, the one who gave a part of his pitiful earnings as share capital – where was he amidst all the din? Whatever essential needs man had were met by nature. Sunlight, rainwater … They had neither shares nor prices associated with them. Where did the fault lie then? Or was everything faultless?

Ramesan locked the door and walked out. He planned to wander around for some time. His mind would calm down a bit. The tranquillity of the sleeping city would hopefully spread to him.

A long, interminable procession. A rabble of men and women, both young and old, and children, punching the air, yelling and shouting slogans. They were standing on the street, the only other thing there being Mini's Fiat. The mob surrounded the vehicle. Share certificates clutched in their fists. Shares of Dhanwantari. Asokan, Zacharia, Adiyodi were all part of the crowd. When the horde started hurling their fists at her and shaking the share certificates right in front of her face, Mini jolted awake from the nightmare, shouting: 'Amma!' Mini's mother came running. 'What happened, dearest?'

'I had a nightmare!'

Amma caressed Mini's hair tenderly.

'I'll sleep with you tonight.'

Mini laid her head on her mother's lap.

'Don't worry, dear. Lord Dhanwantari will take care of us. Sleep well. Tomorrow we shall pray at our family temple.'

Mini slept peaceably.

Her mother did not sleep. Neither did she wish to.

~

Shankaran Kutty struggled to sleep. There were several lodges in the city which let out rooms for cheap. Shankaran Kutty returned from Savitry's hostel and booked such a single room for himself. He took a quick shower, dressed in his old clothes, and set out in search of Vinayan.

Vinayan was his lone hope.

His vendetta would be complete only after selling the shares bought on the advice of Savitry's boyfriend. He wished to call her tonight and announce his victory.

'Fellows like Vikas are never to be trusted. The share prices are falling. But I have disposed of my shares without any loss.'

Shankaran Kutty sought out Vinayan. Without revealing that the share prices of Dhanwantari were dipping, he said: 'I shall give you ten thousand Dhanwantari shares. You're close to the management, aren't you?'

'At what price?'

'Twenty-seven.'

'Share delivery?'

'That will be done. No problem.'

'Sure. I'll buy. But if you plan to square-up without offering the share certificates, that won't work here.'

'No way.'

Shankaran Kutty sold his shares. He did his calculations.

Purchased three thousand shares at twenty-four rupees.

Four thousand at twenty-five.

Three thousand at twenty-five and a half.

Sold ten thousand at twenty-seven.

Profits, twenty-one thousand five hundred rupees.

Good.

Shankaran Kutty immediately called up Savitry at her hostel.

'I sold all the ten thousand shares. Got a decent profit too. Good night.'

Shankaran Kutty was sure that Savitry would not sleep tonight.

The anxiety began when he returned to the lodge.

Vinayan was entitled to ten thousand share certificates. Savitry had to be given five thousand shares. In the evening, he had bought ten thousand shares from three people. They were speculators. They were talking about adjusting the losses during the time of settlement. What should he do now? Vinayan had insisted on the share certificates.

Vinayan represented the company's management. They needed the certificates for voting purposes.

'Ettumanoorappa!'

The Lord of the Ettumanoor temple did not grant Shankaran Kutty a peaceful sleep. The mosquitoes of Ernakulam, the bed bugs, and the noisy ceiling fan joined forces against him.

~

Zacharia reached home. The lights inside the house were on when he pushed open the gate.

Prabhu opened the door.

'What happened? Couldn't you sleep, Prabhu?'

'No, sir.'

'Worried about the Dhanwantari shares?'

Zacharia stepped inside and shut the front door.

Prabhu spoke:

'Well, can anyone sleep during such a time? So many are turning into lakhpatis overnight without sweating a bit. But though I live with someone like you, sir, I gain nothing.'

Zacharia grinned.

'Prabhu, this is my profession. Some miners steal gold. A few are caught by the cops while the rest evade them. Yes, some of these fellows become filthy rich. Does that mean every miner starts stealing?'

'You're right,' admitted Prabhu.

Zacharia removed his shirt and stretched out on the bed. Then he said:

'Companies and their shares play a significant role in human progress and economic growth. The share market is the easiest way of garnering capital. If someone can spare a thousand rupees, he can invest it well in shares. When he does that, as a stakeholder, he's aware where his money is and how it's being used. The Stock Exchange plays a crucial role in this process. And the brokers are vital in its functioning. They help in distributing the accumulated savings in an efficient way. They will charge their commission due to them. It's just a profession, like an engineer, doctor or an advocate. The trouble begins when the broker steps out of that line. The Stock Exchange is not a gambler's den. Never should it turn into one. Even you, Prabhu, don't get sleep when such a metamorphosis occurs. Please go and sleep.'

Prabhu went away.

But Zacharia could get sleep only after 2 a.m.

He imagined five fighters in the arena, ready for battle.

An anonymous, faceless north Indian.

A herd of Bulls using the takeover bid as a cause for speculative trade.

Aniyan Raja, with all the nets he had cast.

Mohandas, Asokan, and the young revolutionary, Ramesan.

Mini, with a gaze that seemed to ask him: 'Uncle, what should we do now?'

Zacharia smiled by the time the clock struck two. Nobody saw that in the darkness. After drinking some water from the bottle kept near the bed, Zacharia went off to sleep.

~

Matthews started for Ernakulam from Aniyan Raja's house. Unni had requested him to spend the night there. But Matthews wanted to get back to Ernakulam as quickly as possible. The plan of action should be implemented right in the morning. The maximum shares were in Madras and Cochin. He had to ensure their sale. Matthews, however, could not reach Ernakulam on time.

After ten kilometres, the taxi developed some trouble. The driver tried his best but in vain. There was no workshop nearby. The closest was at Changanassery. Apparently, it was open in the night. How would they move the vehicle there? Would the mechanic come here in the middle of the night?

Matthews declared: 'I have to reach Ernakulam tonight at all costs.'

The driver hitched a ride in a passing lorry and went to the town. Later, he returned with a mechanic. By the time the car was repaired, it was two in the morning. By the time they dropped the mechanic at Changanassery and reached Ernakulam, it was a quarter past four. Where was the time to sleep?

Matthews took a shower. Then he sat down on a sofa and waited for the newspaper. Inadvertently, his eyes closed.

After bidding farewell to Matthews, Unni and Sreedevi went to their respective rooms. After ten in the night, the telephone receiver was placed in its cradle. That was the custom.

Aniyan Raja dialled a Calcutta number at 10 p.m.

Mahesh Chand Bhartiya, his brother-in-law, was reading an interpretation of the Gita.

Aniyan Raja said: 'Mahesh, I need some urgent information. A company that's listed in Cochin, Dhanwantari Herbal Products, is a permitted security at Bombay and other exchanges. Someone's trying to take over the company. I need to know who it is, his financial capacity, the liquid assets at his disposal, company structure, all the details.'

'By tomorrow afternoon, possibly.'

'No, I need it in two hours' time. By midnight.'

'Saala, you call me only when you have some dire need. No wonder your asthma remains aggressive!'

Aniyan Raja asked about the family, discussed his asthma, and conveyed his regards to his aged mother-in-law.

At midnight, he called the Calcutta number again. The information Aniyan Raja had wanted was delivered to him.

Bhartiya said: 'Now you sleep. I'll call at five-thirty in the morning. Got some work to do.'

Aniyan Raja went to bed. But sleep eluded him. The asthma was not to blame. In half an hour, the phone rang.

Aniyan Raja was taken aback. Who would be calling at such an odd hour?

He was surprised on hearing the voice.

Afterwards, Aniyan Raja could not sleep. He tossed and turned on the bed. Then he tried to read a book.

He thought of Dhanwantari's shares at five o'clock when the temple bells rang indicating the hour for the morning puja.

At five-thirty a.m., when he sat near the telephone, Aniyan Raja knew exactly what he should do regarding Dhanwantari Herbals.

46

The News Report

Matthews awoke hearing the thud of newspapers hitting the front door. The vendor usually bundled three newspapers into one and hurled it with all his might.

A greyish light, a prelude to the ending darkness, was visible.

Matthews opened the first page of the business section. Nothing extraordinary. Normal news of the share market. The share prices of prominent companies, including Dhanwantari's. Updates on three or four IPOs, snippets on the shares of TISCO and Apollo Tyres.

Next, he checked the sports page. Accidentally, the front page caught his eye: 'Bullish Game Wreaking Disaster'.

Lord! The first page was filled with news about Dhanwantari's shares. All three newspapers carried the same headlines.

There were specific lines on the history of Dhanwantari Herbal Products and an outline of their present-day activities. A paragraph about the trade union strike. In India, it was rare to come by women-led public limited companies. In Kerala, it was rarer. The company, a family enterprise, focused on researching the traditional Ayurvedic methods of healing.

The management's priority was not merely profits but commitment to an idea of service. If the Malayalis allowed the sheer avarice of outsiders to take over such a company, it would be a portent of disaster.

A north Indian company was behind the takeover bid. The three newspapers proclaimed that pertinent fact unequivocally. The broker of the adversary was doing line business with other share brokers across the stock exchanges of India, causing a spurt in share prices. The speculators were on the loose, buying shares in the hope of selling them to the combative north Indian company or the aggrieved Dhanwantari Herbals. Another piece of unconfirmed news was floating in the air. There were a couple of local players who were trying to take advantage of the situation. There was no overt mention of Aniyan Raja's name. But those familiar with the scenario would understand the innuendoes. There were also insinuations about Mohandas.

One newspaper openly pointed out that if the Stock Exchange authorities did not wake up in time, their credibility would be at stake. The trading hall of the Stock Exchange should not become a legalized gambler's den.

Matthews deliberated on the impact of the news. Though the articles were well-intentioned, the effect would be the opposite. The brokers who had been reluctant to test the waters until yesterday, would also jump into the fray. Such a bullish market meant that the prices would skyrocket. There would be no trouble in selling off the shares purchased yesterday. Should one wait and watch, or sell immediately?

What would the Stock Exchange authorities do?

Bombay was the nerve centre of all the share markets. Having registered a public limited company, one could list its shares in any stock exchange in the country. However, there was a prestige connected with listing it at the Bombay Stock Exchange. The company could also seek a special permission for the trading of its shares in any exchange. Such shares were referred to as permitted securities. Dhanwantari was listed in the Cochin Stock Exchange but fell under the permitted securities category in Bombay. Naturally, the trading in Bombay affected the overall share prices. The Cochin Stock Exchange authorities could not control the entire trading process.

Every stock exchange functioned as an independent limited company governed by specific regulations. The sphere of action was very small in reality. Typically, one stock exchange had jurisdiction over one district. The Cochin Stock Exchange was in the district of Ernakulam. The Coimbatore Stock Exchange had jurisdiction in Kovai district. Usually, the Bombay Exchange disregarded the checks and balances taken up by comparatively smaller stock exchanges.

Matthews remembered the story of a local company that became a victim of a speculation game. The conspiracy started in the Bombay Stock Exchange.

The company was registered in Delhi and was working in Kerala and many other states. It was famous in its field and held fifteen per cent of the shares. It was doing well and had bright prospects. The dividend on the ten-rupee share was nearly seven rupees. A young stockbroker based in Bombay started buying the stocks of the company silently from all the stock exchanges. The share prices went up steadily. The youth purchased almost five per cent of the company's shares. The share price hit a hundred rupees. The company management became jittery. A foreign organization had one-tenth of the company's total shares and the government, a stake of twenty-five per cent.

Apart from the fifteen per cent shares the management held, almost half of what remained were distributed among the public. The Bombay broker published an advertisement in all the prominent newspapers. 'I am buying the shares of this company because it is a wise investment idea. I have no intention of acquiring the company. I support the management in every way.' The advertisement achieved its purpose. The share value skyrocketed.

The company had a number of shareholders in Kerala. The Kochi brokers, doing line business for Bombay, started a buying spree. The bullish game went on, with local brokers joining the melee. In a fortnight, the price crossed two hundred rupees. One should settle the money on the second Friday of every month and submit the authorized share certificates.

The Bombay party insisted on share certificates on the agreed amount. Or else the broker had to cover the losses. The one who sold the shares at hundred would have to pay an additional hundred. Those who made gains during the settlement clamoured loudly regarding the sanctity of agreements and the legal responsibilities of a stock exchange. They shouted themselves hoarse that the investor's faith should never be compromised.

Those who were devastated pleaded about unscrupulous speculation by the Bombay fellows. They pointed out that the share prices did not reflect the true state of the company's financial status. And reminded everybody about the ethical and moral responsibility of the Stock Exchange authorities. They beat their chests about how the scales favoured avaricious speculators, while disregarding the hapless, unknown investors!

The Stock Exchange took the view that nothing was amiss. Speculation was part of the game, wasn't it? Some lose, some win. However, they took a decision. The average of the share prices of the company over the past few weeks was calculated. It came to a hundred and fifty rupees. With that as the base, the profit and loss were recalculated, reducing both marginally. Both parties howled 'Unfair! Unfair!' The Bombay stakeholder was intractable – he either received the share certificates or the equivalent money.

What next? Courts and cases?

Then the Bombay Stock Exchange decided that further trading of the company shares would be allowed only upon producing original share certificates. Spot sales. The share prices rose again. Three hundred, four hundred...

Many laughed that day. More people wept. Later, those who laughed ended up crying and those who mourned, smiled.

Due to such a precedent, one thing was clear. The Cochin Stock Exchange authorities would take some action today. Matthews was determined to sell the shares before such a step was initiated. One should recover the amount spent. That's what Aniyan Raja had meant: Get out before one's hand got burned.

Matthews did some quick calculations. He had spent more than twenty-five lakhs including the share purchase during curb trading. If he were to get thirty rupees per share, that would be perfect.

One needed a buyer.

Vinayan and Zacharia were trying to help the Dhanwantari management, were they not?

Matthews decided to sell the shares to Vinayan.

~

Though Zacharia had slept at two in the night, he woke at five in the morning as usual. Following his ablutions, he prepared tea. Without waking up Prabhu, he wore his sports clothes and shoes. Then he locked the door and stepped out with his tennis racket.

The city was waking up, freeing itself from the blanket of coolness. The autorickshaws were trundling along. The bicycles of milk-sellers and newspaper boys were whizzing past.

Zacharia was blind to the bustle around.

What should a company management's goal be? To create maximum profits for the shareholders? The liability of the shareholders was limited to the point of their investments. They wanted to harvest the maximum gain and wished their investments should be safe all the time. Did the company owe its loyalty only to the shareholders? What about the nation and society?

Dhanwantari's vision was closely associated with providing solutions to the healthcare concerns of the common man. What should the management of such a company aim for? Research, development, low-priced medicines, newer treatments, easy accessibility. All of these were significant. Most of them might not directly add to the profit margin. Menon never saw Dhanwantari Herbal Products as a mere money-making machine. The takeover bid would upend his benevolent vision. Whoever was trying to acquire the company was only aiming at profits.

Zacharia decided that it was his solemn duty, not just as the broker who served as the company's advisor but also as a humanitarian, to take the challenge head on.

It was time to play a game in the stock market. Before that, on the tennis court.

By the second set, Vinayan stood waiting on the sidelines. Zacharia lifted his racket to acknowledge his presence.

'Let me finish the game.'

Last game.

Thirty-Forty.

A player from the opposing team was serving. It could become a deuce.

Score four-five.

Five all.

At the first service, Zacharia moved forward from the baseline. The opponent hesitated momentarily. Changing his usual fast serve, he tried a slanted spin. Zacharia stepped back swiftly and smashed the ball across the court with his backhand. The opponent was demolished.

Game and set over.

When Zacharia sat down on the chair, Vinayan asked: 'Sir, how could you foretell the guy would chop?'

Zacharia grinned. 'We should determine how the opponent plays. If he gets to decide, he will win.'

'Right,' Vinayan said. 'Now take a look at the newspapers. One has mentioned you by name.'

Zacharia browsed through the papers swiftly.

'Good! The brokers too are becoming respectful! Until now, it was only the politicians who'd hog the headlines. This is progress.'

Vinayan asked: 'What should we do now? The news reports will provoke another surge in the share prices. Those with share certificates shall wait for the prices to still climb higher. Our Matthews and company are retreating from the battlefield.'

'Who, Aniyan Raja?'

'Yes, they have almost one lakh shares with them. They are willing to sell to the management.'

'Price?'

'Thirty rupees.'

Zacharia thought for a while.

'Tell them that we are sellers of two lakh shares. Today is Friday. We are bringing the two lakh shares at the opening price of the Bombay Stock Exchange at twelve o'clock.'

'Are you serious?'

'Serious. Now, something which is not to be shared with Matthews or anybody else. Engage four or five brokers to buy all our shares. We are both the sellers and the buyers. Take all caution that nobody suspects a thing.'

'Price?'

'Let it rise.'

Vinayan was silent for a few moments.

'I'm on it.'

'Small lots as much as possible. In a gap of ten minutes, ideally. The share price should keep increasing. No one should get a whiff of what's happening.'

Zacharia got up and picked up his racket.

Vinayan said: 'I'll drop you.'

When they reached Vinayan's car, a boy came running from the club. 'Phone for Zacharia sir.'

Zacharia looked at Vinayan questioningly. He shrugged. It was Mini Balachandran.

'Uncle, are you there?' She was bubbling with excitement.

'Yes, what makes you so upbeat?'

'Uncle, please don't do anything until I reach there.'

'What happened? Where are you calling from?'

'Mavelikkara. From an STD booth.'

'Mavelikkara?'

'Yes, I'll tell you everything when we reach Ernakulam.'

'We? Who is with you?'

'Amma. She's in the car.'

'What's all this? Where did you go?'

'We will reach in an hour and a half. Don't do anything until I meet you, please.'

Zacharia laughed. 'You mean, no shower or breakfast?'

Mini laughed too. 'Don't tease me, Uncle. Nothing about shares. I am cutting the call now.'

'Is it bad or good news?'

'Good. Good bye.'

Zacharia walked thoughtfully to the car.

Vinayan asked: 'Who was it?'

'Mini. She says that I should try a leisurely oil bath.'

47

The Financier Makes an Entry

Dawn was yet to set in, and a crowd started thronging Avarachan's house.

Stock Exchange member Avarachan was now an established financier. 'Badla Avarachan' was his nickname. He rather liked his sobriquet. 'Badla' stood for doing something deceitful. Depending on the fluctuations in the shares, the financiers who loaned money were given the moniker 'Badla'. Speculation was dependent on these key players. Both the buyers and the sellers indulging in speculative trade needed money. The accounts had to be settled on Fridays. Most of them would not have the required certificates. As per Stock Exchange rules, the price difference of the agreed amount between the buyer and the seller and the Friday share-market prices should be paid upfront. Or carried over to the next Friday. In order to tide over the contingency, the financier stepped into the arena.

The financier would arrange the required funds. There would be a surreptitious arrangement of money for two weeks, at two per cent interest. Irrespective of whether the borrower used the loaned funds or not, the interest had to be paid to the financier.

Avarachan and his ilk were doing annual deals of 'Badla' financing worth two or three crores. In the accounts, it would be shown that Avarachan bought all the shares at Friday's prices and sold them at a two per cent higher rate on Monday.

Avarachan would proudly claim: 'I am the main eye of the Stock Exchange. Observing those who approach me, secretly or openly, for borrowing money, I can predict what's going to happen in the share market next week.'

Avarachan was in Bombay in his youth. He was working with a jobber. The 'jobber' was an expert broker who specialized in dealing with specific shares. In India, almost four thousand companies had listed their shares in twenty-eight stock exchanges. A market of nearly three lakh crores. Ninety of these companies were the aristocrats in the fray. A Class, Blue Chip, and so on were the common names for such premium companies. Speculation happened mostly in their shares. The 'Badla' brokers who loaned money and the jobbers who worked with the shares of such companies were considered aristocrats at the Bombay Stock Exchange.

Avarachan learned the tricks of the trade in Bombay.

He had been expecting visitors after reading the newspapers. His palatial home was located in the outskirts of the city. Avarachan's home boasted of every luxury except a telephone. His philosophy was that the ones who needed money should put in the necessary effort for it. Let them seek help directly.

Even 'Badla' Avarachan did not expect the crowd that poured in eventually. Fifty people dropped in before nine in the morning. Authorized assistants were more in number than brokers. All of them sought financing for Dhanwantari shares, wanting to buy more and more.

Avarachan promised to finance everyone. The documents were prepared accordingly. He calculated his future gains at two per cent interest rates. Fifty lakh had been borrowed already.

In a fortnight, irrespective of who won or lost the game of control over Dhanwantari, Avarachan would make a neat profit. He decided to stock more money.

The 'Badla' financiers had another strong financial ecosystem supporting them. Typically, this involved commercial banks. Earlier, even nationalized banks were ready to offer loans for 'Badla' deals. Based on certificates of credit-worthy brokers, banks would lend handsome amounts of money at high interests for a few days. When the government stepped in to control the overdraft rules of banks, they joined hands with prominent brokers to create subsidiary companies. The banks would lend money to their own subsidiary companies. When trouble started raising its head, other ways of financing came into play.

Avarachan arranged his 'Badla' financing using three methods. The first strategy involved foreign banks. To an extent, these banks were not subject to the Indian regulatory framework. So, they would lend him money at exorbitant rates for a few days. The second method involved gold smugglers. The third, the drug market.

The gold smuggling and drug market could not be trusted. When the customs authorities carried out harsh checking, gold smuggling was affected. The Tamil Tigers and their confrontation with the naval forces had also played a prominent role in the slowdown during a specific period of time. The inflow of gold slackened. The money kept aside for trading in gold was invested in the share market. Almost twenty crore rupees flooded the share market unexpectedly. That was one reason why the share prices increased in the Indian stock market.

When the armies of Pakistan and India increased their surveillance of the borders, especially in Punjab and Kashmir, the marijuana that flowed in from Afghanistan via Pakistan was checked for some time. The drug market money was also used for short-term financing in the share market. The share prices shot up. When marijuana cultivation and gold smuggling gathered forces in Kerala, the money went back to the original markets. Even so, 'Badla' Avarachan did not find it difficult to arrange for funds.

~

Mohandas woke up Ramesan when the newspapers arrived.

'Look at this!'

Ramesan read the papers. Dhanwantari Herbal Products, a synonym for a beautiful, gentle and smart young woman. Some wicked hunter from north India was going to abduct her! Some local villains were abetting him. The article had all the alluring elements of a tragic love story.

Ramesan loathed that sort of journalism. All news, horrid or pathetic, was transmuted into fiction.

'Uncle, you've turned into a villain.'

Mohandas smiled.

'Do you know what's about to happen? The share prices shall shoot up now. Today is Friday. No trading for two days. If what one read is right, there are two players apart from us. The Bombay party and Aniyan Raja. Speculators with money shall enter the arena today. There's a difference between the three players and others.'

'What's that?'

'Speculators don't need share certificates. They aim at the profits made by price differentials. The three main players need share certificates. Only then can we assert our entry into the company's management.'

'What should be done?'

'Make a plan with our share brokers. Make it absolutely clear that share certificates are non-negotiable. Even if the price is one or two rupees higher, they should agree only to those cases with actual certificates. We'll need more money, of course. Let me see.'

Mohandas called up the person who helped him with short-term loans.

'The market is very tight now. I got a request for one and a half crores just a while back. Can you wait for a fortnight?'

'No, I need it today.'

The financier was silent. Then he said: 'Let me check with a few others. The interest might go up to even four. Hope that's okay with you.'

Mohandas did his calculations. Four per cent for fifteen days. Ninety-six per cent annual.

'That's a bit too much.'

'Sir, the rumour is that the rates can go up to five today.'

Mohandas responded: 'All right.'

'How much do you need?'

Mohandas added and subtracted mentally. Two lakh shares. The price should stop at thirty. Maximum thirty-five. Seventy lakh.

'Fifty lakh now. I will let you know later whether I need more money.'

'Okay, let me see. Will call you back, sir.'

Ramesan was busy calling up the brokers.

'Look, we need Dhanwantari's share certificates. Even if it takes one or two weeks, it doesn't matter. But no changes in the condition that we need the share certificates.'

Most were sceptical when it came to getting the share certificates. They would buy shares and ensure no losses. They could possibly procure two thousand or four thousand share certificates. But more than that was doubtful. In a day's time, it was next to impossible.

One said: 'Mr Ramesan, the shares of this company have not actually come to the market. This is an old organization. Some received share certificates in the initial stages. Later, they got bonus shares. God alone knows how many marketable lots there are.'

Public limited company shares had a face value of ten rupees per share. A person or an institution could buy these. Companies make marketable lots of fifty or hundred when they list their companies in the share market. Shares are bought and sold in multiples of fifty or hundred accordingly. When bonus shares are issued by the company instead of dividends, the investor benefits, since the money stays within the company.

During the issuing of bonus shares, the stakeholder with two shares gets a single additional share, someone with three shares gets two, and so on – based on a fixed ratio. Sixty-six bonus shares for a stakeholder with one hundred shares. He shall receive dividends for a hundred and sixty-six shares in the future. But he will face a problem in the share market. His one hundred and sixty-six is not a marketable lot. The person will need to purchase another thirty-four at the day's price!

The major shares of Dhanwantari were not marketable. Two or three bonus issues had taken place in the past.

'I have no idea about that,' Ramesan remarked. 'What's the way out then?'

Everybody gave the same answer: 'We will try.'

~

When Savitry woke up, it was 7 a.m. As she was brushing her teeth, a friend called out from nearby: 'The front-page news is all about your Stock Exchange!'

Savitry could not read or write Malayalam properly.

'What's the news? Good or bad?'

'Go on, read for yourself!'

Savitry freshened up fast and went to pick up an English daily.

'My god! The Bulls will start a rampage!'

The Cochin edition newspaper would not reach Bombay. Vikas would be clueless. Should she buy more shares under such circumstances wherein share prices were shooting up like crazy?

Savitry went to her room hurriedly and got changed. She needed to speak to Vikas quickly.

Vikas had once escaped unscathed in a similar Bull-run situation at the Cochin Stock Exchange.

Gujaratis and Marwaris were doing brokerage at the Bombay Stock Exchange across generations. Their working style was extremely traditional and based on their beliefs. They would check an auspicious hour for trading. They would study the company thoroughly before entering into the share market. Not just from the perspective of the balance sheet but also from the family angle. Who ran the company? Was the heir a woman or a man? Were the products likely to be priced higher in the future? Such prominent families used marriage as a tool for hiking the prices of products and controlling the markets. As a part of the dowry, the companies creating competing products merged with each other. When such marriages were on the anvil, the share prices of such companies would become 'hot' in the Bombay Stock Exchange.

A group of young Gujarati and Marwari businessmen had taken over in such a background. The financial capital of non-resident Indians gave them confidence. They leased huge office spaces, hired qualified MBAs and CAs. The team analysed the historical data of every company. Every aspect of a company underwent intense scrutiny: their assets, movement of products, cash flow, short-term and long-term loans, and relationship with other companies. Then they chose companies to invest in through the share market.

When such a company, based in Kerala, was selected once, Vikas had asked Savitry to purchase as many shares as possible. But Savitry had not followed his instructions. The settlement date for submitting the money was a Friday, the same day when Vikas called. On Saturday, Vikas went ballistic. He spewed abuses, and Savitry gave it back as good as she got. On Monday, the prices crashed. Vikas had called in the evening and apologized profusely. 'How did you get the divine insight, dearest?' Savitry replied wryly,

'Well, call it the Kerala magic.' However, following that incident, Savitry had never dared to follow her hunch without Vikas's approval.

Savitry called Vikas.

'What should we do now? The Dhanwantari takeover is front-page news. First time such a thing is happening.'

'Don't lose your cool, girl! Check the market reaction. Watch what the brokers working for the management are doing. If they're selling, you buy all of those. At whatever price. If they're buying, you go ahead and sell at the highest price. Keep your eyes and ears open. I shall call your phone in the Exchange sharp at ten. Bye.'

Vikas disconnected the call.

Savitry felt a pang of dismay. Vikas had not asked a word about her. But then she realized that even she had not bothered to ask him anything special.

Shankaran Kutty was waiting outside the booth. He came closer and said: 'Savitry, I have something to tell you. Purely personal.'

'Oh Lord! Let me rush to the hostel and take a shower. I have to be at the Stock Exchange before ten.'

Watching Savitry cross the road hurriedly, Shankaran Kutty muttered to himself: 'I will kill that fellow!'

48

The Dhanwantari Trust

Tulsi plants peeked from the stone platform that stood in the middle of the courtyard. The small temple carved out of granite was situated at the western part of the house. The black-hued idol of Lord Dhanwantari was enshrined therein.

Dhanwantari had emerged from the ocean of milk, when the devas and asuras churned the waters for amrit. The Lord was depicted holding the pot of that divine nectar in his hand. There was a consoling tranquillity in the deity's eyes and a smile on his lips. A flaming lamp lit up the space in front of the idol.

Mini sat leaning against the pillar. She did not avert her eyes from the divine idol, even for a moment. Amma was praying, her eyes closed. Thirumulpadu Chittappan, Mini's granduncle, was conducting the puja rituals. Mini felt that she was surrendering her whole self before Dhanwantari in those moments.

'I am your slave. You personify healing. I am an inseparable part of you.'

The bells jingled. The single-wick lamp was being circled reverentially around the deity.

Mini woke up from her trance only when Amma patted her shoulder. Chittappan offered her the prasad.

When the huge Contessa had arrived at the gate early in the morning, the old man remained impassive. He had simply smiled at them.

'Let me take a dip in the river. I'll be back in no time.'

Mini's father had always considered the family home as the seating place of Lord Dhanwantari. He would make it a point to visit the place at least twice a year. Never did he undertake anything important without the blessings of the Lord. Amma had asked Mini to visit the family temple before taking charge as the managing director. Somehow, she had been too busy for that until now.

Chittappan asked: 'Are you in a hurry to leave?'

'Yes, I have to get back quickly.'

'But have breakfast with us first.'

Idli and chammanthi – grated coconut, green chillies, and multiple herbs crushed and moistened with coconut oil. It was absolutely mouthwatering.

Mini asked: 'Amma, do you know the recipe of this chammanthi?'

Chittappan smiled.

'This is your father's discovery. He searched for some herbs in the southern yard and made a unique mixture out of them.'

While they were finishing their breakfast, Chittappan spoke:

'Mini, fifteen years ago, your father had offered an envelope at the Lord's feet. When I'd asked about the contents, he had said, "That is the Lord's property. Keep it safe." He had made a Trust in the name of Lord Dhanwantari and the envelope has the relevant documents. "Hand it over to my son after I pass away." Never did I know that both father and son would part so tragically from us one day.'

Mini's acchan used to speak about the Trust often.

The Lord Dhanwantari at the family home had fifty per cent shares. Acchan and Chittappan had twenty-five each. After their lifetime, the shares were to pass on to the legal heirs.

Mini remembered seeing the deed document of the Trust. There were intriguing clauses. Mini's father insisted that his legal heir worked to propagate Ayurveda. Chittappan's legal heir should do the daily puja. Only then shall they receive the quarter of the total shares. In case of any defaulting, the shares would revert to the deity, Dhanwantari! Whoever was the eldest among the living members would be the managing trustee and the representative of Lord Dhanwantari in the Trust. Chittappan held the position as of now.

But Mini's acchan had never mentioned such an envelope.

She opened the envelope inside the car. It was the original document of a legal agreement entered between the Dhanwantari Trust and the company Dhanwantari Herbal Products, executed fourteen years ago.

Mini's eyes skimmed through the words. Having read it, she sat gazing at the paper for a few, stunned moments. Then she spoke excitedly:

'Amma, have you seen this document?'

'What is it?'

'Amma, Lord Dhanwantari had blessed us! This agreement … Lord!'

'Read it aloud.'

Mini obeyed.

'*Dhanwantari Trust has purchased fifteen per cent shares of Dhanwantari Herbal Products Company, three lakh shares exactly, at the current share price, the total amounting to thirty lakh rupees. Fifty acres of land near Thodupuzha, three hundred acres of forestland in Nelliyampathy, and land and buildings at almost ten locations have been transferred to Dhanwantari Herbal Company for the same amount. The goals of this transfer of properties include ensuring due publicity of Ayurveda, the production of local medicines that the common man can afford, spreading the traditional healing practices of Kerala far and wide, research work, etc. If the managing trustee, for whatever reason, concludes that the company is working against the aforementioned goals, Dhanwantari Herbal Company shall take back the fifteen per cent shares and return the immoveable property, including land, estate, et al. to the Trust. The shares shall be distributed as bonus shares to the company's shareholders at that point of time.*

'Amma, do you realize the implication?' Mini's voice was eager. She was thrilled to bits. 'This agreement will protect us. No matter who comes to take over our company, they will bolt.'

The car was speeding eastwards, through the Mavelikkara town. Mini felt the speed was not good enough. Seeing an STD/ ISD booth sign, she signalled the driver to stop.

'Let me call Zacharia uncle.'

Mini knew his routine very well. He would be at the tennis club right now. The line connected.

'Uncle, please don't do anything until I reach there.'

Much later, Mini remembered that she had not revealed the reason to Zacharia.

~

Asokan woke up first. Usually, he would prepare tea. Then the routine of brushing his teeth and working out would begin. Half an hour exactly. By the end of it, the newspaper would have arrived.

But today, his whole regimen went for a toss.

Asokan was not sure when he had slipped off to sleep last night. His mind had been vexed by many anxieties. When he shifted loyalties to Mohandas, he had only one goal. Become the managing director of Dhanwantari Herbal Products under the new dispensation. He was the only one with knowledge enough to run the company once Mini was removed from her position. But Mohandas was proposing to bring his nephew in as an executive director. Ramesan had apparently been an erstwhile revolutionary.

Asokan complained to Aswathy at night: 'That fellow joining the board means trouble.'

Aswathy was still caught in the thrall of Mohandas's promise of the top job.

'Who?'

'That bearded young man. Didn't you hear Mohandas talk about making him in charge of production after setting him up as executive director?'

'How does it matter to us?'

'He will become the next managing director, that's all.'

'Ramesan is training to take over as MD of a new company after six months.'

'It always starts that way.'

Aswathy caressed her husband's chest.

'No, Mohandas sir will keep his word. You will become MD.'

'How can you be so sure?'

Aswathy did not answer.

Asokan tried to sleep. Somehow, he could not bring himself to trust Mohandas.

Had there been any vested interest in sending him off with Zacharia after dinner? But Ramesan was with Aswathy, wasn't he?

Asokan reached for Aswathy's body in the dark.

Should he ask her? *No, it will sound weird. Did Mohandas…? Tch!*

Half asleep, Asokan thought he heard oracular prophecies from his own mind. *Asokan, consolidate your position firmly. Create your own space.*

He woke up to the sound of the newspaper falling on the verandah. Aswathy was sleeping soundly. Asokan quickly scanned the headlines. Then he rushed to the bathroom forgetting his usual cup of tea. He was ready in ten minutes. Aswathy woke up at the commotion.

'Listen, I'm going to the office. Will be back soon.'

'What happened? What about your tea?'

'Later.'

Asokan dropped a kiss on Aswathy's cheek. He smiled at her.

'Nobody can beat me so easily. Let me see what I can do.'

Aswathy watched him with curious eyes.

'Tell me dear, what happened?'

'Hot news on Dhanwantari in today's papers. If someone wants to take over Dhanwantari, he should have a sufficient number of shares. The north Indian predators, Mohandas or Mini herself – all need share certificates, not just the shares. Or a proxy certificate. Ninety per cent of the trading at the Stock Exchange is speculation. The remaining ten per cent is done in the hope of tracing the share-certificate holders. Who has that information? Tell me.'

Aswathy smiled.

'Only you know that, I guess.'

'Correct. I have the share register and the list of shareholders. Let's put in our best effort. You get ready. Mortgage the gold in the locker. I will borrow more money. We will contact the shareholders directly. We shall lose nothing. Before exchanging our share certificates, we will insist on our conditions.'

'What do you mean?'

'I won't accept anything less than the post of MD.'

Aswathy got up.

'When you're back, let us visit the temple. I'll take a shower now.'

Asokan drove away in his car.

The rush on the road was yet to begin. The buses coming to the city were chockablock with people. Asokan started calculating.

He should reach out to those holding less than a thousand shares. In all likelihood, the ones with more than a thousand were not going to sell. They were mostly hard-core investors and would wait for the share price to rise. The small shareholders would be in need of money. From the list of shareholders, one could make an intelligent guess about whether the person would sell or not.

Usually the parking space was full of vehicles. Now, it was empty. Nobody had arrived in office as yet.

The watchman had just opened the cubicles. The sweeper woman was carrying her broom and basket. She was yet to get started.

'Namasteji.'

Asokan acknowledged the watchman's greetings wordlessly. He opened his office door and made his way in. The share register and list were in the bottom drawer of the rack, if he remembered correctly. But there was nothing!

Asokan started searching high and low.

Where was it? He had locked the rack's bottom drawer with the share register and list in it. How could they simply vanish?

Asokan was distraught with sadness and anger. He scoured every corner of his office, opened every almirah – nothing. Asokan almost wept in frustration. What should he do now? What happened?

Someone had visited his office.

He was about to reach for the telephone when he noticed an office memo kept folded under the device.

> Mr Asokan, I am taking the share register and the list with me. The MD wants them urgently. In case you want these documents in the future, please get in touch with me.
>
> Adiyodi
> Finance Director

Asokan could not believe his eyes.

'Bloody bugger!' The cuss word resounded in the room.

The watchman came running to the door.

'Sir, do you need some tea?'

49

The Charging Bull

The second floor of the Cochin Stock Exchange became active on Friday morning. The trading would begin on the third floor, only three hours later. But curb trading happened all the time.

A crowd of two hundred-odd young men and women. The rush was increasing by the minute. The news in every prominent newspaper in the city, about the potential Dhanwantari takeover bid, had stoked much provocation in the share market. Everybody wanted to reap a fine profit in the melee. It was every broker's dream, every speculator's too.

Usually the pattern of share trading could not be predicted. Consider two companies making similar products. Well-managed companies with no financial or labour problems. Dividends distributed to the stakeholders annually in a comparable pattern. Unexpectedly, the share prices of one company start rising in the stock market. The reason? The management or some speculators were trying to raise the share prices intentionally. Fortune seekers would flock towards it like moths to a flame. But most ended up with their wings burned.

But when a takeover bid was on, the risk was lesser.

The north Indian company was on the verge of swallowing a local company. There were some rich natives in the arena. There was no chance of the share prices going down. Even if they went ballistic, those with money and determination to win would not retreat. Under these circumstances, it was better to buy as many shares as possible. One could sell in the evening or on the next day, at a huge profit.

In a matter of ten minutes, the share prices rose from twenty-five to twenty-eight. Savitry had sold twenty thousand shares at twenty-six rupees by then. The same mantra was being chanted all around:

'Dhanwantari.'

'Dhanwantari, Buyer.'

'Dhanwantari, Seller.'

'Twenty-seven fifty.'

'Twenty-eight.'

'Thousand.'

'Two thousand.'

The voices were muted at the curb trading. Since the sellers were few in number, the share prices kept rising. Suddenly, a few speculators started selling the shares they had bought a while ago. At a higher price. Buyers turned sellers and vice versa.

The cacophony of ringing phones flooded the cubicles abutting the curb trading area. Fellows rushed to the devices, unsure about which of them was ringing. Those attending the calls had one ear covered and the other affixed to the receiver; they spoke at the top of their voices. Nobody bothered to pay any heed to their conversations. The eyes around were ablaze with eagerness; the lips muttered: 'Buyer', 'Seller', 'Gross', 'Twenty-eight', 'Twenty-seven'…

The moistness of the morning melded with the sweaty ambience. The fans scattered the air in all directions.

A sudden rumour spread in the crowd. No one knew from where it had sprung. Perhaps it surfaced at the Bombay Stock Exchange and then spread via the brokers engaged in line business. Maybe from Kerala House in Delhi. A prominent politician used to indulge in share trading often. He might have informed his broker. There were newspapers with huge investments in the share market. They might have got the information via their secret sources. Whatever it was, the news soon spread like wildfire.

It was a famous Lucknow-based Ayurvedic medicine manufacturing company that was trying to take over Dhanwantari. They were very close to the political leadership in both Uttar Pradesh and at the Centre. The state government of Kerala would play neutral during such a game. The probability of government financial institutions supporting the Dhanwantari management was very low. If the Lucknow company bought twenty per cent shares, they would acquire Dhanwantari easily. The state government's financial institutions, with their thirty per cent shares, and the company would join forces. No question of the takeover bid failing. The company would buy the shares, even at the highest prices.

The prices hit the sky during the curb trading.

There were three fortresses of power controlling the share market: the financial institutions associated with the government, the money that financed smuggling and other illegal activities, and the investment in NRI accounts.

It was not easy to conjecture when the last two would influence the share market. For instance, when border checking was intensified, when naval patrolling became strict, when the likelihood of a war increased, when gold prices shot up in international markets, when the Interpol caught some international drug smugglers, or when the US government fortified its efforts against the Colombian drug mafia, the course of events changed accordingly in the financial markets across the world. In scenarios where gold smuggling or illegal drug trade could proliferate, the money would not flow into the share markets. The share prices would fall. When the controls were strong, the money was routed to the share markets. However, there was no clear model to predict when this phenomenon would occur.

The same pattern was seen with the NRI deposits. The RBI rules and laws applied to these accounts. Typically, the value of Indian rupees was lower in the market than the official rates. The exchange rates played a role in whether the money found its way to the stock market. There was no predictive algorithm for such a scenario either. Hence the financial institutions played the most vital role in controlling the Indian share market.

The common man's savings in banks, the post office accounts, unit trusts, life insurance and so on were used by the government in many ways. When most of the private banks became nationalized, the investments in the banking sector came under the control of the government. Banks created subsidiaries for promoting investment tools like mutual funds. Most financial institutions encouraged the officers handling the investments to take independent decisions. These institutions and their head honchos invested thousands of crores in various companies. They played a very significant role in controlling the dynamics of the share market. Every player in the stock market knew that there was a nexus between political parties and top corporates. The appointments and transfers of the top management of financial institutions were under the government's thumb.

Consequently, nobody disbelieved the rumour that the Lucknow company had the support of the top financial institutions of the government.

The share prices of Dhanwantari shot up.

Vinayan, following Zacharia's instructions, made agreements to sell seven thousand shares of Dhanwantari in three separate lots. Three different share brokers were entrusted with the task. The prices kept escalating. Vinayan took the help of a few of his friends. They did not have to do much. At one quarter commission, they signed papers stating they were repurchasing whatever they had sold a few minutes ago.

Savitry's attention was arrested when the third lot was sold. She approached the young man who bought the third lot at thirty rupees.

'How many?'

'Three thousand shares.'

'Price?'

'Thirty.'

Zacharia was Dhanwantari's official share broker. Vinayan was his Man Friday. Vinayan was selling Dhanwantari's shares! Was the company selling off its shares looking at the profit margins? If so…?

There was a ruckus among the curb trading crowd.

If Dhanwantari gave up, the buyers would have a field day. The Dalal Street brokers would buy the company shares at any exorbitant cost.

The costs clambered higher and higher.

At ten o'clock sharp, Vikas called Savitry in her cubicle.

'What's the update?'

Savitry replied in Hindi: 'It's pandemonium here. No idea where this Bull-run shall end.'

'What about the company's broker?'

'They sold some shares. I think they are watching the market's response. What should I do?'

Vikas answered a few moments later: 'What's the price now?'

'Thirty-two.'

'What do you think? Has the company decided to sell its own shares or are they trying to force a further escalation of prices?'

'I don't know.'

'Your gut feeling? The Kerala magic?'

'No, I can't guess anything.'

The line went silent for a long time.

'Vikas, are you there? This is an STD call.'

Vikas replied: 'Savitry, give an offer when the price hits thirty-five. One lakh shares. Spot delivery. At forty rupees. You'll know what their true intention is. Go ahead. Then call me back. I'll be waiting by the telephone.'

Savitry put the receiver down.

She was still grappling with the implications of what Vikas had said. One lakh shares at forty rupees each. The shares that cost fourteen rupees each yesterday were forty rupees each today. Twenty-six lakhs more in worth over a single day. Spot delivery implied taking over the share certificates with an immediate settlement of money. Savitry strategized where and how to confront Vinayan.

She noticed Shankaran Kutty only when he started complaining.

'I should not have sold off the shares yesterday. Now the share price is thirty-three rupees. Savitry, I was so upset yesterday. When I hear unpleasant news, it affects me badly. It runs in my family. My father was also like me.'

Pausing for a moment, Shankaran Kutty continued:

'But I can change.'

'Change what?'

'You didn't hear what I said. Was the call from Bombay?'

Savitry did not deign to reply.

'I know this is not the appropriate time. But Savitry, I purchased four thousand shares at twenty-four rupees in the morning. I will show you what I have achieved by this afternoon.'

Shankaran Kutty waited for five minutes. When Savitry did not react, he got up to leave.

As he walked through the corridor, he shouted: 'Dhanwantari, Buyer.'

'Buyer.'

'Buyer.'

The hordes were thronging the corridors. But the din had subsided a bit. As if a tempest had calmed unexpectedly. Nobody responded to Shankaran Kutty's calls. Some uncertainty was in the air.

Shankaran Kutty asked the man next to him: 'What's the matter?'

There was nothing of significance. Another rumour. A conjecture. The Stock Exchange authorities were about to control the chaotic Bull-run of Dhanwantari's shares. Though the president was empowered to take a call, the board members were arriving from different places for a consensual decision. They would reach the headquarters by noon.

What pronouncements could the authorities make? Many options were available.

One: Sell only by spot delivery today. That would mean that only those holding share certificates could trade.

Two: The settlement of today's shares should be done today instead of the second Friday.

Three: The speculators could be asked to settle at a compromise price, after taking an average of the lowest and highest prices.

Four: No more trading in Dhanwantari's shares for a few days.

Whatever the authorities decided, everybody would rant. The protests of those losing out on profits. The laments of those who lost in a big way. Remonstrations were the quintessential crown of thorns that the authorities had to accept as a part of their job.

Irrespective of the decision taken at the Cochin Stock Exchange, there would be buyers in Bombay. The pronouncements of the Cochin authorities did not have any effect on the Bombay Stock Exchange.

Dhanwantari's name resounded yet again at the Exchange.

'Dhanwantari, Seller.'

'Seller, thirty-five.'

'Buyer, Buyer.'

'Thirty-three.'

Vinayan called Zacharia.

He was in Mini Balachandran's office.

50

Adiyodi's Sincerity

By nine in the morning, the office of Dhanwantari Herbal Products was bustling. Though working hours began at nine-thirty, the newspaper reports had triggered the staff to arrive early. Some north Indian company was trying to take over Dhanwantari! Nobody believed it at first. But why? Weren't there several other companies in Kerala that had better credentials than Dhanwantari? They were making profits too. Usually when such rumours spread, newspapers would carry various opinions. However, in the case of the takeover, all of them were shouting in the same voice: Dhanwantari was in danger!

The phone rang when Adiyodi reached office. From his very first day at Dhanwantari, there was a ritual that Adiyodi performed unfailingly in the morning. A small puja room was located in the middle of the new office rooms for working directors. It was originally the abode of the deity Nagayakshi, in the sacred serpent grove of yore. The idol had never been removed. The new building was built around it. Everybody considered it to be a modern puja room. Marble walls, electric lights and many more idols. No one ever suspected it to be the holy relics of an ancient serpent grove. From the time Adiyodi joined Menon sir's company as an accountant clerk, he had taken over the task of lighting the morning lamp. Unless he was away on leave, he never delegated the job to anyone else.

Ever since he read the morning news, Adiyodi had been experiencing acute consternation. Apparently an attempt was being made by some unknown enemy to take over the company he considered his own, one where he was the finance director and the managing director was a helpless young woman. Adiyodi could not bring himself to trust the news. He read the newspapers with great care.

Adiyodi called Mini Balachandran as soon as he read the news. The servant informed him that both Mini and her mother had left very early for a temple. They would be back before breakfast. Though Adiyodi tried to get in touch with Mini twice or thrice afterwards, it was in vain. He was furious. A takeover bid which the finance director was unaware of! The MD, equally clueless, had gone for worship early in the morning! Adiyodi brooded that women, in general, were supposed to take care of the household and visit temples. The whole thing went for a toss when they set out to run companies and manage businesses.

Adiyodi remembered that Zacharia would be fully aware of the happenings. He was responsible for managing the company's stocks. Wasn't Zacharia accountable to the company when it came to informing the top management about such a nefarious takeover bid? That was his solemn duty, wasn't it? How come the company's broker was uninformed when all the journalists had got their scoop?

Adiyodi called Zacharia. Prabhu answered the call.

'Sir is taking his bath. It will take some time. A luxurious oil bath.'

Adiyodi felt enraged. Look at the day the fellow chose for his oil bath! The man was supposed to be running to them with his expert counsel. Instead, he was relishing an oil massage? This was a Friday. Weren't oil baths supposed to be taken on Saturdays, as per custom?

Adiyodi dialled the marketing director Asokan's number. Apparently, he was not at home either. He had left early, possibly gone to the office as soon as he read the news. Aswathy informed him that Asokan had driven off without even having a cup of tea. She assured him that Asokan would call Adiyodi when he returned home.

Suddenly, Adiyodi remembered a vexatious problem which had confounded him the day before. Matters were certainly grave.

When Mini asked him for the share register, Adiyodi had not been able to retrieve it. When she reminded him once more, he had taken great pains to check each and every almirah in the office except the ones in Asokan's room. After Asokan left, Adiyodi had entered his room and, using the duplicate key, opened the bottom-most drawer of the rack. The share register was lying there. A typed list of shareholders, their addresses and the percentage of shares they owned, was there too. The question of how the marketing director came to possess the share register had befuddled Adiyodi. What was the need of such information? Now he felt suspicious. Nay, Adiyodi was sure that Asokan had prepared the list for somebody. The list of shareholders was extremely valuable information to someone trying to take over the company. As the saying went, 'The thief is verily on the ship.'

The telephone rang right then.

Usually he would start work only after he lit the lamp. Today, things were topsy turvy.

It was the vakil who was a director on the board.

'Where is Mini, Adiyodi?'

'Visiting some temple…'

'Listen Adiyodi. Tell Mini that I'll head straight to the court from office. I shall proceed as we planned yesterday. Since the newspapers have published the details, that strategy is better.'

'What's the matter, sir?'

'Mini Balachandran knows about it. You tell her. She'll understand.'

Even after the lawyer disconnected the call, Adiyodi stood there flabbergasted.

Mini was very much aware of the goings on. That was why she had called up the vakil yesterday.

Adiyodi presumed that Mini must have called him too, after office hours. But where was he then? He broke into a mischievous grin remembering his own location.

'I should take the lady to some nice place like Ooty or Kovalam. There are too many acquaintances in the places nearby. Somewhere not too far, where I can drive myself. And then…'

Adiyodi could not indulge in his fantasies for long. The phone rang again.

'Mr Adiyodi!'

'Yes, sir.' Adiyodi had recognized the voice of the company director, the retired vice chancellor.

'Where is Mini?'

'Hasn't arrived yet, sir.'

'Tell her that I forgot to mention one pertinent fact yesterday. There is a method to discourage the takeover attempt. A new idea that I wish to share with her. Somehow, it struck me after I spoke to her. It was too late at night to call her back. And I am particular about my sleeping time, you know?

'We should buy back our own shares. This is called leveraged buyout, or LBO. It's a popular technique in the American corporate sector. From a legal perspective, it is devious. But then, it's not all wrong. A scheme to buy our own company. Buy the shares and sell off the company assets showcased as low priced in the balance sheet. Like a well-oiled machine, every move should be smooth, that is all. We take over our own company. Got it?'

Adiyodi understood nothing. But he gasped: 'Of course, sir.'

'I have two company board meetings at ten and twelve. Two-thirty is the hour for my afternoon siesta. Maybe three would be an ideal time. Ask Mini to call me then. I'll speak in detail with her.'

'Yes, sir.'

Before Adiyodi could gather his wits, the phone rang again.

It was an unknown voice. 'Adiyodi here.'

'Sir, I am calling from Kurukutty.'

'What's the matter?'

'Read about the company in the papers. Thought I would call. My wife and I have two thousand and two hundred shares of Dhanwantari Herbal Products. We will make a lot of money if we dispose those today. Actually, we decided to sell those to you. Give us today's price.'

'But nobody is buying shares here.'

'Huh! The newspapers are screaming out loud that someone or the other is on a buying spree to take over the company. So why should we sell to outsiders? We prefer giving them to you. It will strengthen your position, won't it?'

'The Stock Exchange handles all that. Try to sell them through some stockbroker. That's the rule.'

'I know all that, sir. But who will chase after them now? You do one thing. Take a month's time to give us the money.'

Adiyodi thought for a moment.

'There's a broker called P.T. Zacharia at the Stock Exchange. He works for the company. Get in touch with him. We will ensure that you get paid as soon as possible. How about that?'

'Sure, no worries. Even if it is at a loss of one or two rupees, we would rather that Dhanwantari gets our shares.'

'Okay.'

Adiyodi gazed at the phone after the caller cut the call. Would it ring again?

By the time he returned from the puja room, both the phones were ringing and the intercom too was buzzing.

Adiyodi wiped his face with a towel. One phone stopped ringing.

He poured Menon sir's patented water into a glass and gulped it down. The intercom stopped buzzing.

Adiyodi sat down in his chair and focused on the pranic healing spot in the middle of his forehead. The second phone ceased ringing too.

There was a knock on the door.

'Yes, come in.'

Asokan walked into the room.

His face was flushed. The door closed behind him. He took a chair opposite Adiyodi.

Asokan's voice was trembling in fury and agitation.

'Sir, by what authority did you take confidential papers from my room? What's the meaning of this memo?'

He hurled Adiyodi's note on the table. Adiyodi picked it up calmly.

'The share register is a document that should be with the company secretary at all times. He's on leave now and the charge is with the finance director. So the register is my responsibility right now. There's no reason why the marketing director should keep it. If you want any details, inform me in writing. I shall check with the legal department and get back to you.'

Asokan wanted to say many things. But no words emerged.

Adiyodi spoke:

'You should know this. I am going to move a note to the managing director today. An agenda should be presented in front of the board of directors about this matter. Under the peculiar circumstances we are facing today, how did the share register end up with you? Why did you prepare a list from the document? It will be beneficial for the board to be cognizant of the facts.'

Asokan slammed his fist on the table. 'Stop this nonsense!'

For a few moments, nobody spoke. Then, Asokan apologized to Adiyodi.

'Excuse me, I am very upset. Why are we bickering anyway? Today, the company is getting away from Mini's hands. We must take care of ourselves, shouldn't we?'

The phone rang then, terrifying them both. Adiyodi picked the call. It was Mini Balachandran.

'Uncle, you must have seen the papers. I'll reach office in half an hour's time.'

'Where did you go?'

'We went to the family temple. Just returned home.'

'There's been a flurry of calls since morning. Vakil sir and VC sir from the board of directors called.'

'They are in a panic after seeing the newspapers. We will face it. There is no other alternative.'

Adiyodi wanted to tell Mini that he would take care of everything and that she should not worry. But he did not have the courage.

'Okay, Mini.'

After putting down the receiver, Adiyodi confronted Asokan.

'Asokan, do not misunderstand me. I am old. It was Menon sir who made me what I am today. The moment someone takes over Dhanwantari, I shall leave the premises. Till then, using my limited abilities, I shall battle for this company.'

Asokan got up slowly.

As he walked out of the room, Adiyodi felt a pang of sympathy. Poor fellow!

51

Battle Moves

'Mini, let's face it! There are four forces in the battlefield that can defeat us easily. One, the north Indian company. I feel it's Sharmaji's company in Lucknow behind this game. He was very close to Menon sir, wasn't he? Logically, Dhanwantari Herbal Products cannot be chosen after analysing its balance sheet. It has to be someone who knows our organization inside out. Besides, Menon sir always used to discuss our future projects with Sharmaji.'

The red lamp outside Mini Balachandran's room blazed at ten o'clock sharp.

The 'Do Not Disturb' sign.

Mini called Adiyodi through the intercom.

'Uncle, come to my office at eleven. I need the minutes of the board meetings for the last ten years, along with the letters sent to the Registrar of Companies. Zacharia uncle is here. By the time we finish talking, do get those documents.'

Adiyodi pitched in eagerly: 'Mini, I recovered the share register.'

'Okay.'

Adiyodi felt bad that Mini did not ask anything more about it. 'Pity, she is a naïve young girl!'

He wished to reassure her, saying, 'Go on, hear Zacharia out. We'll have a discussion to decide on the course of action after that.' But Adiyodi could not say anything. Mini Balachandran had turned off the intercom.

Mini called Asokan next.

'Please come to my office at ten-thirty. Kindly bring along the updated details of all the immoveable properties that we are planning to buy across the country. I have an idea that I wish to discuss with you.'

The intercom went off before Asokan could respond.

Zacharia's analysis, meanwhile, was going full steam ahead.

'Aniyan Raja and Matthews are a team. They have money, but I'm not sure if they want to take over Dhanwantari. If they get a chance to make some decent profits, they might retreat. We will get to know their next step soon enough. Next in line is Mohandas. His intention is to take over the company, no doubt. He knows each and every secret of Dhanwantari. He is alert to every movement of ours. But if the share prices go up beyond a point, Mohandas is likely to withdraw from the fight. The third force, which can devastate us, is our own reality. The fact that we don't have liquidity. You need money to handle every opponent in the market. Going by the share price of Dhanwantari now, even if all our shares are mortgaged, we shall not be able to procure more than four per cent of the total shares. The Lucknow company, Aniyan Raja and Mohandas are all stronger than us. So, what should we do? Like a laser, focus all our strength on a single point.'

'I don't think Sharmaji would have that sort of money,' remarked Mini.

'He must have found some source. Maybe he borrowed money. We should immediately take action to implement the terms of the document you have in hand. Execute the agreement between the Trust and the company management. I'm not sure whether it's legally valid. If questioned in a court of law, anything can happen.

But it's a good tool to scare our foes. In case the company is taken over by someone, inform the managing trustee that the properties and estates given to the company are not being used for the benefit of Ayurveda. Following the terms of the contract, request him to take back the immoveable properties and return the fifteen per cent shares. These shares shall be distributed among the existing shareholders. The board of directors should take a call at once. Of course, it will unleash a hurricane. But we can't go ahead with just one strategy.'

The telephone rang. It was Vinayan.

'The Stock Exchange is unsettled. The prices are going berserk. New rumours are afloat every moment. Speculations and conjectures flying around.'

'Aniyan Raja?'

'Matthews' brokers are selling shares now. But we can't trust them.'

'All right, I'll call you later.'

Zacharia turned to Mini.

'I have a plan in mind. A throw of dice. Big gamble, so to speak.'

'Tell me.'

'It's mandatory for anyone who wants to take over Dhanwantari to have share certificates. The speculator shall pay up the price differential and escape from the consequences. Let's not bother too much about them. Who has the share certificates? Thirty per cent are with us. That comes to six lakh shares. Another six lakh are with government institutions. The remaining eight lakh shares are with three thousand-odd people. The takeover attempt shall be successful only after half of these fellows are traced and the certificates are obtained from them. Not exactly impossible for a filthy rich person. If such a situation plays out, and the agreement between the Trust and our company fails in court, we shall lose. Let me say, we have a thirty-five per cent probability of failing.' Zacharia paused.

'So, what's left for us to do? Our core strength is the six lakh shares we have, right? Keeping aside the three lakh shares of the Trust, we still have three lakh. Let's make an offer in the share market. Two lakh shares ready for spot delivery today. At a price of eighty rupees. We shall start at hundred and bring it down to eighty. If the takeover party is strong, they will fall for the bait. Maybe some big-time speculative traders will step in. There is also a chance nobody will come forward. If so, the share prices will go down. If the offer is accepted, they will rise. We will end up with one crore sixty lakh rupees. A clean profit of one crore forty lakhs. Then we shall implement the Trust's agreement. The market will go wild. The takeover party shall flinch. There's more than a fifty per cent chance that it will try to sell its shares. We will use our liquidity to buy back our own shares at a lower cost. We shall have enough cash as reserve.'

'Uncle, what if events don't unfold as expected?'

'We'll lose the company. But we will make a killing.'

'But the company…?'

'Yes, the emotional bruises will remain, that's true. But if we don't act, we shall still end up in the same situation.'

Mini Balachandran sat silently for some time. Then she gazed at her father's photograph.

'I shall get back to you by eleven-thirty. Is that okay?'

'Of course. It's a hard choice. But I know you're capable of making the right decision.'

'Thank you, Uncle.'

Mini's eyes became moist.

Zacharia got up.

'I will be at the Stock Exchange at eleven-thirty.' The red lamp outside the managing director's room dimmed when Zacharia left. It was twenty-five minutes past ten. Mini Balachandran pulled out a coin from her bag. A one-rupee coin.

Head or tail? Yes for head. No for tail. Ready, one, two, three.

Mini tossed the coin in the air. It fell gently on the carpet.

Head.

Mini closed her eyes and leaned back into the soft chair.

Asokan opened the door and walked in.

The door shut automatically behind him. Mini pressed the foot button. The red lamp above the MD's door came on.

Asokan started gabbling even before taking his seat.

'Mini, I warned you yesterday. Someone is eyeing our company. You did not believe me when I told you about the planted news in *The Times of India* yesterday. Now, look! All the newspapers are screaming about the takeover bid.'

Asokan placed a file on the table. Mini opened it. The list of properties purchased by Dhanwantari Herbal Products from time to time to expand its marketing network.

Asokan elucidated:

'Seventeen properties. Twelve of them are on lease. Three were purchased. Two of the properties are completing the lease term this month. Apart from the working capital, in order to utilize these properties, we shall need an investment of one crore twenty-five lakhs. Menon sir's dream project, setting up healing centres in picturesque places, shall become a reality. Branches can evolve with those centres and generate capital. It's a beautiful idea. Menon sir and Suresh—'

'Neither of them is with us now,' Mini interrupted. 'We are here.'

'Mini, I want to assure you about something. So long as I am there, you can work fearlessly. I will be with you. If you feel at a loss with something, leave the matter to me. I shall save the company from this calamitous situation.'

Mini smiled gently.

'I know that. But I am slightly apprehensive.'

'Why?'

'Can we trust Mr Mohandas? Yesterday, he laid out a few conditions for cooperating with us. I just met him once. Yet, I feel unsure.'

'What's the matter?'

'I just feel he is not to be trusted. Asokan chetta, you know him well. What's your opinion?'

Asokan did not respond immediately. He suspected that Mini was testing him subtly. Was he in Mohandas's close circle? Aswathy was right. Mini was a smart cookie. Only a woman understood another perfectly.

Asokan replied: 'Simple and straight. One cannot trust Mr Mohandas. He's a hardcore businessman. Mohandas has been eyeing Dhanwantari for a long time. I did not share the fact with you on purpose. You know, I was wondering how far he would go. But when he called us for dinner yesterday, all my doubts were cleared. This fellow is serious. Luckily, Zacharia was there too.'

Mini smiled.

'Yes. What you mentioned is true. Mr Mohandas is untrustworthy. When you went off to drop Zacharia uncle, do you know what he told Aswathy? He should not be invited to any decent home. I could never imagine…!'

Asokan was shellshocked. 'Who? What did he say?'

'Well, I can't repeat it. Listen to this…'

Mini Balachandran switched on the tape recorder that was kept on the side of the table.

The tape started playing. The background music sounded. Asokan's eyes widened in surprise. He stared at Mini's face and the tape recorder alternately.

'What's this?'

Mini gestured to Asokan to be silent.

Aswathy's voice resounded.

'Oh, Mini is pretty good at charming anyone! You don't know her. After Menon sir's death, Asokan chettan should have become the managing director in his place. But the board of directors completely ignored him. All of them fell for Mini's smiles and tricks. Everyone knows about her mediocre qualifications and lack of experience. Why did the directors stand behind her when Asokan chettan was toiling for the company day and night?'

Asokan sat like a living corpse. What was he hearing? Was that Aswathy's voice? No, it couldn't be!

Mohandas's voice: *'Aswathy, we're trying to rectify that error now, aren't we? By the way, when you speak so passionately, Aswathy, you look stunning! So, please stop. Or I might forget that there are people around.'*

Asokan clutched the chair's handle tightly. His face blanched. He could not lift his eyes and look at Mini.

Mohandas's tone became softer.

'We need more opportunities to get closer. I don't know ... For the last one hour, your presence has given me a sense of completeness, a new strength.'

Shit! Bloody bugger!

Asokan started trembling in fury.

Mohandas's voice reverberated again.

'In this battle with Mini, you would have been a better opponent, Aswathy.'

Asokan got up slowly. He looked at Mini.

'What did she say?'

Mini did not reply. Aswathy's reply echoed in the room.

'I am more educated than Mini.'

Mini's face turned grave. Asokan, however, did not notice it.

Mohandas's voice: *'I shall call you tomorrow at eleven.'*

Asokan was shaking with fury. He looked at the tape recorder and then at Mini.

'I will kill him ... I will kill the bastard!'

'Under these circumstances' – Mini's voice resounded with absolute authority; it was firmer than her father's – 'I shall expect your resignation. Submit it immediately to the board of directors. It should reach my table by afternoon.'

Regarding a stunned Asokan calmly, Mini Balachandran spoke again:

'Sorry, I have no other alternative. You have to go. Leave the company right now.'

Asokan heard nothing. His eyes were fixed on the wall clock. It was a quarter to eleven.

'The bugger! He shall call Aswathy at eleven!'

Asokan opened the door and rushed outside.

52

Accident

Though Asokan left Mini's room, she did not turn off the red bulb outside.

It was the benediction of Lord Dhanwantari. He had given her the resoluteness and strength. Mini could not believe that she had spoken so firmly to Asokan a few moments earlier. Poor man! His situation was pitiable. But what else was there to do?

The beautiful black idol in the family temple appeared in her mind.

Suddenly, Mini Balachandran remembered. She was yet to give a thank-you call to the friend.

He was not in his office.

~

Following their early morning temple visit, Mini and her mother had reached home ten minutes earlier than expected.

The young man waiting for them in the verandah had approached her as the car came to a halt.

'Mrs Mini Balachandran, am I right?'

A stranger. Closely cropped head. Muscular form. Sharply dressed in shirt and trousers.

'Who are you, please?'

He extended a packet.

'Sir asked me to hand this over to you.'

'Which sir?'

He mentioned Balachandran's friend's name.

Mini received the packet.

'Thanks.'

'I'll take your leave, madam.'

'What about some tea?'

'No, thank you.'

She saw the parked motorcycle then.

Mini went to her room and opened the packet.

An audio tape and a crisp note. Two lines: *Some interesting parts from yesterday's dinner. Might turn out useful.*

Nothing more.

Mini played the tape.

The conversations between Mohandas and Asokan, Aswathy, Zacharia and Ramesan, during their dinner.

Mini shut her eyes and listened; she focused on the essence of what was being said. When the tape played itself out, there was a sound near the door.

Amma.

'Don't you want to eat something? We have dosa.'

'Yes, Amma. I'm in a good mood. A fighting mood!'

Mini had heard about Mohandas. There was nothing surprising about his behaviour. It was rather natural. Neither could she blame Aswathy or Asokan.

Who was to blame? Were there clear boundaries between right and wrong? Everybody did what they thought was right for them, that's all.

~

The intercom sounded. Mini woke from her reverie. It was Adiyodi.

'Are you free now, Mini? It's eleven.'

'Sorry, Uncle. I forgot to turn off the red light.'

Adiyodi had the share register with him. He looked around cautiously, ensuring that they were alone. He spoke in a low voice:

'Mini, be careful. I'm keeping a close watch. There are conspiracies being hatched in the company. We have to be very alert.'

'What's the matter, Uncle?'

Adiyodi cast another wary glance around.

'Mini, you won't be able to guess from where I recovered the share register! A terribly ill-intentioned manoeuvre by someone. I did not care for office protocol then. Stealing is stealing, whoever high and mighty the thief happens to be.'

Adiyodi was extraordinarily sincere. He trusted that whatever he said was the truth, whatever he did was the right thing. Such people were caught in the rigidity of their own beliefs: they firmly believed that nobody else could be correct. After years of viewing matters through an awfully narrow lens, their intelligence and acumen had rusted. They had lost the ability to grow with the organization. Traditions and legacy were helpful, of course. But a mindset of growth alongside a conservative background was rather rare. There were umpteen men and women like Adiyodi in every organization. Not just in organizations, they were also in governments, political parties, and in every field, including science, the arts and so on. This lot turned out to be the greatest liabilities of their respective organizations. Such dead wood were high in number.

Adiyodi was blabbing.

'Do you know what Asokan told me just a little while ago? Others are out to acquire this company. We should save our skins. He has betrayed us and joined the enemy's camp. He created this list of shareholders and addresses from the share register.'

Mini took the list. Adiyodi continued to fulminate.

'Full of typing mistakes. I think Asokan typed it out himself. Most of the names are of those with less than a thousand shares. They're unlikely to sell their shares by themselves. One has to search them out. It will take time and money. But if we employ sufficient staff, it can be done. Someone will try this strategy if the share prices continue to escalate. They might even win.'

Mini spoke:

'Uncle, study the minutes of the meetings that I asked you to. Ideally, one should consult the auditors and the company advocate. But there is no time for all that. I want your advice.'

'On what?'

'There will be an agenda on transferring our Nelliyampathy estate in one of the minutes. We bought the properties from the Trust.'

'Yes, I remember.'

'There was an irrevocable condition. The immoveable properties should be used only for furthering the company's mission and core objectives. If the managing trustee feels that the condition is being violated, the board of directors shall transfer the shares back to the company's shareholders and return the properties to the Trust. Do you remember the clause?'

'Oh, yes! Even Menon sir was doubtful about its legal validity, though! I remember.'

'Examine the agreement and the clauses again. Let's find out if we can enforce it, if required. I need your counsel quickly.'

Adiyodi toyed with the paper weight on the table unbeknownst to himself. Out of the blue, it slipped from his grasp and rolled towards Mini. She caught it deftly.

'Let me think a bit. Where is the original of the agreement? Not in the legal cell. There is a master file with the company secretary called "Personal Secrets". Would it be there?'

A few moments later, Adiyodi spoke:

'Mini, unless we create a perfect filing system, nothing will work. The files form the nerve centre of an organization. If we don't have a system to tackle that issue, we are bound to suffer.'

'Uncle, you are responsible for creating a filing system.'

'Ah, but I hardly get time to breathe. Labour issues, audit problems, endless grievances of the personnel department. But don't worry, I will do it. I shall reorganize soon.'

The phone rang when Adiyodi got up. Mini took the call. She signalled Adiyodi to take his seat.

'It's Vakil uncle.'

'Mini, I'd called in the morning. Told Adiyodi that I'd be trying to get an order issued by the High Court, directing the Stock Exchange to take some action. A stay order preventing further speculation in our shares.'

'What happened?'

'Didn't work out. The court's not convinced that this trade shall harm the shareholder. In its view, the loss is only for the management. The court is sceptical about jumping in based on a single day's trading pattern. Let the Stock Exchange take a call on the matter, they have the powers. That's what the court opined.'

'So, that strategy failed.'

'Yes. What are you going to do now?'

After a poignant pause, Mini spoke:

'Uncle, I want your blessings. One needs good luck more than intelligence right now.'

The lawyer laughed.

'God always keeps aside some good luck for intelligent people, Mini. I shall call you in the afternoon.'

'All right, Uncle.'

'God bless you, my dear girl.'

After Mini hung up, Adiyodi asked: 'So, Vakil sir's plan wasn't successful, right?'

'Right.'

'Let me study the agenda and the agreement and get back to you within an hour.'

'Uncle, I want your blessings.'

Adiyodi lost his composure. His eyes welled up unexpectedly. He kept the file down and reached out to bless Mini with both his hands. Closing his eyes, Adiyodi said: 'Lord Dhanwantari, Menon sir and all the ancestors shall bless you, my girl.'

Suddenly, the old man started weeping. He sat down heavily on the chair.

'What happened, Uncle?'

Adiyodi's words emerged through his sobs. 'Mini, I'm not a fool. I realize that I'm of no use to you during this crisis. You're tolerating me, that's all. If only there was some capable young person in my place!'

Mini got up and walked to Adiyodi. She gently placed a consoling hand on his heaving shoulder.

'Uncle, I look at you as a father figure. You should be a pillar of strength now. Don't get upset.'

Adiyodi raised his head.

'Mini, I know everything. You don't show the turmoil that you're facing.'

'Uncle, when I'm running a company, I should be ready to handle the challenges too. I don't intend to excuse myself claiming that I'm a woman! Please go and wash your face.'

Adiyodi walked gingerly to the washroom. Mini observed him keenly. The telephone rang. It was her personal assistant.

'Yes, Prakashan.'

'There was a call from the police control room. Some accident. Asokan sir's car. Near Panampally Nagar.'

'Where's Asokan chettan?'

'He's not in office. They called us after checking the visiting card found inside the car.'

'What happened?'

'The driver of the vehicle was unconscious. They have moved him to the hospital.'

Suddenly, Mini recollected.

Eleven o'clock. Mohandas's words in the tape: 'I shall call you tomorrow at eleven.'

God! Did Asokan rush home to confront Aswathy?

Mini instructed her assistant: 'Send a few people from administration to the hospital immediately. Call up the hospital now.'

Mini knocked at the bathroom door.

'What's the matter?'

'Asokan chettan had an accident.'

Adiyodi opened the door.

'Who told you?'

Mini did not tell him about her intuition.

53

Wrong Timing

When the coffee was poured, its rich aroma wafted in the surroundings.

Pothuval looked at the old man, who was dressed in a white uniform and standing obsequiously by the side.

'Swami, this is from your hotel, isn't it?'

'Yes.'

'I can tell from the fragrance.'

Mohandas remarked: 'I think only Swami makes the traditional decoction coffee in Ernakulam these days. Instant coffee has routed the original from the city. Swami is pulling on, somehow.'

Pothuval did not like instant coffee. Mohandas's personal staff knew about this. Whenever Pothuval stepped inside Mohandas's office, someone would run to Swami's old coffee shop.

Mohandas said: 'In today's world, no business enterprise can survive based only on the strength of legacy or a product of superior quality, and Swami is a perfect example of that.'

Ramesan was seated on a side table, calling various brokers. He was handling three corded phones simultaneously. He would cover the receivers of two and mutter into a third. Sometimes he changed the pattern.

Ramesan became alert upon hearing about Swami.

Mohandas continued: 'Pothuval sir, you might remember that my first set-up was opposite Swami's hotel. That small room, eight by nine feet. His hotel was the same size even then.'

'No difference in the taste of his coffee either.'

'It has been ages since I visited his hotel.'

'I went there recently. The same old tables and chairs. The glasses and tumblers are of steel now.'

Mohandas became thoughtful and tried to light his pipe.

'Two years ago, Swami came to me panic-stricken. There was a labour strike at his hotel. He had never expected such a turn of events. Swami considered the workers as part of his family. He sat here and wept. Of course, he could not afford to shut the hotel. Swami did not know any other profession. He asked me for guidance.'

Mohandas paused.

'Well, I told him, "Swami, pay off all the legal dues and send them off. You and your family should run the establishment. You can get good casual workers from Pollachi in Tamil Nadu." I helped him to settle matters financially.'

Pothuval looked at Ramesan meaningfully and smiled.

'That was your first strike, wasn't it, Ramesan?'

Ramesan grinned. 'Yes.'

Ramesan remembered the incident quite well. There were many Marxist and Leninist groups in the party. Everyone was in search of their unique identity. Only one group could create a bright future for India by liberating India's poor brethren. Every faction believed that they were the true representatives of Marxism. At that time, Ramesan's group had only fifteen-odd members. A strike was imperative to prove themselves.

Swami's hotel used to provide the cheapest food those days. Ramesan and his comrades would often go there for lunch. Naturally, they befriended the labourers. The young Communists believed that it was their historical responsibility to free the exploited and empower the proletariat in Swami's hotel. They told the workers that Swami was a bourgeois, exploitative capitalist. Someone who relished the fruits of their labour without doing any work himself. Their youthful eyes were blinded by the letters printed in those fat handbooks and could not see the truth that Swami too was a poor labourer. They carried out a successful class struggle in Swami's hotel. Swami stopped selling lunch. He paid his staff whatever he could and bid them goodbye. Since then, Swami and family were running a coffee shop with the help of two chaps from Pollachi.

Swami removed the coffee cups.

When the old man left the room, the door closed automatically. Ramesan put down two receivers and whispered something into the third. Mohandas lit his pipe.

'I used to have lunch at Swami's sometimes. Personalized service. The ultimate goal of five-star hotels and top restaurants is the same. But somewhere, something went wrong.'

Pothuval laughed.

'Companies and political parties, all aim their activities at the common man.'

'You're right.'

Ramesan put down the third phone.

'I just don't get it.'

'What?'

'I told the brokers that we should get share certificates in a week's time. Even a price of thirty-two was okay.'

'And then?'

'The news reports and Bombay trading have churned up things badly.'

'Hmm?'

'The official trading begins at twelve-thirty. Now it's nearly eleven. Curb trading is going on in full swing. The price of Dhanwantari's shares is rising every minute. I just don't understand.'

'What's the problem?'

'Zacharia is Dhanwantari's official share broker, isn't he?'

Mohandas looked at Pothuval.

'I spoke to Mini Balachandran yesterday. I also had dinner with Zacharia. We had a frank discussion. I made it clear that I was interested in Dhanwantari.'

He turned to Ramesan.

'What's Zacharia up to?'

'Vinayan is his assistant. He has sold three lots of Dhanwantari's shares in the last half an hour.'

'That means…?'

'I don't understand what's happening. If they are selling shares, they will definitely hand over the share certificates too, won't they?'

Mohandas closed his eyes and leaned back into his chair.

Ten seconds.

A beep sounded from Mohandas's briefcase tucked under the table.

Beep, beep…

Mohandas opened his eyes and looked at the briefcase. What did it mean? He could not figure it out.

It was an electronic gadget gifted by a Japanese acquaintance. Very handy. One could programme the time and event. The machine would beep when one had set the alarm for an event. If you pressed a button, the details of what was programmed would appear.

Mohandas retrieved the gadget and pressed the button. Nothing flashed on the screen. The telephone rang.

Mohandas was ruminating. He had some work at eleven today. What was it? Unfortunately, he had not keyed in the details.

Ramesan covered the mouthpiece and spoke: 'Utter confusion at the Exchange. There's a seller with one lakh shares. Price between thirty-two and thirty-five. Should we buy?'

'Who is the party? Find out.'

Mohandas calculated in his mind.

Thirty-four lakh rupees. One lakh shares. The total number of Dhanwantari shares was nearly twenty lakhs. This lot was almost five per cent. If the management started selling, he should buy two lakhs from them too. An investment of sixty-eight, seventy lakhs. The total would be slightly above a crore. Fifteen per cent shares. Why delay any more?

Ramesan said: 'These shares were bought yesterday by someone called Matthews on behalf of Aniyan Raja.'

'Delivery? When do we get the share certificates?'

Ramesan called the brokers again.

'No idea. Our brokers are guessing that this is not speculation. These were shares purchased for taking over the company. They are likely to have share certificates.'

Mohandas's pipe was snuffed out. He lit a matchstick. Gazing at Pothuval, he asked: 'Shall I take a risk? Okay, the prices shall go up steeply if we dilly-dally. Let's buy the one lakh shares. Delivery in a week. Or by settlement date.'

Ramesan conveyed his uncle's instructions to the brokers.

'Sir, what do you say?' Mohandas asked Pothuval.

Pothuval smiled in reply. 'Is there such risk in this game? The share prices are rising every hour. Even without share certificates, it is good speculation. What do you call such a market?'

'Bullish market.'

They laughed together.

Mohandas said: 'But I'm not planning to resell.'

'I know, you're interested in taking over Dhanwantari.'

'Not only take over but run it efficiently too.'

Ramesan finished the telephone business and seated himself next to Pothuval.

'Are you tired?'

'Yes.'

Mohandas was observing Ramesan.

'Do you want to say something to me?'

In fact, Ramesan had much to say. But he preferred to be silent.

What was the need for all this? All the frenzy? Tension? Was it necessary to vanquish more kingdoms? There was so much property already. Eight or nine successful business ventures. Money, fame, good health. What was lacking now?

And still…

Ramesan got up and pulled back the curtains of the west-facing window. He observed the waves of the lagoon inundating the bank ceaselessly. The phone rang again. It was Mohandas's personal phone. He gestured to Ramesan. Ramesan took the call. After a while, he said: 'Just a moment.'

'A call from the police control room. An accident. A car. The man had this particular number in his pocket.'

'Which man? Any idea?'

'A white Maruti. They think it might be someone from Dhanwantari Herbal Products.'

Suddenly, Mohandas remembered that he was supposed to call Aswathy at eleven. That was why the gadget was beeping, since he had programmed it to raise an alarm at that hour.

He checked his watch. Half past eleven.

Mohandas tut-tutted internally. *My memory's started failing! Or is it because I blindly trust electronic gadgets?*

Without batting an eyelid, he responded to Ramesan: 'Which hospital? Find out the details of the person. What if it's a friend?'

54

An Apparition of the Adversary

After leaving Mini's office, Zacharia went straight home. He wished to thoroughly examine the analytical reports of the top ten north Indian Ayurvedic companies that Suryanarayanan had sent him. It was Zacharia's instinctive guess that Sharmaji's company, based in Lucknow, was behind this takeover bid.

Menon and Sharmaji had been good friends. As in business and life, friends turned foes. If Menon's company, Dhanwantari Herbal Products, with its exemplary vision and goals, was restrained to the boundaries of Kerala, Sharmaji might have been its staunchest ally. Maybe he did not like it when Menon stepped into the north Indian region. An irritating word, some exasperating behaviour … something must have happened between them. Sharmaji might have felt mortified. Between close friends, enmity was as fierce as friendship. Menon was no more. Dhanwantari, however, remained the visible adversary. It should be conquered and brought to its knees. One could not blame Sharmaji for thinking in that way.

It was based on these psychological arguments that Zacharia had zoomed in on Sharmaji's company.

Zacharia had given his advice to Mini Balachandran. Yet, he wanted to verify the facts again. What was Sharmaji's motive behind the takeover attempt? Why would a good businessman venture into such a loss-making endeavour? Was it out of sheer mule-headedness? Would someone like Sharmaji, who had a long legacy of running an Ayurvedic business, think of taking such a step?

Zacharia started looking into Sharmaji's company.

Registered office in Lucknow, administrative office in Delhi. The computer printout showed the data analysis of the last three years.

As per Companies Act, every public limited company had to get their annual accounts audited by a chartered accountant. The audit report had to be submitted to the Registrar of Companies. A detailed overview of their financial performance, including income statements, balance sheets, cashflow statements, as well as a report putting together its future strategies and vision had to be presented at the annual general body meeting.

Mostly, companies prepared the reports seamlessly, glossing over the actual state of affairs. It was often next to impossible for the common man to separate the grain from the chaff. Even the auditor's report was skilfully made, taking advantage of legal loopholes. But some brilliant share brokers had their own way of analysing the real financial standing of a company. Only such brokers could give genuine advice to an investor about the shares of a company.

Zacharia dug deeper into the details of Sharmaji's Ayurvedic company. He picked up the calculator.

He calculated the dividend yield, that is, the financial ratio denoting the amount the company pays in dividends every year relative to its stock price. Next, he worked out the price to earnings ratio, which compared a company's market price to its earnings per share. Zacharia verified the company's dividend per share, which was the ratio of dividends to the number of shares. He crosschecked the return on capital employed, to determine how well the company was generating profits from the money invested.

Sharmaji's company turned out to be a fundamentally solid organization.

Zacharia wished to understand the company's assets and short-term liabilities. If the company's assets could be liquidated fast and its liabilities were not significant, it was a dangerous situation for Mini. If Sharmaji's company had sufficient money after paying off its dividends, they would be ready to attack.

Zacharia did his arithmetic. His calculator worked incessantly. He examined the changes in the share prices of Sharmaji's company over the last few years. They had once gone in for a rights issue: where the company invited its shareholders to buy more shares at a discount. That too showcased the financial strength of the company.

Soon, Zacharia arrived at two conclusions:

Sharmaji needed more production units urgently. But they did not have the financial wherewithal to build these or even buy them. The easiest way for them was to do some short-term borrowings and acquire a few well-run production units.

Second, Sharmaji's company did not have assets that could be liquidated fast. They had to seek a loan, after paying heavy interests. Since the company's progress was steady, it would not be difficult to borrow funds from the market on the basis of their shares.

Zacharia breathed a sigh of relief. Yes, it was indeed Sharmaji's company that was trying to take over Dhanwantari Herbals. His advice to Mini to handle the crisis had been appropriate.

Two lakh shares at eighty rupees. Spot offer. Let Sharmaji come with the money. Else, he would retreat. If Sharmaji picked up the gauntlet, Mini would make one and a half crore rupees as profit.

She could try to pass a resolution with the board of directors to implement the agreement between the company and the Trust to take back the estates. That would drive Sharmaji into a corner. Dhanwantari Herbals, without its assets, had very low credibility. He would be forced to sell his shares. Using the same money Sharmaji had borrowed from the money market at exorbitant interest rates, Mini Balachandran could potentially buy back her company shares at half their original price.

Zacharia continued to examine his strategy methodically. There was nothing better that the Dhanwantari management could try in the present circumstances.

~

It was half past eleven when he reached the Stock Exchange. As soon as he entered his cubicle, Zacharia asked: 'Any call from the Dhanwantari office?'

The young female clerk responded: 'No, sir.'

The uproar was audible on the second floor, in the members' cubicles and in the corridors. The newspapers had managed to give the hornet's nest a proper stir.

Four syllables were playing on every tongue.

Dhanwantari.

Dhanwantari.

Vinayan had been waiting for Zacharia. He made his way through the crowd and reached the cubicle.

'Matthews is selling all his shares in curb trading. Even then the price is not going down. I presume that the Bombay players have instructed the line operators to buy at any price.'

Zacharia calmly took out his paan from his bag. The ceiling fan overhead was scattering hot air everywhere.

'Vinayan, get in touch with our trusted friends in Bombay. Find the jobbers dealing with Sharmaji's Ayurvedic company listed at the Bombay Stock Exchange.'

'Sure, sir. I suspect it is Savitry's Bombay connection who's handling it in Bombay. But we'll have that verified once again.'

Jobbers were specialized brokers who dealt with specific company shares. A company might have multiple jobbers too. Typically, investors and brokers got in touch with them directly. The jobbers could procure share certificates easily. However, in stock exchanges like Cochin, they were yet to make their presence felt.

Zacharia spoke again.

'Do check whether Sharmaji's company shares have been fluctuating over the past seven days. Verify it from *The Business Times*. While you're at it, get some young fellows to check the share-price pattern of all these top ten Ayurvedic companies.'

A young man came smiling into Zacharia's cabin. A bearded man accompanied him. He wore a bright coloured T-shirt and jeans. A camera was hanging around his neck. Zacharia recognized them. They were the journalists who had interviewed him yesterday.

'Saw the report, didn't you? Hope you are happy with it.'

'Yes.'

'We need a photo of yours. You, in the midst of the boisterous crowd.'

'Are you sure?'

'Oh, yes.'

Zacharia headed towards the swarming mass. Nobody cast a look at Zacharia or the two journalists.

Zacharia posed in front of Avarachan's cubicle. The camera caught Zacharia, the board on his left and Avarachan's impassive face behind it.

The inscription on the board read 'Ready Cash'.

The camera clicked.

Zacharia introduced Avarachan to the young men.

'Financiers like Avarachan are the nerve centres of our Stock Exchange. They are also brokers. Members of the Stock Exchange.

But they don't buy or sell any shares. If someone wishes to buy or sell, they will help. In fact, they lend money after charging interest.'

Avarachan laughed. 'We're getting old. Not impulsive like these callow youth.'

The young journalist followed Zacharia back to his cubicle.

Zacharia remarked:

'Once, there was a big crisis. Unbelievable speculative trading. The brokers ended up in a situation where they owed crores to one another. Even the Exchange authorities were aghast. Then our dear friend Avarachan made an offer to them. Two hundred crores. Can you believe it? Two hundred crores! He was willing to finance that amount. Let the trading continue. Remember, he did not ask for any security. Avarachan asked the Stock Exchange to convert all the membership cards of those who were losers in the game to the names of his own nominees. Until the debt was repaid, the trading should happen as per his dictates.'

'And then?'

'Even the Stock Exchange authorities are scared of Avarachan. They agreed to his terms. Do you know why I chose that spot for the photograph? It was to highlight the signboard: Ready Cash. The one with ready money is the king here. Even a stalwart in the game of speculation will bow his head before such a king.'

The young journalist grinned and then, lowering his voice, said: 'Sir, may I ask something? Is the price of Dhanwantari likely to rise again?'

'Likely.'

'How far can it go?'

'Can't predict that. Might touch fifty by today evening. It's trading at thirty-two in the curb even now.'

The man almost whispered: 'Sir, I want to buy a thousand shares. I will sell them tomorrow. Even if there is a rise of fifteen rupees, I shall make a decent profit of fifteen thousand, wouldn't I?'

Zacharia shot him a sharp look.

'How much money do you have right now?'

'Nothing at present. I will arrange for it.'

Zacharia explained: 'A share that was priced at fourteen rupees yesterday is now trading at thirty-two. Tomorrow is a Saturday. Now the Exchange will open only on Monday. It might reach fifty then. But there is an equal chance of the prices plummeting and hitting ten rupees. If you spend around thirty thousand today for a thousand shares, you might get fifty thousand on Monday. But you also undertake the risk of the shares going down to ten thousand in worth. What do you want to do?'

The young man's face fell.

Zacharia reflected that even without any money, the mere possibility of profits or losses could rattle anyone's equanimity.

'Brother, gamble carefully. There's nothing wrong in playing a game of dice. But be ready to face the consequences. You can give me the margin money of twenty thousand right now. I shall arrange to buy a thousand shares of Dhanwantari. I guess the maximum loss would be twenty thousand rupees.'

The journalist looked visibly uncomfortable.

The phone rang then. It was Mini.

'Uncle.'

'Yes?'

'Two things. I shall tell you the bad news first. Asokan chettan's car was in an accident. He is in hospital.'

'Where? When?'

Mini mentioned the hospital's name.

'Is he serious?'

'I don't know. A few people from the office have gone to meet him.'

Zacharia was silent.

'Uncle, the second thing. We should proceed as you said. With one small modification.'

'Go ahead.'

'We shall make two tender offers.'

Zacharia listened intently to what Mini was proposing. Tender offers referred to a situation when shareholders were about to sell their shares in a company at a specific price, within a limited time frame.

'Offer two lakh Dhanwantari shares to the north Indian player. First condition: Eighty rupees. No negotiations allowed. Second, we shall also give them the share certificates and signed transfer forms. These would be ready in two hours' time. Third, the money should be transferred to our bank account before that happens. Fourth, the tender offer shall stand only till two in the afternoon. Nothing after that.'

'Okay, Mini, let us battle it out.'

'Uncle, have you identified the adversary?'

'I can state that precisely after thirty minutes.'

'All right.'

There was a tinge of laughter in Mini's voice.

'Something else, Uncle.'

'What?'

'With the same conditions, offer fifty thousand shares to Mr Mohandas. The deadline remains two in the afternoon.'

A few moments of silence.

'Mini, are you serious?'

'Why, Uncle? I have never been more serious in my life.'

'Can I ask why?'

Mini answered after a pause.

'In business, we fight with intelligence. The gender is irrelevant.'

Zacharia replied: 'Okay, boss!'

Mini spoke firmly: 'Thank you, Uncle. I want to show him my mettle. I don't need anybody's pity or special consideration because I'm a woman.'

55

The Computer's Sneaky Game

Twelve o'clock.

The trading started at the Bombay Stock Exchange.

In Delhi.

In Calcutta.

In Ahmedabad.

In Madras.

In a matter of ten minutes, the figures would start dancing on the display screen affixed high on the wall. The changes in the important share prices of the five top stock exchanges would show up on the screen. A prominent television news company had created the system, which was centred in Bangalore. It would telecast the share prices of the exchanges against regular payments. The Investors Club and other informal organizations used the information too.

The Cochin Stock Exchange started working at 12.30 p.m. By a quarter past twelve, the brokers would be noting down the share prices of the other stock exchanges and preparing their strategies.

But Zacharia was oblivious to all this. He chewed some paan again.

When he returned to his cubicle, Savitry was seated there.

Savitry had been eagerly watching the price fluctuations of Dhanwantari. She remembered Vikas's instructions. When the Dhanwantari shares reached thirty-five rupees in curb trading, approach the company's share broker and make an offer.

The price was oscillating between thirty-two and thirty-three for some time. The selling and buying were going at full throttle. Thousands of offers. Savitry became apprehensive of a cartel at play, trying to forcibly raise the share prices. Sellers of ten thousand and fifty thousand shares came into the pitch. The price was thirty-one. In seconds, the shares were sold. More buyers came into the field. The share prices went up again.

The price had gone slightly down when Matthews tried to sell his shares. When Mohandas's brokers bought them, the price went up. The speculators also jumped into the fray.

When the price hit thirty-four, Savitry decided to make her move. No need to delay any more.

Everyone knew that Zacharia was Dhanwantari's share broker. Very intelligent. Among the rare brokers who did not speculate. Honest and popular.

Be careful, Savitry warned herself.

Zacharia queried: 'What do you want? You are Savitry, right?'

'Yes.'

Savitry stared at Zacharia's paan-stained teeth.

'I have an offer for you.'

Zacharia's smile vanished.

'Speak.'

'My client is willing to buy one lakh Dhanwantari shares. Spot delivery. Immediate exchange of share certificates. Or arrange power of attorney papers. The cash shall be delivered directly. Now the curb price is thirty-four. My client is offering forty.'

Zacharia gazed unblinkingly at Savitry.

'Who is your client…?'

'You don't need to know that, do you?'

Both kept quiet for a few moments. The pandemonium around them increased by the second. The figures appeared on the computer screen. A mob thronged the area close to the display screen. An aged man was pushed brutally by the crowd. His hand pressed frantically on Zacharia's cubicle wall. He emitted a helpless shriek. Nobody cared a whit. But a few seconds later, the man was back amid the rabble.

Vinayan stood at the cubicle door. He saw Savitry, who was facing away from him.

Vinayan looked at Zacharia and then spoke with his eyes: *Yes, this is the person I was telling you about.*

Vinayan gestured that he would come back later and disappeared.

Zacharia asked: 'One lakh shares might not be sufficient for your client.'

He knew that Savitry was merely carrying out orders. There was no use negotiating prices with her.

Zacharia explained:

'Here's an offer for your client from Dhanwantari's side. The first and last offer, mind you! You are not going to get many shares from the market. The marketable lots of these shares are few and far in between. We should fix the deal before two in the afternoon, though.'

'What's the offer? It's eleven now. We have three hours.'

'Two lakh shares. We shall exchange the share certificates in exactly three hours.'

Savitry sat up straight.

'Two lakh?'

'Yes.'

'Price?'

'Eighty rupees.'

Zacharia hid a grin and looked at Savitry's startled face.

'Are you mad!'

'Yes, we are all mad, aren't we?' Zacharia said soberly. 'Take a look at that crowd over there.' He pointed at the aggressive men and women near the computer screen. It was like the crowd during some special puja at a temple. Eagerly awaiting the auspicious sight of the deity.

Savitry asked again, incredulously: 'Eighty rupees?'

'Yes.'

'You can use my phone. Ask Bombay about their decision. There's very little time left.'

Savitry was slowly coming to terms with what she had heard.

Two lakh shares. Eighty rupees. Three hours' time.

Zacharia spoke: 'The offer ends at 2 p.m.'

'What happens then?'

'Nothing. Like you said, we're all crazy.'

Savitry got up as if in a dream. All of a sudden, she felt scared. A fear that she was all alone in the world took hold of her. Feral animals were growling all around her, waiting to pounce on her at any moment. Savitry yearned to hear Vikas's voice. More than informing him about Zacharia's offer, she wanted her sweetheart's reassuring words. If only she could be certain that he was by her side, would she be able to fight off all the wild beasts.

Zacharia gazed after her. The number of people thronging the space in front of the computer screen was growing by leaps and bounds.

Zacharia dialled Mohandas's personal number. Ramesan took the call.

'Our Asokan met with an accident.'

'Yes. Not serious, I heard.'

Zacharia smiled to himself. How quickly a revolutionary's compassion and humanity became clouded by business and luxuries! When a colleague met with an accident, it did not trouble the others so long as the main business was not compromised. Why waste time bothering about him?

Ramesan handed over the phone to his uncle, Mohandas.

Zacharia spoke:

'Sir, Dhanwantari shares are still bullish. I have no idea how many share certificates you'll get. It's total speculation.'

Mohandas responded: 'I'm trying. But I doubt if even five per cent of the shares will end up in my hands.'

Zacharia waited for a while. Then he said: 'Mini is willing to sell fifty thousand shares. Two and a half per cent of the total shares.'

'Mini?'

'Yes.'

'But why?'

'I don't know.'

Mohandas went silent. A few seconds later, he said: 'At what price?'

'Eighty rupees.'

'Is she mad?'

Zacharia laughed. He did not say out loud that the tender offer was the lone truth being played out that day. The solitary truth, when wily games and speculation were afoot. Evidently, it appeared as lunacy.

Zacharia explained:

'Two conditions, sir. This is an exclusive offer for you. The money, white money, should reach the bank before two in the afternoon. Spot ready. Share certificates and documents shall be arranged.'

'What happens after two?'

'There is no offer.'

Mohandas asked: 'What's the ruckus in the background?'

Zacharia looked around. The crowd before the display screen was screaming. The name resounded even amidst that messy din.

Dhanwantari.

Dhanwantari.

Zacharia replied: 'Official trading hasn't begun. What you hear is the racket of curb trading.'

'This is your idea, isn't it?' Mohandas enquired.

'No, it's Mini's idea.'

'Is it final?'

'Yes, the offer stands till two.'

'I shall call you back.'

Mohandas cut the call.

~

When Savitry went to her cubicle to urgently call Vikas, Shankaran Kutty was seated in a chair. He seemed to be meditating. Savitry felt a surge of irritation. She enjoyed an infatuated young man chasing after her. It was good fun teasing and provoking him. Make jokes, flirt harmlessly, pretend not to understand his desperate hints of love for her. But this obsession of Shankaran Kutty's was becoming annoying. She could not breathe freely without him making an appearance!

Savitry patted him awake.

'Mister Shankaran Kutty, are you sleeping?'

Shankaran Kutty woke up with a start.

Savitry!

He rubbed his eyes and slowly came back to his senses. Where was he? The second floor of the Stock Exchange. In Savitry's cubicle. Her fingers had touched him just now.

Shankaran Kutty spoke:

'Couldn't sleep properly last night. I was anxious. And all those mosquitoes!'

Savitry laughed. 'Eat some paan. That will drive away your lethargy.'

'Paan?'

'Meetha paan. There's a small shop near M.G. Road, which sells sweet paan. Yummy, delectable Banarasi paan. Eat one, and you'll be full of pep and energy!'

'Really?'

'Really.'

Shankaran Kutty smiled.

'I have never eaten one. But…' Looking yearningly at Savitry, he uttered words brimming with love. 'Savitry, do you need one?'

Savitry smiled at him. The dimples appeared unexpectedly. Shankaran Kutty became acutely discomfited. He was gazing at the lovely face of Draupadi, intoxicated by the enchanting saugandhika flower.

He said: 'Just wait. What did you say it's called?'

'Meetha tambaku.'

'What?'

'It's without tobacco.'

'Is that so?'

Shankaran Kutty got up. After reaching the door, he looked back.

'I'm going to play a game today. Wait and watch. I shall tell you the result afterwards.'

Savitry smiled at him.

She called Vikas. He had been waiting for Savitry's call.

Savitry repeated Zacharia's offer verbatim. Vikas listened intently.

'Is that all?'

'Yes.'

Vikas asked: 'Savitry, what do you think? Do they expect us to buy the shares at such a high price?'

'I don't know, Vikas.'

'No worries. I shall get back after an hour. Wait for my call.'

'Yes.'

Shankaran Kutty came racing by the time she put down the receiver.

'Savitry, did you hear that?'

'What?'

'Dhanwantari shares have reached one hundred and fifteen rupees!'

'What!'

'I made fifteen lakhs in the last one hour.'

'What on earth happened?'

'The computer screen showed it's one hundred and ten at the Delhi Stock Exchange! Some filthy rich fellows are out to acquire Dhanwantari for sure!'

'Hundred and ten?'

'Here, it's reached a hundred and fifteen already! The price will go up further. Not just of Dhanwantari, of others too. I'm heading back now. Just came to update you.'

Savitry got up hurriedly.

Both forgot about the Banarasi paan.

~

Vinayan sat fidgeting inside Zacharia's cubicle, waiting for him to say something.

Zacharia had entered a cocoon of silence ever since Vinayan informed him that Dhanwantari's shares had reached a hundred and ten rupees at the Delhi Stock Exchange. There was no earthly reason for such an occurrence! Dhanwantari prices were twenty-four when it started trading in Delhi in the morning. It was unheard of! The CEO and his team trying to take over Dhanwantari was based in Delhi. Even then, there was no logical explanation for such a phenomenon.

Zacharia looked at Vinayan and tried hard to smile. The phone rang. It was Mohandas.

'Mr Zacharia.'

'Yes, sir.'

'I agree to your conditions. Fifty thousand shares at eighty rupees each. In an hour and a half.'

When the call was disconnected, Zacharia exploded: 'Bloody bastard!'

'Who was that?'

'Mohandas, who else? He knew about the surge in Delhi. Now, he's going to make a clean twenty lakh profit without any sweat! Sell the shares bought at eighty for one hundred and twenty. Forty rupees difference. Fifty thousand shares.'

Vinayan was furious. 'But that is grossly unfair!'

'What? That he agreed to our terms? Is it his fault that the share prices hit the skies?'

'Was it intentionally done?' Vinayan asked sharply. Zacharia just looked at him intently.

'Vinayan, call up these numbers in Delhi and Bangalore.'

There was a jangling of bells that went on for a long time. The hullabaloo outside died down quickly.

Half past twelve.

The trading was starting.

56

The Authorities Intervene

The chamber of the president of the Stock Exchange was beyond the vast trading ring on the third floor. The trading ring was replete with heat, sweat, liveliness and noise. In sharp contrast, the air-conditioned chamber of the president was cool and silent. The fragrance of dawn-fresh pink roses filled the room. The noises outside never reached the chamber. The sounds made in the room ricocheted against its walls. Gains and losses worth crores of rupees pivoted on the decisions made inside this chamber. Cryptic secrets were discussed herein.

The informal meeting of the council began after half past twelve. They could not decide on anything until one-thirty.

The councils across exchanges followed their own by-laws. Typically, the president and treasurer were the main members. A few people elected by the members of the Stock Exchange and two or three government representatives made up the council. The government nominees were from the finance department, the registrar's office, and so on. Formal meetings happened once in two months.

There was a clamour to include more public representatives in a council which took such critical decisions involving the common man's money. Invariably, public representatives meant politicians. Businessmen were afraid of politicians. They did not feel respect or affection for them. Unsurprisingly, stock exchanges tried to avoid bringing on board politicians as members of their councils. Since it was an emergency meeting, the government nominees were absent.

The scent of rich filter coffee and foreign cigarettes hung around the room.

When the discussions began, the focus was on the principles.

The share price of Dhanwantari Herbal Products had become double in a day's time. It was not an unusual phenomenon. On the day of the government's budget announcement, or the day when its economic policy was revealed, such things happened. But the shares of Dhanwantari Herbals had been steady over the last three years. Never before had such a humongous trading happened with its shares. There had been no change in the company's management or in its activities recently. The other exchanges were also involved. Someone was obviously trying to take over the company.

The Stock Exchange allowed anyone and everyone to buy and sell the shares of any company through registered brokers. Even so, it had an ethical responsibility. The trading should not have a deleterious effect on the nation or the company involved. That was the core of the conversation.

The consequence of such aggressive takeover bids was an irrational hiking of share prices. Speculative trade increased. People sold without any shares at hand. People bought shares without a rupee at hand.

As per the Stock Exchange rules, for any such sale to happen share certificates had to be exchanged. If not immediately, then at least by the settlement day the formalities ought to have been completed. Usually, some brokers were 'Short' or 'Long'. Short meant that the broker had sold shares without having a sufficient number at hand; long was the direct opposite – he did not have money to buy, but the share certificates were ready. In either case, the agreed amount had to be settled. Usually, the share brokers shifted the payment date by another week. Or they sought the help of financiers. If the non-payment continued for several Fridays at a stretch, the Stock Exchange authorities intervened.

If the buyer did not have money and the seller had share certificates, the authorities auctioned those promptly. If the amount garnered was not sufficient, the remaining amount was added to the defaulter's liabilities. If he was unable to pay even after some time, he was suspended from the Exchange. The next step was the auctioning of his membership card to make up for the loss. Speculative trade following any takeover bid thus affected many share brokers.

There were numerous steps to rein in speculation. Stop the trading of the specific company's shares for a few days, issue an order that only spot deliveries were acceptable, put a condition that forty or fifty per cent of the total amount involved in the sale of shares should be paid up at the Exchange as margin money.

The council discussed the matter thoroughly. A consensus was reached: they would make a decision at two in the afternoon after watching how the share market worked that day. It was then that someone's eyes fell on the computer printout containing the share prices at the various exchanges. The council was privy to such information. The brokers had to satisfy themselves with the updates flashed on the display screens.

'Look, in Delhi, Dhanwantari is trading at one hundred and ten rupees!'

Everybody looked at the document. They were hardy, experienced share brokers. Someone smelled a rat.

'There's something wrong.'

The council called Bangalore.

The broadcasting company that handled the telecast of stock prices examined the data yet again. No, there was no mistake. It was based on the information received from the Delhi Stock Exchange.

The council dialled the Delhi Stock Exchange. 'Give us ten minutes,' they said. 'We will call you back.'

It was half past one. The members looked worriedly at one another. The chaos outside the room continued. Someone stepped out to the trading ring and returned.

Dhanwantari shares. One hundred and twenty rupees.

The share prices of other companies were going up too.

The members crowded around the latest computer printout.

At the Bombay Stock Exchange, the price of Dhanwantari shares was twenty-six rupees. In Calcutta, it was twenty-five. The Delhi Stock Exchange called.

'Dhanwantari share price is twenty-six rupees and fifty paisa here. A hundred and ten, did you say? Nobody knows about such a figure!'

'What about the printout then?'

'We are clueless.'

The council called Bangalore again. After fifteen minutes, the broadcast company had a response.

'Sorry, a clerical mistake.'

The price of Dhanwantari's shares was twenty-six and a half rupees in Delhi.

When the updated share price flashed on the display screens, a huge uproar began in the trading ring. The prices of Dhanwantari plunged immediately. In ten minutes, it reached thirty-five rupees.

But the computer had already taken account of all the sales of Dhanwantari's shares till then.

Loud screams and high-pitched laughter resounded in the air.

~

Zacharia was on pins and needles.

Mohandas's call came right before 1 p.m.

As expected, he announced: 'I've prepared a certified cheque for forty lakhs. When do we meet?'

Zacharia did not inform Mini Balachandran. When the computer showed one hundred and ten, Zacharia was dead sure that Mohandas would grab the opportunity. He would buy at eighty and sell at a hundred and ten or twenty. Fifty thousand shares. A clean profit of fifteen or twenty lakhs. He would not be able to acquire the company with fifty thousand shares. Why did Mini make such an offer to this man?

Zacharia imagined a smirk on Mohandas's face. Savitry came to meet him then.

She handed over a piece of paper. It was a fax message from Bombay.

'Our client is ready to buy two lakh shares at eighty rupees as per your offer. Please fax a reply. Our client is pleased to convey that the amount of one crore and sixty lakhs shall be transferred immediately. Kindly arrange to hand over the share certificates and enable our representatives to meet the company management in order to discuss future plans.'

The fax was from a famous legal firm in Bombay.

'Call them,' Zacharia told Savitri. 'Inform them that everything is okay. I shall send a fax shortly.'

Next, he called up Mini Balachandran.

'Mini, I'm sorry.'

'What's the matter, Uncle?'

'Both our tender offers were accepted. We have to transfer two lakh shares today. I'm truly sorry, Mini.'

'Uncle, we were expecting this, weren't we?'

'Yes, but I had given it only a low probability. At such a high price? Anyway ... shall I fax the reply? They need the share certificates today.'

Mini Balachandran replied calmly: 'Uncle, we are in a pretty comfortable position. We still have fifty thousand shares in our hands. That's apart from the shares belonging to the Trust. Two crores ready cash. The agreement between the Trust and the company adds to our strength. Please fax our reply.'

Zacharia was silent.

'Mini, I'm actually worried. There are undercurrents that we are unable to gauge. I am nervous about the Bombay party insisting on meeting you today itself.'

'In any case, send the reply. Come over if you have some time.'

'I shall reach your office by three.'

Zacharia sent the fax to Bombay. When they acknowledged receipt, he stepped out.

His head was reeling. Such chaos! Zacharia felt lost. He had no clue about what was going on. Mohandas, the unseen Sharmaji, Savitry, Matthews, Mini ... suddenly, everything was bewildering.

It was half past one.

Zacharia never drank during the day. But today was an exception. He yearned for a drink.

The bar was dark and cold. Abraham Joseph was seated in his usual corner. He gestured to Zacharia, inviting him to join him. Abraham Joseph was a rich man with rubber plantations and farmlands in Thiruvalla. He was a post-graduate, and a member of the Exchange from its early days. He had played in the share market and got burned badly. Liability worth fourteen lakhs. The authorities banned him from trading and Abraham Joseph went to court. Legal notices were exchanged. He would pay a pittance to the Exchange from time to time. Everyone knew Abraham Joseph and considered him a good man. He visited the Stock Exchange regularly. When trading began, the man would retreat to the bar.

'The authorities took a good decision today,' Abraham Joseph remarked. Zacharia refrained from probing further.

Abraham Joseph continued: 'I expected a few to have heart attacks!'

'Who?'

'The speculators, of course!'

Zacharia ordered a large and some soda.

'Well,' said Abraham Joseph, 'given a choice, I would have asked them to cancel all the transactions conducted today. Taking exceptional action only on Dhanwantari does not sound good. What do you say?'

'What action?'

'Didn't you hear? Someone manipulated the computer. A huge figure was displayed. Everybody speculated. Now the Stock Exchange authorities have issued an order. No trading done today shall be accepted.'

Zacharia gaped at Abraham Joseph. 'Is that true?'

'As true as the whisky in this glass.'

Zacharia gulped down his drink. He laughed.

'Mohandas, what will you do now?'

57

Defeat

The authorities at the Cochin Stock Exchange unanimously arrived at a decision.

There was a glaring mistake while displaying the share prices of the Delhi Stock Exchange in the morning. Instead of showing the price of Dhanwantari's shares as twenty-six rupees and fifty paisa, it had shown one hundred and ten rupees! The market became bullish instantaneously. Speculation went through the roof. By the time the mistake was rectified, business worth crores had already been carried out. Dhanwantari's shares were trading at one hundred and twenty rupees. The prices crashed when the error was highlighted. The credibility of the Stock Exchange, the safety of the investors, the integrity of the brokers, all were at stake at this juncture.

A single surefooted decision helped to tackle the situation.

'Every sale and purchase of Dhanwantari Herbal Products' shares conducted at the Cochin Stock Exchange today stands cancelled.'

The trading hours were coming to a close by the time the decision was announced.

Another instruction was issued: 'No more selling and buying of shares today.'

It was a Friday. The hornet's nest was stirred.

All the unofficial trading in the curb on Thursday evening had been updated in the computer on Friday. Everything stood null and void. All the line business done for Bombay was futile.

'Unfair! Unfair!' the profit-seekers shouted themselves hoarse.

'Fair! Absolutely fair!' the brokers facing losses congratulated the authorities.

The profits and losses involving crores of rupees had created havoc among thousands of investors.

Other stock exchanges had traded in Dhanwantari shares. What would they do? The decision of the Cochin Stock Exchange was not applicable there.

But curb trading ceased in every stock exchange across India. Everyone was flabbergasted. They waited and watched.

~

Mohandas was extremely uncomfortable.

Over the last twenty-five years, he had started multiple businesses based in Cochin and, with his Midas touch, made them successful. Facing every hurdle with fortitude, he had laid a strong foundation for his business empire. He turned to Ramesan.

'Net result. We have fifty thousand Dhanwantari shares valued at fourteen rupees, purchased at eighty rupees. The loss is around thirty-three lakhs.'

Mohandas had called Zacharia after the Stock Exchange debacle. He had already given Zacharia a certified cheque. Fifty thousand shares had been handed over with the necessary documents. The deal was complete and legal.

Zacharia expressed his helplessness. 'Mr Mohandas, you own two and a half per cent shares of Dhanwantari Herbals as of now. Sharmaji of Lucknow bought ten per cent today. For the same price of eighty rupees. If you wish to sell your shares, do inform me. I am always there to do the needful.'

Mohandas could detect the mockery in Zacharia's words. Zacharia had sniffed out that Mohandas had already sold the shares.

Ramesan was the one to suggest the strategy when the Dhanwantari share prices shot up.

'We have fifty thousand shares and the certificates. Our investment was forty lakhs. Why not make up for all the losses?'

Mohandas arranged to sell all the shares when the prices swayed between one hundred and ten and twenty. He received nearly fifty-seven lakhs. A straight profit of seventeen lakhs! It was true, he could not take over the company with merely two and a half per cent stake in it. But he got seventeen lakhs in profit within thirty minutes.

However, now it was all gone. A mirage.

Ramesan spoke gravely: 'I feel that Zacharia created the computer error by himself.'

'That's not possible.'

'Everything is possible.'

~

Mini Balachandran was not consoled by the difficulties faced by her adversaries.

It was 4 p.m.

Zacharia and the young advocate who represented Sharma Ayurvedic Company were in the midst of heated discussions.

While gambling, she had had a niggling fear. Shares of Dhanwantari worth fourteen rupees being sold at eighty rupees. Ready cash. Mini had expected Sharmaji to flee in terror. She had the backup of the shares belonging to the Trust. Lord Dhanwantari's benediction would not fail her. Mini had relied on the agreement between the Trust and the company, Zacharia uncle's unassailable self-confidence, and the blessings of her late father.

But the throw of dice had gone awry.

The advocate spoke:

'My client has no intention of interfering in the daily working of the company. He wishes to professionalize the present-day management, that's all. Kerala's traditional way of practising Ayurveda should spread to north India too. Action plans for implementing that vision should be made fast. That's his main goal.'

When he referred to the notes at hand and elucidated further, both Mini Balachandran and Zacharia were stunned.

'My client does not wish to change either the vision or mission of Dhanwantari Herbal Products. Mr Menon, the erstwhile managing director, had discussed an agreement executed between the Trust and the company about its estates and other properties. Though nobody has validated the legal repercussions, one fact is clear. My client wants to push the company towards Mr Menon's original goal. Grow herbs in those estates in a planned way.'

The defeat was complete.

Sharmaji had ten per cent of the company's shares. He had obviously arranged for an additional two or three per cent from the Delhi and Bombay exchanges. Twelve per cent shares were yet to come to the share market. The government establishments would take Sharmaji's side.

Mini felt a strange sense of impassivity. As if she were hurling away something which had never belonged to her. She felt that she had given her full commitment to the company. Intelligence, hard work ... Where had she gone wrong? Some mistake somewhere.

Sharmaji's advocate would come again on Monday. This time, he would walk in confidently. Later, Sharmaji would come to the office. *Daughter, nothing has changed. This is your company. I want you to run it.*

Mini's eyes welled up.

'Uncle, where did I go wrong?'

Zacharia was gloomy too. He had acted with utmost care. He had calculated that even if Sharmaji accepted the extraordinary tender offer, he would be frightened off by the legal challenge of the agreement between the Trust and the company. But the major error was misreading Sharmaji's aim. They had all viewed Sharmaji as a predatory beast; a demon trying to swallow Dhanwantari. Never did Zacharia or Mini consider that Sharmaji's goal was pristine. They could never imagine that Sharmaji had Menon's genuineness and sincerity towards creating new Ayurvedic medicines and healing methods. That was where they went wrong.

A profit of one and a half crore. But that was not success. Tomorrow, Mini would have to hand over the control of the company.

Zacharia raised his head on hearing Mini's question.

'We did not make any mistake, Mini.'

'Then?'

'We ran out of luck. That's all.'

'Luck is very important in everything. Isn't it, Uncle?'

Zacharia responded:

'Of course! There's an anecdote from the Mahabharata. Uttara, Abhimanyu's pregnant young widow, visited Kunti Devi, the mother of the Pandavas, to receive her blessings. Kunti placed her hand on the young girl's head and said: "Daughter, may your son be blessed with good fortune."

'See, she did not bless Uttara with a brave son, a handsome offspring, a son who was always following dharma, or someone who garnered much fame. Kunti, who was beautiful and graced with all the riches as a princess, had prayed for a son as glorious as the sun in her youth. Then she prayed for a son as dharmic, ethical and prudent as Yama. Later, a son as strong and powerful as the wind-god Vayu. A famous, handsome and brave warrior-son like Indra. Karna, Yudhistir, Bhima, Arjuna … worthy sons that any mother would be proud of! But what were her life experiences? What about her sons?

'All their best years were spent wandering in forests. They were denied even basic facilities. War, and endless strife. Their lives were always scorched with pain and loss. By the time she became a great grandmother, Kunti had learned her lesson. It was luck that someone needed most in life.

'Uttara gave birth to Parikshit. An ordinary king. Not very capable or brave. Neither very wise nor good-looking. But he was lucky. Parikshit apparently ruled for sixty years. He laid the foundation of the Kuru dynasty.'

Mini smiled.

'Uncle,' she said, 'you can simplify any defeat.'

'I learned that lesson from sports. One player will inevitably face defeat. If one wins today, he might lose tomorrow. Even a world champion should learn to be equanimous in defeat.'

Mini spoke after a while.

'I'm going to call a board of directors meeting in two weeks. Amma and I shall submit our resignations. Let Sharmaji take over the management.'

Mini herself could not believe that she had said those words. Defeat affected one's consciousness and intelligence.

Zacharia affirmed:

'We are not totally vanquished yet.'

Mini leaned back into her chair and shut her eyes.

'No, Uncle. I cannot fight any more.'

Suddenly she asked: 'Uncle, please tell me. Will Sharmaji guide the company towards my father's vision?'

Zacharia answered a few seconds later. 'Yes, that's what I assume.'

'One more question. Be brutally honest, Uncle.'

'Ask.'

'Will Sharmaji lead the company better than me?'

'No, I don't think so.'

Mini leaned forward and took Zacharia's hands into her own. 'Thank you, Uncle.'

Zacharia's eyes turned moist.

The intercom beeped. It was Prakashan, Mini's personal assistant.

'Madam, you had given a prior appointment. The person is here.'

Mini looked at Zacharia. She wiped her eyes with a handkerchief.

'What appointment? Who has come?'

'Aniyan Raja's representative. He says that you fixed the time yourself.'

Friday, five o'clock. Mini Balachandran remembered.

'Ah, it's Matthews. His visit no longer serves any purpose. But let us meet him. Uncle, please stay.'

'I know Matthews. He is a friend of Vinayan's, who is very dear to me.'

Matthews stepped inside the room. Seeing Zacharia, he was taken aback. But he regained his composure at once. Matthews sat down.

Mini spoke:

'You must know about the trading of our shares at the Exchange today. Under the circumstances, your offer is of no value any more. Though today's trading got cancelled, the brokers are not going to sit and watch on Monday.'

Matthews smiled.

'Yes, I have come with full knowledge of what has happened. We have a new proposal. You can accept it if you like.'

Mini turned to look at Zacharia. She pressed the intercom.

'Please send in three cups of coffee. One without sugar.'

Matthews spoke:

'In the current uncertain scenario, the share prices shall crash further on Monday. You can buy your shares back. All of yesterday's shares shall re-enter the market.'

Zacharia gazed at Mini. Matthews was not aware of every detail. Didn't he know that twelve and a half per cent shares had already been transferred?

'I shall give you the money. As much as you need.'

'What about your security?'

'When the takeover bid fails and the market regains stability, the share prices shall rise again. You should sell the shares when I ask you to. My interest will be four per cent monthly. We can divide the rest of the profits, fifty-fifty.'

'And what if the share prices don't come down on Monday?'

'We should force them to.'

'Okay. Suppose the share prices crash and we buy our shares. What if the prices don't go up?'

'We'll enact a farce. Another takeover bid.'

The coffee arrived.

Mini spoke:

'Let me think about it. I shall call you tomorrow.'

'That's fine.'

Adiyodi was waiting for Matthews to leave. He entered the room. The phone rang again. It was Mini's mother.

Mini listened silently for ten or fifteen seconds. Then she nodded in agreement to whatever Amma said. She replaced the receiver.

Adiyodi approached her.

'Mini, please consider my request for retirement.'

'Amma was suggesting that we should go to a temple if I returned early.' Mini got up and picked up her briefcase. She looked at both Zacharia and Adiyodi.

'Uncle, I'm leaving.' But instead of leaving the room, suddenly, she sat back down heavily on the chair, her eyes brimming with tears.

'I can't do it any more. I have failed.'

Adiyodi gaped at her, unable to comprehend what was happening. Zacharia was speechless.

'Amma has a sixth sense. Never before has she called me like this.'

Zacharia took Mini's hand and gently stroked it.

'Mini, I have failed you. I don't even have the right to apologize.'

'No, no, Uncle.'

Zacharia's eyes overflowed.

58

Turning Point

Ramesan said: 'I'm ready to cooperate in any way. We shall join any plan where we don't end up losing. There's no question of ego or obstinacy here.' He grinned openly.

'I'm being very frank. We are not afraid of losses. After all, the share prices are still climbing higher and higher. The Exchange will be bullish on Monday too. We have fifty thousand shares with us. The ones who are taking over the company would love to get the share certificates. They would actually need them.'

They were in Zacharia's home. Zacharia lay on his cot. Vinayan and Matthews were observing Ramesan. Govinda Prabhu had served everyone tea. Now he stood at the door, watching them all and listening to the conversation.

~

Mini had dropped Zacharia home.

While they were in the car, Mini said: 'Uncle, everything happened for the best. Let Sharmaji run the company. Maybe we can fight a bit more. But what's the use? I want to invest the money in some immoveable properties and also save taxes. Maybe I'll request my husband to quit his job and come home. We can start a proprietary concern of our own. Near the family house. Close to the deity. Something not too ambitious.'

The commotion of the evening rush was visible on the road.

'But the war is not over, Mini,' said Zacharia.

'As far as I'm concerned, it is. Let them run Dhanwantari. If I find them deviating from Acchan's vision, we can use the power vested in the Trust. Remote control.'

Zacharia brooded that he was yet to understand Mini Balachandran completely.

Mini had admitted defeat. Yet, she was intentionally retaining control in her hands. Now, she was planning to start a new business venture.

It was too early to cede defeat in the battle. But as far Mini was concerned, she was calling it quits. Or was it a smokescreen to hide her wounds?

Zacharia remembered the scenes following the deaths of Menon sir and Suresh.

The sky was heavily overcast, but it had not rained yet. It was unbelievably crowded that day. Mini was the cynosure of all eyes. But she disappointed everyone who expected a breakdown. Mini did not look at anyone. Not even the coffins, on which lay a profusion of flowers. It was evident that the impact was deep and grievous. Hers was a silence that contained within it all the storm that raged inside of her.

Zacharia prayed for her as he stepped inside his home.

'Mini, may God be with you always.'

~

It was when he was drying himself after a shower that Zacharia heard Vinayan outside. He felt a sudden lifting of his mood. True friends came to one's aid during setbacks. That was Vinayan's special quality. His father, Lambodaran master, had that unique quality too.

Vinayan had seen it all. Money, luxury, extravagance, poverty … all of it. He was cognizant of the betrayals and losses associated with business. Money was a strange beast. There were only a handful who did not change colours when the beast embraced them. All principles and philosophies became meaningless before the power of money. Every person had a personal boundary that protected them from the influence of money. Vinayan's was very strong. Zacharia prayed that it stayed that way forever.

Matthews was with Vinayan.

'Shall we consider Matthews's leveraged buyout proposal today? I think that's the best way for the management to fight back. What do you say, sir?'

Zacharia asked Prabhu to prepare some tea.

Ramesan had arrived then. He introduced himself to Vinayan and Matthews.

'I have come without informing my uncle. He has a very different nature. I thought I will decide matters before telling him.'

'Do you have a proposal?'

It was then that Ramesan spoke about disposing off the fifty thousand shares of Dhanwantari without suffering too many losses.

Zacharia said: 'I am not sure that the Stock Exchange will allow trading in Dhanwantari's shares on Monday. Even if trading happens, suppose the company attempting to take over Dhanwantari withdraws, what will happen to your shares?'

Ramesan sat staring at Zacharia.

'I really don't know. The share market will ultimately harm the people. The basic bestialities of men are provoked, aren't they? Love, compassion, kindness … these have no place here. Hypocrisy, greed and pride dominate. We lose humane qualities. Does the nation need such a system? What's the use of such a game that forgets humanity?'

Zacharia grinned.

'I have deliberated much on this topic. It was difficult for me, a genuine Communist, to compromise with the idea of a stock exchange. You are right in one way, brother. The share market stokes the evil qualities of human beings. But that can be controlled if we change the very concept of a stock exchange.'

'How?'

'Stock exchanges are imperative for the financial ecosystem of a nation. Economic progress will happen only when the public savings support the enterprises run by private players. For enabling that, stock exchanges are needed—'

Vinayan cut in: 'I've always felt that we should make them more people-friendly and democratic.'

Zacharia explained:

'The first step is to reduce speculative trading. It's said that the share price during speculative trading acts as the litmus test for a company's financial health. But unregulated speculation has become a curse for the Indian stock exchanges. Even in Cochin, which is in its adolescent stage, there is rampant speculative trading.'

'Speculation, gambling ... these are as old as humanity. They are in our very life-blood. How will you stop it?'

'Let us not stop it. Simply declare that insider trading is illegal. In America and England, brokers can never buy shares for themselves. They are just agents of the investors. It goes against the core ethics of a broker's job to rake in money by trading without shares, after being privy to insider information. In India, insider trading is uncontrolled and leads to huge speculation. Weren't two prime ministers in Japan forced to resign and face legal proceedings before the courts? Insider trading was the reason.'

'What else?'

'As Vinayan mentioned, make stock exchanges people-friendly. Reach out to the public. Open a stock exchange in all the district headquarters of the country. If possible, at the tehsil level too. The computer systems are becoming cheaper day by day. Can you imagine two thousand or three thousand exchanges being set up? The cost of membership will go down drastically. New brokers will emerge. They shall search for new markets. In the United States, there are brokers known as "market makers". They publicize and popularize the shares of companies. We can copy that model in our country too.

'We can follow the model of the Madras Stock Exchange. It's simple and straightforward. Reduce the settlement time. Exchange the share certificates in three days' time. The carry-over period is restricted to a fortnight. Legal action will begin afterwards. Just this lone condition can check speculative trade to a large extent.'

The doorbell rang, ending their discussion.

Prabhu went to greet the visitor. Seating him in the drawing room, he returned to Zacharia's side.

'Somebody called Shankaran Kutty. He said it's urgent.'

'That must be Shankaran Kutty the share broker,' Vinayan offered.

'Please ask him to come.'

Prabhu detested the idea of calling an ordinary man inside the room where great discussions were taking place. But he could not disobey Zacharia.

Shankaran Kutty hesitated at the door. He gazed at all the faces nervously.

'Come inside, please. Take a seat.'

Shankaran Kutty stepped inside.

'Tea?'

'I did not want to disturb you, sir. But the situation…'

'Go ahead.'

'Very urgent matter.'

'Please tell me.'

Shankaran Kutty looked at Vinayan, Matthews and Ramesan. Savitry's words resounded in his ears with intensity: 'You should convey the message only to Mr Zacharia. This is top secret.

Shankaran Kutty, you shall receive a commission of half a rupee per share tomorrow. Ready cash, mind you.'

Half a lakh shares. Twenty thousand rupees.

Shankaran Kutty felt that the Lord of Ettumanoor had come to his aid. Savitry had chosen him among hundreds of others in the Stock Exchange. Maybe her opinion about him would change soon. Wasn't Savitry ignoring that young Marwari chap nowadays? Somehow, he must accomplish the task she had assigned him.

'Private matter, sir.'

'What is it about?'

'Dhanwantari shares.'

Zacharia got up. 'We'll come back soon,' he said, addressing the others. 'Please wait.'

Shankaran Kutty and Zacharia went outside.

Shankaran Kutty said: 'Sir, you gave a spot delivery of two lakhs to a Bombay party at eighty rupees. I'm representing the same share broker Savitry.'

'Yes.'

'We heard that another party was offered a spot delivery of fifty thousand shares on the same terms. Is it correct?'

'It is.'

'Who was it, sir?'

'That's a secret.'

'Okay, sir. Can you buy back those shares for eighty-five rupees for the Bombay party? Five per cent commission for you. I have no objection to whatever you may decide to give me out of that.'

Zacharia thought for a moment. Soon, it would be public knowledge that Mohandas was the second buyer. Shankaran Kutty might approach him directly. Let the battle be fought on an open field. It was better that way.

Zacharia smiled.

'I shall try. Let's go inside.'

When they entered the room, Zacharia pointed towards Ramesan.

'This is the person who bought half a lakh shares of Dhanwantari. Tell him about your conditions.'

Shankaran Kutty folded his hands respectfully and greeted Ramesan.

'Sir, my client is willing to buy the half lakh shares at eighty-five rupees. The money shall be transferred to your bank by eleven tomorrow. Please arrange to give us the share certificates and other documents. But if you wish to give me some commission, I shall happily accept it.'

Ramesan looked at the faces of all present with astoundment. Zacharia grinned.

'The ball is in your court now, Ramesan.'

Ramesan dithered for a second. Should he check with his uncle once? Then he decided to play the game on his own terms.

'Agreed. But the price will be hundred rupees. We lost quite badly on the first day's trading. That has to be recouped, you see. If it works out well, Shankaran Kutty, you shall end up with two and a half per cent commission. Cash spot.'

Shankaran Kutty blanched. 'Sir, they want…'

'Go on,' said Ramesan, 'give it a try. Inform me by ten in the morning.'

Shankaran Kutty shut his eyes. 'Ettumanoorappa! Please take care of me. Please grant good sense to Savitry, that Marwari "friend" of hers, and the company coming to take over Dhanwantari!'

Shankaran Kutty got up to leave.

'Sir, I will try to call you soon.'

Ramesan gave him the telephone number.

When Shankaran Kutty left, Zacharia congratulated Ramesan. 'Ramesan, I think you have done the wisest thing.'

Zacharia continued with a grin. 'I'm backing out. I think my hands will get burned if I play too much.'

He called Mini Balachandran.

'Uncle,' Mini said, 'a girl called Savitry rang me just now. She is a share broker, the agent of Sharmaji's Bombay broker.'

'Okay...'

'She asked if we were interested in selling them the rest of our shares. Spot delivery.'

'And what did you say?'

'No point in fighting any more. We already have the Trust's shares with us. The agreement between the Trust and the company will be sufficient to ensure that the company does not deviate from my father's vision. We can think about starting a new venture near Mavelikkara. We have enough money at hand.'

'You agreed to sell the remaining half lakh shares, did you?'

'Yes.'

Zacharia took some time to respond.

'Mini, Sharmaji is buying the shares that we sold to Mohandas. At a higher price.'

'How much?'

'Hundred rupees.'

Mini laughed.

'I have better business sense than Mohandas. I sold them for one hundred and twenty rupees.'

Zacharia did not reply.

'Uncle, are you there?'

'Mini, I was thinking about you. You are so nonchalant. As if you don't care about losing the company.'

Mini answered after a poignant interval: 'I'm going to call my husband in Shillong. Good night.'

Zacharia put the receiver down. Then he announced to all:

'It is over. Sharma's Ayurvedic company in Lucknow has taken over Dhanwantari Herbal Products. Everyone has benefitted – everyone.'

59

New Dreams

'Uncle, do you know where one can find the best fish in Kerala?'

Zacharia was startled out of his wits. The sound, the tenor, the mellifluousness – it was as if Menon sir were asking the question. The late man's words through his daughter's voice.

The dawn was painting the darkness of the Arabian Sea with a shimmer of silver. The car was moving fast.

Mrs Menon, Mini's mother, sat on the back seat, with her eyes closed.

~

Mini had called Zacharia late at night. When his young friends had left the house, Zacharia had felt lonely. And he experienced a terrible sense of failure. As if he had been devastated despite playing his best in a football final. Every fact about the enemy was known to him. His brilliance, determination, stubbornness, style of playing, literally everything. Even then, the plan had failed. He had forgotten to foresee a small detail. Zacharia had never calculated the possibility that the enemy also could be genuine like oneself. He had missed out the detail that the enemy could also be interested in Ayurveda, could possibly be more sincere and enthusiastic than one's own self. His goal was not to defeat anyone.

Zacharia was terribly flustered. He sipped a large whisky and stared mindlessly at the television screen. Prabhu nodded off to sleep, leaning against the wall. It was then that Mini Balachandran called.

'Uncle, hope I did not wake you up. Sorry, it's rather late.'

'Not at all.'

Mini's effusive words made Zacharia's dazed brain come alive.

'I have an idea, Uncle,' she said. 'We have already sold off all our shares to Sharmaji. Amma is asking me why we are holding on to the three lakh shares of the Trust? Isn't it better to have most of the money at hand when we are thinking of starting a new organization? What's the use of keeping the shares of the Trust then? Amma is speaking sense.'

Zacharia kept quiet.

Perhaps Mrs Menon, far removed from the business world, could see straight. Unlike him and Mini, who were too embroiled with the matters at hand.

Mini continued: 'I tried calling Chettan in Shillong. The call is not going through. So I decided to go ahead anyhow. We shall sell the shares belonging to the Trust too.'

'Should I speak to them?'

'Yes.'

'What is the price you expect?'

'Maximum. Uncle, negotiate for the maximum. But I need the money by tomorrow morning. Call me when they agree. Even if it is very late.'

Zacharia shrugged away his stupor. A spate of phone calls followed. Savitry, Shankaran Kutty, Vinayan, Vikas in Bombay, the jobber related to Sharmaji, the financier, Sharmaji in Delhi, Sharmaji's broker ... all were wide awake at that late hour. Negotiations, rate of commission, interest, calculations.

At half past twelve, Zacharia called Mini Balachandran. She picked up at the first ring.

Zacharia said: 'Mini, done!'

'Fill me in, Uncle.'

'I started at one hundred and fifty. They began at eighty. I spoke directly to Sharmaji's company secretary. Told him that unless he bought the Trust's shares, he would not be able to handle the estates and properties easily. The market value of these properties is twenty times more than what's shown in the balance sheet. Sharmaji knew about it. They agreed after half an hour.'

'For how much?'

'One hundred and twenty rupees.'

'Fine. That means…'

'At eighty, we sold two and a half lakh shares. That's two crores. Another fifty thousand shares sold at one hundred and twenty rupees. That's sixty lakh. Now we have sold an additional three lakh of the Trust's shares at one hundred and twenty rupees. Three crores and sixty lakhs. A total of six crores and twenty lakhs.'

'Yes, that's right. We need not go begging around for our new project.'

Zacharia did not reply.

Mini did not want to escape the family legacy. Perhaps she wished to be free of her father's ways of doing business. Is that why she sounded so happy? Or was it another smokescreen?

Mini spoke:

'Uncle, please come with us to the family home. We'll pick you up in the morning, at four-thirty. I need Chittappan's signature too. We can also inform him about the new project. Hope you won't find it inconvenient.'

'Not at all.'

~

Mini and her mother arrived precisely at half past four in the morning.

Mini said: 'I was able to talk to my husband at night. Discussed all the problems with him. He takes everything very sportingly. Because I insisted, he agreed to take a week's leave. He will reach Delhi tomorrow and take a flight home on Monday.'

Nothing in Mini's speech reflected any turmoil of having lost her company.

When the car started speeding through the NH, Mini became silent.

Zacharia observed that the eastern sky was golden red in colour. The canopy of coconut trees hid the morning sun occasionally. How long since he had witnessed the sheer beauty of dawn!

'Uncle, do you know where one can find the best fish in Kerala?'

Zacharia woke up from his reverie.

'Let me tell you. My father told me about it. It's here that we get the best catch. The three rivers – Achankovilaru, Pamba and Manimalayar – boast of a rich variety of fish in their depths. When they flood, the waters flow west. In the olden days, the fish use to move to the bay, through the Vembanad lagoon. Now the bund at Thanneermukkom has stopped that natural drift. The river waters reach the spillway. In the small waterbodies and farmlands of Kuttanad, one can see the abundance of fish.'

The sun assumed its full glory.

The car continued to move eastwards, towards Mini's family home at Mavelikkara.

~

Matthews went to bed close to dawn.

By the time he dropped Vinayan home and returned to his own place, Matthews' mood had turned sour. He had no dearth of money or luxuries. Yet, a project he had planned very methodically had failed. There were inexplicable incidents during the takeover of Dhanwantari Herbal Products.

Matthews did not even feel like taking a drink. He randomly picked up a business magazine and started browsing. It featured a young maverick, a share broker, at the Bombay Stock Exchange. 'Aladdin and the Magic Lamp'. He was hardly thirty, and had made a name for himself in the stock market. The man aced the game, handled shares worth crores, and recently paid income tax advances of twenty-six crores. An alligator, patiently lying in wait, its jaws agape. The article said that companies were terrified wondering on whom his glance might fall on next.

Matthews read the article thrice.

'If someone can do it in Bombay, why can't I do it in Cochin?'

Enough money to play with for a month. Aniyan Raja's support. Unni's expert advice. Vinayan's friendship.

Why not? There was no reason to feel discouraged.

Matthews picked up the list of prominent companies in Cochin and nearabouts. Now, he had to study them thoroughly. Their financial status had to be analysed. Suryanarayanan should be asked to prepare a report using his computer system. Matthews intended to choose a company and buy its shares over a period of three or four days. When the share prices started rising, news about a potential takeover bid from Bombay would spread. One could get in touch with a line operator from Bombay rather easily. With the hike in prices, aggressive trading would ensue. Speculators would troop in. Again, the share prices would shoot up. When the margin became promising, he would sell off the accumulated shares. One could end up making nearly a crore in just seven days. Nothing astounding about it.

Matthews felt a new energy filling him. He busied himself with creating an index of the companies. He was lost in work. It was when the newspaper was hurled by the vendor and it fell noisily on the foyer that he came back to the world.

He decided to meet Suryanarayanan before ten and collect more details.

After setting the alarm for a quarter past nine, Matthews went to bed.

~

Ramesan strolled through Mahatma Gandhi Road at night. The boards of the shut shops glimmered in the dark. There was an allure to the road, lit by multiple lights. A few vehicles whizzed past. He felt hungry. Ramesan decided to visit his erstwhile comrade, who was a street-food vendor. His small shop, next to a movie theatre, sold dosas and omelettes.

Ramesan's friend was happy to see him.

'Dosa?'

The comrade was also a revolutionary. He engaged in political activities during the day. At night, he worked as a street-food vendor. There was one helper. A ramshackle, moveable set-up. Three small stools.

The helper addressed the comrade as 'Boss'.

'Hardly get to see you nowadays, Ramesan. Where are you based now?'

'Very much in the locality.'

The friend offered him a fresh dosa on a leaf, placed over a plate. He poured chutney on it. A special mixture of spices mixed with oil.

'We had some discussions today. A strike against the ammonia plant. We need to intensify it. A mass movement is being visualized.'

'Might be tough to gather people.'

'We will see.'

Even after Ramesan reached home, the taste of the dosa did not leave his tongue. He read some magazines. Mohandas came to wish him good night. He enquired whether Ramesan had had his dinner.

Ramesan decided to speak to Mohandas in the morning. He thought about what he would say.

'Uncle, the project you intended for my future has collapsed. I have not made much loss. The shares bought at eighty rupees have been sold at hundred. From now on, I shall decide my own path. You may please focus on building your business empire. I shall build mine in the manufacturing sector. However, I shall do it my way.'

There were many STD booths that stayed open round the clock in Cochin. The world was virtually at your fingertips due to their existence.

Savitry and Shankaran Kutty got in touch with Vikas from one such booth. Half lakh shares at hundred rupees. Shankaran Kutty's joy knew no bounds when Vikas agreed.

Shankaran Kutty called Ramesan.

'Everything's okay, sir! The money will reach your bank in the morning. Please keep the share certificates and transfer form ready. I will meet you in the morning, sir.'

Shankaran Kutty gazed at Savitry, who was talking inside another booth.

It was the Lord of Ettumanoor's grace that such a windfall had come his way! A commission of one lakh rupees. Besides, he did not have to share that with Savitry.

'Let's go. I have to see that watchman's grouchy face when I reach my hostel,' Savitry said peevishly while paying her bills.

When they boarded the autorickshaw, Shankaran Kutty said: 'I'll be going to the Ettumanoor temple in the morning. We need the Lord's grace for any success. I'll start by six and be back by half past nine. Savitry, who don't you come along?'

Savitry smiled.

'I don't think I will wake up before eight tomorrow.'

When she disembarked from the auto, Savitry turned to Shankaran Kutty.

'Conduct a Pushpanjali ritual for me. My birth star is Chithira.'

'Sure.'

'One more Pushpanjali. Name: Vikas. Birth star: Kartika.'

60

Night's End

'Chakyar Koothu and cricket should not happen on the same day! That's the only condition I have. I specifically instruct Unni to ensure that the Koothu performance at the temple should not coincide with a cricket match telecast. The Chakyar himself is a cricket fan! How will he concentrate on his dance drama then?'

It was a huge hill with vast plain areas looming beneath. Shrubs and weeds amongst red rocks. A winding pathway. The new tiles of the old temple gleamed brightly.

Aniyan Raja was leaving the temple premises after attending a Chakyar Koothu performance. Mini, Amma and Unni accompanied him.

Aniyan Raja was speaking to Mini's mother.

'Devaki, whatever you said that day ... I had my own reasons to reach the same conclusion. God's benevolence. More or less things have happened as we wished. I can hardly travel nowadays. Hope I did not cause much inconvenience to you.'

'No.'

'I also wanted to see all of you. Call me selfish.'

The afternoon sun was hot. Mini covered her head with the free end of her sari. Her feet were getting scorched as the pebbles were hot.

'Nothing much to say about the old temple-dances now. Yet, this fellow seems to be good. Disciple of the famous Ammannur Madhava Chakyar. Did you like his performance, Devaki?'

Mini's mother nodded.

~

Mini Balachandran was busy on Saturday. She and her mother had gone to Mavelikkara to procure her chittappan's signature for the power of attorney. The Trust's shares had to be transferred to Sharmaji's company. Mini had been occupied with arranging for the documents. Her granduncle encouraged her when she proposed a new venture. However, Zacharia was gloomy. He could not stop himself from thinking that it was his wrong guidance that had caused Mini to lose the company. Mini requested Zacharia to spend the weekend with his family.

Sharmaji's local advocate came to meet Mini Balachandran on Saturday again. They exchanged share certificates and the other relevant papers. The new board of directors would be selected in a fortnight's time. The money reached the bank.

Mini slept in peace. Not even a single dream troubled her.

Amma woke her up at six o'clock on Sunday morning.

Seeing her radiant mother, fresh from a bath and dressed in white, Mini had wondered aloud: 'How come you look so beautiful today?'

'Get ready soon. We have to go somewhere.'

'Where?'

'To Aniyan Raja's place. He had called me yesterday. There is a performance of Chakyar Koothu in their temple. Let's go watch it. By the way, he also wishes to speak to you directly.'

'Amma, you informed him that we sold our shares to Sharmaji, didn't you?'

'I didn't tell him anything. Just agreed to pay them a visit.'

Mini gazed sharply at her mother. A few moments later, Amma looked away.

'I have asked the driver to come after half an hour.'

On the way, they visited Asokan at the hospital. He was still in the ICU. Asokan had a bad knee fracture. They planned to shift him to the special ward in a few days.

Aswathy consoled Mini: 'I got to know about the company. It's all fate. So unfortunate that Asokan chettan met with the accident. Otherwise he would have devised some way to save the company.'

Mini did not respond.

The doctor taking care of Asokan was Mini's father's friend.

'The fracture will take at least six months to heal completely. Asokan will be fine afterwards. Nothing to worry.'

The car moved through Alappuzha.

'How do you know Aniyan Raja?' Mini asked her mother.

'I know him. That's all.'

Amma was in a distant island of memories. Mini waited.

'When I was in my first year in college, Aniyan Raja was doing his BA degree. He was the magazine editor that year.'

'Did you write a poem that the editor declared terrible?'

Amma smiled. 'I wrote a poem that was published.'

'Really? You actually wrote a poem?'

'In English. Even your father never knew about it.'

A few moments passed before Amma spoke again.

'That was my first and last poem. When I called Aniyan Raja on Thursday, he asked me whether I still wrote poems.'

'Why did you call him, Amma?'

Amma took some time before responding.

'Your Acchan always used to say that we can never succeed in business without the help of others. I felt that we needed help.'

'Then?'

'Aniyan Raja did not give any answer. He simply said that he will look into the matter. But he called last night.'

Mini held her mother's hand and forked their fingers together.

Unni was waiting for them at Aniyan Raja's house.

'Uncle has gone to the temple. We will join him after a coffee break. My sister has gone to Trivandrum for an interview.'

The Chakyar Koothu was held inside the temple. The audience was meagre. It included three or four women. Aniyan Raja was leaning against a pillar. The story being enacted was 'Subhadraharanam': the abduction of Subhadra.

After the performance, Aniyan Raja approached Mini.

'I have heard about you. Smart girl.' Then he turned to Mini's mother. 'Does your daughter write poetry too?'

~

Matthews was waiting for them at Aniyan Raja's house. Aniyan Raja welcomed him warmly.

'I'd say it's all due to good luck. God's benevolence. A teacher of biology in my school got a rare herb for me. Ottamooli. A few crushed leaves. But it really helped with my asthma. I won't say that it's going to work with all asthma patients. But I have not been wheezing for the last three days. I realized that there are likely to be many more such herbs waiting to be discovered. Who has the time to do research? Ninety-five per cent investment goes waste usually. But that five per cent that is effective ... I was thinking about it when Devaki's call came.'

Mini looked at her mother. Amma must have helped Acchan too, in moments of crisis. Nobody was complete by themselves. Suddenly, she felt a heavy burden weighing her heart down. Her husband must have reached Delhi now.

Aniyan Raja continued to speak:

'It was only due to divine grace that the call connected that night. Mahesh happened to be in Calcutta at the same time. Great coincidence, what else? My brother-in-law is usually not there at home. See, the brokers were his acquaintances. God helped since Menon's purpose was always pure. Else, how could everything fall into place so quickly? What if Sharmaji had not mortgaged his own company's shares to borrow money from the market? In such a case, Mahesh too would have found it impossible.'

Mini looked askance at him. She did not understand a word. Matthews, too, was taken aback.

Aniyan Raja smiled at them.

'Didn't Unni tell you about it?'

Unni replied gently: 'No.'

'Oh, so you're clueless. Watching a performance without knowing the story. Interesting!'

Aniyan Raja got up.

'Unni, explain our proposal to Mini. If she agrees, go ahead with the plans.' Then he looked at Matthews with a smile. 'What do you say, Matthews?'

Matthews could not help laughing.

'Why are you laughing?'

'You haven't forgotten my name! That is priceless.'

'Devaki, come with me. You can meet my sister. It is an old tharavadu. You have never been here before, have you? Let the children talk about business...'

Mini watched Aniyan Raja and Amma walk slowly through the front yard. The colours and scents of memories became brighter as age and solitude intensified. But yes, it was all divine grace.

Mini asked: 'What's the new proposal?'

Unni spoke:

'We have the power of attorney and the option to buy thirty-five per cent of Sharma Ayurvedic Company's shares. The deadline is tomorrow evening.'

'What are you saying?'

Matthews stared in bewilderment at Unni.

Unni explained: 'Only fifty-one per cent of Sharma Ayurvedic Company's shares belong to his family. The rest are with the public. Sharmaji mortgaged three quarters of whatever shares he possessed to borrow money from the market in order to take over Dhanwantari. My uncle Aniyan Raja's friends have loaned him the money. They have the option and the power of attorney to buy those shares.'

'That means?'

'You can take over Sharma Ayurvedic Company tomorrow. Become its owner.'

Mini closed her eyes.

'Sharma Ayurvedic Company owns Dhanwantari Herbal Products. But you can own Sharma Ayurvedic Company! Effectively, Dhanwantari will be yours.'

'Conditions? The cost?'

'It's going to cost six crores. Cash to be ready by morning. You have cash in the bank, don't you? Some for sundry expenses.'

'What else?'

'Nothing. My uncle has one goal. A heartfelt wish, rather. There has to be a specialized cell to conduct research for curing asthma. It can be undertaken by either Dhanwantari Herbals or Sharma Ayurvedic. If you do it together, all the better. Uncle will be delighted.'

Mini walked to the verandah. The rocks of the hill far beyond glittered in the sunlight. A green tree was covered with white blossoms.

Sharma Ayurvedic Company.

They had retail outlets in almost every north Indian city. A decent production unit, though not very modern. Her father's words came rushing into her memory. Whenever he came to meet her at her Delhi home, he would wax eloquent about how

Sharmaji and he planned to undertake joint efforts to create herbal plantations in the Kullu Valley in Himachal Pradesh and the Pachmarhi hills in Madhya Pradesh. The ultimate goal was to provide healthcare using nature's own gifts. Money and intelligence were simply the means to an end.

The Lord was giving her whatever her father had always yearned for!

Mini plucked a leaf from the tulsi plant nearby. Closing her eyes, she whispered: 'Yes, if it falls with its face upwards.'

An inner voice reminded her serenely: 'Yes, even if it doesn't.'

Mini Balachandran tossed the leaf into the air. She did not wait to watch which way it fell.

Returning to the room, Mini gave her answer: 'Okay, agreed. We shall transfer the money before noon tomorrow.'

Unni smiled.

'Can I use your phone, please?' she asked.

'By all means.'

Unni checked the phone connection with a grin.

'My uncle usually disconnects the telephone.'

Mini called Delhi. She could get through on the third attempt. She was bubbling over with joy.

'Listen, please don't catch the flight yet. I'm reaching Delhi on Tuesday. I have some great news for you! Will share the details when I reach home at night.'

Balachandran's voice streamed through the line. 'What's the matter, Mini?'

'Later. Do not cancel your leave. We will spend a week in the Kullu valley. Please arrange for a helicopter.'

'What are you up to?'

'I'm calling from the middle of the wilderness. I promise to tell you everything at ten in the night. Now, Balachandran should simply obey Mrs Mini Balachandran, that's all.'

Balachandran laughed.

'Okay, madam. Can I ask something?'

'Quick.'

'When we roam around the Kullu valley, will there be others around?'

'The pilot. Nobody else.'

'What about the Manali resthouse?'

'Ah, there will be an old man there. Mr Sharma from Lucknow. Then a bearded young man from Kerala. He's a scientist.'

Balachandran's guffaw resounded through the phone.

'Yes, I was right.'

'What?'

'My wife is actually loony.'

Mini cut the call with a smile.

61

Dawn Again

On Mondays, the roads to the city would be choked with rush-hour traffic. Mini's car was crawling at a snail's pace, taking twenty minutes to cover a few hundred metres from the Vyttila junction. When she reached the south overbridge, Mini Balachandran sighed with relief.

'Guruvayurappa! Please help me with the climb now.'

The Lord did not take much pity on her. She was forced to stop right at the middle. Iron rods protruded from the lorry in front. There was a jeep behind the car. On her right was a motorcycle. Astride the vehicle was a family of three. The child wore a maroon-coloured school uniform.

Mini helplessly shut her eyes. 'I can't take this tension any more.'

From now on, she decided to ask the driver to drop her to work in the mornings. No more driving.

Mini remembered Adiyodi unexpectedly. She decided to do two things right after reaching the office. One, accept Adiyodi's request for retirement. The board should pass the resolution in the next meeting. Second, Ramesan should become the head of the production unit for three months. It would be a sort of trial.

Zacharia had a high opinion about the young man. Ramesan was also yearning to wriggle out of Mohandas's control. Let Mohandas's defeat be complete.

Yesterday, during lunch at Aniyan Raja's house, he made his vision clear: 'Like the managing director, let there be young blood in all the departments. As of now, Dhanwantari has an aged face. That has to change.'

Then, Aniyan Raja had turned to address Amma. 'Our time is over, is it not, Devaki?'

Amma looked full of life. Also, more beautiful.

Mini recalled the phone call from earlier that morning.

A strange voice. English with a thick accent of Hindi.

It was Sharmaji from Delhi.

'From now on, let us collaborate with each other. I shall return Dhanwantari's shares to you. Please give me back mine. No more enmity. What's done is done.'

Mini wished to ask him why he had considered her an adversary. But she kept quiet. This was business, no child's game.

Aniyan Raja had spoken on the topic.

'Dhanwantari is not just a company or a business. It is all about preserving health. Never lose the service aspect. Smartness lies in making profits while providing service to the public. There are so many medicines yet to be discovered, lying hidden in the herbs and plants of our yards and forests. Invest in research. Take advantage of Sharmaji's know-how and wisdom.'

The lorry slid a few inches backwards. Mini was startled. Instinctively, her foot left the brake. The car moved backwards on the slope. There was a blaring of horns from behind. Finally, the lorry moved forward. Mini prayed while driving the vehicle. Luckily, the engine did not stall.

In her briefcase, she had the leaves that Aniyan Raja had given her. They had greatly helped with his asthma. Mini decided to get those analysed. The doctor from Nelliyampathy would be around today. A young man who radiated confidence and enthusiasm. He would be perfect for the task. She should create a scheme.

When Mini had joked with Balachandran about the bearded young man who would accompany them in Kullu, the doctor was in her mind. What was wrong in coming up with a new scheme for research, after consulting Sharmaji? There was sufficient cash in the bank.

Did my father ever attempt to acquire Sharmaji's company, Mini wondered. Was that the provocation behind Sharmaji's attack?

Mini's car reached M.G. Road and slowly moved west.

The energy of the outside world infected Mini's spirits too. She increased the car's speed. Seeing the crowd crossing the road at the junction, she gently pressed the brake.

Mini's car moved forward when the pedestrians, including Savitry and Shankaran Kutty, crossed the road.

Mini and Savitry had never met each other.

Shankaran Kutty and Savitry were trying to make their way through the footpath that was peppered with vendors selling smuggled goods.

'So what's your opinion, Savitry?'

Savitry smiled.

'I called Bombay. The share prices of Dhanwantari are crashing in the curb trading. The Friday trading of Dhanwantari at the Cochin Exchange has been declared void. Listen to me. Try to sell every share you bought on Thursday, as quickly as you can. You'll be able to manage the losses better.'

Shankaran Kutty felt miffed.

'I'm not talking about shares. And I didn't suffer any losses.'

'What?'

'Come, let's have a cup of coffee. I want to discuss something with you, Savitry.'

Savitry stopped walking.

'Not now! I am going to the Stock Exchange now. Vikas will call me at ten o'clock sharp. Why don't you come along?'

Then she lowered her voice: 'He has some inside information. Vikas will call after verifying it. You coming or not?'

Shankaran Kutty yearned to say a categorical 'No'. But when Savitry got inside an autorickshaw, he followed her.

Shankaran Kutty said to the driver: 'Stock Exchange.'

~

Mohandas spent Sunday in the house at Aluva, near the river. It was the first formidable defeat he had ever faced in life. Of course, there had been minor setbacks before. But this was an unequivocal devastation. Thanks to Ramesan, he had not suffered any monetary loss. But Ramesan's words had provoked much pain.

Ramesan had told him: 'Valiyacha, you are doing many things that I don't agree with. Huge mistakes. I sincerely want to run a successful manufacturing enterprise here. But I shall do it my way. You should not misunderstand me.'

Ramesan had gone to Ernakulam in the morning.

When the mid-day sun started getting hotter, Mohandas shifted his garden chair to the shade. He opened a can of beer.

Mini's lissom body refused to leave his eyes.

Mohandas had forgotten Aswathy, Asokan and Dhanwantari Herbal Products.

~

Matthews was doing his calculations. On Sunday, after talking to Unni, all the accumulated frustration and agony of the past two days had left him. They had made fifty lakh in profits in the Dhanwantari company deal.

Unni suggested: 'Matthews, try a new scheme where we can invest the money sagaciously.'

Both of them examined Matthews' new ideas.

'Try a few companies that are not listed in the Stock Exchange,' Unni said. 'Maybe we can get in touch directly and buy the shares.'

Matthews had collected the details before ten in the morning. He shortlisted five companies based in Ernakulam and in the surrounding areas. They planned to take over one company from the list and bring the shares to the stock market.

'I shall become one of the ten richest businessmen of Kerala in less than ten years.'

Matthews felt extremely confident.

~

Zacharia had his breakfast and went to the office. While he was planning a luxurious paan break, Tarlok Singh approached the door with an open smile.

Removing his shoes, the Sardarji greeted Zacharia: 'Sat Sri Akal.'

Zacharia wished him back.

'Zachariaji, please sell the Dhanwantari shares in the morning promptly.'

'Price?'

'The change of price is determined by the Lord above, Zachariaji. If there is profit, there is also loss. Sell at whatever price you get.'

'And then?'

'Buy one thousand, or maybe one thousand and five hundred shares of this particular company.'

Zacharia stared at the bit of paper handed over to him.

'This one…?'

'Some NRIs based in Hong Kong are planning to take over this company. We won't lose anything.'

'The current market price of a ten-rupee share is forty-one.'

'So what?'

Zacharia replied: 'Okay then.'

Tarlok Singh got up.

'Do you need more margin money?'

'No.'

Zacharia decided to reach the Exchange early. There were a few matters regarding the curb trading of Dhanwantari's shares that needed untangling.

Mini had updated him at night about the latest sequence of events. No loss, no gain. Just a little sorrow.

Everything was like that, wasn't it? Between our arrival in this world and our departure, all profits and losses tallied up. Like on a balance sheet. Only an emotion endured.

People started crowding the Stock Exchange by 10 a.m. Arguments regarding the decision by the authorities – to cancel all Friday trading of Dhanwantari's shares – still boomed from the cubicles on the second floor. There were many sellers of Dhanwantari's shares in the curb. No buyers. The share prices crashed.

Dhanwantari, Seller.

Twenty-five.

Twenty-three.

Eighteen.

The crowd increased. Other names started ringing loud.

TISCO.

Reliance Capital.

Apollo Tyres.

Videocon.

Seller, Seller.

Buyer, Buyer.

The calls for Dhanwantari were losing steam.

Dhanwantari, Seller.

Fourteen.

Suddenly, a new name sounded: Sri Hari Bank. Buyer, Buyer.

It caught Vinayan's attention.

He had never heard of such a company before. It wasn't listed in any Stock Exchange. But now?

The face value of the share stood at ten rupees.

Vinayan moved towards the person shouting.

Savitry was calling out. 'Sri Hari Bank … Buyer, Buyer. Twelve, twelve.'

Vinayan shouted. 'Seller, fifteen.'

Savitry looked at Vinayan. But she did not see him. Just watched his eyes and lips.

The sound of money.

'Thirteen.'

'Fifteen.'

'How much?'

'Two thousand shares.'

Savitry hesitated for a moment.

'Done.'

Vinayan agreed.

'Done.'

Minutes passed.

Everybody forgot Dhanwantari. It would appear only on the second Friday when the accounts were settled: as a profit or loss, long position or short position.

Those who could not bridge the losses would be morose. Those who gained would be happy. Now, nobody had the time for anything.

A rumour was in the air. A north Indian company was trying to acquire a local bank.

The line operators of Bombay were already in the arena.

By the time Zacharia reached the second floor, the cubicles and corridors were flooded with people.

The numbers were growing on a daily basis.

New faces. Eyes glinting equally with greed, fear and enthusiasm.

Zacharia keenly listened for someone to yell 'Dhanwantari'.

No.

New names.

Buyers.

Sellers.

Zacharia entered his cubicle. Slowly, he opened his packet of paan.

On the computer screen flashed figures and letters.

The Stock Exchange became active.

A new day began.

About the Author and the Translator

K.L. MOHANA VARMA is the multi-award-winning author of over seventy-five books, in Malayalam and English, a number of which have been translated into multiple Indian languages. Of his works, *Ohari*, the first financial thriller ever to be written in Malayalam literature, remains a milestone. K.L. Mohana Varma won the prestigious Kerala Sahitya Akademi Award in 1993 for the novel.

He lives in Cochin.

MINISTHY S. works as an IAS officer in the Uttar Pradesh cadre. A literary translator too, she translates between three languages: Malayalam, English and Hindi. Her translations, including those of works by V.J. James, Benyamin, Sheela Tomy, Sonia Rafeek and K.R. Meera, have been shortlisted for the JCB Prize for Literature and the Crossword Book Jury award, and made it to the longlists for the VoW Book Award for English Translation, Green Book Award and DSC Prize for South Asian Literature. She has also transliterated four cantos (Sundar Kanda, Kishkindha Kanda, Aranya Kanda and Lanka Kanda) from Tulsidas's *Sri Ramcharitmanas* into English.

Ministhy lives in Lucknow.

HarperCollins *Publishers* India

At HarperCollins India, we believe in telling the best stories and finding the widest readership for our books in every format possible. We started publishing in 1992; a great deal has changed since then, but what has remained constant is the passion with which our authors write their books, the love with which readers receive them, and the sheer joy and excitement that we as publishers feel in being a part of the publishing process.

Over the years, we've had the pleasure of publishing some of the finest writing from the subcontinent and around the world, including several award-winning titles and some of the biggest bestsellers in India's publishing history. But nothing has meant more to us than the fact that millions of people have read the books we published, and that somewhere, a book of ours might have made a difference.

As we look to the future, we go back to that one word—a word which has been a driving force for us all these years.

Read.